THE
OTHER
WOMAN

Tania Tay is an advertising copywriter whose debut adult novel, *The Other Woman*, won Headline's inaugural Modern Stories Open Submissions initiative. In her writing, Tania likes to explore female friendship and the relationship between mothers and daughters. Tania is also a children's author, writing under the pen name of Crystal Sung, and has written a screenplay, developed with BBC Writersroom London Voices. Tania is second generation British Malaysian Chinese. She studied History of Art at the University of Edinburgh and now lives with her husband and children in East London.

THE OTHER WOMAN

TANIA TAY

ACCENT

First published in 2024 by Headline Accent
An imprint of HEADLINE PUBLISHING GROUP

1

Cataloguing in Publication Data is available from the British Library

ISBN 978 1 0354 0598 5

Typeset in 11.25/15.25pt Bembo Std by Jouve (UK), Milton Keynes

Printed and bound in Great Britain by Clays Ltd, Elcograf S.p.A.

MIX
Paper | Supporting
responsible forestry
FSC® C104740

Headline's policy is to use papers that are natural, renewable and recyclable
products and made from wood grown in well-managed forests and other
controlled sources. The logging and manufacturing processes are expected
to conform to the environmental regulations of the country of origin.

HEADLINE PUBLISHING GROUP
An Hachette UK Company
Carmelite House
50 Victoria Embankment
London EC4Y 0DZ

www.headline.co.uk
www.hachette.co.uk

For Matt,
Anushka, Jasmine and Louis,
With all my love x

Prologue

My hands shake as I fumble for my keys, dropping them twice before landing on the right one and turning it in the lock. I burst through the front door, and my elbow knocks into the post piled on the windowsill. Envelopes fall and I trample over them like leaves.

The first thing I notice is the empty corner by the shoe rack, the usual sprawl of shoes and muddy trainers is missing. 'Leo! Eddie! Amber! Are you here?' My voice sounds harsh, unfamiliar, my breathing is ragged.

No answer.

I often complain I can't hear myself think, but right now I'd give anything to hear the children shouting back.

I dart around the house, throwing open doors, checking behind curtains, as if I've lost them in a game of hide and seek. But I know they're not here. The kitchen smells of bleach and the usual scattering of books and toys have been tidied away.

I can't breathe. My throat's tight and my lungs refuse to draw air.

There *has* to be a logical explanation.

Please let it be some stupid game. Please, Leo, jump out shouting 'Boo'.

I kick off my wedges before sprinting upstairs, taking two steps at a time. My head and shoulders push forward too quickly, and my legs almost give way as I reach the landing.

I half stumble into Amber's room, which is immaculate; her duvet neatly shaken out and pillow straight. But her denim jacket, dressing gown and backpack are missing from the back of the door. I open the wardrobe. Half her clothes are gone. An eight-year-old Amber, at the beach two years ago, smiles at me from a photo frame on her desk. I feel another blow to my chest. *How did I not keep her safe?*

One by one, I wrench open her drawers. Empty.

I cross the landing to the boys' room where their toy boxes bulge with cars and action figures. But, like Amber's, their wardrobes are half empty. Eddie's overnight case is missing. So is Leo's Trunki. My heart slams against my ribs. I want to throw up.

Blue Bear is peeking out from underneath Leo's bed, his arms reaching forward, his stitched smile looking worried. I pick him up and squeeze him to my chest. Tears stream down my face as I collapse onto Leo's bed, breathing in the smell of his camomile shampoo.

Leo will miss you tonight, Blue Bear. He won't sleep without you.

Why did I leave the house last night? However late, however angry, I should not have left.

Now the thing I fear most in the world has happened. My worst nightmare.

My children are gone.

Chapter One

Jade

If you stay at home with your kids long enough, it's easy to lose the person you once were. Parents and teachers are the only adults I speak to most days, and to them I'm Amber's or Eddie's or Leo's mum. Or I'm Mrs Callahan. Sam's wife. I've put my family first for years, so by default I've come last. I don't regret it for a minute, and I wouldn't change anything for the world. But I'm not sure who I am anymore.

I'm buttering bread for the kids' packed lunches when a text message arrives from Christina, confirming she can make coffee at ten. I reply with a thumbs up, fizzing with excitement at the prospect of seeing my old flatmate again.

Leo crashes into the kitchen, still in his pyjamas, chasing after seven-year-old Eddie. At three, Leo's the youngest and noisiest of the family.

'Rarrrhhh!' He screeches in his best dinosaur impression.

'Get off me, stop licking my leg,' retorts Eddie, giggling. His hair's sticking up and his shirt's untucked from his school trousers.

'Dinosaur gonna eat you UP!' growls Leo.

'Stop shouting, I'm trying to read,' scolds ten-going-on-eighteen-year-old Amber from the table. She's munching on her cereal, eyes glued to her book – the latest Agent Scarlett mystery.

Leo pouts and I smother his chubby cheeks with kisses. He stops bothering Eddie and tugs my arm, chanting his favourite refrain. 'Hungry, Mummy, I'm hungry, want brek brek, want pancake.' He drags a stool over to the cupboard and reaches for the flour, nearly sending it all over the counter.

Mummy influencers with their picture-perfect lives don't convey the unrelenting reality of motherhood. I adore the little monsters but sometimes I'd give anything to get out of the house, even if it means going to work in an office. I'm not patient by nature. Sometimes I could do with a break from the endless giving, the anxiety that one of them will hurt themselves, and the constant guilt that I'm not a good enough role model.

'OK, darling. Pancakes it is.' I put down my phone and scoop flour into the blender – a fancy one I bought when we'd built our light-filled kitchen extension. Sam would say I'm spoiling them by giving in to Leo's demands – and he's probably right – but pancakes for breakfast are my way of proving I'm a good mum.

Sorting my kids' breakfasts wasn't always my life, as I remembered when, a couple of weeks ago, Christina's name popped up on Instagram as a new follower. We'd met in halls, the first day of Freshers' Week, and we'd immediately connected – maybe because we're both British Chinese. She'd known me back when I was Jade Chan. Not a mum or a wife, but myself. When I could just roll out of bed and run into lectures. When I wasn't responsible for anyone else but me.

But we hadn't spoken in years, not since she dropped out of

4

medical school. So I was thrilled to hear from her, and we've been messaging ever since. She's in London visiting her mum, so we arranged to meet in a café near me, in Wanstead.

I'm just switching off the blender and pouring the thick batter into a jug when Sam's sandalwood aftershave wafts into the room. 'Daddy!' Leo runs over and swarms up Sam's legs, like a monkey climbing a tree. Sam swings him into the air, blowing a raspberry on his tummy.

Sam looks good for his mid-forties: tall and broad-shouldered, with well-muscled arms and strong thighs. Only a slight paunch shows his love for fine food and wine over his infrequent visits to the gym. He puts Leo down and is about to squeeze past me, but I pull him close and snatch a kiss, tasting minty toothpaste. I snuggle into him. 'You were back late. I feel like I hardly see you these days.'

'Sorry. Loads going on at work. You're not usually down so early.' His blue eyes crinkle at me briefly before flicking to the fridge.

'I promised Leo pancakes.' I keep hold of Sam's arm, and eventually his hands travel under my pyjama trousers, and I shiver with pleasure.

One last kiss and he moves away. 'Sorry. Have to get going.'

I get it. Mornings are far too busy. It's been a long time since he could sweep me back to bed and get to work late.

'Do you want to make a smoothie? Take me two minutes to wash this up.' I wave a hand at the blender.

'No, you're all right.' He pours a glass of orange juice, draining it as he crosses to the table, kissing Eddie and Amber on his way out of the kitchen. 'Early meeting. I'll grab something on the way.'

5

'Bye-bye, Daddy.' Leo waves, sprinkling flour over the counter and making Eddie sneeze.

I follow Sam to the hall for a last smooch, but there's only time for a peck on the cheek and he's out of the door, his mind already on work.

The smell of burning butter calls me back to the stove. I ladle in batter, which sizzles as it hits the pan. 'Yummy pancake!' Leo cuddles my legs. 'Thank you, Mumma, love you.' Moments like this make it all worthwhile and I ruffle his tousled brown curls, glinting with gold highlights – a mix of my black Chinese hair with Sam's blond.

I stack fluffy pancakes onto plates, drizzle them with maple syrup and usher Leo over to the table to join Eddie and Amber. As the boys tuck in, my mind wanders to Christina and the futures we'd planned for ourselves. I longed to be a writer, she a surgeon. Has she moved as far away from her dream as I have? Had she recovered and completed her degree somewhere else? Her Instagram and Facebook profiles don't reveal much; nothing about a partner or kids, just moody shots of landscapes and interesting architecture, plates of food and inspiring quotes. Nothing personal to help me understand her better.

I never got to say goodbye to her when she left Edinburgh. She'd left our flat so suddenly. One minute she was there, ensconced on the sofa with a fruit tea, and a medical textbook. The next, she'd gone. I came back to our flat after a few days hanging out with my then boyfriend, Tom, and she'd been whisked off home. A medical emergency, she'd said in her brief letter, explaining how she wasn't coming back, and where to send her deposit.

I've always wondered if her parents played more of a role in her leaving. They were so strict, a part of me was surprised she was allowed to study away from London in the first place. I called her parents' landline more times than I could count, but no one answered. I wrote her a letter, but never got a reply. After a while, I gave up trying. But I've always had a nagging sense I should have tried harder, that I could have been a better friend. I've thought of reaching out to her so many times over the years, but I wasn't sure what to say, or if she'd want to hear from me.

'Leo, you're splashing milk on me!' Amber's voice brings me back to the present. 'Mummy, we need to go.' She scrapes back her chair and skips over to the door.

I interrupt the boys' slurping contest and rush them upstairs to brush their teeth. 'Who can get ready the fastest?'

I wrestle Leo into his nursery joggers and polo shirt. 'Ow, Mumma! Leo dress Leo!'

'We don't have time, darling, don't want to be late.' Back downstairs we play hunt-the-trainer, unearthing one from a plant pot, while I thank the shoe gods for Velcro straps.

Out on the street, I clutch tightly on to Leo's shirt to stop him rushing off on his balance bike while we cross the road to the school. Amber runs ahead to her friends and Eddie joins the queue for his class. Leo weaves through the crowd leaving the playground, while I jog after him. I'm relieved to deposit him at the nursery gates.

Back at home, I haphazardly shove bowls and mugs in the dishwasher, run a cloth over the cream quartz countertops, then load the washing machine.

At ten, my headhunter, Nina, calls. I haven't had a job in years, but Leo will be full-time at school from September, and

I've been thinking about returning to work. After Eddie was born – with all his allergies – Sam said it was easier if I stayed at home. At the time, I'd wanted to, I was so worried about Eddie. And Amber loved me taking her to nursery rather than a childminder. But while I've loved having time with the kids, I can't help worrying that my career has suffered as a result. Just the thought of an interview terrifies me, and I'm trembling with nerves as I answer the phone.

'Hello, darling girl.' Nina's voice pours down the line like treacle. 'How's life as a domestic goddess with your two – no, three – kiddiwinks, so your gorgeous husband tells me?'

That jolts me. 'You've . . . spoken to Sam?' But why wouldn't she? He hires through her agency. I take a breath and smile even though she can't see me, faking confidence. 'We're all well, thanks. My youngest is about to start school full-time in September . . .'

'So you thought you'd dip your toe back in the water? Good girl,' she oozes.

'What's the market for copywriters like at the moment? Do you think I could go back part-time?' I bite at a loose cuticle.

'Well, to be honest . . . it's not brilliant. You know the advertising budget is the first thing to go in a recession.' Someone asks if she wants tea. 'Lovely – no sugar,' is her muffled reply.

'Is there anyone who wants to job-share? A-another mum maybe?' My voice breaks, revealing my worry.

'Goodness, darling – Sorry, but no. People tend to arrange job-shares with people they know.' Her voice drips concern but the click of a keyboard tells me she's not totally focused on our conversation. 'Why don't you freelance? Can't you ask Sam?'

'Oh, you know how it is, we'd rather keep work and home

separate.' I hear the pity in her voice and I want to hang up. 'Look, I've got to go, but keep me in mind if anything comes up.'

'Absolutely, darling. You take care now, and look after that gorgeous family of yours.'

I ring off from Nina, my mood low. A message arrives from Christina.

Just arrived in Wanstead – see you soon!

She's early, but she always was punctual. I run upstairs to change out of my stained top and baggy leggings, a far cry from the vintage dresses I used to love twenty years ago. I slap on make-up and throw on a pair of cropped trousers and a top that's not covered in food stains.

I wonder how much she'll have changed.

Will I recognise her? Will she recognise me?

Chapter Two

Jade

Wanstead High Street is buzzing with people pushing buggies and walking their dogs. I avoid looking too closely at anyone, wary of bumping into someone who'll want to stop and chat.

By the time I arrive at The Kitchen, I'm out of breath and sweat is running down my back. I should have worn a lighter top. It's building up to be a warm day. There's no one East Asian sitting outside – just an older couple with their poodle. I hold the door as a woman with a double buggy backs out with difficulty. That was me, not so long ago.

'Cappuccino, please.' I smile at the bearded barista, and scan the room. A group of people are taking up the main table. For a change it's not one of the book groups that often congregate there and which I long to join if I ever get time to read more than a page at a time. This seems to be a training talk for estate agents, all in crisp blouses or shirts, and tailored suits. Looking at how smart they are, I feel that full-time employment is as far away as Mars.

A few lone customers sit in front of laptops, tapping away,

staring intensely at their screens. On another table, a tired-looking mother feeds a curly haired toddler who's smearing orange goo round his face. I smile at her sympathetically.

I find a quiet table at the back and while I wait, I pull out my notebook to jot down some story ideas. When I left my job as a copywriter, I'd planned to give fiction a go. But being a full-time mum means I rarely have space in my brain for stories – which leaves my notebook pretty empty. I turn to a fresh page of my Moleskine, smoothing the creamy paper with my finger. I uncap my pen.

'Jade?' a low voice says.

'Christina!' I jump up. For a moment I don't recognise the dark-haired woman in front of me, wearing a cream silk dress and carrying a Prada handbag. She looks different, older, even though her skin's smooth and unlined. I'd been expecting a studious type in cords.

'It's been years!' She gives me a nervous smile, showing even, white teeth, instead of train-track braces. I'm sure she's noting all the differences in me too. I must look older, more worn out. I hold in the spare tyre bulging round my middle.

'You look fantastic!' I lean in to hug her, then draw back, remembering she's not keen on hugs. She's obviously got over that, as she squeezes me tightly. As I breathe in her light lily perfume and clasp her warm, slim frame, a wave of emotion floods over me.

I draw back and there's an awkward pause. We sit down, and a nervous giggle escapes me. 'Wow, look at us – all grown up!' An older woman at the next table glances over at us. 'Haven't seen each other for years,' I say and the woman smiles politely before turning back to her screen.

11

'So much to catch up on ... where do we start?' Christina's saying when the barista brings over our drinks.

What I really what to know is why she left Edinburgh and what she did afterwards. But it's a sensitive topic – I won't bring it up unless she does. I smile and launch into small talk. 'How are your family? Your mum, dad, brother?'

'Oh yes, they're all fine.' She rolls her eyes. 'Austin, the Golden Boy, is annoying as ever. Wife, two kids, he's a financial director in Hong Kong now.'

Of course. Austin. Her accountant brother, who her parents compare her to, just as my parents are always comparing me to mine. My brother excels as a lawyer, and I've often heard my mum on the phone to friends, saying how much he earns. She never really got what I did, as a copywriter. She doesn't understand that people are paid to write the marketing leaflets that come through the post, or that writing is a valid career.

As Christina fills me in on her family, I marvel at how chic she looks. When we were students, I could hardly ever get her to wear make-up, apart from pale pink lipstick. Her plum lip colour suits her much better.

'My father's gone pro-China in his old age. My mother can't get him to come back from Hong Kong, which is why I'm here ... What?' She catches me staring at her.

'Nothing!' I smile, feeling my cheeks grow warm. 'I was just thinking – how different you look.'

'I'm not nineteen with plaits anymore.' Her voice is dry. 'I finally cut them when I grew up.' We laugh.

'It's not just the hair. You look really great.' The years have given her a patina of confidence. She's not the shy student who I'd encouraged to come out of her shell.

12

'So what about you? Are your family all right? How are your mum and dad?' she asks.

Of course – how would she know? 'They've split up,' I say. 'Happened while I was at uni.' The pain of Dad leaving our family home stabs me, like a broken splinter I can never remove.

'Oh, I'm sorry.' She only met them once or twice. But I'm sure if we'd still been friends while my parents were splitting up, she'd have been the one to help me through it.

We'd spend hours discussing our families. Christina understood what it was like to live under the weight of your family's expectations. Always feeling like you were letting them down. I'd felt it was my fault that my parents had split up. My mum always complained about the trouble she'd gone through, having children. She blamed me for the pain of my birth, and the hours she'd spent trying to stop me crying and waking my father in the night.

'Your mum . . . is she happy you're visiting?' I ask. Christina's mother hadn't liked me much. She was even more controlling than my mum, and I doubt she'd changed.

Christina makes a non-committal face. 'Maybe. Does your mum like being a grandmother?'

'Oh, you know . . . My mum loves telling me all the ways I'm doing it wrong.' I shrug. 'But let's not talk about them.'

There's a short awkward pause before we both speak at once. 'Are you with anyone?' I say, at the same time as she asks, 'You're married, I see from your Instagram?'

We laugh. 'You first,' I say.

'No, you go first. You've got three children, right?'

'Yes, who'd have thought it, eh?' I sip my coffee, thinking of the years I've lost, devoting my life to my three kids. *Who would I be without them?*

'When your name came up – when I saw your photo with your adorable children – I couldn't believe it!' She chuckles. 'Jade the party girl – a mum! What are their names?'

'Amber, Eddie and Leo.' My heart softens, thinking of them. Sam had captured a rare, perfect moment. Amber's smiling at me, kneading dough. Eddie's cutting out a gingerbread man. Leo's eating raisins. All of us with flour on our noses. Hashtag PerfectFamily.

'They're so gorgeous,' she enthuses. 'I'd love to meet them one day. How'd you meet your husband? At Edinburgh?'

I shake my head. 'Oh no. Sam did go to Edinburgh, but he was a few years above. I didn't know him then. No – we met at work. I was a copywriter, and he was a suit, an account director. Oh God, such a cliché – an office romance. Straight out of a romcom. I hated him at first. One of those annoying good-looking posh guys. Everything handed to him. And he'd been brought into the agency to make cuts.'

'So what changed?' She leans forward and the end of her nose twitches.

'Oh, I don't know,' I shrug. 'Maybe because we worked late – it gets pretty intense on a pitch. We drank a few beers, smoked a spliff. Suddenly his jokes seemed funny. By the time we won the pitch and went out celebrating, I was smitten.'

From the start of the pitch presentation, no one else in the room had mattered. Sam's intense gaze had made me feel like I was the most fascinating person alive. *Does he still think I'm fascinating? Or has familiarity bred boredom?*

'Sounds like you're made for each other,' Christina comments. She blows gently on her latte.

I smile. 'Yes, I suppose we are.' Things might not be perfect

14

but young kids are a struggle for most families. *I know I'm lucky.*

'And, after you married, did you carry on working together?'

'I went back part-time after Amber, but when Eddie arrived . . . He has so many allergies, and nurseries cost a fortune. Then came Leo, who's a ball of energy.' *And I haven't had a life ever since.* But I don't want to sound like I'm complaining.

'Are you back at work now?'

I sigh. 'I had a meeting with a headhunter this morning, but I'm not sure we can justify the cost of childcare. What about you? Any kids?'

'No. I don't have children.' She looks down at her cup and her tone is neutral so I can't tell whether she wants them or whether she's avoided having them. She always kept things close to her chest. It would take a while to get her to confide in me. Whereas I'd tell my problems to anyone who'd listen.

'Are you married or with anyone?' I ask.

'Michael.' She looks at me through her lashes and smiles. I remember that shy smile from when we were students. I'd tease her for having crushes. She would admire boys from afar, rather than talk to them. 'I met him while I was training. He was my supervisor.' I wonder at the flush in her cheeks. Her face is quite pink. Could she be embarrassed she still fancies him? What's it like, to be madly in love at our age? Of course, they don't have kids.

'So you went back to medical school?' I ask.

'Yes, but in London, not Edinburgh. My parents wouldn't let me go back to the university.'

'But you live in Scotland, right?'

She nodded. 'I was fond of Edinburgh, so when a training

position in a hospital came up I took it. My parents couldn't really say no – it was a job. Then I met Michael, and I've been there ever since.' She stirs her drink, and the cocoa smudges a dark stain into the white foam.

I can't avoid the subject any longer. 'You know, I tried to call you, after you left, but no one answered. I left a message . . .'

She puts her hand on my arm. 'I know, I'm sorry. I . . . I wasn't in a good place for a while. I . . . still find it hard . . . Do you mind if we don't talk about it? Not now, when we've just found each other again.'

I nod, wishing I could know what happened. There's an awkward pause and we both turn to study the watercolours on the walls. For a minute we study the landscape of a Scottish loch. Then Christina speaks. 'Jade, do you remember our week in the Highlands? In Izzie's aunt's house? It was magical.'

I nod, grinning. 'Oh yeah, so much fun! I haven't seen Izzie for years either.'

'Do you know, it was the most wonderful week of my life.' Her eyes are glowing. 'I never felt so free. My exams over, but no holiday assignments yet. No parents telling me what to do, how to live.'

'Off wine and crisps, I seem to remember.' We laugh and reminisce. The weather that week had been great for Scotland, and we'd sunbathed every day. Talking about what we'd got up to all those years ago smooths over any awkwardness.

'So what are you doing in London? Just down for a visit?' I ask.

'I'm thinking of moving back, for mum. I need to talk to Michael . . . I'm planning to arrange some job interviews – test the waters while I'm here.'

'So you're at a crossroads. Like me.' I grin then I catch sight of the time on her Rolex. 'Oh crap, sorry! I didn't realise the time. Have to get Leo from nursery.' I drain my cup, pick up my bag. 'Maybe we could link up again before you go back to Scotland? How long are you here?'

'It depends on my mum. How long we can bear each other. Maybe another week? But ... what are you doing this afternoon?'

'I'm taking Leo to a play centre.' I stand up and she does too.

'I'd love to meet him!' She puts a hand on my arm. 'I'm free this afternoon, Mum's out. I could join you if you like?'

I hesitate, not sure the play centre's the right place to meet the little hooligan. But I can't think of an excuse. 'Er, I guess. If you're sure? It can get quite noisy, but the café there does good coffee.'

'Sounds perfect. Text me the address.' We start walking towards the door.

'I'm so glad you found me, Christina.'

'Thank social media,' she laughs.

As we say goodbye the awkward pauses are forgotten and I hug her tightly, happy to see her. It feels amazing to be with someone who knew me when I was my old self.

When I was Jade, and not just someone's mum.

Chapter Three

Jade

Rumble Jungle's heaving when we get there. Screeching pre-schoolers charge around a huge play cage, lined with safety mats and divided into climbing areas. A central slide drops into a massive ball pit.

Leo kicks off his shoes and tears up a tunnel to his favourite shooters, barging past a baby who starts to bawl. The noise and bright primary colours are a sensory overload. Christina won't know what she's letting herself in for.

I'm lucky that between them, my group of mum friends know everything there is to know about bringing up children. But they're so efficient that I often feel a bit crap by comparison. And it can get boring, talking about potty-training and schools.

It'll be lovely to talk about something other than kids with Christina. She won't give a toss about school catchment areas. I just hope she gets on with the others. But the mums will be busy with their children, so maybe I'm worrying about nothing.

Leo shoots sponge balls into the ball pit while I hover outside the play cage and snap a few photos. A familiar redheaded boy bombs past me and I turn to see Kate and Fran have arrived. They pause their conversation when they see me.

'Wonderful to get out of the house.' Kate envelops me in an apple shampoo-scented hug. 'Daniel was in meetings all morning and Ollie was driving him insane.'

I met Kate at prenatal yoga. Her 'earth mother' vibe – the drapey scarves and paisley kaftans – belies her efficient attitude to parenting.

'So Daniel's working from home?' Fran says to Kate, once I've kissed her dark cheek. She's a part-time teacher, and the pencil skirt and blouse she's wearing suggests she's come straight from school.

'I should be grateful Dan's at home, away from temptation.' Kate's jaw stiffens. She and Daniel went through a dark period a few years ago and nearly split up. He was flirting with someone at work and eventually he'd confessed it to her. She's told us how they've been to marriage counselling.

'How is the dashing – sorry, dastardly – Dan doing?' Fran often refers to Daniel as the Silver Fox, but generally out of Kate's hearing, so she settles for a sympathetic smile.

'The pandemic actually helped, and subsequently he's mainly worked from home. It's brought us closer together,' Kate says.

Fran rolls her eyes. 'Glad I wasn't stuck in our flat with Zac's dad. If we hadn't been history by then, that would have finished us off.'

'Did I tell you I confronted her?' Kate's voice wobbles. 'Some young thing at Reuters. Such a cliché. She's rather plain, but apparently super intelligent. I imagine she won't be ready to have children until Daniel's nearly sixty. We've had a run of counselling sessions. He claims it never went beyond an emotional affair.

Nothing physical. He felt cut off from our lives. I handle every-thing to do with the children, so he felt there was no place for him.' She pauses to call to Ollie. 'Careful – mind the little girl.' She turns back to me. 'I mean, forgive me for being an efficient mother.'

I nod, but privately, I can almost understand Daniel, even though it doesn't justify what he did. It must be hard for him to contribute to their family life sometimes – apart from finan-cially. I guess the flirtation boosted his ego.

Fran sighs. 'Relationships don't last for life these days. Don't fifty per cent of marriages end in divorce?' She catches herself. 'Oh, sorry, Jade. You and Sam'll be in the happy fifty per cent, of course.' They both smile reassuringly. But I know Fran's not always been loyal to the sisterhood. She had a fling with a mar-ried man last year.

'When I found out about that girl, I took a long hard look at myself in the mirror.' Kate's upper-middle-class voice carries over the children's squeals. 'The truth is, four children have thickened my waistline beyond redemption. Everything in my life has been about the children. Music lessons, drama school, tuition. I handle it all. So if I don't have the energy to get more than a home haircut every now and then, so be it.'

Her words echo how I'm feeling. We make soothing noises and tell her she's brilliant. Is it my imagination or does Fran roll her eyes at me? I wonder if Fran has a nickname for Sam when I'm not in the room? 'Hot Dad' probably. I smile, think-ing of his striking blue eyes and blond hair that could do with a cut.

Leo's squeals pierce the air. He's with Ollie, climbing up the slide. 'It's OK when no one's coming down, right?' I ask, deferring to the others' more experienced judgement. My rule is to let Leo climb up the slide if no other children are waiting. It's good for him to explore a different way to use it. But other parents can get funny about the slide. Offended parent number one is shaping out to be a pregnant mother in dungarees, guiding her tiny daughter up the steps. The toddler stops at the top of the slide, chewing the end of a pigtail. She stares at Leo and wails.

'Leo,' I call. 'Come down, darling. The little girl's waiting to go.' I smile at the pregnant mum. 'It's fine, he won't push in.'

Leo doesn't totally ignore me. He stops climbing up the slide itself. But the slide is set on a slope lined with mats. Leo starts climbing the slope instead, using the slide as a handrail to pull himself up. He pushes his way to the top of the slide, making the little girl take a step down. The pregnant mother frowns. I sigh, kick off my wedges, wade through the ball pit and scoop him up.

'Slide!' Leo squawks. He kicks furiously at my thigh.

'Jade!' The voice comes from where I was just standing. I look round.

'Christina! You made it!' Relieved for a distraction away from the slide, I climb out of the cage, Leo wriggling under my arm, bellowing. 'Shush, Leo! I did warn you when you wanted to meet here!' I laugh to cover up how stressed I am, but she knows me too well.

'Are you OK, Jade?' she asks in a low voice.

'I'm fine. Leo's having a bit of a moment.'

I introduce Christina to Kate and Fran, who stand outside the ball pit, to avoid taking their shoes off. Their boys are running around too, but of course it would have to be Leo who barged the toddler.

'Lovely to meet you, Christina. And where's your little one?' Kate glances around.

'Christina came to meet Leo,' I say quickly. 'We were at Edinburgh together, and she's visiting her mum.'

Zac and Ollie run to the basketball court behind the play cage. 'Sorry – we better check on them.' Kate gives us a wave as she and Fran follow their boys.

Leo's feet thrash at my shins. I put him down, but he clings to me, pushing his face into my thighs, pulling at the stretchy fabric of my leggings.

'Who's this little cutie?' Christina leans down and waves at Leo.

'Not little,' he mutters, turning his head away.

'This big boy is Leo. Leo, meet Mummy's friend, Auntie Christina. And no climbing slides when people are trying to slide down,' I add loudly, for the pregnant mum's benefit.

'There should be no climbing up slides *ever*,' the woman snaps, scooping up her daughter.

I roll my eyes unapologetically. 'Oh, sorry, I didn't see the signs turning our toddlers into sheeple. I thought this was a play centre not a one-way system.'

Leo wriggles out of my arms and bullets up the slide again. I sigh as the pregnant mum glares at me.

Christina says loudly, for Leo's benefit. 'I'm sure a big boy like Leo would like to show the little girl how to go down the slide nicely. And then I think Mummy said something about the café? Maybe a yummy hot chocolate?'

Leo slides down headfirst on his belly. He forward-rolls into the ball pit and wriggles his way to my legs, stretching his arms up to be carried. 'Café, Mummy!' he orders.

'How do we ask?' I raise my eyebrows at him.

'Pleeease, Mummy?' He gives me a cheeky grin and I scoop him into my arms.

At the front of the hall, there's a counter with tables and chairs dotted about. I plonk Leo in a booster seat and order coffees, hot chocolate and chips. Leo's fascinated by Christina cleaning the table with a wet wipe or three. She's always had a thing about germs. She gives him a wet wipe to clean with and he giggles.

I fetch our order when it's ready. 'Careful, chips are hot. Blow!' Leo ignores me, dipping his chips in his drink and splashing hot chocolate everywhere. 'Look, Mumma, choc choc chip.' He shoves the chip in his mouth then he rubs his palm across the table, smearing chocolate over the surface. I rescue the cup before he knocks it into Christina's lap. 'Let Mummy have that before we have an accident.'

'Don't worry, it's nothing that won't come out in the wash,' Christina assures me. Does she not know that chocolate won't wash out of cream silk?

A nearby toddler screams and I wince. 'Sorry, I warned you!' I can't imagine why anyone without kids would want to come here.

'It's fine, don't worry. It's nice spending some time with you.' She gives my arm a squeeze.

'Finished – go play.' Leo wriggles out of the chair.

I grab my bag and stand up. 'Sorry, I have to keep an eye on him with all these babies around.'

We take our coffees back to the play area where Kate and Fran are in a deep discussion about SATs. Leo chases Ollie and Zac around the play cage to some monkey bars. He clings to the first rung, attempting to swing. My heart swoops, worried he'll fall.

'So maybe this wasn't the best place to carry on our chat,' Christina admits, laughing. 'But I'm glad I've met Leo. He's a real character.'

'Is it any surprise that headhunter thought I wasn't ready to go back to work?' I blurt out. 'I – I feel so worn out and haggard these days.' Tears of self-pity are pricking at my eyes. Leo roars at another little girl. 'Leo, nicely, please.'

'It can't be easy, being a full-time mum,' Christina sympathises. 'But Leo's super confident – he has great leadership skills.'

'That's one way of looking at it.' When Leo wants something, he bashes anyone in his way. But I'm grateful for her positive spin.

'Oh, he's sure to be a CEO one day.' She raises her eyebrows. 'Look how he charges forward. Some people don't see obstacles.' Her tone's dry, and I wonder who she's thinking of.

'He's like his dad,' I say. 'Sam worked his way up to become partner of the agency. He's always known what he wants. Whereas I . . . Well, I'm not getting any younger. I barely have time to trim my own hair.' It's a relief to voice my fears. Christina won't judge. She'd always been a good listener.

Leo runs up to the shooters with Ollie and Zac. Sponge balls rain on my head. I collapse, faking dead, and they scream with laughter. I crawl out of the ball pit, groaning as if in agony.

'Mummy dead,' yells Leo. 'More.'

'No more. You killed Mummy.' All three boys pull at my arm, dragging me back to the ball pit.

'You know, it might be easier to chat properly without

children?' Christina suggests when I extricate myself. 'How about meeting for dinner one evening?'

I sigh. 'Evenings are difficult. Sam's working late a lot.'

Kate turns from her conversation with Fran to interrupt us. 'You need to make sure that Sam does his fair share of babysitting.'

Fran joins in. 'Sorry — that's another thing that winds me up — why do we say "babysitting" when it's *their* child too?'

'Apologies!' says Kate. 'Bad habit. You're quite right.'

'Can't your mum babysit?' Christina suggests.

I shake my head. 'Last time she did, it was a disaster. Leo clung to my legs and wouldn't let go. I was so stressed I couldn't enjoy myself. When we got back, the kids were still up, watching telly. It was the only way she could get Leo to stop crying. Never again.'

'I could do with a night out,' Fran says. 'Time Jordan pulled his weight. There's a salsa bar in Soho I like the sound of. What about it, Kate? Up for some salsa?'

Kate shakes her head. 'I'd love to say yes but I'm focusing on "couple time" at the moment.' Fran raises her eyebrows suggestively and we all laugh.

'I feel too haggard to hit a West End bar,' I say.

'How about I book us into a salon first?' Christina suggested. 'Like old times, except we can afford more than a five-pound cut.' When we were at uni, Christina and I had made the most of the Toni&Guy student cuts although she never did more than trim hers.

'I'm so ready for a night out in Soho!' Fran grins. She flings an arm around me and one around Christina.

Fran's a good laugh — it'll be a good night. 'Sure you can't join us, Kate?'

'Another time,' Kate says, picking up her bag. 'Time to go.'

A loud scream interrupts the chatter.

'Oh my God, LEO!!' He's run smack into Ollie and they're both wailing. 'I'm sorry, my darling – Mummy wasn't looking.' I sweep him into my arms and cover him with kisses but he wails on. 'We better go, too.' I slip on my wedges and wrestle with Leo's trainers against his will.

'So – the salon?' Christina asks. 'Shall I book us in? I'm desperate for a haircut.'

I know she's talking about herself, not me, but I'm suddenly aware of my scraped-back, messy bun. I hoick Leo onto my hip. 'I'll check Sam's all right with the kids.'

'I'll text you the salsa bar deets,' said Fran. 'They do tapas. Let me know a time.'

'Brilliant. Say bye to everyone, Leo.' I wave to Kate and Fran and walk to the car park with Christina.

'It's been so lovely to catch up, Jade. Let me know what Sam says.' Christina hugs me goodbye.

'I'm so glad you found me.' It *has* been good to catch up, after all these years. Leo pushes my head away from her. 'Bye, I'll text you ...'

I turn to wave before I get into my car, but she's already disappeared.

Chapter Four

Christina

Then

C hristina had never lived away from home until she started
at Edinburgh University. After a ten-hour coach journey,
she dragged her suitcase to Pollock Halls and her tiny box room,
which had just enough space for a bed and a desk.

She was exhausted and trying to ignore her growling stomach, but her mother's complaints echoed through her mind. 'So
expensive, halls of residence. You better make sure you don't
miss any meals, get our money's worth.' Dinner finished at
seven, she'd read in the handbook, so she was just in time.

There were clear signs to the dining hall, but the reek of
boiled cabbage alone could have directed her. The smell took
her back to school dinners when she'd sit on her own, bolting
her food before escaping to the library.

She joined the queue to the counter, her neck hot and sticky,
as if everyone's eyes were on her. *No one is paying any attention
to you*, she repeated to herself. *Everyone's more concerned with
themselves.*

Her pulse raced. Peering from under her fringe she wondered if anyone would talk to her. Would her school lunchtime experience be extended to every meal? She kept her head lowered so no one would ask what subjects she was taking. She never felt like she belonged. Why would it be different here?

Students sat in pairs and groups as if they'd known each other forever, even though it was only the first day of Freshers' Week. She glanced at a jostling group of Scottish students. They could have been at school together. There were a few English accents, generally over-privileged voices, even posher than the girls at her school. A few girls were in flowery summer dresses, others wore peasant blouses and vintage flares. Christina usually shopped for clothes with her mum. She wished she'd bought denim jeans instead of the corduroy skirt she had on.

At the counter she took a tray and pointed to baked beans, chips and sausages. Comfort food but unhealthy. There'd be time to investigate healthier options later. At home food was simple. Plain rice, stir-fried vegetables with slices of meat or tofu, always with half-cooked onions.

She turned to brave the tables, aiming to scuttle to the back, where she could hide.

Someone tapped her shoulder. 'Could you pass me an apple juice?' The London voice reminded her of home and her heart squeezed.

She picked up another carton and turned round. A British East Asian girl stood behind her. The apple juice slipped from her fingers.

'Hi, I'm Jade.' The girl's voice carried over the hubbub of the hall. 'What's your name?'

'Christina.'

Christina's face burned. Everyone must be listening. To hide her red cheeks, she knelt to pick up the carton. It was leaking, so she grabbed the paper napkin from her tray to soak up the liquid. When she stood up, Jade threw out slim arms adorned with dozens of thin metallic bangles, and hugged her hard. 'Lovely to meet you. Where are you from?'

'London.' Christina's voice croaked. She hadn't spoken to a soul since her dad had dropped her at the coach station.

A smile split Jade's face. 'Great to meet a fellow Londoner on my first day. Which side's your room? I'm on the north side.'

'Me too.' Christina's heart was beating hard. She held her breath as the last of the evening's sun slipped through the windows enveloping Jade in a golden nimbus of light. Christina dared to hope for a friend, even though Jade would probably reject her once she met other more interesting people.

'We're on the same side? Amazing!' Jade smiled, looking directly into Christina's eyes instead of glancing over her head like the other students.

Christina's eyes slid away. It wouldn't last. Jade's perfume was the sweet lily scent that had been all the rage at school, and it took her straight back to the common room and the popular girls who'd always ignored her.

'I don't know anyone here. Thank God I found you.' Jade squeezed her arm and turned to find a table. 'Come on, let's eat, then we can go into town and explore.'

Chapter Five

Jade

After the fun afternoon, I'm brought back to reality pretty quickly. The traffic's terrible on the way back from Rumble Jungle and I'm late picking up Eddie and Amber. Eddie hurt his knee in football and, unlike him, was tearful and whiny. Amber was fretful and anxious about being the last child left with her ballet teacher. She stomped all the way to the car.

Once home, I cook dinner in a rush, hoping food will make them less grouchy, but I undercook the pasta. 'Mumma. No want 'mato.' Leo pushes his bowl back at me. Even Eddie, who's normally obliging, puts his spoon down and refuses to eat.

Amber makes a face. 'The pasta's hard.'

'Oh gosh, really?' I take their bowls back, scrape off the bolognaise sauce and tip the bow ties back into the pan. I add more water from the kettle, then stick the pan back on the hob.

After they finish eating, I rush them upstairs to get ready for bed. My mum phones while I'm trying to get Leo into the bath. I'm tempted to ignore the call, but I know she'll keep ringing until she gets me, so I answer.

'Jade, I never hear from you,' she complains, before launching straight into a story about an auntie in Malaysia.

'Mum . . . can I call you back tomorrow? Sam's working late and I need to get the kids to bed.' I agree to have dinner at hers the weekend after next, then pass the phone to Amber while I carry on with bath time.

Leo runs round naked and giggling until Eddie tempts him with a dinosaur game, then he refuses to get out. He lies kicking and splashing, fingers wrinkling. I pull out the plug and the water drains with a slurp. He rolls around the empty bath on a bed of plastic alphabet shapes, with his T-rex and squeezy submarine. Eventually I scoop him up, wet and slippery, drenching myself while I wrap him in a towel.

I'm exhausted by the time Sam texts to say he's on his way home, so I speed-read three Mr Men books, forcing myself to do the cute voices the kids expect.

'One more, Mumma.' Leo holds up a finger, looking so adorable my heart melts despite my tiredness.

'I'll read to him, Mummy,' says Eddie. 'You go and rest.'

I kiss him. 'You sure?' He nods.

I pause at the door, listening to Eddie's Mr Tickle which soon has Leo giggling. I hope they won't be up all night. Usually, I'd change into PJs and collapse in bed. But I bet childless Christina isn't in PJs by nine.

It's been great to re-connect with Christina, but it's made me see myself through her eyes. As a student she'd been quiet and anxious, but she's grown into her own skin while I feel a wreck.

It's like we've swapped places.

I shrug off my damp clothes and pick out a taupe sleeveless shift dress. Years old, but its classic shape hasn't dated. I brush my hair and pin it in a loose knot. Remembering Christina's floral scent, I spray my wrists and neck with the Jo Malone perfume the kids had given me last Christmas and hide my tired eyes with a dab of make-up, feeling my spirits lift instantly.

The kids have quietened by the time I go down. I pour myself a glass of wine and sink into the leather sofa with my iPad. Christina's right. I'll feel more myself after a haircut. Sam can look after the children for a change. I send her a text, asking her to book me an appointment.

I flick through pages of hairstyles. Should I try an asymmetric bob? Long layers? The hair stylist will know best.

I've finished my glass and poured myself a second by the time the front door opens and Sam's shoes click across the hall-way. A moment later, he appears in the living room. 'Hiya – kids OK?' He leans down and kisses me. It's been a while since he's greeted me with more than a perfunctory kiss, but I'm often in bed by the time he gets back. I detect the yeasty odour of beer and a hint of smoke. 'Surprised you're still up. And at the vino?' He picks up my glass and takes a sip.

'Oi, get your own.' I push him off, but he nibbles playfully at my neck in the way I love, and I relax against him. It was a good idea to come back downstairs for a change. 'How was your meeting? Been boozing?'

He chuckles and sits down. 'Wayne ordered pizza and beers and we thrashed around ideas with the creatives. We're getting there. Bloody need to.'

Twelve years ago, I'd be the one sharing late-night pizza with him, working on a pitch. We'd giggled over stretchy cheese, and stole kisses when the rest of the team weren't looking. But since the kids arrived, we've forgotten we're anyone other than parents.

Recently, he's been getting in later from work. We used to eat dinner then watch a bit of telly before bed, but we've hardly had a glass of wine together in a while.

He looks over my shoulder at the iPad. 'Planning a new look?'

'I met up with Christina, my old friend from university. We're going for a haircut on Saturday, so you'll have to sort the kids. We might go for some food.'

He puts the iPad down and combs a strand of my hair through his fingers. 'Fine, but don't cut it all off, or I'll have words.' He pulls me in for a kiss. 'Mmm. You smell good enough to eat.' Shivers of pleasure ripple through me. He rarely compliments me these days and I'm glad I stayed up, sprayed on perfume. 'When are we going out, just the two of us?' His hands sweep up my skirt, squeezing my buttocks.

'You've had a lot of late meetings lately,' I remind him gently, hoping it doesn't spoil the mood.

'I'm sorry, darling – work's been crazy. If your mate can babysit, we can hit the town.'

'Sounds amazing.' I can't remember the last time we had a date night. He's been rather distant lately. Maybe we just need time on our own, to remember what we love about each other.

He's unzipping my dress and pulling down the top. 'There's the summer party coming up next week – you could meet me there ... we could go on somewhere?' The agency summer party wasn't quite what I had in mind, but his hands are cupping my breasts and I'm finding it hard to speak.

'Shall we ... go up?' I drag myself from the sofa, my dress hanging off me. Sam follows closely, a hand on the small of my back.

We peek in on Amber, and then the boys. They're asleep and don't stir. There's no time to drink in their cuteness as Sam nuzzles my neck, making me giggle, then drags me up to the loft.

When we reach our room, he pushes me onto the bed. His lips find mine, his tongue tasting my mouth. As we kiss, he sheds his clothes. Suddenly we're crazy for each other again. It's a relief. All we need is more focused time together. He pulls down my dress, his hands tweaking my nipples roughly. It's been ages, over a month at least, and I'm craving the touch of his bare skin on mine. My nails dig into his back, fingers kneading his muscular body.

After an initial rush of passion, we slot into our well-practised routine. Twenty minutes later, it's over and I lie snuggled in Sam's arms, as his breathing turns into snores.

Chapter Six

Jade

Christina and I meet outside the hair salon in Covent Garden on Saturday afternoon. We're ushered into a sleek waiting area with abstract art on the walls. A fashionista assistant with an asymmetric dress and pink and turquoise hair offers us coffee, juice or champagne. She waves a limp hand to an array of tablets which we can use to browse looks. Then we're whisked off by our respective stylists. It's certainly a step up here, compared to my local salon, but Christina looks perfectly comfortable in this world, and eventually I start to enjoy myself.

We emerge with hot new looks – Christina's crisp bob giving her a 1930s Hollywood look of a young Anna May Wong. Mine is more Hollywood of today, layered and blow-dried for extra volume. I gaze in the mirror, delighted, swishing from side to side. I catch Christina's eye, and we giggle like teenagers.

Afterwards, we find a cute boutique where Christina insists I buy a new rose print dress with a sweetheart neckline and a circular 1950s skirt. It's a lot more glamorous than the simple black dress I'd put on this morning, and I feel ready for a night out. She finds a sequinned 1920s shift dress that suits her new bob perfectly.

Fran's waiting for us at the restaurant that's art deco-styled, with smoked glass and velvet furnishings. It's like walking into a jewellery box. Excitement bubbles through me. She's wearing a polka dot wiggle dress and envelops us in a perfume-scented hug before stepping back to admire our new looks. 'Wow, you both look fabulous,' she says, moving back to her seat. I sink into the velvet banquette next to her, slipping off my heels and sighing with relief. Christina slides in opposite. 'So, nice day, pampering yourselves?' Fran asks, handing us the extensive menus.

'Wonderful. It's such heaven not to be Mummy – for the whole day.' I grin, feeling a little closer to my old self, before kids.

Fran chuckles. 'Sam won't know what's hit him.'

Her words knock me slightly. *Do I normally look so awful?*

Christina notices my face drop and quickly waves over a waiter. 'Bottle of Moët, please. Make sure it's cold.' She's obviously used to finer things these days. I'm just wondering if my bank account can stand the expense when she adds, 'It's on me. First time out with my best friend in – what? – twenty years? We must celebrate.' Her eyes sparkle, like the sequins on her dress and I let her joy melt away my insecurities.

I beam at her. 'Thanks, Christina. Won't say no.'

Fran cheers at the pop of the cork, and I clap.

'Thank you, Christina – it's been amazing. I feel truly indulged.' I clink my glass to hers and then Fran's. 'And here's to the rest of the night!'

'It's been a pleasure.' Christina sips and sighs. 'There's nothing like a West End salon to make you feel fabulous.'

The champagne fizzes on my tongue, leaving a warm glow.

My phone beeps with a text from Sam. I sigh. 'Sorry. Sam can't find the oven chips. He wasn't happy to be left with the kids this morning, hungover from Friday night's drink with the guys.'

Fran barks with laughter. 'Men, eh? Go ahead and call him. I'll just check on Zac.'

'I should text my mum,' says Christina, picking up her phone.

I turn to one side and dial home. 'It's Mummy!' Eddie calls out.

Leo in the background shouts, 'Me, me! Want speak to Mumma! My Mumma!'

My heart squeezes with love. 'Hello, my darlings, I've missed you.' Suddenly I feel guilty for leaving them all day. But Christina's right. It's my turn for a treat. 'What've you been up to?'

'We took Amber to ballet and went to the park . . .' Eddie managed to get in before Leo snatches the phone off him.

'Disney, Mumma. Chips, ice cream!'

I laugh. 'Sounds lovely. Can you pass me to Daddy?'

Buoyed up on champagne, I launch into him before he's had a chance to say hello. 'For God's sake, Sam, can't I have one night out with my mates, without you bothering me for the goddamned baked beans? All right, oven chips, whatever. Middle drawer, back freezer, which you'd know if you ever did a thing.' Christina glances at me and I realise I'm speaking too loudly. 'Sorry,' I mouth and lower my voice. 'And don't forget to put the fish fingers on a separate tray to the chicken. Don't text me again unless it's an emergency.' I ring off and put my phone on the table. 'Honestly.'

'Everything OK?' Fran raises her eyebrows.

'Eddie's allergic to fish,' I tell them. 'But Amber loves fish fingers. I hope Sam doesn't cross contaminate anything. I'll just send him a last text.'

'Surely Sam remembers his own child is allergic to fish?' says Christina.

Frans empties the bottle into our glasses. 'Right, put your phone away – the kids are safe with Sam.'

I send the text, then stow my phone in my bag and zip it up. Christina picks up her glass. 'Are you always the children's main carer? Doesn't Sam take over on the weekends?'

Fran chimes in. 'You might not be a single parent, but you do most of the work.'

'To be fair, Sam's job is pretty demanding. But while my mate's back in London, he'll have to take his turn at the weekend.' I squeeze Christina's arm, and she clinks her glass on mine. It's great to have her back in my life. A friend who doesn't have children, who knows me from the good old days, not just the haggard-mum version of me. Apart from Fran, the mums I know rarely go out, and when they do, all they talk about are their kids.

In the bar downstairs, there's a live salsa band. So, after we've filled up on garlic prawns dunked in aioli, patatas bravas and chorizo we move to the basement. Fran's hips are wiggling to the beat. 'Come on, girls, ready to rumba?'

The basement's dimly lit, and looks like one of those jazz caves in Paris with red velvet banquettes and stone walls. The black-and-white tiled floor is filled with dancers. A Latin guy with slicked-back hair, in a black shirt, dress trousers and Cuban-heeled boots, tips his alluring partner backwards. Scarlet flounces sweep the floor as she kicks a shapely leg.

A group of women in matching pink T-shirts – adorned with

the word 'Hen' in glittery print – draped in cerise feather boas and clutching pink penis-shaped cups, giggle and whoop, salsa-ing with more enthusiasm than skill. They're led by the bride, who wears a sparkly tiara.

Back at university, I would have been the first on the dance floor. But it's been ages since I've danced to anything except the *Paw Patrol* theme tune, and my confidence isn't what it used to be. As Christina and I stand to the side, Fran is already moving to the beat, and soon she's pulling us onto the dance floor and teaching us the steps. Christina soon gets the hang of it, but I feel self-conscious, my arms and legs stiff. *If only Sam would come to a salsa night.* But it's not his thing. Hanging around kids in their twenties gives him a fear of not looking cool.

Fran's soon partnered up with the Latino dancer, spinning around like a pro. Christina won't let me retreat to a table in the shadows. When we were younger, she was the one who needed persuading. But now, she's the one encouraging me to twirl.

Whilst Fran continues to salsa, Christina pulls me over to make friends with the hens. They're ordering vat-sized jugs of frozen margaritas, dripping with condensation, the rims crusted with salt. The bride holds up one of the vats. 'Up your bum, chuck!' she says with a strong northern accent.

Another hen joins in. 'Here's to the bride – and a lifetime of happiness!' One of them offers me a jug and I grab a straw and suck. The salty lime slush is refreshing but makes my head spin. I turn to Christina and offer her the straw, whispering, 'More like a life sentence . . .'

She hides her snigger with a polite smile. 'Congratulations.' She bends down to the jug, but her lips don't reach the straw.

'Don't worry,' I whisper. 'The tequila kills any bacteria.'

I take another slurp. My head whirls. The hen party swirls me onto the dance floor. Soon, we're bopping around, inhibitions loosened by the margaritas. I'm feeling sexy for a change. And I'm loving it.

Time speeds by when you're having fun and soon it's nearly ten. Fran's in a clinch with the Latino. The hens are bopping. The crowd blurs, then splits into two.

I stumble to a table at the back and Christina joins me. Her phone's buzzing. The screen casts a glow on her frown.

'Everything OK?' I ask. I wonder if it's Michael.

'Oh, it's nothing. You don't want to hear about my problems.'

'Come on, Christina – you know you can tell me anything.' I throw an arm around her. She's listened to me, and I want to return the favour.

She's about to say something when her phone buzzes again. 'Oh, I'm sorry. I have to go before my mum locks me out.'

Once in the summer break, I made Christina lie to her mother about going to the library so we could go to the cinema. Her mother still seems to be controlling her fun. 'Don't you have your own keys?' I ask. 'It's only ten. The night is young.'

'Mum only feels safe at night when she bolts the door. Although if I'm locked out, I can always sleep in my car.'

'In the car?' I squeal. 'You can't sleep there!'

She gives me an awkward smile. 'It's fine. I should get back in time if I leave now.'

The music changes to the samba. I long to carry on dancing. 'Look, why don't you stay at mine? There's a sofa bed in the study. Come on, we haven't been out together for . . . over twenty years.'

The barman appears with another vat of margaritas.

I clap my hands. 'Who ordered this?'

'I did, before my mum texted,' Christina admits.

'That's that. We can't leave now. Stay at mine.' I pick up the jug. I offer Christina the straw and I take the other one. We slurp. I catch her eye and grin, glad she's not worried about my germs.

Three hours later, we're the last to leave. Fran has disappeared with her Latino. After heartfelt goodbyes to the northern hens and promises to look them up on Facebook, Christina and I pile into a cab.

Everything's a bit of a blur after that. I remember leaning back on the leather seat, feet aching, my face stretched in a huge grin. '*Such* a brilliant night. I'm so glad you're back. Can't believe Fran copped off. If I didn't have kids, I'd come dancing every week.'

'It's been fun,' she nods. 'Do you remember dancing by the loch? It was magical.'

'I remember,' I say, thinking of the Highlands holiday again. 'Oh, it's *so* good to get out. The two of us together again.'

Chapter Seven

Jade

A beep wakes me. *Is that my phone?* Head pounding, I emerge from the duvet and squint at the sunlight flooding the loft. Sam's side of the bed is empty.

I vaguely recollect pulling out the sofa bed in the early hours and Christina making me drink a glass of water. Just like old times.

The phone beeps again and I reach for it. Not a reminder or the alarm, but a text. I peel open my eyes and read the words in the grey box before I realise this isn't my phone – it's Sam's.

I blink in disbelief. *What the hell?*

Unknown Number:
Dreamed about you last night x

My brain wakes up as my fingers tighten round the phone, Sam's phone.

Who the fuck is this? And why are they dreaming about my husband?

Heat floods my face. My heart thumps wildly. The grey box

stares at me, black type blurring. Pain stabs my chest and it's hard to breathe.

I slam the phone on the bedside table.

Footsteps thud, the door opens and Leo bounces in, arms swinging importantly. 'Mummy, wake up! Kisstina here.' He tugs me out of bed, before running downstairs.

Numb with shock, I stare at my new rose print dress, a crumpled heap on the floor. Yesterday's shopping and dancing feels aeons away. Another lifetime. But manners demand I ignore my pounding head and go check on Christina.

Chatter and a peal of laughter drifts from the kitchen. I take a breath before I push open the door.

'Mummy!' Leo barrels into me, followed by Eddie. They drag me to the table.

Sam wolf-whistles. 'Good morning. The dancing queen awakes.' I blink, staring at him like he's a stranger. He takes a tray of croissants out of the oven and puts them on the table.

My thoughts are scattered in pieces. *Should I say something about the text? Am I even sure about what I've read? It could be a wrong number.*

'Daddy make brek brek!' Leo runs up to him, hugging his legs.

'Who's my best boy?' Sam blows raspberries on his belly. Leo is squealing with delight.

What should I do? My mind floats, watching us, as if we're actors on a screen. I play the wife, paralysed with doubt, as the devoted father nuzzles his giggling son.

Sam comes over to me and kisses me, and Leo joins in kissing my other cheek. Sam doesn't seem to notice my stiffness. Or he mistakes the reason for it. 'Mmm, I approve of the new look. But someone's feeling a little worse for wear, methinks.'

'Shut up.' I nudge him away before I'm tempted to scream at him.

'What's "Methinks"?' asks Eddie.

Amber looks up from reading *Agent Scarlett*. 'It's from olden times. Like Shakespeare.'

'Daddy's talking like Shakespeare now.' Despite my clenched jaw, I manage to fake a smile for the children's sake. 'Morning, Christina, do you feel as rough as me?'

'Good morning!' Christina smiles from her seat at the table next to Amber. She looks fresh in yesterday's slacks and silk blouse. Anyone would think she's had a full night's sleep instead of rolling in with me at gone four.

I sit in my usual seat, conscious of my baggy dressing gown and tangled hair. I suddenly see our kitchen-diner as a guest might. The shimmering silver cabinets I'd loved at the time look dated. The cream quartz breakfast bar is stained and chipped. The walls are crammed with faded handprints, crayon scribbles and moulting nature collages, blu-tacked at odd angles, overlapping one another.

A seashell-framed mirror Amber made for a school project throws back my reflection. I jump back. My eyes look shadowy and tired. When did I get so old? My pyjamas, once pink, are tinged with grey from the wash. Sam's so late back these days that he mostly sees me in night clothes.

Is the text from someone at his office? Looking smart in designer office wear, her face covered in make-up? One of the account execs? A client? Or is she a new recruit, straight from college, with young, dewy skin?

I'm dimly aware that Christina is talking to me. 'Thanks for having me. Your sofa bed is incredibly comfortable. I slept like a baby.' Her eyes shine with gratitude but then she pauses. 'Is everything all right, Jade?'

She must think I'm being so rude but it's hard to act normally when a potential bomb could be about to hit my marriage. Still, it's not her fault. 'I ... er ... I'm just hungover.' I attempt a smile even though I want to be sick.

Sam brings a cafetière and a basket of croissants over and sits down at the head of the table. '*Et voilà! Café et croissants, mesdames.*' He pours coffee into mugs with a flourish. Christina and the children giggle.

His hammy French-waiter impression is making my skin crawl. Anger flushes through me, heating my cheeks. All very well him acting the perfect father for Christina's benefit when he's hardly been around lately. Hanging out with whoever sent that text no doubt. I open my mouth, about to ask if he knows who the 'Unknown Number' is, but the words stick in my throat. I can't ask now. Not in front of Christina and the kids. 'My head is banging,' I mumble instead. *Could he be having a mid-life crisis?*

Sam places a mug of coffee in front of me. 'Awww ... Mummy had too much vino?' he teases. I have to bite my lip to stop myself snapping at him.

'Champagne followed by margaritas,' Christina admits, looking like nothing but mineral water passed her lips all night.

'Will Fizzy C make your head better, Mummy?' Eddie asks, cuddling up to me. 'Like you give to me when I'm ill? I missed you last night.'

I avoid Sam by snuggling into Eddie's neck. 'I missed you too, my darling.' I kiss him.

'Me, me!' Leo clambers on my lap and puts something in my

hands. It's the tube of fizzy Vitamin C. I kiss him too. 'Thanks, darling.' I breathe in their love, hiding from my rocky emotions. I wish I could stay cuddled into them all day, and escape thinking about that text.

Leo wriggles off and drags a stool to a cupboard. He fetches a glass, and with Eddie's help manages to fill it with water from the Brita jug, only sloshing a small puddle on the counter. He carefully carries the glass over to me and climbs back into my lap, pushing Eddie out of the way.

'Oh wow. Thank you.'

Eddie opens the lid of the tube, and Leo tips out a vitamin tablet, dropping it into the water and staring in fascination at the fizzing.

Sam passes round the basket of pastries. '*Croissants, tout le monde?*' The table's laid, with jam and butter in dishes, the milk in a goddamned jug. I want to shout that this perfect husband act is fake. The text throbs like a bassline to my hangover. My fingers itch to slap his chiselled face.

Leo grabs a croissant and dumps it on my plate.

'Offer one to Christina,' Sam says. But Leo's turned shy. He grabs another and shoves it in his mouth, scattering flakes of pastry everywhere.

'Leo!' Sam scolds but I hug my baby tighter.

Christina flicks a concerned look at me. I know she senses something is wrong, but she chatters on. I'm grateful for the distraction. 'I can help myself, Leo, but which croissant shall I have?' Leo points to a croissant. 'This one?' She picks it up and places it on her plate. 'Mmm! Good choice – this looks yummy! I love your kitchen, Jade. It's so . . . homey.'

I attempt a joke. 'Thanks, is that a polite word for messy?'

I can't help but notice the leaf collages are moulting on the floor and Lego is everywhere. But neat-freak Christina seems to have mellowed with age.

Leo shoves a Lego truck towards Christina, bashing it into her hand. 'Leo, careful!' Sam scolds.

She smiles and takes the truck, running it along the table. 'Thank you, is that for me? I mean it, Jade. There's a lovely atmosphere, just like in your photos. Your house is so – full of life, compared to my mother's.' Her cheeks turn red. 'Sorry . . . I sound like I've been stalking you.'

'Jade's rather obsessed with Instagram,' Sam says. 'I've told her it's a public platform. Anyone can see your pictures, babe.'

'I know how social media works,' I retort, avoiding his gaze and turning to Christina. 'You're welcome to come round anytime. You seem to have turned Sam into Husband of the Year.' I clench my hands into fists.

Sam puts an arm around me. 'Don't know what you mean.'

His arm feels heavy, and I shrug him off. Christina looks away. I know she can tell something's up.

'Amber – how was ballet?' I ask.

'Fine.' Amber doesn't lift her eyes from her book.

'Girls jumping,' Leo jumps off my lap. He stands on his tiptoes and then bends his knees and swings his arms, as if about to take off.

Sam ruffles his hair. 'He insisted on watching, and then on jumping with the girls. He's hilarious.'

'Leo could take ballet, too.' I glare at him. 'They need more boys.'

Amber looks up. 'No way!'

47

Leo sticks his tongue out at her then nuzzles into my lap.

'No gender stereotypes in this house.' Sam winks at Christina, who lowers her eyes to her cup, her cheeks pink. My neck feels hot. *Does he have to lay it on so thick?*

Sam can be an extrovert. It's like he searches for approval from others around him. I often wonder if it's anything to do with his childhood. His mum died of cancer when he was young, and he was left to himself a lot as a teenager. *Could that desire for approval have led to an affair?*

Sam drains his coffee and stands up. 'I'm going to love you and leave you.' He moves towards the sink and I wonder at his choice of words.

'Where're you going?' I say, my throat tight. *Is he going to meet 'Unknown Number'?*

'Meeting some dads down the pub to watch the cricket.' He rinses his mug and plate and tidies them into the dishwasher. Totally unlike him. 'You're always at your mothers' meetings.'

'But you hate cricket.' Is he lying to me? *Surely not.* A quick call to Kate and I'd catch him out.

He explains to Christina. 'The mums get together over cake and moan about their husbands. Us dads are more civilised. We get together in the pub.'

'Without the kids. It's hardly fair.' I'm gritting my teeth.

'Who says it's fair? You'll be fine. The lovely Christina can be trusted to look after you. Didn't you say she's a doctor?' The affected way he's speaking makes me want to hit him.

'Catcha later, gang.' He clicks his teeth and points his fingers in a double gun sign at the children.

'Bye, Daddy,' chorus the boys. Amber looks up from her book and waves.

Heart thudding, I follow Sam to the hall. I have to ask him about the message. I might not like the answer, but I'd rather know.

I take a breath, nausea rising in my throat. 'Sam . . .'

'Fuck's sake, bloody kids.' He exhales hard through his nostrils and pulls at his laces. They're knotted together. 'Leo, have you been playing with Daddy's shoes?'

Leo runs giggling into the hall. He takes one look at Sam and escapes into the kitchen. I can't confront Sam now. Not in front of the kids, and with Christina here too. I let go of the breath I've been holding, relieved I can put it off.

Sam's out of the door and as I watch him walking down the path, I see him check his phone. *Is he keying a reply? Chuckling at the shared joke?*

I'll have it out with him tonight, when the children are in bed. They hate Mummy and Daddy arguing. No point upsetting them.

I go to the kitchen and sit down, avoiding Christina's look of concern by putting my head on the table. 'I feel awful. I blame those bloody vats.'

'What's a bloody vat?' asks Eddie.

'Jug, I mean. I apologise for my husband, Christina. God knows what got into him today. *Methinks*. Humph.' I hope she just thinks I'm hungover.

'He's . . . charming.' I lift my head and see her mouth twisting with something indefinable. Maybe she misses her husband.

My mind flashes back to the club. Christina on her phone. She hadn't looked happy. Was it Michael? Could I ask her? Once upon a time, we'd told each other everything.

I slope to the fridge and pour myself a glass of cold sauvignon blanc from Sam's wine club order. It's nearly twelve so just about the afternoon, and the way I'm feeling, it's medicinal. Sam's at the pub, for fuck's sake, and he won't be drinking water.

'Like a glass?' I offer Christina. 'Hair of the dog? The kids won't notice. Remind me never to drink tequila again.'

She smiles. 'I'd better not – I have to face my mum later. I'll have a fruit tea instead.'

I fill the kettle and wait for it to boil, leaning on the kitchen counter.

'Want *Nemo!*' Leo shouts.

'No. *Red!*' Amber insists.

'Please stop arguing!' Eddie is ever the peacemaker.

Christina glances towards the living room. 'Would you like me to help them decide?'

'My head will thank you.'

She disappears into the living room. I can't hear what she says but her voice sounds calm. Soon, the Disney theme tune blares out.

'You're so good with the children,' I say gruffly when she reappears. I dunk a fruits-of-the-forest tea bag in a mug of hot water and carry it over to the table with my wine. The fruity scent takes me back to those nights in halls. Christina sitting on my bed while I poured out my boy troubles and she analysed what I could do. At uni, she often seemed wiser than me. *Should I tell her about the text?* But I feel bad launching into my problems when she seems to be having issues of her own. I remember now. Last night she'd received some texts and looked upset. I should check on her first.

'Christina, is everything OK?' I take the plunge. 'Last night, you seemed upset? Was it your mum, or . . .?'

She smiles sadly and looks at her lap. I stay silent, giving her space. She always did take longer to open up. Eventually she sighs. 'No.' She fixes her gaze on me. 'It's Michael. We're spending some time apart. He wouldn't travel to England with me. He's . . . been working late a lot.'

'He's a doctor, isn't he?' So I'm right. There is something wrong.

'Yes. We met when I was training. But we haven't worked together for some time. These days, it's getting more and more impossible. He pushes me away. I think I . . . I irritate him.' She stares out of the window. 'I guess it's not uncommon. Couples drift apart. We don't want the same things.' She avoids my gaze by sweeping a few stray crumbs from the table, catching them in her palm.

I nod in sympathy. 'I know what you mean. Sam and I . . . we were so good together at first. Having kids changes a relationship. It's tough.' Self-pity pricks at my eyes.

'Is everything all right, Jade? I can't help noticing – you seem tense. Is it really just the hangover?'

Her sympathy makes a couple of tears spill over. I wipe my eyes and speak quickly before I change my mind. 'I found a dodgy text on Sam's phone this morning. It said, "I dreamed about you last night". From an unknown number. With a kiss.'

'Oh, Jade. I thought you looked upset.' She puts a hand on mine.

'I can't believe someone woke up dreaming of my husband,' I burst out.

She nods. 'It does sound odd. Did you ask him about it before he left?'

'I ... I couldn't. Maybe it's ... a friendly text? I've dreamed about colleagues before.' My excuses sound lame. *Just trying to convince myself.*

'So, you've no idea who she is? Is there someone you suspect – at his office?'

I shake my head. 'I haven't been into the agency for ages. I don't have time to meet him for lunch. It could be nothing. A wrong number?'

Christina raises her eyebrows.

I laugh, bitter. 'I'm kidding myself. All right, I admit I can't face it.'

'First things first,' she says, firmly. 'It could be nothing, as you say. Would it set your mind at rest if you find out who any possible competition could be? Could you make some excuse to go to his office?'

I nod. *Oh, the relief of telling someone!* I let go of the breath I feel like I've been holding since I found the text. And a solution comes to me.

'Actually, the agency's summer party's on Friday. There's an awards ceremony, but I wasn't going to go. My mum finds it hard babysitting all three kids.'

Christina looks at me earnestly. 'What if I came over and helped? If you turn up at the party looking fabulous, it'll remind whoever sent the text that Sam is a married man – with a gorgeous wife.'

I blink at her. 'Is that what you'd do?'

She nods. 'Definitely. The other woman – if there is one – will feel guilty. She'll leave him alone. It's easy to have an affair with a married man if you don't know his wife. It's harder if you see you're hurting a real person, breaking up a family.' She

52

looks out of the window for a second. Something told me she was speaking from experience. *Had her husband strayed? Was that why they were spending time apart?*

'Christina, what would I do without you?' I press her hand, gratefully. 'And you're confident you can handle the children? And my mum? You certainly worked your magic over the Disney channel.'

She smiles. 'Your kids are great. My last job in the hospital was in Paediatrics, so I'm used to children. We'll be fine.' She smooths a piece of hair behind her ear. 'To be honest, it'll take my mind off my own problems,' she adds, glancing at her phone. 'Sorry – I better go. My mum's been texting.' Right on cue, her phone beeps. She sighs and stands up.

'Thanks, Christina. Yesterday was amazing. Sorry I'm a bit worse for wear. Blame the tequila.' I squeeze her arm. 'I'm glad we're in touch again.'

Chapter Eight

Christina

Then

One of the best moments of Christina's life started off as the worst.

'Jade! Jade! Jade! Jade!' heckled Digby and Mungo. Their heads were sleek as sea serpents as they trod water in the freezing loch.

Christina watched Jade edging towards the water, her borrowed black-and-white swimsuit hidden by her flowery sundress. Christina hung back by the boulder, willing Jade not to listen to them. Under her T-shirt, Izzie's aunt's padded and wired orange swimsuit was an exoskeleton that didn't quite fit.

Netball captain Izzie climbed the boulder with well-muscled limbs, before executing a perfect swan dive from the overhanging ledge at the top. Christina watched anxiously until Izzie's head bobbed back up. She found herself releasing her breath, not knowing she'd been holding it.

Please don't get in, Jade. Why, oh why, had she come on this trip? What made her think she could fit in with this public school clique? Jade's exceptional looks and sunny nature bought her instant popularity. But Christina felt her rough edges snagging at every turn. She longed for the security of her room in halls, but it was no longer hers. She'd packed up and emptied the room after the end-of-year exams. She'd been squeezing her books into her suitcase when Jade had come to find her. 'Izzie's invited me to her aunt's cottage in the Highlands. Fancy it? Go on! I won't know any of Izzie's friends.'

Christina and Jade had hung out all first year. They'd spent weekends in vintage shops and cafés and watched theatre shows at the Bedlam. She'd invited Jade to the medics' ceilidh and Jade had brought her to parties. She was pleased to be included in Jade's holiday plans, and said 'yes' without thinking.

Three trains and an extortionate taxi ride later, they'd arrived at a grey stone Victorian cottage, straight out of a period drama. Two scruffy pink-cheeked lads and Izzie were sat around a vast wooden table in a flagstoned kitchen, filled with marijuana smoke. For dinner, Izzie served boiled potatoes, gritty with their skins on, to accompany a sludgy vegetable stew. When Jade offered her the spliff that was being passed round, Christina muttered something about it being late and wanting her bed.

'Oh, OK . . . you guys are in the attic,' said Izzie. 'There's only a single bed, but you brought a sleeping bag, yah?'

'I'll be fine on the floor,' Christina said brightly, not wanting to be difficult. But the attic floor was uncomfortable and dusty, and the weed made Jade snore. Christina barely slept all night.

The next morning, Digby and Mungo passed round a joint for breakfast. Izzie threw Jade and Christina mini packets of cereal. 'Come for a swim?'

'Ooo, yes!' Jade nodded.

'I didn't bring a swimsuit,' Christina protested.

'You can borrow my aunt's,' Izzie said.

After breakfast, they trooped past a couple of apple trees, and out of a gate at the back of the garden. The sun was hiding behind a thick layer of cloud, and the drizzly air was pungent with earthy smells. Rising in the distance were purple and green hills, covered in heather and pine. They followed a stony path bordered by weathered rocks, covered with frilly patches of lichen. A stream chattered alongside, like in a fairy tale, and the undergrowth was studded with baby fir trees. This was the real Scotland.

They turned a corner and the flat mirror of the loch came into view, the grey green water reflecting a steely sky. Izzie pointed out a massive boulder on its shores, maybe five metres tall. 'That boulder's from the Ice Age. Millions of years old. And those pine trees are Caledonian. From prehistoric times.'

Christina shivered at the size of the loch, stretching to the horizon, concealing who knew what monsters in its depths. Around the water, the land rose steeply and was partly covered by pine trees with curling canopies, partly by heather and gorse.

Digby and Mungo whooped. They threw off their clothes and raced each other up the boulder. The protruding ledge at the top hung over deep water, forming a natural diving platform.

'Arrrggghhh!' Both boys launched themselves in at once, spraying Christina's arms with icy droplets, giving her goosebumps.

Izzie followed them and they splashed her for a while. Then they heckled Jade.

'Jade! Jade! Jade! Jade!'

'Coming, Jade?' Izzie called out, pulling herself up the boulder for a second time.

Jade flashed her a smile. 'Give me a minute.'

Christina didn't blame her. The chill in the air didn't make the water very appealing. She shivered as the boys dunked each other, shouting and whooping.

Jade slipped off her sandals and walked towards the shoreline. 'Fancy a paddle, Christina?'

Christina shook her head. No way. Tongues of cloudy water lapped at the grubby shingle and her toes shrank at the idea. 'I . . . er . . . no. I don't like cold water.'

'Don't be such a wuss,' Izzie called from the water. 'Wakes you up.'

Christina nearly added she had her period, her perennial excuse to avoid school swimming lessons.

Izzie waved. 'Come on, Jade. Climb up and jump in.'

Jade smiled, nervously. *She's such a people pleaser*, thought Christina. *Why can't she just say no?* Instead, Jade shrugged off her dress and folded it up on the shore. Then she slung herself up the rock, toes wriggling to find a foothold.

'Jade! Jade! Jade! Jade!' hollered the boys, louder now they'd succeeded in enticing a victim.

Jade scrambled slowly to the top. She paused for a minute, scraping her hair back into a messy bun like Izzie's. The sun emerged from behind the clouds, backlighting her silhouette against the sky.

Don't jump! Christina wanted to shout. But her throat was too tight to utter a sound. She crept towards the shingle and an icy wave lapped over her toes, making her jump back.

Jade hovered, undecided. Mungo waded out, shaking off water like a dog. He bounded up the boulder, ready to jump in again. 'Come on, it's easy,' he encouraged Jade.

She giggled, shrinking away. He stretched his arms above his head, standing up on his toes, as if about to leap. But as he jumped, he grabbed Jade, pulling her with him. Christina's heart stopped.

'Arrrgggh!' Jade's shriek was cut off by the gigantic slap as their bodies hit the water. They disappeared under the surface. Christina stared at the foaming water, unable to breathe.

Seconds later, Mungo reappeared, spluttering and whooping. But Jade was nowhere to be seen.

Jade, where are you? Christina shrieked inside. The others didn't notice anything wrong.

'Izzie!' Christina's voice was weak. 'Where's Jade?'

Izzie glanced around the loch. But just then, Jade bobbed up, her hair slicked back, teeth chattering. 'Oh my God it's freeeeez-ing.' She swam towards the shoreline. Christina grabbed a towel and ran towards her, the icy water like knives round her legs.

She reached the dripping, wheezing Jade, threw the towel round her and helped drag her out. Jade's skin was turning blue.

'She has asthma!' Christina snapped, too angry to notice her own chattering teeth.

'Oh fuck!' Mungo waded after them, frowning. 'I didn't real-ise. Jade, why didn't you say? I'm sorry.'

'I'm O-O-O K-K-K,' Jade chattered.

'That was so irresponsible!' Christina muttered, settling Jade on the shingle, searching in her bag for a dry towel.

'Thank Christ someone here has sense,' said Izzie, climbing out of the water. 'Well done, Christina. Boys are hopeless.' She rummaged in her rucksack and handed Christina a bottle of whisky. 'Medicinal.'

Christina twisted open the cap and helped Jade sip the whisky. It made her cough but stopped the wheezing. She wrapped the picnic blanket around her.

'Oh my God, that woke me up,' Jade said, when she could talk. 'Slug?'

Christina placed her lips round the whisky bottle, just like Jade, and sipped tentatively. The whisky burned and she coughed. They giggled.

'I'm so sorry, Jade.' Mungo couldn't apologise enough.

'Cold water isn't a good idea for asthmatics,' said Christina, sternly.

'Thank fuck we had a medic here. Good show, Chrissy,' added Digby, giving Christina a slap on the back.

No one went back in the water.

The rest of the day was magical. Mungo and Digby couldn't do enough for Jade and Christina. Directed by Izzie, they went back to the house and fetched a picnic of crisps, baguette and cheese, with bottles of red wine. The sun dissolved the clouds and it turned into the perfect summer's day. They lay on the boulder, sunning themselves like lizards. The glow of the wine warmed Christina, making her feel loose and free. Mungo plugged his iPod into speakers and played chilled-out house music from a club in Ibiza.

After a while, Izzie, Jade and Christina climbed down to the beach. Jade started to dance, drawing Izzie and Christina to her. Digby took photos, which he later developed in the village shop. As they posed and danced and drank, buzzing with alcohol, Christina felt like a model in a magazine shoot. Happy. Shiny.

When they packed up to go, she kept a few of Digby's photos. Evidence of the best day of her life.

She felt seen. Accepted. She'd proved herself useful. A future doctor. And she was finally doing what she'd found so hard to do all year. Making friends. Dancing. Partying.

The rest of the week was equally fabulous. They picnicked every day. Drank in the pub in the village. One day they sailed a boat across the loch and walked through purple heather in the hills, snacking on blackberries and drinking from clear streams.

The best thing was that Digby, Mungo and even Izzie – who Christina had thought never really liked her – spoke to Christina like she was one of them. Mungo confessed that he didn't want to work on the family farm in Northumberland. Digby told her his dream to be a travel photographer. Izzie sympathised about the workload at medical school. Christina felt included. An important part of the group.

On the night before they were due to go home, as they drifted off to sleep in the attic, Jade spoke the words that Christina had never dared hope she'd say.

'When we get back to Edinburgh, how about we look for a flat together?'

'Really?' Christina's heart beat hard, and her chest nearly burst with happiness. She'd geared herself up for disappointment, expecting Jade to be sharing with Izzie, whose father had bought her a New Town flat.

'Yeah, it'll be nice, you and me. The others are lovely. But you're a real mate. What do you reckon? Be my flatmate?'

Of course, Christina said, 'Yes.'

Chapter Nine

Jade

On Friday just before six, I emerge from Old Street tube station. Traffic fumes choke the streets, making it hard to breathe. It's only a five-minute walk to The School Bar, the venue for the Bradley & Callahan Agency summer party. A sticky day has culminated in a hot and humid evening, so I move slowly.

My mind keeps wandering to home, where Christina and my mum will be getting the kids ready for bed. Christina had come over in the afternoon and soon after, my mum had arrived. Any worries I'd had that my mum might feel put out by Christina being there soon vanished. Mum remembered her from years ago, and was pleased to hear she'd qualified as a doctor. In fact, they got on only too well. As I left the house, I heard her telling Christina about her latest aches and pains, and saying how proud her parents must be to have a doctor daughter. Mum would have preferred me to study medicine instead of English, as she was always telling me.

When I reach the bar, I find a printed sign to the party and tread carefully in my platformed sandals down a steep, uneven staircase towards the rumble of chatter.

The basement's heaving. Even if 'Unknown Number' is here, this could still be a pointless mission. The agency's eighty-plus staff are squashed into a space designed for fifty at a push. Spilling from the doorway, a couple in checked shirts and turned-up jeans chat to a woman with blonde plaits in mustard dungarees. They press themselves against the wood-panelled wall as I squeeze past, feeling self-conscious and overdressed.

'Cool dress!' the blonde says. Her Aussie accent is friendly.

'Thanks,' I smile, suddenly glad I wore the tulle underskirt.

A huge electric fan stirs the hot air like soup. Perfume and aftershave scents clash with body odour and yeasty alcohol. I slip off my cardigan and tuck it into my bag, sticky under the arms.

Groups sit in beaten-up leather armchairs around tables made out of old school desks. I spot T-shirts with ironic slogans everywhere. It feels like ages since I was one of them. I realise the sender of the text message could be any one of the twenty-somethings in this room.

I spot Sam in front of a display of wooden plaques. He fits in with the hipsters, in his open-necked linen shirt and designer jeans. A young woman hands him a microphone. The roar of chatter bouncing off the hard surfaces is deafening, and he leans close to her ear, touching her shoulder. She smiles politely, her cheeks flushed pink.

'One two, one two.' Back at the mic, Sam's voice booms and electronic kickback squeals. There's a few ironic claps and cheers. He plays the charming Managing Director with an easy smile, blue eyes crinkling attractively. Then he glances in my direction and he turns back into my Sam, his lopsided grin slightly strained. He heads towards me, raking fingers through his hair like he does when he's stressed.

'You made it.' He pecks me on the cheek, nuzzling my neck for a second. 'Hey you,' he murmurs. The familiar smell of his aftershave triggers a jolt of desire, and I'm about to kiss him when he pulls back. 'I've been roped into giving out the awards. Why don't you grab yourself a drink at the bar and I'll see you after?'

He squeezes my hand and turns his megawatt smile back towards the tech woman, now in headphones. I try not to mind. After all, this isn't a date with my husband. My purpose is to find the person who sent that text. It might be over-optimistic to think I'd find her here, but I hope she saw Sam kiss me – not the smooch I'd have preferred her to witness, but there's still plenty of time.

I perch on a stool to wait my turn at the bar and examine the reconditioned slab of oak, covered with graffiti. There are pens laid out, an invitation to scrawl your own message. I scan some of the messages.

Dave 4 Sheri.

We are the CHAMPIONS.

School's Shit. Life's a Bitch.

There are names scrawled too: *Carlie. Jonnie. Si. Molly. Reuben.* But no *Sam.*

'Jade Jai?'

I turn round. I'm surprised but relieved to hear a familiar voice. Jai means 'big sister' in Mandarin and there's only one person in London who calls me that apart from my real brother. 'Anthony! What are you doing here?' Anthony's bob has been cut into a short back and sides and his face has filled out.

He gives me a hug and his soft linen shirt brushes my cheek.

64

I breathe in his citrus aftershave. 'Good to see you, mate.' He has an Australian mum and Chinese dad, from the same town in Malaysia as my dad. We worked together at the agency, before Sam arrived. It was our running joke that he was my younger brother, and I was his older sister.

The barman's waiting for my order. 'The negronis are good,' suggests Anthony.

I nod and soon the barman slides us two tumblers, full of fiery-coloured liquid, garnished with orange wedges.

'Thanks.' Anthony joins me at the bar and we survey the room, sipping on our cocktails. I feel dislocated from the buzz of conversation and I'm grateful for Anthony's company. Once I'd started seeing Sam, our relationship had been all consuming. Anthony had gone to another agency, and we'd lost touch.

He clinks my glass. 'Cheers, Jade Jai. So what've you been up to?'

I smile. 'Oh, you know – kids. But what about you? Back at BCA?' Sam's never mentioned Anthony was working there, but then he'd never liked him.

He grins. 'Just freelancing now and then. I've set up my own marketing consultancy. Just signed a big client.'

My smile freezes for an instant. Even Anthony's moved on. I take a sip of my drink and the bitter-sweet syrup floods my mouth, with a kick of alcohol. 'Wow, get you! Creative turned suit, huh?' I slap him on the arm and grin. I'm about to ask what he's working on when a spoon clinks on a glass and the crowd hushes.

'Hello everyone,' Sam speaks into the mic. 'Welcome to the BCA Summer Party and Awards Night.' There're a few half-hearted claps and piss-takey whoops, and Sam announces the first award. His smile's rather fixed, like he can't wait for the presentations to be over.

I wonder, could I ask Anthony if Sam is particularly close to anyone in the office? But even as I form the words in my head, I dismiss the idea. I'll look like a suspicious wife. *Which is what I am.*

The room sways, the negroni hitting harder than I expected. I need air. As Sam announces the Award for Best Art Worker, I slip off the stool and push my way towards the Ladies.

There's a woman standing by the sinks, touching up her make-up, but the toilets are otherwise deserted. It's a relief to escape the noise and the heat, so I sit on the loo for a few minutes longer than necessary. I'm just about to stand up when the door opens, and another person comes in.

'Hey, Lauren, good night?' The woman with an Aussie accent.

'Bloody strong drinks. I'm falling over. You coming for food?'

'Yeah, try and persuade Mazza? She's a bit down?'

'I wonder why?' One of them hums the tune to Whitney Houston's 'I will always love you' and they both laugh.

'Wifey's a stunner,' the Aussie says. 'Love her dress. Mazza's got no chance!'

My heart thumps hard. The blood rushes in my ears. The Aussie earlier had complimented my dress. Could 'wifey' be me? Who is Mazza? Did Mazza send Sam the text? My stomach heaves like I'm going to throw up.

Heidi continues. 'Classic sign of a crush – bringing up his name all the time.'

'Aw. She's young. She'll get over it.'

The door opens and shuts, and the silence is overwhelming.

I leave the cubicle and wash my hands carefully. Someone called Mazza has a crush on Sam. *Could she be the text sender?*

Back by the bar, Anthony's saved my stool.

'Sorry – long queue,' I lie. I wonder if I could ask Anthony about Mazza? He must know her if he freelances there. I take a breath and try for a casual tone. 'By the way, who's Mazza?'

'She's in production, why?'

I smooth my skirt. 'Oh . . . someone mentioned that she's . . . fun?' And that she has a crush on someone. Possibly Sam. It wouldn't surprise me. He often attracts female attention, and he laps it up. I suspect he's always looking for the attention he never got from his stepmum, Victoria.

Anthony points. 'See that middle table? Long red hair, tattoo. Between the Asian girl in the flowery dress, and the blonde in dungarees.'

My heart beats hard as I clock the Aussie blonde who'd been talking about Mazza and her crush.

Anthony's speaking but I don't catch what he says. 'Sorry?'

'I said, do you want me to introduce you?' he repeats.

'I'll . . . find her later. Cheers.' I crunch on an ice cube, ignoring the sudden brain freeze.

So that's Mazza. She's a splash of colour. Dyed red hair scraped back in a ponytail. A halter-neck sunflower print dress shows off an intricate tattoo, covering her back and left arm. Japanese-style waves, in shades of blue and black. She's far from the glamorous model types that Sam dated before me, with names like Olivia and Sienna, part of the posh crowd at uni.

She's short but animated, waving her arms in conversation, bouncing from one friend to the next. Her Doc Martens say

'Don't mess'. She must be in her twenties, her face is chubby, with pitted acne scars on her olive skin that make her look even younger. Sam's too old for her, but he looks good for his age. I don't feel as relieved as I should.

As I head back to the bar, Sam's voice booms out. 'The Award for Best Production Assistant goes to . . . Marianne Reeves.'

A chant booms out. 'Maz-za! Maz-za! Maz-za!'

My heart races and I squeeze my way to the front.

Sam's holding the award, eyes crinkling in a smile. Mazza flops back in her seat, shaking her head, all mock outrage. 'You bastards!' she shouts, as her friends push her up, cheering.

I watch Sam closely. He shakes her hand, and leans in to hug and kiss her, just as he had with the other female winners. Friendly, but impersonal.

Her behaviour is more suspect. She avoids looking at him, turning her head so he kisses her hair. She bows to the audience and plays to her fans, punching both arms in the air like a champion, before she brings the award to her lips with an ironic kiss.

Mazza's fan club roars. 'Ugg! Ugg! Ugg! Ugg!'

Someone else yells, 'Speech!'

'Yeah, OK.' The room quietens. 'I wanna thank my mum, my cat, and all you lazy shits – don't miss your deadlines or else . . .' She mimes thumping someone with the award and the room roars.

Sam looks amused, shaking his head like an indulgent parent. All evidence points to the crush being one-sided. Sam's not good enough an actor to fake a lack of interest. Plus he'd never fancy a woman who'd inked her skin like that. Once, on holiday in Italy, the beach had been full of sunbathers, covered in body art. 'I prefer a woman with a natural look,' he'd commented, kissing my shoulder.

Mazza hams it up while avoiding looking Sam in the eye. Her friends are right. Classic crush behaviour. There are more cheers and whistles as she skips to her seat.

Sam slaps another winner on the back. The cheering's calmed to a polite level, thank God. After a couple more awards, it's all over.

I make my way to Sam and hand him a negroni. He hooks an arm about my waist, pulling me close. 'Read my mind, babe.' He takes a long gulp, then grins and kisses my cheek. 'That went on forever. Something to do with the free bar. Hope you weren't too bored.'

'Not at all,' I laugh. 'It's good to see the youngsters having fun. I feel ancient, like someone's mum.'

'We're all getting older.' I know he's including himself, but I want him to deny I'm old. Except he doesn't. He rubs his face. 'OK, I've done my bit for tonight. Wayne can take over with the schmoozing.'

'Yeah, it's way more fun once the bosses go home.' I lean into him, breathing in his scent. I should make an effort to enjoy the night. If only I could be sure there was nothing going on with this Mazza.

'Want to come home with the boss?' He nuzzles my cheek and I try to relax. It's good to be here, surrounded by adults, no kids in sight. 'Mmm, I like this new dress.' He fingers the strap, his voice low in my ear as he kisses my neck. I shiver.

I glance at Mazza's table. She seems far from down, but is it just an act? She's telling a funny story to her audience, circling her arms. A poem springs to mind. 'Not Waving But Drowning.'

Crush or not, Mazza must realise she doesn't have a chance with Sam. I remember Christina's advice to make myself visible. When Sam's waylaid by a colleague, I make my way towards Mazza. She's standing next to Anthony, and I give him a hug. 'We're off soon,' I say. 'It's been so great to catch up!' I turn to Mazza and put my hand out. 'Oh, hi! It's Mazza, isn't it?'

'Yeah, who's asking?' She looks at my hand but doesn't take it.

Feeling awkward, I smooth my skirt. 'I'm Jade, Sam's wife – I love your tattoo.'

'Yeah, thanks.' She's perfectly polite, but she doesn't meet my eyes.

'And . . . congratulations on your award.' I keep my voice friendly but she's hard work.

'Yeah, right.'

'You know, Jade and I came up with these awards years ago,' Anthony says and Mazza's face lights up with interest.

'Probably feels like ancient history to these kids.' I joke, feeling the blood rising to my cheeks as they laugh politely, humouring the boss's wife.

'Jade!' Finally. Someone else I know. Wayne was an account director in my day, and like Sam, he's now one of the partners. With his handmade leather shoes, navy linen suit and floral print shirt he stands out in this crowd as a grown-up.

We do the air-kiss thing. 'Long time, no see. Chic as ever. Sorry I've been keeping your man so late recently.' I laugh but my face flames. Are my suspicions written on my forehead in capital letters? Wayne goes on. 'We lost a major client unfortunately. But exciting stuff's coming. Did Sam tell you we're pitching for a pan-Europe yogurt account? The pitch is in Paris. Could be a trip for you lovebirds in it?' He winks.

'Are there many clients here tonight?' I ask.

'To be honest, it's been a tough year. But talking of clients, do you mind if I borrow your sweetheart for just two more ticks?' Sam's coming back from the loo and Wayne points to a new arrival, an older woman with big hair, in a red power suit. 'Incoming, must schmooze. Sam, two minutes?'

The woman in red laughs through her lashes at Sam. His eyes twinkle and he kisses her on both cheeks. Does he always have to be so friendly?

My phone buzzes. It's a text from Christina.

Have you found sender of mystery text?

The negroni leaves a bitter aftertaste. I put the glass down. I'll talk to Sam over dinner. I'm almost certain there's nothing going on with Mazza. At least I'm trying to convince myself of it.

But someone sent that text. I need to find out who.

Chapter Ten

Jade

It's past nine by the time we manage to escape. Sam's polite smile drops the minute we emerge from the bar, tiredness visibly taking over.

'Thank God that's over.' He rubs his face. 'Sorry, babe – rather a yawn for you.'

I shake my head. 'It's fine. Good to be amongst adults for a change.'

The air is thick with traffic fumes. To the west, the sky glows with the last bands of sunset, while to the east, night has already arrived. The third negroni kicks in and I grab Sam's arm to steady myself as we weave through the buzzing Friday night crowd, spilling out from the tube, bars and restaurants.

We haven't booked a restaurant, but we duck into a nearby pub that does pizzas – an old haunt from the early days of our relationship. Sam holds the door open for me, an unusually gallant act for him.

'I can't believe this place is still here.' Inside, little has changed and the usual smell of woodsmoke fills the narrow space. As we make our way to the only free table, I notice that they haven't replaced the carpet, sticky from years of spilt drinks.

Sam pulls a seat out for me. 'Your usual? Chicken and roast veg?'

I nod gratefully, surprised he remembers my favourite, if they still have it. Sam heads for the bar.

My phone beeps with a new message from Christina. She would be staying in the study while my mum was getting an Uber home. The text tells me Mum is home. It reminds me of what I need to do; of the conversation I need to have with Sam. I want to believe the text message was from a wrong number. But, somehow I know it wasn't. So why hasn't Sam told me about it? We used to tell each other everything. My mind somersaults as I consider the options, the room getting hotter by the second as an uneasy feeling settles in the pit of my stomach. My thoughts are interrupted by Sam placing a pint of lager in front of me, dripping with condensation. 'Cold enough for you?'

I prefer wine these days, I think, placing my palms around the glass, appreciating the coolness all the same. 'Lovely.' I take a large swig. Then another. The lager fizzes gently and I'm reminded of the dates we've shared here before. How we fell in love, how we built our life together. It's been hard the last few years – with all our focus on the children. Of course, the hard work's been worth it. I love my kids so much it hurts. Why would he throw all of that away for a flirtation with 'Unknown Number'? Surely it can't mean anything. *Am I blowing things out of proportion?*

Sam downs half his pint and burps. 'Excuse me!' We laugh, his eyes creasing at the corners and for a moment it's like we're in our twenties again. He nods at my phone. 'Who were you texting?'

'Just Christina.' I put the phone in my bag.

'Kids OK?'

I nod. 'All fine. Mum's gone home, more than happy to leave Christina to it. But then again, she's a doctor, the perfect daughter.'

Sam takes my hand, giving it a gentle squeeze in an attempt to soothe my insecurities. 'Well, we could do this more often, if Christina is happy to babysit.' He gazes at me with a loving smile I haven't seen for ages.

By the time our pizzas arrive, the beer is adding to the effect of the cocktails and my head is spinning. Sam deftly slices up his pizza. I roll the cutter on mine, but the blade isn't sharp enough to cut through the strips of chicken and peppers. Oil oozes from the melted cheese. I tear a piece off and take a bite hoping to soak up the alcohol. It's too spicy. I gulp more beer and my stomach churns.

'Needed that.' Sam has demolished his pizza. He drains his pint. 'Another?'

'No – thanks.'

Sam returns with another pint. By now I've lurched from tipsy to drunk. I can't help blurting out another thing on my mind, not caring that it might sour the atmosphere. 'You never told me that Anthony was still freelancing for you?'

'Yeah, on and off. Whenever we need an extra pair of hands.' He looks puzzled, as if I wouldn't be interested.

I've gone past the point of hunger. I push the rest of my pizza towards him, saying, 'If you need help, maybe I could freelance for you?'

'Hmmm.' He starts shovelling the rest of my pizza in his mouth.

'I spoke to Nina the other day and she suggested it. Leo goes full-time in September. I'd like to go back to work.'

He finishes chewing. 'Let's see if we win this new account. We can't really afford any more help right now.'

'Wayne said you lost a big client. Why didn't you tell me?' I blurt out.

He frowns. 'Things aren't brilliant, but we've plenty of pitches lined up. Wayne shouldn't have said anything.'

Irritation flashes through me. Sam should have told me himself, not Wayne. What else could he be keeping from me?

But that tic in his temple flickers and we're on a night out after all. I force myself to paste on a smile and put my hand back on his. 'I . . . I had fun tonight. It's been good to get out.'

'Yeah.' But he pulls his hand away and picks up his glass. Is it talk of work that strains the atmosphere? Is he keeping something from me? *Maybe he detects the coldness in my tone.*

Even though the room is swaying, I decide I need to ask about the text. 'Your production manager. Mazza, isn't it? She seems . . . fun.'

'Popular kid.' He looks away.

Is he really not interested in Mazza? Am I worrying about nothing? 'Do you have much to do with her? Mazza?'

'Not really. She's on the creative side.' He shows no interest in engaging. He downs the rest of his beer.

'Well, she certainly seems like a character.' I try again, leaning towards him.

Sam shrugs. 'Yeah, she is, I guess.'

Is his lack of reaction too careful? I don't know what I'm

expecting. The table next to us bursts into raucous laughter, making me jump. I slump back in my chair.

'You OK?' Sam's voice comes from far away. 'How many of those negronis did you have?'

Too many. The table is spinning but I can't live with the doubt. I'm going to have to ask him. 'Look. Please don't take this the wrong way, but I need to ask you something.'

'O . . . K . . .' His eyebrows knit together, amusement gone.

I take a breath. 'I . . . saw a message from an unknown caller. On your phone, Sunday morning.'

'Oh, OK.' His eyebrows unknit. Is that relief? 'Probably a wrong number.'

Does he expect me to believe he didn't read it? I grit my teeth. 'It said, "I dreamed about you last night".'

Sam looks puzzled. Should I repeat what I overheard in the toilets about Mazza's crush? He takes my hand again. My fingers stiffen, and I pull away. 'Oh God, I'm *so* sorry, Jade. Is that why you came tonight? Were you worried I was having an *affair*?' He runs a hand through his hair, fixing his gaze on me. 'Look,' he continues, sitting forward. 'I don't know who that text was from. I saw it, ignored it, deleted it. Thought nothing more of it. Come on, Jade, do you really think I would do that to you?'

He looks so hurt, I feel bad that I didn't trust him. 'Well, you have been working late a lot . . .' I trail off, my cheeks hot.

He sighs. 'I know. I'm sorry, but as Wayne told you – we're bleeding clients. We're pitching like crazy, but we're in a recession. No one is spending much money on marketing.'

Guilt stabs me. 'I'm sorry. I didn't realise the agency was in trouble.' *Why did I spend so much last weekend?* 'You should have told me.'

He leans forward and strokes my cheek. 'I didn't want to worry you. It's just a blip. All businesses go through ups and downs, you know that. There's no need for concern.'

'I'm sorry,' I mutter, but someone next to us tells a joke and laughter drowns my words. I feel terrible. Sam's always been ambitious – he became a partner in the agency by the time he was thirty-five – and he hates admitting to any kind of failure.

He pulls me towards him, kissing me on the lips. 'Why'd you read my texts anyway?' he asks, rubbing his thumb in circles on my palm. 'Trying to catch me out?'

My face flames and I pull away. 'I thought it was my phone. I would never normally read your texts.'

He doesn't hear me as the DJ turns the volume up on a classic house tune. People get up and dance. *How can they move in this heat?*

Sam yawns and rummages for his wallet. 'I'll go and pay, then.' Heading for the till, he threads through the throng of dancers, resting his hands on the bare shoulders of a glamorous Asian woman, in an attempt to stop her falling into him as he passes behind her.

She smiles after him, then leans towards me, drunk. Her lipstick has bled into the skin above her top lip. 'That your feller? Lucky you!'

By the time Sam returns, tiredness has settled in and I'm desperate to leave. Sam helps me with my cardigan, then steers me past the crowd to the door. I relax, glad of his arm around me. Like the Asian woman said, I'm lucky. I believe Sam, that the text meant nothing to him. *But does it mean nothing to the person sending it?*

★

'Jade! You getting up?' I peel my eyes open, blinking at the sun filtering through the blinds. Sam's dressed and crouched by my bedside. 'The boys are with your friend. I'll take Amber to ballet. I'll bring her back, but then I'm going to meet Wayne for a working lunch.'

'Fine,' I mumble, dragging myself out from under the duvet, before padding to the bathroom.

When I appear in the kitchen, the boys are sat around the table with Christina. There's a disposable tablecloth protecting the wood underneath, and it's covered with bowls of dried pasta, bottles of food colouring and small paintbrushes. Christina looks at home, making pasta jewellery with the boys. She throws me a quick smile before turning her attention back on Eddie, who's threading a piece of penne onto a length of wool.

'Mumma!' Leo bounces over, overturning a bowl. Dried penne skitters across the table and onto the floor.

Eddie abandons his work and joins Leo, hugging my legs. I crouch down, cuddling their warm bodies, breathing in their buttered-toast smell. 'Morning, monsters!'

'We're making you pretty jewellery, Mummy,' says Eddie, letting go.

'Neck-lace.' Leo clambers onto my knee and drapes a string of pasta over my head.

'Wow. Looks amazing.' I kiss Leo, then Eddie. 'Thank you, my darlings.'

'The food colouring's not dry yet, don't spoil Mummy's clothes,' Christina warns.

'It's OK, these pyjamas are old. This is gorgeous!' I examine the string of dyed pasta round my neck. 'Did you do this on your own, Leo? Clever boy.'

'The red pasta's like rubies. Do you like it?' I help Eddie slip the pasta bracelet over my wrist.

'Gorgeous. Straight out of *Vogue*.' I kiss him.

'Leo,' says Christina gently. 'I know you're excited to see Mummy, but you must pick up the pasta before someone has an accident.' She points to the penne scattered over the floor. He burrows his head into my shoulder, but Christina's right.

'Come on. Let's tidy up, shall we?' I kneel down, picking up pasta. Eddie helps, and even Leo kicks some of the penne over to us.

'Do you want to make anything else, boys?' They don't reply. 'I'll pack up then, shall I?' Christina twists the lids on the bottles of food colouring and Eddie helps.

'Want watch *Nemo*,' Leo tugs at my hand.

'We watched *Finding Nemo* last night,' Christina explains. 'I said maybe we could watch *Finding Dory* today?'

I place the bowl of pasta back on the table. 'I don't have any other plans. Eddie, can you sort out Disney? Mummy's just going to have a cuppa. Tea, Christina?' She nods and I fill the kettle.

Eddie runs to the living room shouting, 'Come on, Leo! *Finding Dory*!'

'Yay,' Leo thunders after him.

I down a glass of water while I wait for the kettle to boil. My mouth tastes rank. I make two mugs of tea and bring them to the table. 'Thanks for babysitting,' I tell Christina. 'We don't get out much, I'm grateful you could help.'

She sits opposite me. 'So? Anything to report from last night?' I guess it's natural she's curious. When we lived in halls, I told her everything. But somehow I feel reluctant to do the same now.

'The bar was so cool,' I say instead. 'Remember the desks we had at school? They had those, covered in fake graffiti.'

Christina refuses to be palmed off with discussions about décor. 'What about the text? Did you find out anything?'

'No. Not really. There's someone who works with him who has a crush on him. But she wasn't that chatty,' I explain. 'I made it obvious I was Sam's wife.'

'What does Sam think of her?'

'I didn't ask him. I . . . didn't want to be repeating what I'd heard in the Ladies. But I asked him about the text. He doesn't know who it was from. Must be a wrong number.'

'Well, that's great. You've cleared things up.' Christina tips the leftover pasta tubes into plastic bags, zipping them up efficiently, like there's nothing wrong. But as I watch her, I realise the doubts about my marriage aren't tidied up. I have a niggling sense Sam's not being quite truthful.

Christina picks up her mug and blows on her tea, then she catches my eye, looking concerned. 'Is everything all right, Jade? You – seem tense.'

The camomile fragrance reminds me of our late-night chats when we would share our problems. I blurt out, 'What if . . . what if Sam's not telling me the truth?' Sam's dismissal of the text was so convenient. *Could he have been lying?*

'Are you sure you're not seeing too much into this? Could the text be – I don't know – some kind of work banter . . .' she trails off.

'So I'm overthinking it? It could all be perfectly innocent?' I bite my lip.

'Not exactly . . . just – you're not actually there with him, in the office.'

'You know, I bumped into my old art director last night. Anthony, who's freelancing for Sam. What if I went to work for Anthony? I could end up working for Sam too and find out what's been going on?'

She shrugs. 'Possibly. It could be a way of finding out if you have anything to worry about.' She stood up. 'I have to rush off. My mum needs me. I'm sure you'll know what to do.' She squeezes my arm.

After she leaves, I cuddle up with the children on the sofa watching *Finding Dory*.

If I freelance with Anthony and I end up in Sam's office, I'll be able to see for myself how they interact. Bumping into Anthony last night could be a sign. If Sam won't recommend me to his creative team as a freelance writer, maybe Anthony will.

I leave the children watching the rest of the movie and go into the kitchen to call Anthony.

Chapter Eleven

Mazza

Six Months Earlier

I never thought I was the type of person to do anything really bad, but that was before I met *him*. You know what I'm capable of, and that I deserve better. I'd like to say I feel guilty about it, but I don't. And you're right. It doesn't come down to wrong or right, when you're simply taking something that should be yours.

I enter the boutique on the high street, filled with confidence. I've never stepped foot in this shop, the prices are higher than my usual budget. But I've just been paid, and I need something to wear for maximum impact.

'Hiya! Looking for something special?' calls out an assistant in a burnt-orange wrap dress.

'Yeah. Something for my office Christmas party.'

'Lovely! Can I guess, you're looking to impress people?'

I nod. 'I've just passed my probation.' I can't help a note of pride in my voice. Three months have gone by quick. Three months of willing him to know who I am – three months of biding my time. But now I'm taking matters into my own hands. And I want him to notice me.

'Well then, you need the perfect dress. Let's see . . .' She flicks through one of the racks, '. . . nothing too short, I suppose? What sort of colour are you after? Something to go with that gorgeous hair of yours . . .' She admires the vibrant red of my home-dye job.

'And I guess I should cover my tattoo?' I turn to show off the Japanese waves cascading down my back and arm.

'No need to show the world, right?' She chuckles like we're sharing a secret.

I walk past a halter-neck dress, the kind of thing I usually go for. But it's not suitable for tonight. 'He needs to take you seriously,' I hear you whisper.

'Ah! I have just the thing, my lovely.' She holds out a navy-blue dress, tailored, with white polka dots and a Peter Pan collar. 'Knocks the socks off, but professional.' She winks like she's my mate, and I almost hear you chuckle.

I take the dress, trying not to look at the price tag, and head into the cubicle. It's spacious enough to twirl around in, but the mirror doesn't reflect my confidence. My eyeliner's halfway down my face and my lips are cracked. I slick on fresh lip gloss and smooth back my hair, before shrugging off my denim tunic and slipping on the dress.

The lining rustles like money, feeling cool against my skin. The skirt of the dress has knife-sharp pleats, falling just below my knee, and the cap sleeves cover most of my tattoo. A brand new Mazza pouts back. Sedate. Elegant. Grown-up.

'Fake it till you make it,' you whisper in my ear.

You're right. It suits me.

It's hard to shrug back into my own clothes. Out of shape and worn, like a skin I've outgrown.

'Great choice.' The woman folds the dress in a sheet of tissue. 'Anything else you need? Tights – or stockings?'

I shake my head. The dress alone is a squeeze. Tesco Value tights will have to do.

She rings up the purchase and I take out my purse, bulging with this week's rent, about to go straight to Mum. I hand over my credit card.

She taps glossy red nails on the counter as she waits. She smiles, politely. 'I'm so sorry. That hasn't gone through. Shall I try again?'

'Oh? Of course.' My voice cracks. *Please work!*

She tries again. Shakes her head.

Shame floods my chest. My face burns.

'Maybe you should call your bank.' The pity in her voice is worse than a sneer. 'Do you want me to put the dress aside for you?'

'Er, no, yeah, OK.'

If only the reclaimed parquet floor would swallow me up right now. 'I'll come back.' I scuttle out, hopes deflating like a balloon. 'Shut up, Ben,' I mutter before you say anything. 'It's me, the woman, who matters. Not the clothes.'

Chapter Twelve

Jade

I'm up before my alarm and get the kids to school with time to spare. Back at home, I change my clothes, replacing my stained leggings with a soft blue linen shift dress, my favourite vintage rose print scarf tied round my waist for luck. I have a meeting with Anthony to talk about his latest project and how I might get involved. I'm buzzing at the thought of working again.

The doorbell rings three times, urgently. At the door is Christina, her eyes bloodshot, hair unbrushed. 'Oh my God, Christina, what's wrong?' I hug her. 'Is everything OK?'

'I'm so sorry to bother you.' I notice tear tracks down her face. Next to her are two suitcases, and a Mulberry leather holdall.

I help her heave them over our step, ushering her inside. 'Are you heading back to Scotland?'

She blows her nose. 'I'm not sure. I had a huge row with my mum last night. She's thrown me out.'

I'm shocked. 'Row? About what?'

She looks down. Her blouse is buttoned up wrong. 'She says I make too much mess. And she doesn't like the fact I've been staying at yours so much.'

85

'Oh honestly, it's only been twice!' I sigh. Her mother is so unreasonable. Christina's the tidiest person I know.

'She gave me the "I'm not a hotel" line. She said if I'm spending so much time away, I might as well go back to Scotland.'

'It's my fault. I shouldn't have asked you to babysit.'

She shakes her head. 'I enjoyed babysitting. And besides, it was good to get away from the constant C-dramas. Her hearing's going and the TV volume is always too loud.'

I feel for her. 'I don't know how you've done it. I couldn't stay at my mum's for more than a day. She drives me mad. And there's no way I'd ever go to my dad.' I feel the usual spike of anger when I think of him. He left us when I was a teenager, leaving my mum stressed and angry. It always felt like she blamed me for her disappointing life.

'I'll find my own flat eventually. As long as I can find work, I'd like to move back to London.'

She looks so worried, I nearly ask her to stay with us, but I know Sam wouldn't be keen. 'Look, I'm really sorry, but this isn't a great time. I'm about to meet my old colleague, Anthony, but I can meet you somewhere afterwards.'

She wipes her face and fiddles with her blouse, doing the buttons up right.

'I'm sorry . . . I didn't know where else to go. I'll get out of your way.' She turns to go.

'No, wait! Look, Anthony and I were having a lunch meeting but it's quite informal – you're welcome to join us.' It's not ideal but there's no way I can turn her away, the state she's in. *Anthony won't mind. He's a mate.*

★

86

After the stickiness of the tube, the air-conditioned restaurant is a refreshing change. Anthony's working for Teatro, an immersive dining experience, and we're here for 'research'. I'm immediately entranced at the magic of it all. Roses spill from Murano glass vases, filling the room with fragrance. The circular dining room has high ceilings and spotlights are trained on a round stage where a show's about to begin.

Anthony is sitting at the bar when we arrive, a laptop and a stack of folders in front of him. He stands up when he sees us, kissing me on the cheek. 'Jade Jai.' His aftershave is fresh and citrussy.

'Anthony.' I pull away and draw Christina towards him. 'This is Christina, my old flatmate – from uni.'

Her eyes sparkle, and she holds out her hand to shake his. 'It's good to meet you, Anthony. Thank you for letting me interrupt your meeting. This place is impressive.'

He gives her a polite hug. 'Christina, actually it's perfect. We can make sure Jade has the full customer experience. Lunch with friends. A few drinks. The works.' He walks us over to a table near the stage, his hand pressing lightly on my back.

'The taste of smoked salmon always reminds me of the Highlands,' says Christina when our starters arrive. 'Jade invited me to join her friends on a holiday by a loch,' she explains to Anthony. 'That was the first time I tried it.'

I smile at how much she rates that holiday. It *was* fun, but I don't remember it quite as clearly.

A tangerine waterfall of silk tumbles down, and an acrobat, dark skin covered in glittery body paint, dances onto the stage and starts to climb the silks. Christina turns to me, eyes shining.

'It's incredible to be so close, hear the swish of the silk, see her muscles flex ...'

'Smell her sweat ...' Anthony jokes.

I'm glad Christina's with me. She deserves a treat after dealing with her mum. And this feels so decadent on a weekday. What will Sam say when he hears I've escaped the Monday pile of laundry?

'I wonder how many years of training it's taken her to master those skills?' Christina cuts her lamb deftly, adding potato and crushed peas with every forkful.

'They say it takes ten thousand hours to be an expert,' I say, recalling an article I'd read. 'So what does ten thousand hours equate to?'

Christina consults her phone. 'Three hours a day, for nine years. No wonder I never made Young Musician of the Year. My mum only forced me to practise piano for an hour a day.' Her laugh is bitter. I know that to her mother, playing the piano wasn't for pleasure but to boost her intelligence and ultimately her grades.

'But what about your career?' I reassure her. 'You're a doctor. You must have trained for more than ten thousand hours.'

She flushes. 'I suppose so, but I don't pretend to be an expert.'

'You're being modest. I'm not an expert in anything.' I laugh, but I can't help my voice catching and there's a hollow feeling in my chest.

Anthony raises his eyebrows. 'Now who's being modest? Your copy's won awards.'

It's my turn to be bitter. 'Copywriting awards ... do they count? One day I'd like to write fiction. Something more worthwhile than copy. A novel even. One that reveals – I don't know – the meaning of life . . .' My mood sinks. After ten thousand hours perfecting something else, I'll be nearly fifty. More than half of my life gone.

'You've devoted more than ten thousand hours to raising your children,' Christina remarks. 'You've put your career on pause to stay at home with them.'

I appreciate her giving me a boost, but I shrug. 'Like they care. And who's an expert mother? It's impossible. That's motherhood. Trying to keep everyone happy.' I nod at the stage where a pair of jugglers are throwing skittles, balls and even a broomstick up in the air. 'No one tells you how hard it is. You feel like you're doing everything wrong. I adore Amber but her anxiety makes her temperamental. Your second's meant to be easier, but Eddie has terrible allergies. And Leo's such a . . . a ball of energy. He doesn't listen to a word I say.' Suddenly everything feels too much. How can childless Christina or Anthony understand how it feels?

'Is life getting on top of you, Jade?' There's concern in Anthony's eyes.

I swipe at my face, swallowing the lump of self-pity. *What's wrong with me?* 'Sorry. Ignore me. I adore my kids. But it'll be great to do something else for a change. Forget ten thousand. A few hours would be fine.' I feel like such a killjoy, when his client's treating us to lunch.

Anthony waves over a waiter. 'How about a round of espresso martinis?'

'What a great alternative to coffee,' Christina approves. Her cheeks are pink. 'You're lucky to have Jade to work on your project, Anthony. She's always completely dedicated, whether it's to being a mother or to her career.'

'Thanks, Christina.' I squeeze her arm. I hate blowing my own trumpet, but it's nice she's doing it for me.

Anthony grins. 'I remember – we were a team once. So what do you think, Jade? Up for the job?'

I flush. 'I . . . I wasn't sure you were definitely hiring . . . I mean, you haven't even seen my portfolio.'

'Rack off, Jade, I'm not going to interview *you.*' He holds out his palms. 'The job's yours if you want it. It's a marketing campaign for Teatro's private dining rooms and venue hire. About a week's work initially. More to come in the autumn.'

'Oh, OK, thanks. So it's really happening? I'll need to sort out childcare.' I can't quite believe I'll be working again so soon.

'It's a great opportunity, Jade,' Christina breathes.

She's right. Why do I suddenly have cold feet? 'I don't know,' I find myself prevaricating. 'Everything's moved on. Digital media's a whole new landscape.'

Anthony's nodding. 'Sure, things have moved on, but we need good writers, whatever the media. I'm going back to write the brief this afternoon. Surely you've had enough of being a domestic goddess, Jade?'

'I . . . guess so.' I'm overwhelmed at the speed things are moving.

'Let me know and I can email you the brief. You could think up some ideas before we get together for a meeting. I'll pay your going rate, of course. What are you on? Three fifty? Four?'

'I'll let you know.' Four hundred a day would definitely help pay the bills.

The waiter arrives with a tray of espresso martinis. We toast each other.

'To Jade, and restarting your career.' Christina waves her glass at me.

'Yes, to Jade.' Anthony holds up his glass. 'Lucky I bumped into you.'

His eyes turn intense, and I recall why I'd stopped seeing him. I laugh lightly. 'And to Christina.' I touch my glass to each of theirs in turn. 'To new beginnings.'

Outside, the glare of the sun is a shock after the cool of Teatro. We run for the station, giggling. On the tube, Christina shouts in my ear, over the rattle of the train. '*Jade Jai*. He likes you.'

I fan my top, sweat streaming down my back. 'He needs a writer.'

'It's more than that. He couldn't stop looking at you.'

My cheeks flame. 'Anthony's like my brother.' She gives me a knowing look. 'Oh, all right. He had a crush on me years ago. We went for a drink once – not a date – as friends. Soon after, I met Sam.' Who's always been jealous of Anthony. 'Please don't tell Sam we bumped into Anthony,' I say quickly. 'And . . . to be honest, I wasn't going to tell Sam about Teatro. He – kind of wanted to take me himself.'

She puts a finger on her lips. 'I won't say a word. But you'll have to tell him about Anthony when you start work.'

I shrug. 'I know, and I will, but I need to see what the timing's like before I commit. Leo doesn't start school until September. Anthony needs someone now.'

She frowns in concern. 'That's a shame. He obviously values your work. Can't your mum look after Leo? If you wait until September, he could find someone else.'

She's right. It's frustrating. I nod and change the subject. 'So, now you've left your mum's, what's the next step?'

Christina sighs. 'I need to find somewhere to rent until everything's settled with Michael. If I find somewhere soon, I could help you with childcare.'

I smile at her. 'That's sweet of you, but it's a bit of a trek from Bounds Green, isn't it?'

She presses her lips together. 'Actually, there's nothing keeping me near my mother. While I'm looking for work, I could live anywhere. Actually, would you mind if I found somewhere near you? It's such a nice area.'

'Why would I mind?' I smile. 'I'd love to have you nearby. East London's getting pretty gentrified. There's lots of places to rent.' The tube emerges overground and rattles past Leyton cemetery. The rows of graves make me shiver.

Christina chews her lip, worried. 'I'll start looking for a flat tonight, but meanwhile I can book a Premier Inn.'

'Isn't that expensive?' Her money won't last for long if she moves into a hotel.

'It's fine for a few days,' she insists, but the look in her eyes says it isn't. 'I'm sure I'll find a flatshare soon.'

She blinks quickly, her eyes shiny. 'What's wrong?' I ask.

'Just, well, it feels a bit daunting. Starting again, at our age.' She blows her nose.

'I know what you mean.' The idea of a flatshare fills me with horror.

She looks at me, hopefully. 'You . . . you don't have any friends looking for a lodger? If I'm near you, I could pick your children up from school and nursery sometimes.'

I shake my head. 'No. I don't. But I can ask around.'

'Thanks.' She squeezes my arm and leans towards me. 'And I'm serious about helping. Apart from the occasional job interview I have plenty of time. I could share childcare with your mum. So you could take the job.'

I shake my head. 'Mum finds Leo a handful. I can't ask her to do more than an hour or so. I was actually thinking I'd work at night, when Sam gets back and the kids are asleep.' The train pulls into Leytonstone and most of the passengers get off. It's a world away from the rush hour commute. I can't imagine doing that again.

'But isn't Sam working late these days?' She gazes at me. 'You'll be exhausted before you sit down to work.'

'Mmm, but September will be easier. I'll have more time then, if the job's still going.'

Christina speaks quickly. 'There's a Travelodge not far from you. If I stay there, I could easily get to yours and help you.'

She seems to mean it. 'You really want to babysit for me so I can take the job with Anthony?'

'It'll be better than being on my own, staring at the walls.' There's a sad look in her eyes. I guess she's lonely.

That decides it for me. Christina's one of my oldest friends. I can't let her stay in a Travelodge. 'Look, why don't you stay at mine until you sort yourself out?'

'Really?' Her face lights up. 'That would be . . . so kind of you. But are you sure Sam will agree?'

I smile and put an arm around her. 'Of course,' I say, hoping my uncertainty doesn't leak through my voice. 'Besides, if you're helping with childcare so I can work, Sam can't really say no.'

'I'd rather stay with you than on my own, I must admit.' She wipes her eyes with a tissue.

The tube gathers speed, rattling through the tunnel, making us sway in unison. It feels good to be able to help her now, when all those years ago I hadn't been much use. And the childcare will be a godsend.

I think of Anthony's four-hundred-a-day rate. That'll take the pressure off Sam. If I wait until September Anthony might find another copywriter, and I'll miss my chance.

Chapter Thirteen

Christina

Then

Ba wanted to meet the girl Christina was going to share a flat with.

'She's Chinese-British like us, but her parents are from Malaysia. She lives in Ilford,' Christina said.

'Not far,' said Ba. 'Ask her to come round for dinner so we can meet her.' Christina's father smiled kindly, the good cop, while Ma stared boot-faced at the latest TV melodrama.

But when it came to the summer break and Jade was free to visit Christina, Ba was out, and Ma complained. 'It's your father's idea to invite your friend. Now he is not here. Typical. I am the one who has to cook for her. Easy for him to invite – he does not have to do the work.'

'I can cook something, Ma,' Christina suggested. 'I could roast some chicken pieces and potatoes?'

Ma shook her head. 'No. You make too much mess. You do not clean properly afterwards. I will cook.'

'Or we could go out for something to eat?' But Christina knew it was a mistake as soon as the words left her mouth.

'What?' Her mother looked shocked. 'You have so much money, ah?'

Christina gave up. Nothing she did was ever good enough for her mother. If only Ba had been here to smooth the waters. But it might have caused another argument. Better that he was out and didn't hear Ma's complaints.

The night of the dinner, Jade was half an hour late. 'The rice will be cold by the time she arrive,' Ma grumbled.

Christina bit her lip but didn't say anything. Finally, at half seven, they heard the buzzer.

'Hiya!' Jade stepped in smiling, no apology for being late. She held a bottle of wine and a bunch of supermarket lilies, the waxy petals curling open, spilling dark red pollen. She enveloped Christina in a hug and the scent of lilies clashed with Jade's rose perfume.

Christina pulled back quickly. 'Jade, this is my mum.' She introduced her to Ma, who was hovering behind her in the hallway like a disgruntled spirit.

'Hi, Mrs Lee, so lovely to meet you,' Jade breathed.

Ma's lips twitched, the closest she got to a smile.

'These are for you, Auntie.' Jade thrust the lilies into Ma's arms, giving her no choice but to take them. She held them with an outstretched arm. Christina realised she'd be worried about the pollen staining her clothes.

'I'll put them in water.' Christina took the flowers. 'Shoes.' She pointed at Jade's shoes, before she stepped in any further.

'Oh, of course.' Jade hopped on one foot and flicked off her

96

emerald mock croc platforms. Jade's warm hand gripped Christina's arm for balance. Christina felt an urge to giggle and quickly looked away. Ma would not approve.

'Where's Mr Lee and . . . And Aidan, is it?' Jade asked.

'My husband took my son to a karate competition. It is just us three,' Ma replied.

Jade grinned. 'Great. Girls' night!' She bounced towards Mrs Lee to give her a hug, but Ma pulled away, so Jade grasped the air.

Ma didn't do physical contact. Christina couldn't remember ever hugging her. She would carry Aidan, her younger brother, but only in a functional way, when he was a toddler, not to comfort him when he cried.

'Jade, go and wash your hands then come and sit down. You are late. Dinner is ready,' Ma said.

'Oh, OK.' Jade glanced at Christina, suppressing a smile.

Christina could feel giggles bubbling up but merely pointed the way to the bathroom, then helped Ma carry the food into the dining room.

The table was set with the best plates – the bone china ones with a leaf pattern round the rim. Ma had cooked a few simple dishes. Plain rice. Sliced omelette. Steamed Chinese greens. Fried pig's liver braised in ginger and onions.

'Good for you. Lots of nutrition.' Ma spooned liver onto Jade's plate.

There was a sinking feeling in the pit of Christina's stomach. How could Ma serve liver to her friend? Christina hated liver. But it was cheaper and more nutritious than meat, as Ma often pointed out. As a child, Christina had swallowed the chunks whole, hating the gristly texture.

'You don't have to eat the liver if you don't want,' she whispered to Jade as she passed her the omelette and rice.

Ma glared at her. 'Wasting food is a sin.'

'It won't go to waste. Ba and Aidan will eat it tomorrow,' Christina murmured.

Jade grinned. 'This omelette is so yummy,' she praised Ma. 'What did you put in it to make it so tasty? The choi sum is fresh and delicious. Shall we open the wine?'

Ma's eyes shot daggers. 'We do not drink alcohol.'

Jade gave a nervous laugh. 'Oh, I'm so sorry. I didn't realise. I could go and get . . . some juice?'

'Boiled water is fine. Good for digestion,' Ma replied, taking a sip from her glass.

Christina took a large portion of the liver, hoping that Ma wouldn't realise Jade hadn't touched hers. The aroma of the shao xin and soya sauce gravy mixed with the gristly texture of offal made her nauseous. But she forced herself to chew and swallow, washing it down with sips of boiled water.

Jade chattered on about the flat she'd found. 'It's perfect, Mrs Lee. The ceilings are lovely and tall. Most of the buildings in Edinburgh are Georgian. You must come and visit. There's a sofa bed for visitors.'

Ma didn't respond. She chewed her food methodically, staring at her plate.

Jade smiled at Christina, but swallowing the liver took all her focus and she couldn't return the smile.

Ma looked up. 'What about the rent? Does it include council tax and bills? How much deposit you pay?'

'Oh, I'm not sure, I'll have to check.' Jade knew full well that the rent didn't include council tax or bills. It was rare for a landlord to do that. Christina had already budgeted in an extra hundred pounds a month. Ma knew that. She wouldn't have forgotten. She was being deliberately rude.

'Is there a church nearby?' she barked. 'Anglican church? Very important that Christina continues to attend Sunday service.'

'No worries, Mrs Lee. The Scottish are really religious. I'm sure we'll find a local church.' Jade's eyes brimmed with laughter. She called students who attended Chapel the 'God Squad'. Christina avoided her gaze. She belched, and the flavour of liver mixed with sour digestive juices almost made her gag.

After dinner Christina offered to wash up but Ma shook her head. 'No. You go sit down. I will do it.'

'What about the show?' Jade whispered. 'Are we still going?' They'd planned to go to the cinema.

Christina nodded and spoke to Ma. 'Jade and I are going to the University of London library. It shuts at ten. I need books for my assignment.'

'OK, you better go now.' Ma stacked the dirty plates.

'Can we help with the tidying up?' Jade started to follow Ma into the kitchen, but in the hall, Christina grabbed Jade's arm and pulled her in the direction of her room. Christina slung on a jacket and grabbed her rucksack.

'Thanks so much, Mrs Lee,' Jade sang out. 'Delicious dinner. Christina must come over to my house one day.'

Ma didn't reply. The girls could hear her running the taps. They hurried down the steps, shoulders shaking.

Out in the street, they let loose their laughter. 'Sorry about the liver,' Christina apologised when she could talk again.

'Oh, don't worry. My mum cooks stuff I hate all the time.'

Jade slung an arm around her shoulders. 'Your mum's a bit scary, isn't she? What's this?' She tugged at Christina's rucksack.

'We said we were going to the library.'

'I hope she'll still let you move in with me.'

'I've already paid the deposit and first month's rent. She won't want me to lose it.' Christina stuck her hand in the bag and drew out the bottle of wine. 'You better take this.'

'Oh no – we can drink it in the cinema. Actually, hand it over.'

Giggling, they took turns to swig the wine. Before they'd reached Bounds Green tube station, it was gone. The alcohol went straight to their heads. They hooted and giggled. Oh, the relief of getting out of the flat. Tears streamed down their faces.

In Christina's case, some of the tears were real.

Chapter Fourteen

Jade

Amber's sitting on the doorstep reading *Agent Scarlett* by the time we get back from picking up the boys. She jumps up, nearly in tears. 'Where've you been? I've been waiting ages.'

'I'm so sorry, darling – Mummy went into town and was late.' I feel terrible for making Amber's anxiety worse. I unlock the door and the boys push past, kicking off their shoes, dropping bags and jackets in heaps. Amber arranges her shoes neatly and hangs up her jacket.

'Oh Amber, how tidy you are,' Christina remarks, approvingly. 'The boys should learn from you.'

Amber ignores the compliment, still frazzled.

'Sorry, Christina. She gets really anxious.' I'm ashamed of Amber's rudeness, but I know it's because she was worried. Luckily Christina smiles. She must be used to grumpy children from her job. It's a relief she's so calm and cheery.

Leo screeches. 'Hungry, Mummy, I'm hungry!' He's extra grouchy after a full day at nursery.

Eddie runs a hand on one of Christina's suitcases. 'We going on holiday?'

Christina removes his hand. 'You're very observant, Eddie. Well done for noticing. The cases are mine and ... well, I guess I am having a little holiday of sorts.'

'Holiday, yay!' Leo jumps up and down.

I shake my head. 'No, *we're* not going on holiday. Not yet. Auntie Christina's coming to stay.'

Christina crouches down to Leo and Eddie's level. 'How would you like me to look after you so Mummy can work?'

Leo giggles. 'Silly. Mummy don't work. Daddy works.'

Hot shame floods my face. 'So much for being a feminist. I'm a crap role model.'

'You've had some time off to prioritise your children but you're starting your career again,' Christina reassures me. 'Mummies need to do something for themselves too. Something other than looking after you,' she tells the kids. 'She still loves you.'

Yes, exactly. Filled with renewed confidence, I kneel and look Leo in the eye. 'You know, mummies can work too. Like daddies.'

Eddie nods. 'Adam's mum works, and his daddy works, and he has a nanny – Sheena. She's nice and brings us sweets. You going to be our nanny, Auntie Christina?'

Christina's eyes gleam with amusement. 'Not exactly. I'm helping out so your mummy has time for her work. If it's OK with Mummy, I'll go get you a drink and a snack?'

She looks at me for approval and I nod, gratefully. Whatever qualms I'm feeling about the arrangement, it makes sense. Surely Sam will be able to see that? Other families have live-in childcare. And it's just for a couple of weeks, max.

The truth is, Sam likes to be consulted before major

decisions. I try calling him, but his phone's switched off so I send a text.

Just letting u know – Christina staying for a few days

The grey tick doesn't change to blue. He's probably in a meeting.

Sam's not used to people staying over like I am. My parents would invite Malaysian friends and relatives to stay all the time. Throughout my childhood there was often an auntie or uncle sleeping on the sofa bed.

I ignore my doubts. I'm sure he'll be OK with it. After all, hadn't he mentioned that if Christina babysat, we could go out more? It's just an extension of that idea.

In the kitchen, Christina pours the children glasses of milk. 'Who would like some delicious slices of apple?'

'Want bic bic,' whines Leo.

'There's a biscuit tin in the cupboard above the kettle,' I call to her.

'Healthy habits start young,' she says, decanting a tub of grapes into a colander. She rinses them and cuts up apple, arranging slices on a plate. 'Yummy fruit. And then I have some presents for you.'

'Yay. Pressie!' shouts Leo. Amazingly, he crunches into slice of apple.

Christina disappears for a while and comes back with a paper bag. 'Hey, Leo!' She bounces a sponge ball to him. He catches it, excited. 'Great catch!' She claps. 'Now, Amber – you're such a brilliant reader, you might like these. Eddie – here's some fun adventures with mythological creatures.'

Amber gives Christina a shy smile. She holds up copies of *The Little Princess* and *The Secret Garden*. 'Oh! I've always wanted to read these. I've seen them on DVD.'

'Thanks, Christina,' says Eddie, accepting the set of Rick Riordan books. He runs off to play ball with Leo.

It's incredible how much smoother the evening goes with an extra pair of hands. I'd been planning to throw ready-made pizzas and chips in the oven, but Christina makes a quick dough and shows the children how to roll out their own pizzas with tomato passata, ham and sweetcorn. She cuts up carrot and cucumber sticks for a healthy boost and the children munch on them happily enough.

I find a bottle of Veuve Cliquot, at the back of the cupboard. I wave it at Christina before sticking it in the freezer to chill.

She smiles. 'Are you sure? On a weeknight?'

'We're celebrating, aren't we?' I'm hoping more alcohol will stave off the hangover starting to thud at my temples.

Amber tugs my arm. 'Mummy? Can we watch the Disney channel?'

'Please, Mummy?' Eddie clasps his hands together.

'Please.' Leo shows me his best angelic face.

I don't usually allow TV after dinner on a school night. But my resistance is low. 'Oh, all right. But PJs first.'

'Yay!' they chorus and I melt at their smiles. How can I deny them when I've been having fun all day? Christina helps them into their pyjamas while I fetch ice cream and popcorn. Soon the children are bundled under a blanket on the sofa, watching the live-action *Dumbo*. Even Amber's entranced. She's growing up fast, but Disney isn't too babyish for her quite yet. We've long promised them a trip to Disneyland Paris. Now I'm going to be freelancing, I can contribute.

While the kids watch TV, I set up the sofa bed in the study for Christina. 'Hope it's comfortable enough for a longer stay.'

She looks uncertain. 'Are you sure this is fine, Jade? Don't you need to talk to Sam? I could book a room at the Premier Inn.'

I check my phone. Sam hasn't replied. I think of 'Unknown Number'.

'Please, I insist.' Sod Sam and his late nights and weird texts. This is my house too. I have every right to ask one of my oldest friends to stay.

She hugs me, eyes moist. 'You've been so good to me.'

'Just let me know if you need anything, OK?' I say.

She checks her phone, her forehead creased with worry. 'Yes. Thank you. I really appreciate this. I was seeing if my mum had called.'

'Oh, Christina. I'm sure she'll change her mind. My mum used to threaten to kick me out all the time, but she never meant it.'

'Oh, no . . . my mum meant it, all right.' She looks away, biting her lip.

I squeeze her arm. 'I'm sorry. Come on, get yourself sorted and come and join us in the living room. I'll open the bubbles!'

I'm snuggled on the sofa with the children, sipping champagne, when I hear the front door open. Sam peeps in on us.

'Daddy!' chorus Leo and Eddie.

'Ssssh!' says Amber. It's the emotional bit with Dumbo's mum.

'What's going on? Slumber party?' Sam smiles, but he looks tired.

'The movie's nearly finished,' I whisper, realising it's gone nine. Way past bedtime. I follow Sam into the hall.

His shirt's rumpled and he's loosened his tie. He glances at Christina who's followed me out. 'Oh, hi, Christina. I didn't know you were coming round.' He attempts a smile, but I can tell he's annoyed.

'Didn't you get my message?' I ask. 'I called but your phone was off.'

'What's so urgent?' The set of his jaw tells me it's not the best time to discuss having a guest. I will him to be more polite, smiling reassuringly at Christina. 'I've been in meetings all day, trying to get some new clients, while you're having a rave-up on a Monday.' Sam's vain attempt at a joke reveals his irritation.

Christina murmurs, 'I'll, um, go check on the kids.' She gives my arm a squeeze and disappears into the living room.

I follow Sam into the kitchen, and he clocks the bottle of champagne. 'Someone's birthday?' Now Christina's gone he doesn't bother to hide his sarcastic tone.

I ignore the automatic stab of guilt. Why shouldn't I have a weekday drink? Sam stays late in the pub after work all the time, probably in the company of 'Unknown number'. 'Actually, we're celebrating.' I pour champagne into a glass and thrust it towards him.

He gulps it down like juice, then clatters open the bread bin, before slapping bread in the toaster.

'Sorry, I didn't leave you any dinner,' I keep my voice bright, swallowing my irritation. 'You were so late, I thought you'd eat out.'

He scowls at the toaster. 'Wayne promised Mark he'd be back for dinner.'

I should have cooked something fresh for him. A hangry Sam is unlikely to play nice. 'I could put a pizza in for you, if you like?'

'Toast is fine.'

I open the fridge. 'There's ham and Brie, I could make you a sandwich?' Anything to improve his mood. I want him to be OK about Christina staying, after all.

'I can do it.' He pushes past, grabbing the Brie and a packet of ham. When the toast is done, he concentrates on buttering it evenly. He slaps on the ham, smears on Brie, then finishes it in a few bites, washing it down with champagne. I try not to mind it's a special vintage.

He sits back. 'So, what are you "celebrating"?'

I'm suddenly nervous. 'Christina's left her mum's, and I . . . well, actually I've found a job.'

'A job?' He lifts his eyebrows. 'I thought you said Nina didn't have anything?'

'A freelance opportunity came up.' There's no way I'm mentioning Anthony while he's in this mood. 'It's business-to-business. Not your sort of thing.'

'Weren't you going to wait until September?' He scrapes back his chair, goes to the fridge and pulls out a bottle of Sancerre.

'This job came up. If I wait until September, the opportunity might be gone.'

Sam sloshes wine into his glass. 'So your mum's going to babysit?'

'You know my mum can't manage Leo on her own. He's too boisterous. But there's good news.' I stay upbeat. Sam's not really in the right mood for me to discuss Christina moving in. But she's waiting to hear it's OK for her to stay. I have no choice.

'That's why I was calling you. I'll be working from home, but I need someone to help me with the children. Freelance gigs don't come every day. It's not enough to justify a proper nanny. If Christina stays here, she can help with the kids.'

He stares into his glass. Is he listening? Is he angry? He has to see that it's the perfect solution.

I carry on. 'Christina had a fight with her mum and needs somewhere to live. So it's worked out well.'

His eyes narrow. 'Hang on, you mean Christina is going to be *living* here?'

I nod. 'Just for a couple of weeks.'

'And you didn't think to ask me first?' His eyes are flinty.

'I can't help it if you don't check your phone.' I'm defensive.

He picks up his phone. 'OK, I see your text. You're telling me, not asking.' He sprawls back in his chair, jaw protruding mutinously.

'I'm asking you now.' I grit my teeth 'So, what do you think?'

'You just want me to agree. Your friend's already installed, I don't know for how long, just when we need to economise.' He's scrolling through Facebook, like he's bored with our conversation. Suddenly I'm enraged. I'm sure he doesn't ignore his work colleagues like he's ignoring me.

'She's my friend – I can't see her on the streets.' I grit my jaw. 'I had to move fast on the freelance job, and I need childcare. Can't you see this is a win for all of us?'

'You didn't think I might like to know if a stranger is going to stay at our house?' He finally stops scrolling and glares at me.

'Ssshh, she'll hear you. She's not a stranger. She's one of my oldest friends. It's only until she finds somewhere to rent. It's not like you're here much at the moment.' *Too busy hanging out with Unknown Number.*

'That's because I'm working all hours to save my company!' he explodes. 'You don't understand what's happening in the market. It's a bloody nightmare.'

'I do see! I'm not stupid – that's why I thought you'd be pleased that I could bring in some money.' I don't bother lowering my voice. I'm too cross.

'A few days' freelance?' He's scathing. 'Like that'll pay the mortgage! Or keep you in champagne.'

Bastard. 'That's not fair! That champagne was a present from my aunt.' I clench my fists. As usual when we fight, he uses the fact I'm not earning against me, like I'm some spoilt princess sponging off him.

Who's the one who's given up their career? Looks after the children? Sorts all the crap in the house? I want to scream. Instead, I take a deep breath and try to control myself. 'I'm making an effort to find work, to contribute, and all you can do is put me down.'

He stands, scraping his chair on the floor. 'Well, you've clearly made up your mind. Thanks for consulting me. Carry on *celebrating* with your friend. I'm going to bed.' He stalks out.

I stare at his empty plate, which he hasn't bothered to tidy up. Crusts and crumbs are scattered over the table.

In a rage, I pick it up and throw it in the sink.

Chapter Fifteen

Jade

A champagne hangover's never the ideal start to a school day. My alarm works itself into my dream and I wake with the beep drilling into my skull. I hurry to the bathroom – mouth rank – and brush my teeth.

I sweep down the stairs to the children. Amber's usually up, but when I open her door, the curtain's drawn shut, the duvet over her face. 'Darling, wake up.'

She stirs, mumbling, 'What's the time?'

'Nearly half eight . . . we're late.'

'No!' She flings back the duvet and jumps out of bed. She sways for a moment, blinking. A tangle of hair sticks up like a bird's nest. Registration isn't until nine, but Amber gets anxious if she doesn't get to the playground early.

I can hear Sam in the hall, getting ready to leave, and my resentment towards him grows. *Why didn't he notice that none of us were up?*

'Eddie, Leo . . . Time to get up – school! Nursery!' I fake a singsong tone, disguising my panic. We have just over twenty minutes.

Eddie stumbles to the loo and I carry Leo downstairs, heavy nappy and all.

Sam slings his leather satchel over his shoulder and shakes his head. 'Partying on a school night. Don't say I didn't warn you.'

Bloody annoying. Did he let us be late on purpose? 'So why didn't you wake me?' I grind out.

He leans down and kisses Leo. 'Sorry. Your alarm was going for ages. I thought you must have heard it. At least you can sleep it off when they're at school.' He's out of the door before I can mention I'll be getting the brief for my freelance job today.

'Want pancake.' Leo pushes at my head, directing me towards the kitchen.

'No pancakes today,' I tell him. 'We don't have time, we're late. How about cornflakes?'

'Choc choc PAN-CAKE,' he insists. 'Kiss-tina! I want choc choc.'

'Good morning,' she sings out. She's at the breakfast bar, cradling a floral mug, not one of ours. In a pale pink blouse and white capri pants she's a vision of calm.

'Morning, Christina, you look . . . fresher than I feel.' After I'd put the kids to bed, I'd downed a last glass of wine. Big mistake.

I scrabble through the cupboards pulling out cereal and bowls. 'Want choc choc pancake, Mumma!' Leo whines, striking a nerve in my head.

'Can I do anything to help?' Christina closes the cupboard door quickly before Leo bangs his head.

I shake my head. 'I'm fine, thanks. Shouldn't have drunk so much.'

111

'Alka Seltzer?' she suggests.

'Can I have Coco Pops, Mummy?' Eddie's fully dressed in uniform. Darling Eddie.

'Oh, all right.' I glance towards Christina, embarrassed that I'm such a slummy mummy. 'We don't *usually* have such sugary cereals on a weekday,' I mutter as I pass Eddie the Coco Pops and a bowl.

Christina smiles towards Amber who's just appeared in her uniform, rucksack over her shoulders. 'Good morning, you look ready for school.'

'Quick bowl of Coco Pops, darling?' Amber nods but looks anxiously at the clock.

'Naughty cornflakes.' Leo slaps at the cereal box, and it falls to the floor, scattering cornflakes everywhere.

'Argghh! STUPID boy. I need a bowl!' Amber's eyelid flickers, a precursor to a full meltdown.

'Let me help.' Christina picks her way over the spilt cornflakes.

'Thanks, Christina.' I hand her a bowl and spoon. 'Pass this to Amber for me?' I kneel to clear up the mess while Leo wriggles out of my arms and drags a stool over to the fridge.

Christina nips towards him, unflustered. 'Come on, Leo. Sit down.'

She takes his arm, but he shakes it off. 'Want pancake.' He opens the fridge and pulls out the box of eggs.

Amber yelps. 'Leo!'

Eddie screams. 'He's got an egg!'

Splat. The egg smashes on the floor, before I can get to him.

'Arrrrgggh! Stupid boy!' Amber screams again, on the edge of a meltdown.

112

'Never mind!' I do my best to sound cheery, but the kids pick up on my stress. Leo's face turns red, and his mouth opens – quivering but silent.

If only Christina wasn't here to witness each minor disaster, but she remains unflustered. 'Accidents happen.'

Amber wails. 'Eddie's finished the milk!'

'There's more in the fridge,' says Eddie. 'Stop fussing.'

But Leo blocks the way to the fridge. His mouth is stretched so wide, his face is turning purple. When the wail finally emerges, it's so loud I slap my hands over my ears.

'Ssssh! Stop crying!' I'm fast unravelling. Sod the fake cheery tone.

'Jade, what can I do to help?' Christina's voice is gentle.

'Amber needs her packed lunch. Ham sandwich, juice and apple. Sorry. Not at our best today.' Trust the kids to play up in front of her.

'It's one of those mornings. We all have them.' She steps around Leo, grabs the kitchen roll and begins wiping up the smashed egg.

'Come on, darling. Coco Pops.' I bribe Leo away from the fridge, trying to keep my temper.

'No cereal.' He picks up the carton of milk and deliberately drops it on the floor. It skids towards Amber. The lid's not on properly and milk glugs out, puddling around her feet.

'Leeeeeooooo!' Amber screeches. 'THERE'S MILK ON MY SOCKS! I'm going to be late! I hate you!'

'Kids, please.' I'm losing it. 'Stop being such nightmares. Or I'll ... I'll CANCEL THE DISNEY CHANNEL!'

My threat does nothing to deflate the situation. 'NO, Mummy, no! Want DISNEEEEEYYYY!' Leo's screech is louder than ever.

I slump over the breakfast bar, covering my ears with my hands. A hammer pounds at my skull.

Over the din of Amber's screeches and Leo's cries, I'm aware of Christina moving about the kitchen, opening and shutting drawers, cupboards, the fridge. 'Amber,' I hear her say. 'I've just popped in a piece of toast for you, run up and change your socks and it'll be ready. Eddie – well done for eating your cereal. Could you tidy away your bowl and go brush your teeth? Leo, move away from the spilt milk. Let's get you some Coco Pops.'

Amber and Eddie leave the room but Leo's heaving with sobs, snot dripping down his face. 'I want Mumma! Want Disney!' He runs over and buries his snotty face into my pyjama trousers.

I feel terrible for yelling and pat his back with what little energy I have left.

'Have you any sandwich bags or foil?' Christina asks as she butters bread.

I point to the drawer. 'In there. Why's your head not pounding?'

She pulls out the foil, smiling. 'I drank a glass of water before bed.' She folds the foil neatly over the sandwiches. 'I can drop them off at school, the children can show me where to go.' Leo clutches me tighter. She kneels down with a bowl. 'Leo, you like chocolate, don't you? The best thing about Coco Pops is the chocolate milk.'

Leo peels his face away from my legs and allows Christina to lead him to the table. Soon he's slurping greedily, while Christina mops up the worst of the milk.

Coco Pops and Christina to the rescue. I'm grateful for her help. Peace is restored.

When Amber reappears, Christina hands her a plate of toast

and a sandwich wrapped in foil. 'I've made you a sandwich. Ham and cheese OK?'

'Don't like cheese,' she mutters.

'All right. I'll take it out.' She unwraps the foil.

'I can do it.' Amber snatches the sandwich and takes the cheese out before re-packing it.

I hand Christina Amber's flowery lunch bag and Eddie's *Toy Story* one and she packs satsumas, cartons of juice and the sandwiches.

'Can I go now?' Amber asks.

'Shall we leave together?' Christina suggests before I can answer.

'Mu-um.' Amber looks about to scream again. 'I like to go early.'

I hug her, knowing she's only acting up as she's worried about being late. 'OK, darling . . . you go first.'

Amber runs out before Christina can object.

I explain. 'Amber likes to get to the playground before the bell rings. She's careful crossing the road. She'll be fine.' The front door slams.

Christina helps Eddie with his laces while I take Leo upstairs and dress him in jogging bottoms and T-shirt. 'Quickly, brush teeth.' I carry him to the bathroom.

'No!' he shouts. Oh well, one missed toothbrushing wouldn't kill him.

Downstairs, he clings to me, refusing to let go.

'Come on, Leo, you're a big boy. Come and show me where your nursery is,' persuades Christina.

I crouch down and pick up his trainers. 'No Kiss-tina,' Leo mutters curling his toes away. 'Want Mumma take me nursery.'

115

Eddie crouches by Leo. 'Come on, Leo, we need to help Christina. She doesn't know where anything is. We have to show her.'

'Mummy's still in her PJs,' I add. 'I can't take you to nursery in PJs.' Leo giggles. I take my rose print scarf, which is looped over the banister, and tie it on his bag. 'Look ... why don't you take Mumma's scarf? That way, you have a piece of me close all morning.' I hug and kiss him.

Christina and the boys leave the house just as the school bell's ringing. Eddie's telling her how he goes into a different entrance to Amber, and Leo pulls at Christina's hand, suddenly keen to show her the way.

After they leave, I go upstairs for a shower. But despite the warm flow of water, I can't relax. I get out and throw on a pair of leggings and a stretchy top.

I ignore the mess of the kitchen, make a cup of tea and take my laptop to the living room. I check my email and see Anthony's sent over the Teatro brief.

Dear Jade,

So glad you reached out. Looking forward to working with you again. Attached Teatro brief – let me know asap!

Anthony

I download the attachment and glance through it, trying not to picture what the kids are doing. The brief is pretty dry, and I have to keep re-reading. As I review the target market and competition, worries niggle at me. Is Leo walking nicely with Christina? Will she carry him if he doesn't? He's a dead weight at nearly twenty kilos but she didn't want to take his balance bike.

I try to focus on the words of the brief. Teatro want a corporate brochure and marketing materials for their private dining customers. I pull out a notepad and doodle a few sketches of the circular stage and the trapeze silks, hoping inspiration will strike. But I'm no artist and my stick drawings are puny and pathetic. I sketch a bike on a tightrope wire. It turns into a boy on a balance bike, with chubby cheeks.

Through the open window, the chattering school crowd quietens. A child vrooms down our street, pretending to be a racing driver. *Could it be Leo?* The traffic can be awful at this time. The short walk to the nursery entrance is full of potential hazards.

I cross out the balance bike and sketch a circle for the stage. 'Teatro' means theatre. How about a performance? Juggling clowns? I draw a clown face with crosses for eyes and a down-turned mouth. What can they juggle?

Did Christina hold Leo's hand tight enough so he doesn't go running off? Did Amber manage to meet up with her best friend, Saskia? I usually keep an eye out in the playground.

Why didn't I ask Christina to check on her?

I sigh. It's no good. I can't concentrate.

It's nearly ten before Christina rings the doorbell. I rush to the hall and fling the door open. 'Where've you been? I was worried something happened. Did Leo go to nursery all right?'

Christina's smile is puzzled, and she checks her watch. 'Oh, I didn't realise the time. I got chatting to one of the mums, then I popped to the high street.'

117

'Oh, thank goodness.' I slump against the wall, weak with relief.

Christina slips off her shoes and hangs up her jacket. 'It was lovely to meet some other mums. Shareen – you might know her? – is recruiting for the PTA. There's a summer fair soon and they need help.'

'Was Leo OK waiting for Eddie to go in?' I can't listen to her words about the fair until I know the kids are fine.

'Leo behaved perfectly. He waited nicely and then held my hand walking to nursery. So, as I was saying, Shareen approached us while we were lining up. They need volunteers to run some stalls. I said I'd ask you.'

I shake my head. 'I volunteered when Amber was little. But Leo won't sit still. There's no way I can help unless Sam comes too, which, at the moment, is unlikely.'

She smooths her hair behind her ears. 'Of course. But I'll be happy to help too.' She changes the subject. 'Shall I put the kettle on? I picked up some croissants at the deli.'

I follow her into the kitchen. Cornflakes are still scattered over the floor, the worktop is covered with chocolate milk. 'Sorry it's a bomb site.'

'Oh, it's fine.'

I'm sure Christina's kitchen would never be left in such a state. She must think my hygiene standards are horrendous. I find myself explaining. 'Anthony's email arrived, and I was trying to get some thoughts down.' I pick up a bowl and open the dishwasher. It's still full of clean stuff.

Christina touches my arm. 'Jade, I can sort this out. I'll find where everything goes. Why don't you go work while you're fresh? I'll make coffee.'

'Are you sure?' It seems rude to leave her to clear up.

She steers me to the door. 'Go, leave me to it. I enjoy cleaning – it's therapeutic.'

'Really? All right – thanks, Christina.' I admit it's a relief to leave the chaos behind.

A few minutes later, Christina pops into the living room with coffee and a croissant. 'Shall I pick up Leo later? If you give me your keys, I'll pop to the high street and get a spare set cut.'

Should I ask Sam first before we make a copy of our keys? No. Why should I? This is my house too. 'Good idea, thanks.' I scribble something on my pad.

The pastry and coffee is a brief respite. Soon I'm sweating and there's a sharp pain behind my eyes. I slump lower and lower on the sofa until I'm horizontal. I close my eyes for a second.

The front door slams, waking me. Leo's clear voice calls out. 'Where's Mummy?'

My phone says its 12.30 p.m.

'Ssh, Mummy's working,' Christina murmurs.

'I'm in here!' I open the door to the hall.

'Mumma! I want Mumma to pick me up.' He flings himself at me, grabbing my legs with hot hands.

'Oh darling, I'm sorry. Auntie Christina's helping Mummy while I do some work.'

'NO! Don't want Mummy work!' Leo digs his nails into my thighs.

'Ow! Stop that, Leo.' Guilt overwhelms me. Am I doing the right thing? Should I be working before Leo starts school? Will he grow up thinking my work means more to me than he does?

'Come on, Leo, let's get you some lunch.' Christina holds out her hand.

'Mumma get lunch,' insists Leo, pushing me off the sofa. 'Mumma. Pleeeease, Mumma!'

'Come on, then.' I let him drag me to the kitchen. 'He's used to having me to himself.'

Christina's smile is strained. I know I shouldn't be giving in to Leo's demands. But I can't help it. He's still so little.

'Wow. This looks amazing.' The surfaces are clear and wiped down. The scraps of bills and paper normally strewn over the counters are piled to one side. Herb and spice pots line up on the spice rack. The floor's been hoovered and mopped.

I fetch cheese from the fridge, and slap some slices on bread, and stick it under the grill.

Christina piles sticks of cucumber and slices of apple into a bowl. Leo sits down and she offers him the bowl. 'I can take over from here, Jade. Why don't you go and work upstairs in your bedroom?'

'No.' Leo turns away from her. 'I want Mumma. Yummy cheese toast.' The smell of grilled cheese fills the kitchen.

'Don't you want to come to the high street?' Christina's voice is warm. 'Before we get Eddie, I have a surprise for you.'

'Pressie?' Leo looks up at her.

I leave Christina to serve him his lunch and sneak back to the living room, collecting my laptop, pads and pens before heading upstairs.

There's another email from Anthony.

Just checking to see how you're getting on? Maybe we can go over your ideas on Thursday?

Thursday's only a couple of days away. I better get a move on.

Chapter Sixteen

Mazza

Six Months Earlier

After the shame of the dress shop, I'm in a foul mood. I unlock the door, the leather B for Ben on my keyring swinging. 'Sod the dress. Believe in yourself,' you encourage me.

Mum's got some quiz show blaring from the telly but she's crashed out on the sofa, eyes shut, dribbling and snoring like a train. Since she's been working shifts, I only seem to catch her when she's asleep – in bed or on the sofa.

I pull dress after dress out of my wardrobe. Too faded. Too short. Too tight. The sales assistant said it. I want to look like a grown-up. Someone to be reckoned with. Someone worth a promotion. You get that, don't you?

'Trousers could be classy.'

You would think that. But I pull out a pair of black satin trousers, still with the TK Maxx tags. Cigarette pants, they call them in *Vogue*. They look smart teamed with a flowery blouse.

Remember when I inhaled *Elle* and *Vogue* and *Marie Claire?* Anything to take me away from East London. It was different in those days. Now, you can't move for all the Scarletts, and Tamaras, and Giselles. Yeah. Can hardly believe it myself.

I slope to the kitchen and open the fridge. God knows I need a drink or five after tonight's crap. But I've learned the hard way. I don't want to peak too early. Or puke. Or punch someone. The three Ps the old Mazza was so good at. I could add 'piss myself' if I want to make it four.

Could be sensible to avoid alcohol if I'm to succeed in our mission, right? But it's not often you get free booze on the company tab. It'd be rude to say no to all those empty calories, cost-of-living crisis and all.

'At least line your stomach.'

Yeah, yeah. I tip beans into a saucepan. The party'll be loud and busy enough to hide any windiness. Half the blokes in the studio trump all day anyway, fucking stinkers. Maybe I'll fry an egg, push the boat out, why not?

You always told me you could tell how well a company's doing by the quality of the Christmas party. Not too well this year, some at the agency have been moaning. Not that anyone would notice with all the client schmoozing over boozy lunches and dinners. But tonight, there's no posh hotel for the workers, just drinks and finger food in a club. Hoxton, mind, so not quite the local Palais. The agency's ageing hipsters'll be scoffing crisps and sausage rolls. Ironically, of course, darling, thinking they're slumming it coz we're not in Soho.

I stick a couple of slices in the toaster, and scroll through my socials – you never know, I might've won the lottery or that hot guy I got with at the school prom might have tracked me down, not that I'd tell you. I'm watching a funny cat meme when the reek of smoke hits my nostrils. Shit. Burnt the toast.

I open a window before the smoke alarm goes off. Mum'll kill me if she's disturbed from her favourite quiz-slash-nap. I fish out the charred remains and go to chuck them but the fucking bin's full.

'Mum!' I yell.

She's been saying her job puts her off doing any cleaning at home. Claims she needs a rest or she'll get cleaner's elbow. Cleaner's lazy arse more like.

I pull out the binbag and, fucking hell, it breaks and there's shit all over the floor. Tea bags, potato peelings and rice. And a ton of junk mail. How many times have I told her about recycling? Her fave expression's: 'Roll on global warming, I can afford the Costa del Hackney'.

I put in a new binbag and pick out a load of ripped-up paper.

What the . . .?

It's not junk mail. They're official-looking letters. Pages of them. From the council. Covered in tea stains. But when I piece them together . . .

Oh. Fuck.

You are being evicted . . .
Final warning: rent due . . .

The latest is dated yesterday.

Beepbeepbeepbeep. OH GOOOODDD!

I jump up as my eardrums are assaulted by the smoke alarm.

Crap. The beans have turned to tar in the pan.

'What the bleeding hell's that noise?' Mum screams from the sofa.

I grab my selfie stick, use it to turn off the alarm, and open another window.

Thank fuck. My ears ring in the silence. Hope to God we don't get a visit from the fire warden. Old fart likes nothing more than sticking his nose in.

'Mum,' I say. 'What the fuck's all this?' I hold up the ripped eviction notice.

'Language, Marianne. Why're you rooting in the bin? Not that desperate yet.'

'Why haven't you been paying the rent?' I rage. 'Where's the cash I've been giving you?'

She yells back. 'Oh, sorry, love. It's gone. On beans and bread and milk and tea. Food doesn't magically appear in the cupboards, you know. Even Tesco Value's twice the price. The electric eats money and I'm still freezing my tits off all day.' She wraps her cardigan around her.

'What d'you mean "all day"?' I say. 'Aren't you working the day shift?'

She shakes her head. 'Sorry, love. Lost my job. Got taken over by Romanians. They have their own people.'

'So? There's a labour shortage, case you hadn't heard. Get another job.'

She picks up the remote. 'Marianne. Give your old mum a break. I've been working my arse off since you was old enough to be left. And now you're a big girl, it's your turn.'

I'm shaking with anger, plus a shit ton of fear. I like my home. I don't want to be kicked out, or moved into a hostel. I take a breath. Try to calm down. Yelling at Mum just sends her loopy.

'I'm sorry. Why didn't you tell me? I could've put more aside.'

'How'm I meant to know they're serious about chucking us out?' She leans back, closes her eyes. A roar of laughter bursts out from UK TV Gold. 'Oh, it's the one about the rat.' She giggles, opening an eye. 'Bloody love this.'

'Mum!' I yell, irritated. 'We're going to be evicted in two weeks if we don't pay what's owed.'

Her eyes don't leave the TV. 'Where'm I gonna get nine grand from?'

I shake the letters at her. 'You don't seem to give a shit. Were you just gonna wait until they threw us out?'

'Don't get your knickers in a twist, eh? Auntie Dell'll always have us.'

'No way!' Auntie Dell's house stinks of smoke and that creep she's married to freaks me out with his slimy stare.

'Maybe you could talk to your father if you're that desperate.' She nods. 'Yeah, he owes me years of maintenance.'

'Mum, I'm twenty-three. Too old for handouts from my dad, even if I knew where he was. Which I don't.'

She tugs at my hand. 'Come on, darling, don't be such a grump. It's Christmas in two weeks. They can't chuck us out on Christmas Day.'

'Maybe not, but soon as Boxing Day's over ...'

We've been in this flat since you and me were little, Ben, and she left our dad. From what I remember he slapped her one too many times. No way would I call that arsehole, even if I had his number.

'The council will sort out a payment plan,' you say.

Good idea. I'll call them on Monday. Beg and grovel.

If only you were still here, Ben. Mum was always crap at looking after us. It was you who stopped me being bullied, walked me to school. We'd pass umpteen building sites and none of the sleazy gits dared whistle at me because you'd report them. No one dared mess with you. My big brother.

Mum pulls me close, kisses my hair. 'I know you'll sort it, Maz darling. Just watch this episode. It's a classic.'

She's driving me mad. But it's the most we've spoken in ages, so I sit down and watch *Fawlty Towers*. Mum laughs at Manuel running round looking for his rat until she has tears running down her face.

But we can't ever talk about you, Ben.

Chapter Seventeen

Jade

I emerge from my room at gone five, shoulders stiff and brain drained. I'd been vaguely aware of the children's voices echoing up the stairwell when they got home, but I was buzzing with ideas and since Christina was with the kids I carried on working.

Eventually I pad downstairs, wondering at the silence. I open the kitchen door and look in on a peaceful scene. Eddie and Amber are folding paper serviettes into fans, while Leo sprinkles breadcrumbs over a dish of macaroni cheese. More land on the table than on the pasta, and I chuckle.

Christina grabs the packet of breadcrumbs before it goes on the floor. 'I think that's enough, Leo. Well done. Amber, if you could help the boys set the table, I'll pop this in the oven.'

'Hey, kiddos!' My heart's swelling in my chest as the boys run towards me. Amber waves but skips to the cutlery drawer.

I ruffle Eddie's hair. 'We're earning marbles, Mummy.'

'Treats!' yells Leo. 'Elefun.' He barges Eddie away and throws a breadcrumb-y hug around my legs. I kneel and bury my face in his curls, squeezing his sturdy body.

He wriggles away towards Amber. 'Elefun, marble.'

'Hi, Amber.' I give her a kiss, but she swipes at her cheek. I know she's missed me too but doesn't want to act like a baby.

'Leo's setting the table.' She picks out individual knives and forks, inspecting them for defects as she counts. 'One, two, three ...'

'Four, five.' Leo takes the last of the cutlery from Amber then bangs knives and forks in place on the table while she moves on to the plates and glasses.

I lean over Eddie's shoulder, and watch him fold the paper serviettes. 'Wow! Where'd you learn that?'

Eddie grins, and fans me with the serviette. 'YouTube. Do you like it, Mummy?'

'Fantastic. You guys could run a restaurant!' I hug him and sit in my usual seat. 'Christina, what have you done with my kids? Are these angels mine?' If a tiny part of me feels miffed that they're behaving so well, I ignore it.

Leo climbs onto my lap. 'Marble for the elefun.'

Christina holds out an old Nutella jar. Three marbles roll round the bottom. 'I read about this parenting technique,' she tells me. 'Children can earn a marble every time they behave well. When the jar's full, they get a treat. Things should run more smoothly, especially in the morning.'

Leo stretches a hand towards her. 'Mine. I want elefun.'

Christina places another marble in his hot palm. 'That's for setting the table.' She hands a marble to Eddie too.

Leo plops his marble in the jar and holds it up to me, grinning. 'Elefun soon.'

I kiss him. 'Wow, good boy. How did you earn so many?'

'We ate our breakfast without fighting and put our plates in the dishwasher,' Eddie says.

'I can tidy up without marbles. I'm not a baby,' insists Amber.

'I know, you are very tidy.' Christina hands her a marble. 'But it's only fair that you earn treats too.'

Amber takes the marble, curling her fingers round like she's hiding it.

'Treats do sound exciting.' Despite my misgivings, I do my best to sound keen. 'As long as there's not too much sugar. I don't want the dentist to tell us off.'

Eddie bursts out laughing. 'Not *that* sort of treat, Mummy!'

'Silly Mumma, not choc choc. Elefun.' Leo starts marching, lifting his knees high, his version of the elephant march from *The Jungle Book*.

Christina puts the packet of marbles in a cupboard. 'Who'd like to explain to Mummy?'

Amber put her hand up. 'We made a list of rewards.'

'Which you'll need to check with your mum and dad.' Christina takes a list off the fridge and hands it to me. 'What do you think?'

'New ball, book, trip to the park.' Reward schemes aren't really my thing. 'I guess there's no harm in it.' I shrug. 'But who added "elephant"?'

Leo bounces up and down. 'Elefun, yay!'

Christina's shoulders shake as she hides her laughter. 'Oh, I'm sorry – I suggested a trip to the zoo. That's a big treat, Leo. You'll have to save a lot of marbles.'

'I don't want to go to the boring old zoo,' says Amber. 'I want to go the cinema, with popcorn and ice cream.'

'And I want a Nerf gun,' says Eddie. 'Please. I've been saving up.'

'Well, hopefully, we can do all those things.' They run off

with their jars and something flickers in my chest. The children don't seem bothered that I haven't been around all afternoon. Christina certainly has a knack with them.

I should be grateful her system seems to be working. I tried a sticker sheet when Amber was two and had terrible tantrums. It worked for about three days until the novelty wore off. If she'd built up to a tantrum, nothing would stop her.

But marbles to earn treats are more exciting than stickers, even if they feel a bit like bribes ... Well, who doesn't like positive rewards? I make a mental note to find out more about the marble system, ask some friends what they think.

'Jade?' Christina touches me on the shoulder. 'Shall I cook some chicken for you, me and Sam later? You could go back to your work if you like?'

'Thanks, Christina.' I smile. 'I guess we could eat later rather than with the kids. Not sure when Sam'll be back though.'

'Mummy, you're spoiling my fan!' I look down to see I've unpleated the napkin. Eddie snatches it off me.

'Maybe you could let Sam know I'm cooking dinner? It's the least I can do after you've all been so kind to me,' Christina says, ruffling Eddie's hair but he squirms away to join Leo loading cars onto his transporter.

'You're looking after the children.' I smile at her again. 'That's more than enough. By the way, did you manage to check the local hospital for locum work?'

'I found an agency covering East London. I'm just updating my CV. Staying here has given me a breathing space. I'm so grateful.'

'Aw – it's good you're here!'

She lowers her voice. 'So,' she glances at Amber reading her book and the boys rolling cars on a ramp. 'Have there been any more texts from the unknown number?'

It's an unwelcome reminder. 'Oh God, I hope not,' I say, brightly. 'I told you, it was nothing. And Sam's so busy, he'd hardly have time for an affair,' I joke, though I can hear the tension in my voice.

'Mmm.' She doesn't look convinced.

'What are you talking about?' asks Eddie, listening to our every word.

'Nothing!' I say. 'Time to wash hands for dinner.'

Chapter Eighteen

Jade

On Thursday morning, I leave the children eating breakfast with Christina and take the Central Line to Holland Park. I feel strangely nervous as I walk to Anthony's flat. As I approach the white corniced block, ornamented by wedding-cake-like columns, sweat prickles my neck. *Will he like my ideas?*

'Jade! Come on up.' Anthony's voice crackles through the intercom. His flat is an early inheritance from his mother, who'd remarried after his father died, and spent her time between New York and Hong Kong. My heels sink into the plush carpet as I walk up the stairs to the second floor.

'Good to see you!' Anthony's waiting at the door and his muscled arms pull me into a warm hug. Gone are his skinny arms and cheeks marked with acne. The hug lasts a beat longer than feels natural. *Is Christina right?* Does Anthony consider me more than a friend? Something makes me reluctant to tell Sam I'm working with him. Is it because I don't know the truth behind the text from the unknown number? If Sam's keeping a secret, now I have one too.

'This is where the magic happens.' Anthony winks, leading

me into a high-ceilinged living room that doubles as a design studio. The kitchen wall has been knocked down, the units relegated to a corner, and sunlight streams through the tall sash windows. Wooden floors and Ercol furniture give it a contemporary look.

There's another guy sitting in an ergonomic office chair in front of a large screen in the corner. Anthony introduces me. 'This is Jonno, visualiser extraordinaire. Jonno, meet Jade – the copywriter for Teatro.'

Copywriter. It feels good to hear. I stand straighter.

'So you're the legendary Jade? Hi.' Jonno rolls his chair towards me and, without getting up, pumps my hand with a meaty paw.

'Hi, Jonno.' I snatch my hand back, conscious of my damp palms.

Anthony pulls out a chair, and I hang my linen jacket on the back. On a nearby desk in silver frames are photos of Anthony's family and guys I recognise as his Cambridge mates.

Anthony grins. 'Cup of the old brain fuel, yeah?' I must look puzzled. 'Caffeine fix?'

I give myself a shake. 'Oh yes, lovely. Thanks.' I duck down and take out my sketch pad, hiding my red cheeks.

He scoots over to the kitchen area, returning with two mugs and a cafetière a few seconds later. He adds milk to my mug, but no sugar. *And his is black, with no sugar.* Weird, how some things stick.

I open my sketch pad, mouth dry with nerves. Yesterday the theatre concept seemed perfect. But were the masks too old-fashioned? It's so long since I've thought about anything other than children's activities.

'Teatro means theatre.' My voice cracks and I clear my throat. 'So my concept's based on "All the world's a stage". Headline: *Find the right stage for you.* A party or private dining experience is, in its own way, a performance . . .'

Anthony's brow creases. Not the reaction I was hoping for. A sinking feeling replaces the flurry of butterflies. 'A bit too obvious?' I swig my coffee and it scalds my mouth.

'No. No – it's a good idea.' He's nodding. 'Anything else?'

'Er . . . anything else?' I repeat. The roof of my mouth is burning.

'You brought more than one concept, right?'

Why didn't I come up with a few alternatives? 'I . . . Sorry. I've drawn out the brochures, posters and leaflets to show you how the campaign could work across the different materials.'

'Can I see?' He flips through my pad, face serious. 'Yes. Thanks. This is great. But . . . sorry, my fault, I should've shown you these.' He hands me a leaflet. 'They ran something similar five years ago.'

I flip through the leaflet. It's a more traditional take. But they've used the comedy and tragedy masks, with a striped curtain as a frame.

'No matter!' I say brightly, hiding my disappointment. 'I'll think of something else.' Ideas are thrown out all the time, but I've forgotten how much it hurts.

Anthony hands me the folder. His eyes are kind, but I still feel like I've failed. 'Since you're here, why don't you check the past campaigns?'

I flick through various leaflets. There's a concept with jugglers and I'm speaking before I have time to think. 'How about . . . circus acts blended with foodie dishes; a surreal mash-up?' I grab my sketch pad and draw a big top and scribble a line: *Your turn to take a bow.* I add a plate of bow-tied pasta.

He grins. 'I think you're on to something. Let's bounce a few ideas around. I'll get Jonno to fetch us some lunch. You're fine to stay?'

'Sure.' Thank God Christina's picking up the kids and I don't need to rush back. It's a huge relief.

He hands me a marker pen. 'Dream Team – remember?'

Dream Team. Anthony's cheesy nickname for us, back in the day. It's kind of him to boost my ego instead of bawling me out. He's always been kind. Once our old creative director had thrown out concept after concept. We'd slogged our guts out, all weekend, until Anthony had come up with a cool headline and, finally, we had a decent concept. But he never told our boss the words were his, and he let me take the credit.

The truth is, I should have brought more concepts – at least three – even loosely sketched out. Will he think I've lost it?

'Right . . . more coffee. Clip this to the board, will you?' He hands me an A2 pad and a bulldog clip.

Once he's sorted a fresh pot, Anthony draws a mind map, with TEATRO in the middle. 'So, think back to lunch the other day. What was going on? Close your eyes. Remember.'

'OK.' I lean back and close my eyes. It's a relief to shut away the brightness of the studio.

'What did you see, hear, smell?' Anthony's voice is low in my ear.

I imagine being back at Teatro. The coolness after the heat outside. 'Bebop saxophone. Clink of cutlery. A cork popping. The scent of lilies.'

'What did you taste?' I sense Anthony crouching by my chair.

135

'Umm – salty smoked salmon, sharp horseradish, cold dry Sancerre, creamy bittersweet chocolate mousse.' I open my eyes. Anthony's face is near mine. I laugh lightly, edging my chair away. 'I might need another lunch to remember.'

He bounds back to the board and scribbles. 'Lunch on me, when we crack this.'

'I'm sure we will ...' On a fresh page, I sketch a circular stage and bottles of champagne. 'Love is in the air. Clowns could juggle the bottles?' I make a face. 'Too obvious?'

Anthony peers at my drawing, his breath rustling the paper. 'Cute. Circus props'

'And maybe ... wheels of brie?'

Nothing's too silly or crazy, or rude. The best advertising creatives rarely stick to their roles. It's all about the idea. He jots down words and headlines. I'm drawing trapeze artists swinging off chandeliers, clowns juggling steaks and slices of watermelon.

After a few hours, Anthony passes my sketches to Jonno. 'Can you draw these up? So our visuals don't look like someone's dog has drawn them.' He winks at me.

I throw a ball of paper at him. 'You saying I can't draw?' We've slipped back into our old banter.

'Too right. Stick to what you know.' He pings a pen at me. 'Work on a tagline and leave the visuals to the artists.'

'Oh my God, you can turn the creative into a suit all right,' I tease him. 'Do you boss your clients around like this?'

Anthony's right about Jonno. In a few strokes, he turns our garbled ideas into arty visuals that capture the quirky humour of our campaign. Clowns juggling food and trapeze silks swooshing fill our concept with personality.

Now for the perfect tagline. I roll my shoulders, stiff from hunching over my pad. 'I have a few crap lines. "*Parties de vivre*"?'

'Like *joie de vivre*? Mmm, maybe. Work on it.' Anthony walks behind me. He presses his fingers into my sore shoulder muscles. 'Another day like this and we'll crack it. Watch out, awards!'

My face burns. His fingers rubbing my shoulders feel too intimate. I move away, gathering my jacket and bag. 'If you don't mind – I'd like to catch the kids before they go to bed.' It had been a fun and productive afternoon, but I didn't want to give him the wrong idea.

'Sure – same again tomorrow?' He waves.

'Yep. Bye, Anthony, Jonno.'

Feeling like I've escaped an awkward moment, I skip down the stairs and out to the street. I'm buzzing from too much caffeine and sugar. I make a note to myself not to encourage Anthony's flirting. He knows Sam and I are married. I'm sure he doesn't mean anything by it. He was just playing the little brother and I'm his Jade Jai.

At Wanstead, I hurry up the escalator, longing to see the children, hoping to read them a story. I open the front door, bubbling with energy, but the house is quiet, the lights dimmed. 'Hi, I'm back!' I sing out.

Christina pads into the hall, finger over her lips. 'The children are in bed.' Her voice is hushed. 'Best not disturb them.'

'Bit early for bedtime?' It's only just eight, but maybe they were tired. Disappointment bursts my excitement. I have a sudden urge to run upstairs to kiss them goodnight, but it would be unfair to wake them, and I'd never get them back to sleep.

I follow Christina into the kitchen. Everything's been put away, the surfaces wiped down with bleach, the pungent scent warring with savoury smells from the oven.

'I didn't know how long they'd take to settle so I started bedtime early. How'd your meeting go? Anthony like your idea?' Christina opens the oven and takes out a foil-wrapped dish.

I sink into a chair. 'Yeah, it was fine. I forgot how intense it gets. I'm shattered.'

'Are you going back tomorrow?'

'If that's OK? What about you? Any sign of a job interview?'

'I spent the day applying to a local hospital, so no word yet.' Christina fetches a bottle of wine out from the fridge and fills two wine glasses. 'I'm fine to look after them tomorrow.'

She puts a glass in front of me and I take a swig. 'Wow, thanks.' It's ice cold and refreshing. Just what I need. 'Something smells good.'

'Lasagne. I waited for you to eat.' She serves up the lasagne and we tuck in.

'Now I know how Sam feels, coming home to a well-cooked meal,' I joke.

Christina puts her fork down. 'Even when I worked at the local GPs surgery, I liked to cook every night.'

I'm about to ask what happened with her husband when I hear the front door open. 'Sam!' I call out. It's the first time we've seen each other properly since our spat. 'Come and have dinner. Christina's made a lasagne.'

Sam walks into the kitchen, looking relaxed. 'What's that amazing smell?' He leans down to kiss me, all traces of yesterday's bad mood gone. A hint of smoke and alcohol tells me he's stopped at the pub.

'How's your day been?' I want to ask if he's started smoking again, but I don't want to argue in front of Christina.

'OK, usual crap.' He accepts a glass of wine from Christina, then sits in his place at the top of the table, next to me. 'And how are the little angels?' He flashes a smile at Christina, softening his sarcastic tone.

'Good as gold. And Jade had a brilliant day at work,' Christina reminds him. She places a plate of lasagne in front of him and sits opposite me.

'Oh, yeah – your freelance gig. How's it going?' He doesn't wait for my reply before turning to Christina. 'This tastes fantastic.' He shovels up another forkful. 'Sure this isn't M&S?'

'I cooked it from scratch. It's not that hard if you have the time and the children are good at sprinkling cheese.'

I try not to mind that Sam is showing more interest in the food than my job. 'I had a good day. We came up with a great concept.' Now's the moment to mention I'm working for Anthony. But I'm not in the mood to fight my corner if he doesn't like it.

'It must feel good to be back at work, Jade,' Christina comments. 'You're a great role model for Amber.'

'Thank you, Christina.' I flash her a smile. 'I couldn't do it without you.'

She looks down at her plate and focusses on finishing her food. She's never been keen on compliments. It's the Chinese way, to ignore praise.

Sam hides a belch. He fetches another bottle and fills our glasses. 'Cheers. That was delicious.' He grins at me, and it feels like a truce after our fight the other night.

I grin back. 'I did say Christina was a better cook than me.'

Sam turns the full force of his smile on Christina and puts his hand on her arm. 'You can stay as long as you like, if you cook like that!'

She smiles shyly through her lashes. 'I do like to cook. I enjoy cooking all sorts of cuisines. Italian. British. Chinese. Indian. Thai. But there are plenty of other talents just as valuable.' She nods at me. 'Jade's doing a fantastic job. Raising three young children, restarting her career.'

I smile. It feels good to have Christina stand up for me, someone in my corner at last.

'Of course. Jade's amazing,' said Sam, pulling me towards him. But I move away, and his kiss brushes my ear. I'm relieved Sam seems to be warming to my friend finally. He's certainly enjoyed her home-cooked meal. I relax, enjoying the glow of the wine after a satisfying day's work.

Sam turns to Christina. 'So, are you planning on staying in London rather than freezing in Scotland?'

I nudge him. 'Sam! It's none of our business.'

He shrugs. 'Just saying. If you're a canny investor, it's a good time to buy, with house prices falling. And I know Jade would love a mate nearby.' He stretches out a hand and squeezes her shoulder.

His phone buzzes with a text. He checks it and frowns, then leaves the kitchen.

'Sorry Sam is being rather nosy about your plans. Take all the time you need,' I say. I can't help feeling suspicious of the text.

'No. It's time I thought about the future. I can't stay here forever.' She sighs.

I should ask her about her problems with Michael, but selfishly I don't have the energy right now for an emotional conversation. I should make the effort to spend time with Sam, since he's home at a decent time for once.

When I join Sam in the living room, he's in front of the TV, absorbed in a documentary about the economy. We might not be at odds any more, but it's a long time since we really connected.

His phone buzzes with another text. He turns his phone off without looking.

'Who's texting you at this time?' I can't help myself asking.

'No one important,' he says.

Is it the unknown number? Could it be Mazza?

Suspicion settles in my gut like it's here to stay. I have to find out who texted him.

Later that night, I wait for Sam to fall asleep so I can check his phone. He turns his back to me, and curls onto his side. I lie on my side too. We're like two inverted commas, our backs against each other, our days of spooning long gone. I listen to the sound of his breathing. Lightly at first, then getting heavier.

When I gauge Sam's asleep, I reach over him and check his phone. There's a text from Wayne about a meeting the next day. But the last text is from 'Unknown number'. Just as I suspected. *We need to meet. Soon.*

My heart is thudding hard. My stomach churns. Hands shaking, I scroll through the message thread. 'Unknown number' and Sam have been chatting. The chain begins with the original message. So he hadn't deleted it, like he'd assured me. *Dreamed about you last night x*

Sam replies: *Don't text me.*

Later there's another message: *Howz it going?*

Sam replies *Busy.*

Finally, that last message: *We need to meet. Soon.*

It's nothing exactly incriminating. But a coiled-up feeling in my gut tells me it's another woman. He'd told me it was no one, that he'd deleted the message and blocked the number.

If he's lying about that, what else is he keeping from me?

Chapter Nineteen

Jade

I want to hammer my fists on Sam's back and demand to know why he lied. Instead, I replace the phone and collapse back into bed, drawing the covers tightly around me.

I toss and turn for hours, listening to Sam's heavy breathing, analysing our every interaction from the last few weeks. He's been distracted – supposedly busy with work. But what if he's been spending time with the sender of the texts?

I finally fall into a restless sleep, full of anxious dreams. I wake to find Sam – and his phone – have already gone.

As I drag myself out of bed, my body creaks and aches in protest. It's Friday and I'm working at Anthony's again. I shower and dress before the children wake, then leave Christina preparing their breakfast in the kitchen. I'm too preoccupied to say much to her. Thoughts chase round my head. Should I text Sam? Ring him? But no. We need to talk, face to face.

I believed him when he said he didn't know who the text was from. But the thread proves he lied. I think of the sex we had the other night. *Did it mean nothing?*

There must be a logical explanation. Unknown Number

could be an old friend, someone he hasn't caught up with for a while. Or maybe a colleague.

Then why didn't he explain properly when I asked him?

Before I know it, I arrive at Holland Park. At the studio, Jonno tells me that Anthony's had an unexpected emergency at the printers. 'He'll be there all day. You can reach him on his mobile if you need to talk to him, but he said you have brochure copy to get on with?'

'Yes, thanks, Jonno.'

Jonno's absorbed crafting a mock-up and it's a relief not to have to talk. I stare at my screen, writing and re-writing the same paragraph. I find myself sifting through the agency staff I met at the awards night, wondering who could be Unknown Number. I keep coming back to Mazza. The only person I know who has a crush on Sam.

At lunchtime, I nip out for a sandwich and walk round Holland Park to clear my head. One thought is stuck in my brain. *Anthony's been working at Sam's office.*

Could I ask him to check up on Sam for me? Anthony and I go back a long way, and I've always felt I could trust him. But would it be a step too far? In the old days we'd ended up talking about anything and everything. But not since Sam and I got together.

Anthony must know if there's any gossip. He knows Mazza. Does he know about her crush on Sam? Could I just ask him? But I think of how he massaged my shoulders the night before. Will it give him the wrong idea if I start questioning my marriage? No. It's not appropriate to ask for Anthony's help. Not a good idea.

The Unknown Number could be anyone. It's Sam I need to talk to. There's no need to involve Anthony.

Back in the studio, I carry on butchering the brochure copy. Towards six, I'm about to give up and leave when Anthony arrives.

'Hi guys, thanks for holding the fort. Sorry I've not been around. Nightmare with the colours. How'd today go? Copy done?'

'Nearly . . .' I don't want to admit most of the draft was rubbish. 'Do you want a read?' I add reluctantly.

'No rush, Jade, next week's fine if you're not quite there. By the way, Jonno and I go for male-bonding beverages on a Friday. Wanna join?'

'Not tonight, Ant,' Jonno interrupts, slinging his messenger bag on his shoulder. 'Dummy brochures are on your desk. I'm off to a comedy night.'

'No worries. Jade'll save me from a night of drinking on my own, right?'

'Yeah, why not?' I roll my aching neck. 'A drink sounds lovely.' After all, Sam would be living it up on a Friday in Soho – he could even be with Unknown Number. If I go straight home, I'll just stress even more. I text Christina to let her know I'll be late.

All fine here, Christina replies. *Stay as long as you like.*

Should I bother texting Sam? I resent telling him my movements when he's been lying to me, but I force myself to send him a quick text.

Sam replies with a thumbs up emoji, probably from the pub. *Why did I even bother?*

The Castle's bustling with a mixture of the after-work crowd and tourists. I find a corner table and Anthony threads his way to the bar. He returns with a bottle of Chardonnay and some crisps. He pours the wine.

'Here's to our fantastic concept, and to completing the brochure next week.'

'Cheers.' We clink glasses and I take a large gulp of wine, which numbs some of the pain.

Anthony chats about his plans for his design studio, how his mum's been nagging him to pivot to banking. After a while, he runs out of words and there's a pause. 'Is everything OK, Jade? You seem a bit quiet? I'm sorry I abandoned you today. You could've worked from home ...'

'No ... It's not that,' I say. 'I've a few things on my mind.'

'So ... work? Kids? Family?'

The Chardonnay loosens my tongue. I sigh. 'Actually, it's Sam. He's been so busy lately. I hardly see him.'

'Yeah – they're pitching at lot. That's why I was called in.'

'I'm surprised Sam didn't mention you're freelancing for him. He knows we were mates.'

'Yeah, well ... It was the production manager who arranged it.'

My heartbeat quickens. 'Mazza? The girl with red hair, in production?'

'Yeah – of course – you met her the other night.' He shifts uncomfortably, and I wonder if he knows something. Mazza's crush on Sam seems common knowledge at the agency. Her friends had been gossiping quite openly. Anyone could've heard them.

'Do you ... Do you think it's worth me talking to her about freelancing there?'

He opens his palms. 'I guess. But why don't you ask Sam?'

146

'I did. Sam says he can't afford to employ me right now. They need to win a pitch or two.'

He gazes at me intently. 'It wouldn't be any use talking to Mazza if Sam said that.'

'What's she like? She seems fun. Popular.' I pick at a cuticle.

'She's a good laugh. I like her.' He picks up the menu and scans it. 'Do you fancy getting some food?'

'I hear Sam gets on with her. Do you know – if Sam hired her, or Wayne?'

He puts the menu down and gives me a sharp look. 'Why're you so interested in Mazza?'

'Anthony – you'd tell me, wouldn't you, if there was any . . . gossip about Sam? And maybe Mazza?' We're old friends – his loyalty lies with me, I want to add.

'What?' His jaw drops open. 'Jade, I . . . I don't know? I'm not at the office that much. Mazza and I – we go for a drink now and then. I could ask my mate Baz if you're really suspicious. He knows all the gossip.'

'Would you? I'm sure it's nothing. But I want to set my mind at rest.'

Chapter Twenty

Mazza

Six Months Earlier

I read online that the nightclub, Fusion, has been around since the nineties. You probably came here, Ben, back in the day. As I make my way across the room, I wonder whether it's had a revamp since it opened. The 'warehouse chic' décor is dated. But it makes me smile.

Remember that retro-themed bar you wanted to open? The one I sketched out? We'd made so many plans – but there hadn't been time, in the end.

I wouldn't have this job if it weren't for you. You always encouraged me at school – unlike Mum, who didn't give a fuck. You bought me a laptop, so I could apply to colleges. You used to tell me how you flunked out of school; all you could do was work in a bar. 'Good money, shit hours,' you'd say. You wanted something better for me.

I've always been good at art and designing stuff on the computer. But none of us knew just how hard it would be. I left college in 2020 when the world was plunged into the pandemic.

There weren't any jobs. I had a BTEC in graphic design, but no experience and creative industries were going bust.

Thank fuck your mate Steve hired me to work in his print shop for a while. It was the best I could do, taking orders for flyers and fitting customers' designs to the templates. I was lucky to have a job, but I was bored.

Luckily, you were always a people person. You liked to chat to the punters who came into the bar – find out what they did and what companies they worked for.

Remember what you used to say? 'It's not what you know, it's who you know.' Your bar was bang in the middle of Soho, near all the media companies. That's how you met Sam and Wayne, persuaded them to give me an interview and when everything opened up, they hired me as a production assistant. It was all down to you, Ben.

There are murmurings that the agency is in trouble, but looking around tonight, it's hard to believe.

'Blue Lagoon?' An out-of-work actor dressed as a mermaid offers me a frosted martini glass full of blue liquid, welcoming me to the private area the agency have hired.

'Thanks!' I wink at her and take two, knocking one back and handing her empty glass. My throat burns and the room spins.

'Hey, Maz!'

'Mazza, you're here!' Heidi and Lauren hug me, giggling.

'Hiya, gals,' I say. By the way they're swaying, I've some catching up to do.

I follow them to the bar, wobbly on my kitten heels. 'Heidi, where are the sausage rolls?' She's on the party committee, in charge of catering.

'Vegan canapés,' she corrects. She waves over another mermaid holding a tray of tiny hamburgers. 'Fake beef, but real char-grilled,' Heidi assures us. I grab a couple as Heidi and Lauren pull me to the dance floor. I immediately regret my choice of shoes and kick them off, soon as I can.

Propping up the bar with the designers are Wayne and Sam. As soon as I clock them, blood rushes to my cheeks and I can't take my eyes off Sam. His blue eyes are piercing, stubble frames his square jaw, a lock of blond hair flops over his forehead. When he talks to someone, he stares straight in their eyes, like no one else matters. He's the guy you want to get with, or be mates with at least.

He glances over and catches me staring. I gulp at my drink, hiding my red cheeks. Heidi and Lauren will only tease me again. My head's spinning, and not just from Sam's attention.

I grab Heidi's shoulder. 'Whatddyya put in that drink?' My eyeballs are going in different directions.

'Nothing – just some MD,' Heidi laughs. 'Merry Christmas.'

So much for being taken seriously, that's out the window. But fuck it. It's a party. *Chill, Maz.*

But soon the night's a blur. 'Yep,' I hear you say. 'The dangers of a free bar.'

As the MDMA kicks in, and I'm rushing with love for everyone, things start to go downhill. I remember necking a negroni – mouth numb enough not to mind the cough mix-ture taste – then I'm sat outside, waiting for a cab with Lauren. Heidi's gone off with some guy.

'Come on, Sam,' Baz bellows. 'You've the keys to the office.'

My heart beats faster when I see Sam trailing behind us.

He's slung a leather jacket round his shoulders and looks dangerously hot.

'Let's go, everyone! Afterparty in the office.' Baz piles us into the seven-seater that's just pulled up.

I'm squashed next to Sam, his sharp cheekbones and chiselled jaw inches away. The cab goes round a corner, and he leans towards me, pressing his muscled weight to my side. I can smell his aftershave, a waft of clean sweat. My pulse quickens, my blood racing with adrenaline.

Our plan's back on track.

Chapter Twenty-One

Jade

Saturday morning, I wake to find a note from Sam to say he's working with Wayne all weekend. I take Amber to ballet and spend an hour in the park with the boys. Christina stays at home, searching for flat rentals.

Is Mazza working overtime this weekend too? Is she sending the texts? Whoever it is, Sam told them to stop. There could be a perfectly innocent explanation. Or so I keep telling myself.

We're meant to be going to my mum's for dinner but when it's gone five and Sam's not back, I ask Christina to come instead. She's delighted to be invited.

It's just past six when we arrive at my mum's. She's still living in the terraced house in Ilford, where I grew up. After my parents' divorce, Dad let Mum have the house, while he used their savings to buy a flat.

I ring the doorbell. Next to me, Christina adjusts her jacket. Behind us, Amber's eyes are glued to her book, while Leo and Eddie jostle each other on the doorstep. Mum opens the door and the boys squeeze past, stopping only to kick off their shoes.

'Hey, aren't you going to say hello to Por Por?' Mum catches the boys for a cuddle. 'Jade – you don't teach your children to greet me? You say six o'clock, but you're late. You look tired. You sick?'

'It's only ten past six.' I swallow my irritation. *Let me survive the next couple of hours without a row.* 'I got to bed late last night.' I touch my cheek to hers for a brief kiss.

'Hello, Por Por.' Amber hugs her, then runs upstairs. She's working her way through a shelf of my old books.

My mum sighs. 'No Sam? I cook his favourite, lamb curry.'

'Sorry, busy working.'

'On Saturday night?' She raises her eyebrows.

I quickly nudge Christina forward, avoiding Mum's question. Christina kisses her cheek. 'Hello, Auntie, how are you?'

Mum beams. 'Come in, come in, Christina. We were a good team last week. Cannot believe so long since you at university with Jade. Time flies. Getting so old.'

Christina smiles. 'Nonsense, Auntie, you're looking younger than ever.'

Mum's flattered, and I'm glad Christina's here. We remove our shoes and follow Mum into the kitchen, welcomed by the aroma of fried garlic and ginger.

A few years ago, my mum extended the kitchen and dining room, turning it into one large space, with marble flooring, cream tiles and a state-of-the-art range cooker, where there are various pots simmering away. Bi-fold doors open out onto a manicured garden.

Christina is suitably impressed. 'Auntie, your house is gorgeous – so modern.'

'Aiya, I forget how light colours show the dirt.' Typically Chinese, Mum always negates a compliment.

'But so much easier to clean.' Christina runs a finger over the marble worktops. She walks over to the sideboard and gazes at the photos. She stops by a framed photo of my wedding day, studying it closely. Sam and I are surrounded by family and friends. There's a strange look on Christina's face. 'You have a large family, Auntie Chan. And more beautiful grandchildren too.' She looks at my brother, Derek, with his wife and new baby. They live in Manchester, and we never seem to have time to meet up.

Mum ignores her praise. 'But you know, none of my children study medicine. Your parents must be very proud.'

Christina's mum wouldn't show her pride. It's the Chinese way, to be humble about your own children. You don't stick your head above the parapet, a habit left over from centuries ago, when death came easily. People believed that what the gods couldn't see, they couldn't take away. They play down achievements, and kill their children's self-esteem as a result.

'I want to be a doctor, Por Por,' says Eddie, appearing in the kitchen-diner with Leo, who jumps on the cream sofa and throws a cushion at him.

'Aiyo, boys! No jumping inside. Go – garden.' Mum shoos them off. She's never had much interest in playing with the children. She likes them to do what they're told.

'Come, Jade – open wine for Christina.' Mum hands me a bottle of Petit Chablis from Aldi.

'Can I do anything to help, Auntie?' Christina asks.

'No, no!' Mum laughs, suddenly in her element. She guides Christina to a seat. 'You're our guest. Sit down, relax. Jade, serve drinks.'

I pour wine into three glasses, handing one to my mum,

another to Christina and taking a big slug from the third. One glass won't take me over the limit, and I'll need it if I'm going to make it through the next couple of hours.

'Mummy, come and see Gong Gong's new fish,' Eddie calls, and I'm happy to escape.

The garden is gorgeous, packed with blooms. My dad comes back to look after it, though I haven't seen him for some months. The way he left my mum is hard to forgive and I avoid his visits.

I sit on a bench under the apple tree, soaking up the evening sun while the boys kick a ball on the lawn. A sweet-scented rose climbs the fence. The occasional bird tweets. The raspberry canes are heavy with ruby fruit and bees buzz around the lavender.

Memories crowd in. The tart taste of the first strawberries Dad would pick for me and my brother. We'd eat them in the garden, juice running down our chins. How I'd loved to tend my own small plot, planting marigolds and sunflowers. Until Dad left, when I stopped going into the garden and let the weeds grow.

'Dinner in ten minutes,' Mum calls. 'Boys, come, eat!' Leo chases Eddie round the garden, squealing. 'Aiya, when your Mamma go out, you behave much better.' She can never resist a dig at me.

'Come on, boys – or I'll eat all the crispy pork!' I chase them into the kitchen and take off my sunglasses, blinking while my eyes adjust to the change of light. Mum's filling bowls, and Christina's carrying them over to the table, heaving with our family favourites. Ginger chicken, braised duck, lamb curry, crispy pork, fried meatballs, rice and noodles. For a minute,

Christina looks like the incarnation of the obedient daughter my mum's always wanted.

'Noodles!' Leo runs in and kicks off his shoes.

'Meatballs, my favourite!' Eddie's hand shoots towards the plate.

Amber sits down, eyes not leaving the Chalet School book.

There's never any need to coax them to eat at my mum's. The room's filled with the sounds of chomping. No matter how hard I try, my Malaysian dishes never turn out the same.

'Christina, more wine?' My mum tops up her glass. 'So glad you meet up with Jade again. Eh – Jade – Christina's brother is financial director. For a bank.'

'Right,' I say, uninterested.

Christina mouths 'Sorry!' at me.

'Accountancy is a good career,' my mum says. 'Your parents have good fortune. Good children.' She glances at me and tightens her lips.

When I refused to be a doctor, she'd suggested accountancy. She still can't understand why I bothered with an English degree. I could read books on my own, without going to university, she'd complained. This from someone who rarely reads anything but gossip mags.

I stare at my plate, chewing methodically. It still hurts that neither of my parents had valued what I'd studied. Unlike my brother, I'd let them down.

I drain my glass. That's my quota gone, since I'm driving. And it's only taken the edge off.

'Eh, Jade-ah, Christina tell me you go for haircut last week,' my mum nods at me. 'Why you not cut short style like her one? Very practical, easy to manage.'

My inner teenager raises her head and I roll my eyes.

'Jade's layered look is bang on trend.' Christina's quick to defend me.

My mum looks puzzled. 'Aiya, not so different from before.'

'Well, it looked great when they blow-dried it.' I dig my nails into my palms.

Mum turns back to Christina. 'You are a good daughter to visit your mother. At our age many health problems. Lucky she has a doctor in the family.'

'There's nothing wrong with you, Mum.' I take a swig of water, wishing it was wine. I hope she's not going to bore Christina with her hypochondria again.

'Jade knows I have high cholesterol. I take statins. Jade doesn't approve.' Mum looks at Christina for advice.

'You're meant to cut down on fatty food.' I pop the last piece of deep-fried pork in my mouth. The kids have scoffed most of it.

'You can do a lot with diet, Auntie,' Christina agrees. 'But if the doctor prescribes statins, you must take them.'

'Aiya, at my age, I want to enjoy life. Eat what I like. Can I ask you? I keep getting pain here . . .' She presses a hand to her side. 'You think could be kidney problem?' She's feared getting cancer or dropping dead of a heart attack ever since I was a child. 'If not too much trouble, can you take a look?'

Oh God. Here we go.

Christina nods. 'Of course, Auntie Chan, but you must promise to consult your doctor as well.'

After dinner is over, the boys run outside, and Amber goes back to her book. Christina examines Mum while I make myself a camomile tea. Mum listens intently to Christina's advice. She ignores me every time I ask her not to eat deep-fried food. But when Christina tells her to, she nods.

I can't help feeling a stab of jealousy. Christina has become yet another peer my mum will compare me to, unfavourably, along with my successful cousins and family friends who are doctors, lawyers and bankers. Mum considers herself unlucky to have a daughter with no fancy job.

'We better head off.' I make an excuse to leave. 'The kids have homework.'

Mum tuts. 'Not yet finished their homework? OK, go. You better go.'

I round up the children while Mum insists on ladling leftovers into plastic tubs for Sam. I wouldn't have bothered. In the hall, she presses a few folded banknotes into my palm. 'Jade, Come. Take.'

'What's that for?' I try to push them back.

It's a ritual we play. She gives me money. I refuse. She'll force me to take it, adding some kind of emotional blackmail, like making sure I care for her when she's old.

'Buy yourself some new clothes, come on, Jade, please. I worry about you.' She lowers her voice but I'm aware Christina can hear us. 'You know, some men, they see nice girls, dress smart in office, wear make-up. Don't let Sam look elsewhere.'

She says stuff like that all the time, and usually I ignore her. But today, it's too close to the bone. It reminds me Sam is quite possibly 'looking elsewhere'. Of course, she doesn't know about the texts. But I don't need her to rub in the fact I've let myself go, that this could all be my fault. My throat tightens.

'Mum, I'm fine. I don't need your money.' I push it back into her hand and hide the tears leaking down my face by kneeling to fasten my shoes.

'Come, aiya, take.' She slips the notes into my pocket. 'Don't spend on the children. This is for you.'

Christina looks away to give us space, but I can see her lips twist with pity.

A wave of shame floods my chest. I'm a complete failure. Not only could my marriage be in trouble. But I should be keeping my mum comfortable in her old age, not the other way round. 'Mum, I said NO.' I reach in my pocket and take out the notes. I try put them back in her hands, but she refuses to accept them, forcing me to throw them at her. Two twenty-pound notes flutter to the floor.

Mum scoops up the money, a frown between her eyebrows. 'What? You can afford to throw away money? I cook for you, and you shout at your mother? So ungrateful.' She flushes, biting her lip, leaving me hot with guilt.

'Bye, Mrs Chan, thanks for dinner.' Christina steps between us and gives her a hug.

'See how your friend behave?' Mum tries to involve her, but Christina refuses to be drawn into our argument. She rounds up the boys.

I'm shaking as I pick up my bag, scrubbing at my face with a tissue. 'I'm sorry, Mum. Thanks for dinner, but I don't need your cash. Come on, kids, let's go.'

So much for avoiding a fight. I can't drive away fast enough.

Chapter Twenty-Two

Jade

I don't get a chance to talk to Sam alone until Sunday. I hear him come in around four in the afternoon, so I leave the kids watching TV and find him in the kitchen.

Christina's there, too, and the kettle's boiling. She's laughing at something Sam's said, and putting biscuits on a plate.

'Here you go.' She puts a mug in front of him. 'Can I make you a tea, Jade?'

'Christina ... Sorry, do you mind leaving us a moment? I need a word with Sam,' I say, biting my lip.

'Of course.'

As soon as she's gone, I take a deep breath. 'OK, Sam, I am just going to come out and say it. That text message, from the unknown number ... I noticed you didn't delete it like you told me. And you've since received more texts. What's going on?'

Sam puts his tea down like it's scalded him. 'What? What texts ... oh! Look, I don't know who they're from. I guess I forgot to delete them and block the number. But ... if you've read them, you'll see I told them to stop.'

I nod, unable to speak for a moment, my throat tight with tears. It's true. He told whoever was texting to stop. But the thread of texts, starting with the one saying they'd dreamed of him, implied he knew who was texting him. He wasn't asking them to stop out of respect for me. He was asking them to stop so I wouldn't find more evidence of whatever was going on. *That was right, wasn't it? Wasn't it?*

He gazes at me, his pupils like dark liquid. 'Jade . . . why were you looking through my phone? Don't you trust me?'

I don't know what to think. I don't know if I trust him. I don't know if I trust myself. *Could I have mistaken the meaning of what I read?*

Sam pulls me towards him. 'Come on, darling, why would I look at anyone else when I have you?'

I let him fold me in his arms. I lean on his chest and feel the beat of his heart. Then I pull away. I look him in the eye, saying fiercely, '*Promise* me you don't know who these texts are from?'

'I promise. Jade, why would I lie?' He hugs me close again. 'Look, I'm sorry I haven't been around lately. I have a crazy week – the pitch is hotting up, and you know what it's like. But Christina was telling me about the rewards for the children. How about I book tickets for Colchester Zoo for Saturday? We'll have a good day together. We need it.'

I nod, swiping at the tears that have leaked onto my cheeks. 'All right. Leo really wants to see the elephant.'

'And I'm going to delete and block that number now.' He stabs at his phone and shows me. 'Look – the number's blocked. There's all sorts of weird messages that come through these days. Who knows what it was about?'

*

On Monday, the hamster wheel of the week begins again. Anthony had said I could finish the rest of the project from home, so I work in the living room while Christina helps with the kids. Looking for a distraction from my doubts, I decide to go to Kate's for our Tuesday mums and tots group. While Christina drops the kids at school, I roll out some ready-made dough and chuck a tray of cookies in the oven before jumping in the shower. I'm just getting dressed when the smoke alarm's high-pitched beeping assaults my eardrums. I throw on my dressing gown and rush downstairs towards the stench of burning, covering my ears with my hands.

Christina's in the kitchen, flapping a tea towel at the smoke pouring from the oven. The cookies are black and frazzled. My head's exploding from the alarm until I find the broom handle and poke at the reset button. My ears ring in the silence.

'That'll teach me to multitask.' I mop at my sopping wet hair with a towel.

'I'm sorry. I should have kept an eye on them for you,' Christina apologises. She hesitates a moment. 'Jade, did you mean to set the oven to 250 degrees?'

'What? I set it to 160.' I look at the dial, but she's already turned it off. *Did I check?* 'I'm sure I did, but ...'

'These things happen,' she says brightly. 'I've a great recipe for a coffee and walnut cake I've been meaning to try. Kate will love it. Did she mention she'd invited me?'

'Oh. I didn't realise you'd want to come.' I flush. I hadn't meant to leave her out, but I'd been preoccupied with Sam and the texts.

'I bumped into Kate yesterday in the high street and she

mentioned you were all meeting at her house. I presume it's all right if I come with you?'

'Of course – we'll pick up Leo and go straight there.' If I was childless, there's no way I'd enjoy being around a load of mums, moaning about our first-world problems, but maybe she's lonely.

'It would be lovely to meet more people.' Her eyes gleam with excitement. 'I'll get on with the cake then.'

She looks so thrilled I feel bad for not asking her before Kate did.

'Jade, Christina! I'm so pleased you could both make it.' Kate pulls me into an apple-shampoo-scented hug, the sleeves of her paisley kaftan brushing my face, before doing the same to Christina, then bending down towards Leo. 'Ollie's in the garden waiting for you.' He threads past my legs towards the back of the house.

Kate's 1930s detached house is nearby, in South Woodford. The wide hall is decorated with William Morris wallpaper, which complements the tiled flooring and oak staircase perfectly, giving off a level of glamour I can only hope to emulate.

'Hi Kate,' Christina turns on the charm. 'Thank you for inviting me. I've baked a coffee cake.' She thrusts the cake tub forward eagerly and I don't mention the burnt biscuits.

'Wonderful! I adore coffee cake. Do come through; we're celebrating!' Kate leads us down the hall and into a large, country-style kitchen, where the cream-coloured walls are a perfect match for the Aga and KitchenAid appliances that adorn the marble-topped surfaces. Huge bi-fold doors open onto the Cotswold-stone patio where Fran, Melinda, Naseem and Agata are sitting at a teak table under a parasol.

I met Kate and the other mums when I was on maternity leave with Amber. For a couple of years, the six of us would meet every Tuesday morning to compare notes and provide each other moral support. Apart from having children the same age, we don't have much in common and our parenting styles differ, but we bonded all the same.

The usual tea and coffee have been replaced with bottles of champagne, chilling next to a bowl of scarlet strawberries and chocolate brownies stacked high on a glass cake stand. We swap hugs and air kisses and I introduce Christina.

Fran smiles and hugs her. '*Hola*, Christina, *chica*. You should all come to salsa next time.'

'Fran got lucky,' I tease, and she slaps my arm playfully.

Christina places her coffee cake on the table next to the brownies.

'What's the occasion?' I glance at the champagne.

Melinda beams, flicking her dark curls. 'My dream's come true.' She claps her hands together and her brass bracelets jangle. 'I've signed a publishing deal for my blog.'

'Oh my gosh, that's amazing!' I hug her, ignoring the hollow feeling in my chest.

Melinda writes a blog about her and her wife's journey with IVF, giving birth, and raising triplets. She's a magazine journalist, and her light-hearted yet meaningful posts have struck a chord. The curly-haired triplets rack up thousands of views on Instagram, and she's something of a 'mumfluencer'.

'How amazing! Congratulations,' says Christina. She throws me a look and mouths 'OK?'

She must notice the pang of envy shooting through me. My cheeks grow warm. *Is it that obvious?*

'Bellini?' Kate hands out glasses of champagne and peach juice.

'Thank you, Kate.' Christina accepts a glass.

'Just a small one,' I say. 'I'm driving.' No one'd mentioned we'd be drinking champagne. I could've walked to Kate's but it's a good twenty minutes and Leo never wants to leave. It's easier to get away in the car. I sip a mouthful of Bellini. It's not quite cold enough and the peach juice leaves an aftertaste like vomit. I knock it back anyway. *I can come and get the car later.*

'I'm going to be celebrating all day.' Melinda can't stop smiling and I don't blame her. It's a huge achievement. 'Laura and I are going for dinner at Tom Kerridge's latest place.'

'Amazing.' I stretch my lips in a smile. 'And well deserved, you've worked so hard for this.'

Kate chimes a spoon on a crystal glass. 'Congratulations, Melinda. Cheers. To dreams coming true.'

I lean forward to clink my glass with Melinda's, but a gust of wind whisks at the serviettes, and she bends to pick them up.

Will my dreams ever come true? Do I know what they are anymore?

'Trust Mel to land in the jam, lucky cow!' heckles Fran. As a teacher and single mum, her life's far from easy but her smile softens her words.

'Triplets must be a handful,' Christina remarks.

'Oh, I'm very fortunate.' Melinda settles back in her seat, and arranges the skirt of her maxi dress. 'When we decided to go for IVF, I insisted on having a full-time nanny. A distant cousin came over from Trinidad to help. Laura agreed, thank God. I couldn't do it otherwise.'

Melinda has it all. A successful career and adorable children.

She makes me feel bad about my own sagging career. If she can do it with triplets, why can't the rest of us?

'Are you going to have to rewrite your posts into a novel or a memoir?' *Even with a nanny, how on earth will she manage?*

'Fran's right, I *am* lucky,' Melinda purrs. 'They love the blog as it is. My editor's a darling. I won't need to do much. Just a little tidying. Suits me fine, with these three around.'

We look at the triplets, who are tying a skipping rope around Kai, Naseem's boy.

'Rather you than me,' drawls Agata, pushing her sunglasses up her nose. 'I'm not sure that I'd like everyone reading about every messy poop and bout of mastitis.'

Too right. I wouldn't want to reveal my life, warts and all, to the world, which is why I prefer to write fiction. Or I would if I ever get time one day. I never get a chance to write anything apart from shopping lists in my notebook.

I'm about to mention my new copywriting job but one of the triplets starts wailing. Melinda and Naseem get up to see what's happened and Agata throws a ball to her son – three-year-old Dommi.

Leo and Ollie run around the manicured flower beds, so different from the tangled weeds in my garden. They're whacking each other with wooden swords. Thankfully, I don't need to watch Leo so closely here. I relax and let the champagne work its magic.

Kate hands round the snacks. 'How's things with you?' I ask her.

'Oh, the usual running around. There's never enough time.' Kate's earth mother look is deceptive. 'Emma's doing a couple of GCSEs early and they're piling on the homework. It's hard to fit it in, what with netball practice. And she insists on keeping both the violin and the piano going.' I nod along. *Shoot me if I'm ever that pushy.*

Christina gazes out at the lawn, her Gucci shades hiding her expression. I hope she's not too bored, but she wanted to come.

'Emma won a music scholarship, didn't she?' Naseem asks Kate. 'I'm wondering whether to give Kai music lessons.'

'We turned down the scholarship, actually,' Kate admits. 'Daniel's doing pretty well these days. So we thought, why not let some other child from a less fortunate background have it?' I glance at Christina, hoping she can't hear Kate's patronising tone. She was a scholarship pupil.

Dommi's ball lands in the bushes. He runs to his mum and hides his face in her denim flares. Agata pats his back and carries on talking. 'Lucky you, having the means to give up a scholarship. I'd like Dominic to play the piano. How old should he start lessons?'

'What do you think, Christina?' I draw her into the conversation. 'Piano lessons are the one creative thing Chinese mothers approve of. They're meant to increase your intelligence,' I tell Agata. 'Christina's living proof – she's a brilliant pianist and a doctor.'

Christina gives a self-deprecating laugh. 'You're too kind, Jade. I'm not sure about brilliant.'

Agata tucks her hair behind her ears, looking at Christina. 'Interesting. You know, we have a piano in our house, inherited from the previous tenants. Dommi likes to play. Could he start lessons?' Dominic shyly folds pleats in Agata's smock.

Christina waves at him and he pulls the smock up to his face. 'You'll have to wait a few years,' she says. 'I started piano lessons at eight.'

167

'Eight's rather old, surely?' Agata sounds sceptical. 'I met a mother whose daughter is six and has already passed her grade one. Dommi would have to get to scholarship level by eleven.'

Kate nods. 'Yes, it's good to start early with music. Emma started the violin at four. She's a natural.'

'Didn't Mozart start at three?' Agata carries on.

Christina's jaw tightens. 'Children are often naturally musical.' She's perfectly polite but there's an edge to her voice.

'I'm sure he played "Baa Baa Black Sheep" the other day, didn't you, darling?' Agata's pretty competitive about Dominic's achievements.

'Incredible. A musical prodigy.' Behind her shades I sense Christina's eyes are rolling, but Agata's oblivious to her sarcastic tone and prattles on. 'You know, I'm thinking that music lessons could be a worthwhile investment if he wins a music scholarship to Forest.'

At the word 'investment' my heart sinks. Christina often said her mum had ruined the piano for her with her strictness about practice and grades. *What's she going to say now?* But she answers Agata's questions about music lessons politely enough and soon they are chatting away.

Naseem pulls me aside, shuffling her chair near mine. 'Jade, someone told me your other son suffers from food allergies? Can I ask your advice?'

'Sure,' I smile. 'Is it about Kai?'

Naseem's worried as her youngest, still breastfed, develops rashes when she eats eggs. I explain about allergy testing and the alternative therapies we've tried for Eddie. While we chat, I'm aware of Christina asking the way to the bathroom.

While she's gone, I turn back to the group. 'What do you all

168

think of Supernanny-style reward schemes for good behaviour. Sticker charts. Do they work?'

'We use them at school,' says Fran. 'Better than nothing!'

'We can all do with positive rewards – the carrot and not the stick,' says Agata.

'I must say, I've never been keen on these schemes,' says Kate. 'Children should learn to be helpful anyway. What happens if there's no reward? They refuse to help?'

'I worry about the children who don't win a sticker,' added Naseem. 'Won't they feel bad about themselves? Not everyone can be the Star of the Week.'

Their opinions reinforce my feelings about Christina's marble scheme. But how would she react if I told her I didn't like it? I don't want to upset her while I need her help, and I suppose it won't be for much longer.

Kate moves over to the sliding doors. 'Hello, darling. Come join us. We're toasting Melinda's success.'

Daniel, Kate's husband, waves at us. 'Afternoon, ladies!'

'Oooh, it's the Silver Fox,' Fran whispers loudly. Naseem and Agata giggle and Kate's cheeks turn pink. It's true his laughter lines are as attractive as George Clooney's.

Christina emerges after him, eyes sparkling, all traces of boredom gone. 'Did you know Jade's a writer too?'

She drags Daniel over to me. 'Ah, of course, Jade, Leo's mum. How are you?' He leans forward to kiss my cheek, and I smell musk and a hint of sweat. 'I'm "Ollie's dad" to her,' he explains to Christina. 'Us parents are mere attachments to our children.'

'So you're not the astute financial editor of a national newspaper?' Christina teases him. 'I couldn't believe that I got lost going to Daniel Sharp's guest bathroom. I've followed your column for years.' She touches his arm, her head tilted towards him.

'Oh, stop, you're making me blush.' But his eyes crinkle in appreciation. 'I hear congratulations are in order.' He raises his glass. 'Christina tells me you've landed a gig freelancing for Teatro – one of our favourite restaurants.'

Kate moves over to us, but her eyes are flinty. I sympathise with her, knowing Daniel's tendency to stray. He's certainly lapping up Christina's flattery. 'How exciting for you, Jade. Yes, we adore Teatro. We celebrated our last anniversary there. Congratulations.' She tops up my glass and then Christina's before steering Daniel towards the table. 'Come and have a brownie and some strawberries, darling.' She stands with her back to Christina, blocking her from following Daniel.

I bite into a strawberry. It's mushy and flavourless. Somehow, I feel responsible for Christina flirting with Daniel. She's single and attractive, and he was obviously enjoying it. I think about Sam in his office, laughing and joking with young, single women. Like Daniel, I'm sure he'd enjoy the attention.

Kate turns to question Fran about GCSE grading and I down the rest of my Bellini. It's half two. If we leave now, we can walk. I'm not keen on using Christina's marbles, but at times only bribery will do. 'Come on, Leo, time to go home.'

'Going already?' Kate sounds relieved.

'Congratulations again, Melinda.' I hug her. 'Have fun tonight.'

'Yes, congrats on your achievement,' Christina says sweetly, kissing her cheek. 'Goodbye, Daniel – lovely to meet you.' She kisses him too.

In the hall, Leo grips a Transformer in his fist. 'Leo, give me that,' I hiss.

He shoves it in his pocket, and I shrug on my jacket, hoping to get away with returning it next visit. But Ollie screams, 'Tran-former – mine!'

Kate holds her hand out to Leo. 'Oh my goodness, Leo. You know, you don't take other people's things. Ollie is good at sharing his toys when you're at our house. You can play with it the next time you come.'

'Leo.' Christina takes his hand and leads him outside. 'Maybe you could put a Transformer on your treat list.'

Kate gives us a limp wave and shuts the door. I can tell she's relieved to see us go after Christina's flirting with Daniel, and I guess I don't blame her.

Soon after we've put the kids to bed, and while Christina is dishing up pasta, Sam gets in. 'Oh hi, Sam! Fancy some spag bol?'

'Fantastic, yes please.' He sinks into his usual seat, and I fetch him a glass. I find myself watching his reaction to Christina's attentions.

She places a plate of pasta in front of me, and then one in front of Sam, with a fresh bottle of Malbec. 'Red OK?' She touches his arm and hands him the bottle to open, then sits opposite me, on Sam's other side. Was she always this tactile? Or has her flirting with Daniel alerted me to this trait?

'Smells wonderful and garlicky, Christina.' He winks at her, appreciative. 'Good thing we're all eating it!'

I'd been tempted to eat with the children earlier, but I'm glad I waited. Sam's explained about the text message, but I'm still not sure I can totally trust him.

'I've hardly seen you lately,' I say, aware that my tone is colder than usual. 'How's the pitch?'

'We're meeting the yogurt people in Paris soon.' He leans towards me and squeezes my arm. 'Once it's over we'll have more time together.'

'Paris. Lucky you,' says Christina, wistfully. 'The City of Romance.'

'*Bien sûr, mademoiselle,*' he jokes, eyes gleaming.

'Oh! You speak French?' She flicks me an amused glance.

'*Mais oui,*' he's saying. 'The language of lerrrrve!' He takes my hand and kisses it.

A flash of anger travels through me and I snatch my hand back. But Christina giggles. She's gazing at him through her lashes like when she chatted to Daniel. As a student, she would smile like that because she was shy. But if you didn't know her, it could appear flirtatious. Her cheeks are flushed from the wine and her giggles encourage Sam to speak more pidgin French, getting even more silly. She's laughing so much she has to wipe her eyes. *He's not that funny.*

I chew the pasta, but the wine has numbed my tastebuds. This is what I wanted. Sam and Christina getting on. I should be glad he's charming her. After all, she's my oldest friend. But instead, I feel my anger growing.

Chapter Twenty-Three

Jade

CRASH.

Eddie and Leo's screams travel up to my room where I'm drafting copy for some Teatro marketing emails. I rush downstairs.

The living-room floor is a bombsite of Lego.

'Mummy!' Eddie throws himself at me, shoulders trembling with rage. 'Leo's ball hit my Millennium Falcon!' No wonder he's upset. It took him and Sam three days to build after Christmas, the last time Sam had a proper break from work. We'd thought it would be safe on the top shelf.

Leo barrels into me, rubbing his snotty face into my trousers. 'Mumma – want marble, want elefun!'

Where on earth's Christina? She's meant to be looking after the kids, and now there's a hundred quid's worth of Star Wars Lego scattered across the floor.

Sam will go berserk, although I'm sure he won't yell at Christina. I shift with suppressed rage as I remember how impressed he'd been on Wednesday, when she'd cooked a lamb pasanda complete with home–made naan, reheating it for him when he got back late.

Christina appears at the door, holding two jars. 'I've removed five marbles from each of your jars, boys.' Leo wails, stretching his arm towards the jar, and she holds them high above his head.

Eddie shouts. 'That's not fair!'

Those bloody marbles. I hate them. God knows some sort of order is needed if I'm going to get any work done, but it didn't stop the Lego getting smashed.

Oh, I know I'm being unreasonable. Christina can't keep an eye on the boys every single second. She's only human. But the slow drip of jealousy is starting to corrode my relationship with her. Since the visit to Kate's, I can't help noticing how she responds to Sam's compliments. His praise of her cooking. The way he can't seem to pass by her without stroking her back or touching her arm. Of course, he's always been tactile, and I've never felt it as a threat before. But then I've never felt as ungrounded in my marriage as I do right now. Every one of his actions feels suspect.

'Leo, stop that noise,' Christina commands calmly. 'Mummy should be working and you're disturbing her. Or I'll put you on the naughty step.'

'What?' I say, while Leo turns up the volume, hitting a nerve in my skull. I look at Christina. 'What happened?'

'Leo's upset that he won't be able to have his reward.'

'I'm sure it was an accident. And now he's in a state . . .'

'He broke my Millennium Falcon, Mummy,' whines Eddie, quivering at the unfairness of it all. 'Why am I losing my treat, too? Leo's naughty, not me!'

'OK, darling, don't worry, you're not going to lose any treats.'

Christina's gaze is icy. 'Jade, he really should. Eddie used some nasty language in retaliation. We don't speak to each other in that way.'

'Look, Christina.' I pat the enraged Eddie on the back. 'The naughty step is pretty draconian.' Christina's methods are punishing them for being kids, when even adults would get upset by what's happened. How does that make them better people?

'Leo's been responding well to the step. And Eddie's language was awful. They do need to learn boundaries. Afterwards they can help pick up the Lego.'

'No one's going on the naughty step!' I force myself to breathe deeply to control my temper. 'That's not what we do in this house.' I move the boys to the sofa, Eddie clinging round my waist while Leo climbs on my lap.

Once they're calmer, I draw Christina into the hall. 'Can I have a word?'

A tic pulses in her temple. Enraged though I am, I need to tread carefully. Without her help, I'll never be able to finish my work. But this is exactly what I've been scared would happen – withdrawing treats feels like withdrawing love. She hadn't consulted me on the marble scheme which was bad enough. But the naughty step! Isolating an upset child is sure to make them feel unloved. I can't let her instigate these techniques.

'Please, Christina. I have to insist there's no naughty step. And about this marble reward jar,' I say. 'It may have its benefits, but it's done its job for now. As far as we're concerned, the children filled their jars. Sam's free this weekend, and we promised the zoo as a treat. We've already booked the tickets.'

She folds her arms. 'But they've behaved so badly. You can't reward them. How will they learn?'

'What's going on?' Amber slopes up, munching a bag of crisps. 'Daddy says we're going to the zoo and cinema tomorrow. We are, aren't we?'

Christina smiles tightly and shakes her head. 'The boys need to re-fill their jars first, I'm afraid. Another week should be enough time.'

'What?' Amber scrunches up the crisp packet. 'That's not FAIR!' Her bottom lip trembles.

Not a meltdown from Amber as well. I clench my fists. I don't want to upset Christina, but she's going directly against me. It's too much when she doesn't have children herself. She doesn't know the reality of being a parent. 'Christina, it isn't fair if Amber's punished for the boys' mistakes,' I say. 'What if Leo and Eddie say sorry?'

Her stare is icy. 'We must stick to the rules. They can earn more marbles for next weekend.' She goes back into the living room, places the jars on a shelf, and starts to pick up Lego.

A wave of irritation travels through me. They're my kids not hers. 'We're not free the following weekend.' My voice is cold. 'The trip has to be this Saturday. Sam's bought the tickets. He'll be annoyed if he's wasted his money.' I immediately regret mentioning Sam. She should listen to me anyway.

Leo hiccups as his sobs die down. But Amber looks like she's about to explode. 'Amber, darling, would you take Leo and Eddie and get them some ice cream? Mummy ordered different flavours this week. Go get some tubs out of the freezer.'

Amber nods and dashes out.

'Ice cream, yummy,' sings Eddie, following her.

'Yay!' Tears forgotten, Leo chases after them. 'Want strawberry, want choc choc.'

I kneel to pick up the Lego with Christina. We work in silence, but I have to say something about the marbles.

'Look, Christina,' I try to sound reasonable. 'You know, it's really kind of you to help me. And I appreciate all you're doing. But I'm not sure if I'm quite comfortable with this marble scheme. I don't want the children to equate treats with love. If we end up withdrawing treats, it's like we're withdrawing our love. Just like the naughty step, it's damaging to their self-esteem.'

Christina deposits a handful of Lego on the coffee table. 'My methods have been working. The children have behaved well all this time.'

'Exactly.' I attempt a smile. 'So, you agree this is just a blip? They're tired. It's the end of the week.'

Christina's arm moves methodically over the rug like a robot. 'You need to show zero tolerance for tantrums or children think they can scream for what they want.' Her voice is flat.

'Sorry, Christina, I don't agree.' My heart beats hard against my ribs. I hate confrontation. 'Reward schemes, the naughty step . . . I don't like these methods. They're children, not—Not dogs.'

Christina's lips twist in a smug, superior smile. 'The trouble is, Jade, you don't have a method, do you? You're never consistent. You say one thing, but you never enforce it.'

My face flames. How dare she? 'Parenting isn't about . . . reading some book. You don't even want children. What makes you the expert?'

She jolts back like I've slapped her, face set and white. 'What makes you think I don't want children?'

I feel awful. What have I said? She must think I'm such a bitch. 'I'm sorry, Christina – I didn't mean it like that . . .'

'I do want children. At least . . . I did. But I can't have them, as you'd know if you'd bothered to ask.' Her voice trembles.

'I'm sorry. That was so insensitive of me.' I apologise but she doesn't look at me. 'I have no right to talk to you like that—'

'No,' she grinds out. 'You don't. And your children, like you, don't have clear boundaries. No wonder they behave badly.'

'What?' I can't believe how judgemental she's suddenly being. Now I'm the one shaking with rage.

I stomp out of the room, calling to the children. 'Any ice cream left for Mumma?'

Chapter Twenty-Four

Mazza

Six Months Earlier

We pull up in front of our office block. Sam has the keys, and he reassures Rafael, on security, that we're not causing any trouble. Just having a few quiet drinks.

The building's eerie and dark. Sam leads the way to the conference room and flicks a switch, lighting up the room as the others troop in behind.

Soon, it's out with the black Amex and he's racking up lines on one end of the glass table, like he does this every day. Maybe he does. He rolls up fifty quid and hoovers. Then it's Baz's turn and before long, all eyes are on me. I sway for a minute, but one look at Sam gives me the courage I need. No harm having a bump, before I make my move.

I lean over the table and pause, pointing the rolled-up fifty at the slug of white powder. Charlie's not really my drug. My personality's too addictive to get into something so expensive. But this is courtesy of the boss. It'd be rude not to. I close off my right nostril and snort with the left one. Bitter chemicals sear my nasal lining, shooting poison to my brain.

Later, I find myself next to Sam, having made my way around the table. 'You know what, Sam? You are the fucking man!' I tell him.

Sam grins. 'I've got big plans for the agency. Huge. If only you knew. We gotta streamline, and that means we won't be popular. But you gotta do what you gotta do.'

'Yeah. Yeah,' I grin back. 'Great business brain.'

'What must you think of us, eh, Mazza? Pitching, pitching, pitching. But not for much longer. Soon they'll come to us. Branding kings of Europe, eh?'

My cheek muscles ache. I can't stop grinning.

Sam racks up the last of his coke and we go again. Round two.

'When – and not if – our agency wins these pitches, our campaigns will go global. No more cash-flow issues ...'

The coke flow's stopped though.

'Want me to call my dealer?' Baz says.

'Go on then.' Sam hands Baz a wodge of cash and he disappears.

The art directors have gone by now. Me and Sam are left alone. I hover by the door. He paces up and down. He's chucked his wallet onto the table, and it's fallen open on a photo of his wife and kids. She's gorgeous, but is she enough for him?

'So – what's the story about cash flow?' The coke in my bloodstream makes me bold.

When I listen to him talk, it feels like he cares. About me. About the agency. How could the agency be in trouble? Sam's so passionate, so confident, so convinced of his own greatness.

You reckoned Sam's agency was a good career move, didn't you, Ben? And you're not often wrong.

'All businesses have cash tied up,' Sam's saying. 'You have to re-invest to grow.' He rubs his nose. A few white grains fall out.

'Sure.'

He flings an arm around my shoulders and squeezes, a matey hug. We grin at each other. His pupils are huge. Mine must mirror his.

This could be the only chance to say what I have to say. I'm not really in a fit state. The night's run away too quickly. I drank too much, and the coke was a mistake. I'm sorry, Ben.

I test the waters. 'You . . . you like me, don't you, Sam?'

He squeezes my shoulders. 'I like you, Mazza, course I do!'

'I mean . . .'

'Come on, tell him how brilliant you are,' I hear you say.

So I take a breath and try again. 'Don't you think I'm a good worker?'

His pupils are so huge you can hardly see any blue in his eyes. 'You're amazing, Maz.' He laughs and I find myself laughing along. It's doing my head in, pretending to be mates, when my feelings are way different. 'But tell me,' Sam carries on. 'How are you finding the agency? What do you think of us?'

'What do you think of me?' The coke makes me bold. 'Did you notice how much I saved you on that last job? The flyers?'

He nods, like he's taking me seriously. 'Kevin told me printing costs were lower than normal.'

'And guess who negotiated for you? Yours truly.' I stand up and bow.

Sam claps. 'Wow – brilliant. I knew you were a good hire. Amazing, Maz.'

'I'd actually make a brilliant production manager,' I say quietly.

But Sam doesn't seem to hear me. 'Yeah, so why can't Kevin cut us a better deal?'

This is my chance to stick the boot in. 'Oh, Kevin ne-go-ti-ates.' I put about ten thousand syllables in that last word. The coke's loosened my lips and I want to prove how clever I am. 'There's all sorts of deals that go on in production,' I tell him. 'The printers often cut a discount. It's up to the production manager how much of that discount you see.'

'Really?' Sam's interested. 'Tell me more.'

'Come on, Sam. Don't tell me you don't know? The deals that go on? A canny business guy like you?' Call me a bitch, but I get a buzz from dobbing in that jobsworth 'You're-five-minutes-late-from-lunch' Kevin.

You guessed the deals Kevin was making, didn't you, Ben? You overheard Kevin and a printer, sorting out a deal in your bar.

'I'm going to have to keep a closer eye on Kevin.' Sam stands up, pours himself more whisky, sloshing a fair amount on the table.

'Kevin was off sick in November, if you remember? I did the deal and I passed on the savings to the agency. No cut.'

'You've got a lot that Kevin doesn't have. Maybe Kevin could be ready for retirement.'

But his eyes are red, and the mood has changed. Maybe it's the coke. It's a nasty drug. One minute, you're on top of the world. You feel like you can do anything. The next . . .

And then I feel it. His hand on my bum. I freeze. This wasn't what I was after.

'I've been wanting to do that all night.' His voice is low, husky.

Where's everyone gone? There's no one in the conference

room but us. I fucked up. I made a mistake coming here. Should've left after the party.

I'm suddenly stone-cold sober. I pick up my bag. Time to go.

Sam's eyes are bloodshot, the pupils still dilated. He moves towards me. 'Don't worry. Only us left.' He pulls me to him and buries his head in my neck. Events are speeding up. It wasn't meant to happen like this. So I feel inside my bag for my phone. Time for me to get out of here.

I hold up my phone. Press a button.

'What you doing?' Sam's curious, then suspicious. 'Put that away, I'm camera shy.'

'Look . . . you got the wrong idea, mate.'

'What's going on, Maz?' he protests. 'It was just a bit of fun. Come on.' He reaches for my phone. 'Get rid of it.'

I hold my phone out of his reach. 'I've got something to show you,' I speak clearly. 'And I'll send it to your wife if you touch me again.'

'Whoa!' He holds his hands up, empty palms towards me. 'Now hang on. This was mutual.'

'Touch me again and I scream for security.' I back away slowly.

'You fucking bitch . . . give that to me . . .'

I record his face, all twisted and ugly, my heart hammering as I edge to the door.

I feel for the door handle. Open it and run.

I'm out of the conference room, down the corridor, out of the building.

I run all the way to the bus stop.

I've let you down, Ben. Sorry. But I can still go back to our plan.

Chapter Twenty-Five

Jade

It's Sunday morning and nearly eleven by the time Eddie and Leo bounce into our bed.

'Hungry.' Leo's hot hands reach for 'mumma chub', the roll in my belly that countless sit-ups can't seem to shift, while Eddie snuggles in next to Sam.

Saturday had been a good day. Colchester Zoo, followed by Nerf-gun shopping at Lakeside, pizza and then the cinema. Bar a tantrum or two, everyone enjoyed themselves. In normal circumstances it would have been brilliant for the four of us to spend time on our own. But much as I try to enjoy the day, the distrust between me and Sam is like a piece of grit in my shoe. I can't take a step without wondering – has he been lying to me about those text messages?

Now Kate's fears are rubbing off on me. Her paranoia about every attractive woman who comes within a metre of Daniel is catching. I don't want to be like her, but I suspect Sam isn't too different from Daniel, enjoying the flattery of a flirtation too much.

'Brek brek.' Leo drags me out of bed. I throw on my dressing gown and follow him downstairs.

The oven's on and a savoury aroma fills the kitchen. Christina's chopping onions by the sink. She pauses to wipe her streaming eyes with a tissue. I haven't seen her since the row on Friday, after which she'd disappeared into her room. I was relieved not to see her all day on Saturday. I feel it's time for her to move out.

I try to ignore the tension in the room and sing out an upbeat 'Good morning!'

'How was your day out?' She concentrates on chopping onions but the air between us feels heavy.

'Knackering,' I sigh. 'But fun. I haven't been to the zoo for ages.' I'm glad we hadn't invited her along. I don't know how long I can keep pretending that nothing is wrong.

'Elefun!' Leo side-eyes Christina. He hasn't forgotten she threatened to take away his treat. He burrows his head into my legs and drags me to the cereal cupboard. I pour Coco Pops into a bowl. He climbs on my lap to eat, and I cuddle him close.

'Morning all! Is it feeding time?' Sam has Eddie on his back. He's freshly showered, wearing a graphic printed T-shirt and jeans. He joins us at the table, puts Eddie down and kisses me before I can move away. His stubble rasps my skin and I shiver with distaste. Sam had been like a little kid at the zoo. Oblivious that anything was wrong, he'd lost the tense frown he'd been wearing lately.

The oven timer beeps, and Christina takes out a tray of cheese straws.

'Fantastic!' Sam charms her with a smile. 'They look and smell incredible. Bet you enjoyed the peace and quiet without these animals.'

I watch him closely, wondering if he'll stroke her arm, but instead he turns to tickle the squealing Eddie and Leo. He makes an elephant noise and the boys giggle, clambering over him. Leo smacks his head. 'Naughty elefun!'

'Arrgggh!' screams Sam, laughing. 'Help!'

If only I could wind back to the time before I discovered the text messages. I would have enjoyed quality time with Sam and the kids. Instead, it's like we're putting on a play for Christina's viewing. Sam's acting looks mannered and unrealistic to me. Only the children carry on as normal.

Christina calls out, 'Would anyone like to play with some dough? Make your own cheese biscuits?'

'Yes, please – me!' calls Eddie.

'Me! Me!' shouts Leo. She brings a lump of dough to the boys, and they climb up to the breakfast bar. She hands them mini rolling pins, and they roll out the dough.

Sam straightens, raking his hair back. 'Oh jeez, this elephant game!'

He slaps a hand on Christina's shoulder. 'Thanks for rescuing me.'

She turns away, cheeks pink. 'Of course.'

Is she developing a crush on Sam? Is she flirting with him like she had with Daniel?

I say loudly, 'By the way, how's your flat-hunting going, Christina?'

'I went to a viewing for a flat in South Woodford,' she replies, a serious look on her face. 'I've left a message to say I'd like to take it. I wondered, if you're free today, I'd like to cook Sunday lunch for you all, to show my appreciation before I leave.'

'Oh Christina, you've been a lifesaver, there's really no need.' I busy myself re-tying the belt around my dressing gown to hide my cool tone.

Sam grins. 'After yesterday's craziness, lunch at home sounds perfect.'

Christina darts a nervous smile at me. 'Jade?'

I guess it would be churlish to refuse her peace offering. 'Yes, that sounds . . . nice.'

'It's the least I can do, after you've welcomed me into your family.' She twists her fingers together. 'I popped to the high street yesterday. I have everything prepared. Please. My treat.'

'All right. But can I do anything? Peel potatoes?' I offer, relieved that she's actually leaving.

She smiles. 'No, no. Please, you relax.' The timer beeps. 'Oh! The croissants. Shall I make coffee?'

'You read my mind,' Sam says. 'But I'll do the coffee.' He stands up and heads towards the kettle. As he passes, he pianos his fingers on Christina's shoulder to get her to move so he can squeeze past. The space between the island and the counter is narrow, so it's perfectly natural, I tell myself. His flirting, and the way she seems to lap it up, is getting on my nerves. But she'll be gone soon.

Christina brings a basket of croissants to the table, with butter and raspberry jam.

'Elefun,' Leo mumbles hiding his face in my dressing gown.

'You liked feeding the elephant, didn't you, Leo?' Sam's oblivious to any tension between Christina and Leo. We still haven't told him about the broken Millennium Falcon. It's been the last thing on my mind.

'The giraffe ate my sandwich!' Eddie tells Christina. 'He saw lettuce sticking out, and thought it was his cabbage.'

'Elefun – shower,' mutters Leo.

Sam nods. 'That water was muddy, wasn't it?'

'Talking of showers, I'm going up for mine.' I kiss Leo and Eddie.

'I wondered what that smell was,' Sam jokes.

Christina giggles and I flush. *Did Sam have to make that joke?* She follows me to the hall. 'I'll have lunch ready by two, Jade. By the way, are the children OK with spice? I'm thinking of doing a spicy coating to the chicken. There's chilli paste in the fridge.'

'Fine, I guess,' I answer shortly. 'But not too much.'

I think of the Neal's Yard lavender shower gel the kids gave me for Mother's Day. I'd been saving it for a special occasion but why not open it now? The lavender would help me relax.

At two o'clock precisely, Christina calls us for lunch. As we drift to the table, I'm shocked to see she's used our Royal Doulton dinner set and the crystal wine glasses we received for our wedding. They only come out at Christmas and birthdays, and the linen napkins folded into swans are a gift we haven't even used. Before I can ask where she found them, she hands me a glass of chilled Sancerre. 'Your lovely dinner set was in the back cupboard. I hope you don't mind?'

Sam grins, cutting across me. 'That's what it's there for.'

I hate the idea of Christina rifling through our things. 'We usually keep the posh china for celebrations,' I say.

'I told you to ask Mummy,' Amber scolds Eddie.

'You like the posh plates, don't you, Mummy?' Eddie's brow is creased.

So it was Eddie's idea? 'It's fine, darling ... Looks wonderful,' I quickly reassure him.

He clinks his glass of sparkling elderflower on mine. 'Cheers, Mummy!'

'Cheers!' Leo and Amber join in, and the awkward moment passes.

'Mmm, these cheese straws taste fantastic.' Sam shovels a couple in his mouth.

We're in our usual places, Leo next to me, Amber and Eddie opposite. Christina serves up a golden-skinned chicken with crispy roast potatoes, parsnips, stuffing balls and pigs in blankets.

'Will you carve?' She hands the knife to Sam, smiling shyly through her lashes. Now I've noticed this habit, it seems she does it all the time.

'It's like Christmas,' says Sam, slicing and dishing out portions of meat.

'By the way, your father called when you were out yesterday,' Christina tells him. 'He said he's waiting to hear about Devon. His holiday place sounds wonderful. I told him to call your mobile?'

'Thanks, yes, I got his message – but in the middle of the penguin show.' Sam turns to me. 'We have to let him know our answer.'

Fresh irritation stabs me. Sam's dad and stepmum, Victoria, have a holiday home in Devon, and they've offered it to us in the last week of term. I didn't want the children to miss school, but before I can remind Sam I don't want to go, Eddie starts coughing.

I leap up, worried he's choking. 'Eddie, what's wrong? Do you need water?'

Bright red hives are erupting round his mouth. My heart hammers. Hives signal an allergic attack. *Oh God oh God oh God . . .*

'What's he eaten?' My voice is hoarse with fear. I run to get his medication from the cupboard. 'What's in the food? Pesto? Sesame?' I rifle through pill packets, and vitamin pots to get to the bottle of Cetirizine which is my first point of call. I grab it and rush back to Eddie.

'No, no pesto, or sesame or nuts.' Christina's voice shakes.

Hands trembling, I slosh liquid everywhere as I spoon it into Eddie's mouth, and he gasps faintly as it trickles down his chin.

'Eddie ate a chicken wing,' says Amber. 'Covered in yucky stuff.'

He coughs, wheezing, like he can't get enough air.

'Oh God oh God!' I scream. 'What did you use?'

Eddie's face is covered in red blotches. With every wheeze my throat tightens in sympathy.

Christina's voice is faint. 'A tub of chilli paste in your fridge.'

'What? The Thai curry paste?' I yell. 'Oh my God – there's fish sauce in it! Eddie's allergic to fish!'

Eddie coughs and the antihistamine projectiles out, splashing my hands. I lower my voice, soothing him. 'Sorry, darling. Quick, Sam – the sofa.'

Sam lifts Eddie and carries him to the sofa. Leo wails, burrowing into my legs. Christina hands me a plastic syringe from when they were babies. The syringe gets the antihistamine in him. He coughs and chokes, but eventually he swallows. He lies back weakly, chest heaving, like breathing is too much effort. His skin has a grey tone. The hives are spreading to his chest.

'Where's his EpiPen?' Christina says. 'He needs adrenaline.'

'It's never been that serious ...' I say. But I've never seen Eddie react like this.

'Come on, Jade, she's a doctor.' Sam puts an arm round me, but I twist out of his hold.

I point to the hall. 'EpiPen. My bag.' I force the words out, a band of fear gripping my chest.

Seconds feel like hours as Sam searches for my handbag. Back in the kitchen he shakes the bag's contents on the floor. The yellow EpiPen box is battered. I've never had to use it. His hands shake as he rips at the cardboard and holds up the plastic tube.

I snatch it from him. 'Hurry!' I claw off the lid, and tip the pen out. I turn to Eddie and stab it into his thigh. He screams, thrashing away, but Sam pins him down so I can hold the pen steady and count. 'One, two . . .' I hold it in for ten seconds, like in the training video, while Christina counts with me. When I withdraw the needle, Eddie collapses back on the sofa and I syringe more Cetirizine into his mouth. Snot, saliva and tears stream over his blotchy face.

'Eddie, want Eddie!' I've forgotten about Leo, wailing and kneading his nails into my stomach.

'Shall we go to the living room, Leo? Leave Eddie to get better with Mummy and Daddy?' Christina takes his hand, but he pulls it away, pressing his face into me.

'Mumma cuddle Leo, not Eddie!' he whines.

Amber crouches down. 'Leo – do you want to come and play Sylvanian Families in my room?'

He lifts his head. 'Sylvanian?' He's tempted by the prized toys he's not normally allowed to touch.

'Yes, you can look inside the caravan,' says Amber. 'I'll let you.'

'Amber darling, what a wonderful sister,' Sam praises her.

Leo trots off, holding her hand. *Thank God.*

'I'm so sorry.' Christina crouches next to me. 'I should have checked the ingredients of that paste. Let me check him over.'

'No, thanks.' I resist the urge to push her away. 'You know

191

he's allergic to fish. Thai curry's full of fish sauce. You must know that.'

Sam murmurs gently. 'Come on, Jade. It's not her fault. She *is* a doctor – maybe she can help?'

'No!' My voice is harsh. 'I don't trust her. She knew about his allergies. Call an ambulance. They can check him out.'

Sam dials the emergency services. There's a worrying wheeze in Eddie's chest, but at least he can breathe. Hives are still appearing on his arms and legs.

Christina disappears and I'm glad. I can't help but blame her. Who puts bloody curry paste on chicken? She might as well have poisoned him.

But there's a small voice at the back of my mind that won't stay silent.

You should've checked which chilli paste she was using. This is your fault.

In hospital, Eddie's dosed with strong antihistamines, and they keep him under observation.

I barely leave his side. He's tiny and frail, lying against the hospital pillows, eyes closed, face pale, red marks where he's scratched the hives. There's an oxygen mask on his face and a needle taped in the back of his left hand. As his chest moves, there's a wheeze in his lungs the medication hasn't managed to shift.

The door opens and Sam comes in, face creased with worry. He leans down and his lips brush my hair. 'How's he doing?'

'Better. Leo and Amber OK?'

'They're fine,' he says. 'Your mum's cooking them noodles.' He pulls over a chair and sits next to me. Our differences are temporarily forgotten as we gaze at the sleeping Eddie, willing him to get better.

'Curry paste on chicken . . . who does that?' My voice breaks. 'We could have lost him.'

Sam touches my hand. 'Come on. It was an accident. Are you sure she knew he's allergic to fish?'

'I told her several times. Didn't she say she cooks Thai food? She should have known about the fish sauce.' I pull my hand away as anger courses through me. 'She's a doctor, for God's sake – she of all people should know the dangers.' Tears leak down my cheeks. 'You were right, Sam. I shouldn't have asked her to stay. None of this would have happened. Eddie would be fine.' Losing a child would be like a part of me dying.

'Look, you've had a shock. She didn't do it on purpose,' Sam says softly.

'Why are you defending her?' I look at him properly for the first time. The lines on his face have deepened and he looks his age.

He spreads his fingers. 'Jade, Christina feels terrible.'

I take a sharp breath. 'You would say that. You seem to care more about Christina's feelings than mine.' A hurt expression flashes across his face but he tightens his lips and says nothing. Maybe I'm overreacting, but Sam's defending her enrages me.

He puts an arm around me. 'She's your friend and you need her support now more than ever. Especially now you're freelancing. She could stay until the school holidays. Until we know Eddie's totally better. And then my dad and Victoria have offered us the Devon place.'

I shrug off his arm. 'I told you. The dates don't fit. The kids are still at school that week.'

193

'Yeah, well, they can miss the last week of school,' he insists.

'No.' My heart thuds. 'Amber won't like that. She loves all the end of term fun.'

'Let's not decide now, eh?' Sam strokes my hand. 'We'll think about it. It'll be a break for us too. We can't afford to go abroad this year. Not until we win some new business.'

'You're right,' I say. 'This isn't the time to talk about it.' For a second, I let myself lean into his arms. But before I can relax, I remember all the ways I don't trust him and push away from his muscled chest.

'Christina could stay until the school holidays. We can decide if you need her help after that,' he murmurs.

He finally seems to appreciate that I need help.

I'm just not sure I want it from Christina anymore.

Chapter Twenty-Six

Mazza

Six Months Earlier

The night bus crawls along Hackney Road, thoughts running round my head like rats in a maze. If only I could reach into my skull and rip them out.

So . . . I botched that up, Ben. Not quite what I was after. Sorry. It's my own fault. Coke's never a good idea. But I still plan to get what I can out of it.

I'm so wired, I get off the bus two stops early so I can walk it off. I march down the quiet streets, wishing I could stomp tonight out of my brain.

At home, Mum's on the sofa, exactly where I left her. You'd think she hadn't moved all night. A dirty plate on the floor's the only evidence she's eaten. The telly's playing some crappy comedy even she wouldn't watch. I turn it off and chuck a blanket over her.

In my room, I download the video on my phone to my laptop.

This could finish Sam. But I need to play it to my advantage.

I wasn't expecting that grope. I wanted him to take me seriously. But it happened. I can't change that. And it might just give me the edge now I know he fancies me.

Have I got the guts to do what you would do, Ben? Can I be cold-hearted and calculating enough?

It's a tough decision.

What am I prepared to do to survive?

Monday morning, Sam and Wayne are at a meeting, taking a brief for yet another pitch. It gives me time to practise what I'm going to say.

The office is quiet. I guess people are recovering from the party. Heidi messages, asking to meet in the pub. She'll want a debrief about Friday night, I'll have to think of something to say. She can't keep a secret to save her life.

'Why not threaten to tell her?' You put the suggestion in my brain and it's perfect. If Heidi knows something, so will the whole world. Sam knows that.

We sit in the pub with our drinks and chips, and Heidi lowers her voice to a dramatic whisper. 'Baz said you were doing charlie on the conference table.'

Baz is another one who likes to gossip and I'm not happy he's talking about me. I deflect the conversation. 'Yeah. But what about you and a certain Ponytail, eh? What happened after you left?'

Heidi smiles smugly. 'We came back to mine, too wasted to do much, but . . . well, let's just say we didn't get out of bed all weekend.'

'Aaahh!' Lauren squeals.

'Dirty stop-out, you,' I nudge her. It's just the effect she's after.

Lauren adds. 'So what about you and boss man?' She hip bumps me.

Heidi makes an obscene gesture. 'Someone's got the hots for Maz.'

'Nah, fuck youse.' I give them the finger. 'Not into older men.'

'Apart from a certain Aussie . . .' teases Heidi.

'Yeah, what happened to Anthony?' says Lauren.

'Went home early,' I say.

We chit-chat on about who did what at the party. Luckily Heidi's happy to go on about Ponytail for ages. She even buys him a brownie in the deli before we go back to work. 'He's a chocoholic, like me,' she says.

'Why don't you get him a haircut, while you're at it,' I say. 'Although, to be fair, the man bun's making a comeback.' We cackle as we get in the lift.

All afternoon I wait, but Sam doesn't make an appearance.

The council call me and I make an appointment. They put the eviction on hold meanwhile. They're not going to chuck us out straightaway, thank fuck. By the time I pay off what we owe, I'm not going to have a whole lot left in my pay packet. It'll be beans on toast for the foreseeable. Lucky I love beans, but a few hundred a month would come in handy.

Have I got the nerve to ask Sam? But what choice do I have?

I check Sam's diary. Tomorrow morning's wide open. I schedule myself in. Won't take long. Even if he comes in late or hungover, I'll be waiting.

Tuesday at eleven, I knock at his office with his favourite Starbucks Grande. 'Come in.' His glance flicks to me and then back to his screen. He's in a linen suit, with an open-necked shirt.

Clean and fresh compared to the state he was in Saturday night. *Did he really put his hand on my bum?*

'Morning.' I put the cup on his desk, forcing my hand to stop shaking. 'Er . . . How'd yesterday go? Good meeting?'

Sam takes the coffee without looking at me. 'Just working out the brief. Not ready for creative yet.'

I sit down in front of him and clear my throat. 'I . . . er . . . I'm not here to talk about that.'

He looks up, his handsome face creased in a frown. 'So . . . why are you here?'

I give him a knowing look.

He sits back in his chair, hands behind his head. 'Come on now. If it's about the other night . . . Look, we'd all consumed too much. Things got out of hand.'

My eyes narrow. 'Oh, don't worry. I'm a big girl. Your secret's safe with me. But thing is, my mum's got us into a spot of bother with the rent. I could do with a pay rise. A generous one.'

He leans forward and opens his palms. 'If only I could. The agency's not doing too well right now. My hands are tied.'

'Oh really?' I rest my elbows on his desk. My phone's in my right hand.

He sighs. 'Wayne and I are talking about cutting costs. Redundancies. I'm trying to leave it till after Christmas. But unless we win the next pitch . . .'

'Five per cent would do, to tide me over. You can afford that. Less than your coke bill for the month.' I tap the screen on my phone.

His face turns red. 'Look, we were talking about slimming down our operation. Keeping a skeleton staff and using freelancers means we save on pensions and healthcare.'

Cold shivers through me.

He's answered my threat all right.

He's talking about making me redundant.

'I don't care about pensions and healthcare, but I need a decent monthly salary, say another couple of hundred a month, so I'm not thrown out of my flat.'

His smile doesn't reach his eyes. 'And if I can't afford to give you that?'

I take a breath, hope my voice doesn't wobble. 'This might change your mind.'

I hold up my phone and press play.

Chapter Twenty-Seven

Jade

On Tuesday morning, we're finally allowed to leave the hospital, after staying in an extra night to keep Eddie under observation. I've spent the last two nights dozing in the armchair next to his bed, so I'm dying for a night in my own bed.

As soon as we're through the door, my bones sag with relief. Eddie and I kick off our shoes. My nose wrinkles. The house always seems to reek of bleach since Christina moved in. She walks out of the downstairs loo with a bucket and wearing a familiar Glastonbury T-shirt over old leggings.

'Oh, hi.' I manage a weak smile. I'm doing my best not to blame her for Eddie's attack. I shouldn't have left the sauce in the fridge. It's as much down to me as it is her.

'Hi Jade, Eddie. So glad you're back!' Christina steps forward, like she might hug me but for the rubber gloves. 'I thought I'd do a deep clean.'

I focus on her T-shirt. I have one just like it. 'Were you at Glastonbury in 2006? So was I.'

'What?' She glances down at the T-shirt. 'Oh! I hope you

don't mind. I didn't have any old clothes suitable for cleaning. I found these in the utility room. Hope that's OK?'

I want to say *No, it's not OK*, but that would be unreasonable. She could hardly ask my permission while I was at the hospital. 'You don't need to clean my house,' I blurt out.

Eddie pipes up. 'But don't you always say you wish someone else would help clean, Mummy?'

'Yes, sweetheart.' I hug him. 'But I meant Daddy, not Christina.'

'It's only right that I contribute while I'm living here.' Christina disappears into the kitchen.

I flick through the pile of post and find a brown envelope addressed to Christina. 'Letter here for you,' I call out. It looks pretty official. A new job, I hope. Or something that finalises her divorce.

'Mummy, I'm hungry.' Eddie tugs at my hand.

'Come on, let's get you some food.' I lead him into the kitchen.

Christina's been busy. The dining table and the granite worktops are immaculate. She's stowed away all the jars of herbs, spices and vitamins. The piles of paperwork, bills, receipts and school notes usually strewn everywhere are in a basket. There's a pink begonia in a hand-thrown pot on the table.

'Shall I make tea? Eddie ... would you like a drink? Some cake?' Christina asks.

'I'm sorry I shouted at you the other day,' I say.

'Understandable. It was a shock,' says Christina. 'I can't apologise enough.'

'I know. But why didn't you check the ingredients? You know more about cooking than I do. You must have known

there would be fish sauce in an artisan Thai curry paste ...'
Eddie gives me a worried look. I stop talking. I'm sure she
wouldn't have deliberately given him fish. But she should have
known.

'I'm sorry. It won't happen again.' She looks so apologetic; I
feel like a bitch.

Still, I have to tell her what I've decided. 'If you don't mind,
I'll take care of the children's food – at least Eddie's – from
now on.'

'I understand.' She turns away to swipe at her face with a
tissue. 'Can I at least make you some tea?'

I pour Eddie a glass of water and sit down, overcome with
exhaustion. I guess there's no harm her making tea. Sam said
he'd checked the fridge and cupboards, in case anything else
dangerous was lurking.

'And I ... er ... I baked while I was waiting for you to come
back.' She opens a plastic tub and a citrus scent drifts out. 'Lemon
drizzle cake. Would you like some?'

'I just said, I will cook the kids' food,' I remind her.

'There's no nuts in it, I promise. There's nothing in it but
eggs, sugar, butter, flour and lemon.'

Eddie looks at me, eyes wide. 'Please, Mummy! I love lemon
cake.'

'All right, but Mummy's cooking your dinner.'

Christina slides out a delicious-looking sponge onto a plate.
'Jade?'

'Thanks.' I don't have the energy to refuse. After the stress of
the hospital, I'm not fit for anything. Sam's right. For another
few days at least, I need her help.

She cuts two slices and passes one to me and one to

Eddie. I stab at the slice with a fork and chew. The sponge is light, the lemon syrup lovely and sour, but it's toothachingly sweet.

Eddie takes a bite of cake and slumps back in his chair. I kiss his hair. 'You OK, darling? Shall we flop on the sofa?'

'Can I watch TV?' He attempts a smile which turns into a yawn.

'Yes, of course, darling.' I'm so relieved he's better, I'd say yes to anything. He runs off to the living room. I turn to Christina. 'Have you heard anything more about the flat you were interested in?' *Will she get the hint it's time for her to leave?*

'I'm waiting for the agent to phone me back.' She picks up Eddie's empty plate and glass, takes them over to the sink and turns on the tap. The running water stops any further conversation.

I take my tea into the living room. The books stand straight on the shelves, the cookery books in alphabetical order. The CDs and DVDs are in their cases, lined up in order. The coffee table is polished, the cushions plump and straight, and the sofa blankets neatly folded. The mirror and windows lack their usual frosting of fingerprints and even the felt-tip scribble on the wall has been miraculously cleaned away.

I have an urge to mess everything up, turn it back into my home.

Voices are murmuring.

'You look exhausted, Sam. It must be all the worry. Why don't you go and sit down? I've opened a bottle of red. I'll heat up dinner.' Christina. She's taking care of my family.

Someone whines. 'I want Mumma!'

'Come on, Leo, leave Mummy to sleep.' Sam – I can smell his aftershave.

'She really needs to rest.' Christina again. 'Leave her. She was exhausted when she got back from the hospital.'

'She's been asleep since then?'

'Mum-my!' It's Amber. Why's she shouting?

'Mumma! Wake. Up.' Hot hands shake me.

I feel weighed down, but I force my body up. 'Leo?' I'm sitting on the sofa, the blanket tangled around me. I blink my eyelids open. My mouth's claggy with sleep and my head hurts. I was meant to pick up Leo from my mum's. *How'd he get back?*

'Jade?' Sam hovers over me.

'How long have I been asleep?' I mumble.

'Yay!' A warm chubby body barrels into me and holds me tight. Leo.

'It's nearly eight o'clock,' Sam says. 'Poor darling – why don't you go to bed?'

Brain fog threatens to close in on me. 'Who brought Leo home?'

'I got him,' Sam says gently.

'Sorry.' My head feels full of cotton wool. *How could I have forgotten?* 'I was watching TV. Must have passed out. Oh – Eddie's dinner. Don't let Christina cook for him.'

Sam kisses my cheek. 'Ssh. Don't worry. Eddie's already in bed. Fell asleep in his clothes. You're both clearly exhausted. Why don't you go to bed?'

I heave myself off the sofa and follow Sam into the kitchen. The light's dimmed and the table's set for two. The begonia I'd noticed earlier gives the setting a romantic air.

Christina stirs something at the stove. A smile lights her eyes when she sees Sam and the kids. Then she notices me, and her cheeks turn pink. 'Oh, hi, Jade. Would you like some pasta? I tried to wake you several times, but you were out for the count. Leo and Amber have eaten. Eddie took himself to bed.' She lays another bowl, spoon and glass on the table.

'Christina, can I have cake?' asks Amber.

'Cake, please, Mumma,' Leo asks sweetly.

'I guess so, if you brush your teeth after,' I say.

'Smells great.' Sam sits down and pours himself a glass of wine. Christina serves up. Did she cook for him yesterday? Sunday evening too?

She turns back to the counter and slices up lemon cake. 'Jade, sit down. Glass of wine?'

'Want Mumma give me cake,' Leo cuddles into me.

'Let Christina do it for you, Leo. Mummy's tired,' Sam says.

'I'm fine. I can slice up cake.' But I feel strangely cut off from them, like I'm still dreaming. My head aches, even though I slept a good few hours. I stumble to the cupboard and take out a plate. The floor tilts, and the plate slips, smashing on the floor.

'Whoops!' shouts Leo.

I kneel to pick up the pieces, dizzy.

Sam crouches next to me. 'Come on, guys, move away safely.'

'Mumma, you're bleeding.' Leo's voice pierces the fog.

Tears scald my cheeks. Someone hands me a tissue.

'Why don't you go rest in your room?' Christina murmurs. 'I'll take care of this.' She exchanges a look with Sam.

Why did I invite Christina to stay?

Sam helps me up. 'Come on, let's get you to bed. Do you

205

think Daddy's strong enough to carry Mummy?' The kids giggle as he lifts me into his arms. I nestle into his chest, and he mock staggers. 'Whoops, maybe not quite strong enough.' More giggling. He carries me into the hall and up the stairs. Soon I'm under my soft cotton duvet, sinking back into sleep.

Chapter Twenty-Eight

Mazza

June

Y ou'd be proud of me, Ben. Sam paid up. He refused to give me a pay rise and make it official, but an envelope filled with cash appeared in the top drawer of my desk on the first of the month. I have to admit, cold hard cash is better than I'd hoped for. It means I can sort a payment plan for the rent we owe the council.

January, February, March, April, May, the cash appears.

But it's June now, and there's no envelope. For the past few mornings, I've been checking my drawer religiously, but there's no sign of the cash. I do the only thing I could think of – I send a text. Something that hits the right bunny-boiler tone. He'll get the message.

Dreamed about you last night x

It does the job. The envelope appears in my drawer, stuffed with the usual notes. But that afternoon, Sam visits me in the production department. He leans over my shoulder like he's looking at my screen and hisses in my ear. 'My wife saw that text. You need to be more discreet. She's coming to our awards night. I better not see you anywhere near her, or no more envelopes.'

On awards night, I'm shitting bricks. When Sam's wife enters the crowded bar, I recognise her straightaway. Pink lips, glossy updo, a 1950s style dress covered in pink roses. Her net under-skirt makes it look like she's floating in her own bubble. She spots Sam, and a smile lights up her face like the sun.

I've too much at stake to ignore Sam's instructions. I keep to the opposite side of the room, tracking her movements out of the corner of my eye so I don't bump into her. I'm not the only one eyeing her up. While Sam's busy with the techie, I notice Anthony winding his way to her. She's happy to see him and they hug. They make a good-looking pair.

I hang out with the studio guys. Their jokes are shit, but they provide a buffer against Sam. Not that I look at him. Even when they call me up for an award, I manage to avoid looking him in the eye.

Once or twice, I feel the back of my neck prickling. I turn and see Wifey looking at me daggers. She turns away, but not before a brief moment of awkward eye contact.

Maybe Sam's right about the text dropping him in it. Maybe she's not such a pushover. Does she suspect that text message was from me? Is that why she's looking like she wants to kill me?

Oh. Fuck. After the awards are given out, I'm chatting to Anthony when she heads over and gives him a hug goodbye. I'm too close to avoid her and my heart races as she introduces herself. Sam's told me not to talk to her. I hide my panic with a blank face and quickly eyeball Baz. He's telling a joke about his brother-in-law. I laugh like it's the funniest thing I've heard, even though I want to puke.

Poor thing.

Her perfect marriage is a sham.

But does she know it yet?

Chapter Twenty-Nine

Jade

It's eight in the morning, and Christina looks like she's been up for hours, dressed smartly in tailored trousers and a blouse, while I've just about managed to throw on a pair of jeans and a T-shirt.

I slept so deeply, my head's groggy and there's a dull ache at the back of my skull. Thinking I'm dehydrated, I gulp a glass of water, and stare vacantly at the boxes of cereal before reaching for the muesli.

'I can take the children to school if you're tired?' Christina hands me a cup of tea. 'I added a spoon of honey for energy.'

'I'll be fine.'

I'm not keen on honey in tea but I drink it, wincing at the strange taste. I gather up the kids and we leave for school. Leo refuses to walk halfway, so I have to carry him to nursery. 'I did tell you to take your balance bike.'

'Kiss-tina say big boys walk, not bike.' Christina had said she couldn't control him from running into the road with the bike. Her methods are not the same as mine, but it won't be for much longer.

I arrive home exhausted from carrying Leo, to see an Ocado van parked outside our house. I step over bags of shopping on the floor in the hall. In the kitchen, Christina unpacks groceries onto the counter.

'Did Sam do a shop?' I ask.

'Sorry, you'd run out of everything,' Christina explains, examining a jar of pasta sauce. 'I was going to pop to Sainsbury's, but Sam gave me your log in. I used a suggested order. They make it so easy, don't they?'

'Christina, you really don't have to do that.' I take a carton of milk over to the fridge.

'As you said, I should have checked the sauce. I'm making sure it won't happen again.' She peers at the label. 'You'd be surprised what contains traces of nuts and fish. It's best to be safe. I feel so guilty. I know you told me about Eddie's allergies, but it was a shock to see such a severe reaction.' She picks up a packet of sausages and comments. 'These are full of additives.'

'I do check labels.' A defensive tone enters my voice. Christina isn't actually accusing me of being negligent, but guilt tightens my chest. 'Anyway, I'm going to be cooking the kids' food from now on. I'd feel more comfortable this way . . .' I trail off. My meaning is all too clear. *I don't trust her.*

'Let's do it together, it'll be quicker. The chilled food needs to be stored in the fridge ASAP . . .'

'Please, Christina.' I bite my lip. 'I'm really grateful for your help, but I can take it from here.'

'I'm sorry.' She blinks and there's a wobble in her voice. 'I feel like I can't do anything right. Sam thought you were overtired after the hospital. He suggested I look after you for a few days.'

They've been discussing me? So I hadn't imagined the air of collusion the night before. *I need her to leave my house.*

'Look, Christina, why don't you call the estate agent about that flat in South Woodford? Find out what's happening?'

She looks at her hands. 'I – I missed it. I should have put down a deposit at the viewing. But it was the first place I looked at, I didn't realise how quickly things move. I'm so sorry – I would book a hotel but – I hate to admit this ... I'm rather short of cash ... Michael's not being co-operative and the hospital never got back to me about locum work. You'd think the NHS were crying out for doctors.'

Much as I want the house to ourselves, I can't throw her out with no job and nowhere to go. I'd feel too bad. 'What about your mum?' I suggest.

'Knowing her, she'll have changed the locks.'

I sigh, wanting to be supportive, but my patience is running low. 'You could call some other estate agents. You don't have to live in this area.'

'Don't worry, Jade.' She smiles bravely. 'I'm sure something will come up. It ... It might take a few days. If I could stay here until next Monday?'

I nod. 'Monday's fine.' I feel guilty, pressuring her, but with how I'm feeling about Sam, I need my space back. Only then can I work out what to do.

She wipes her eyes. 'Thank you,' she smiles. 'How about I babysit on Friday so you can go out?'

I look at her, blank. 'Why Friday?'

'It's Sam's birthday on Saturday, isn't it?' She points to the calendar where I've marked the occasion in red felt tip. 'You could meet him from work on Friday night?'

I'd completely forgotten. 'God. I haven't had time to think about it.' The last thing I want to do right now is celebrate Sam's birthday, but the kids will expect it.

'Anything else planned?' Christina asks.

I shake my head. 'Not much, to be honest. I'll have to order him something on Amazon. I think he wanted a hip flask.'

'It's understandable – you've been so busy. Let me help. I could book a bar in town. What about that salsa bar we went to?'

I shake my head. 'God no – he hates salsa.'

She chuckles, her tears forgotten. 'Don't worry, I'll do some research, find somewhere suitably hip. Have a night out together. It's the least I can do.'

I breathe out. 'Thanks, Christina. That's so helpful. But ...' I hesitate, but I make myself say it. 'After the weekend, I'm going to need my study back.'

'Of course.' Her smile trembles.

I harden my heart. But it was never meant to be forever. She can stay till the weekend, and it's kind that she's offered to baby-sit for Sam's birthday.

But by next Monday, she has to go.

Chapter Thirty

Mazza

July, the envelope's late again. I try another text, but there's no reply. I check the drawer daily, but the envelope doesn't appear. I'm well into my overdraft and it's only the first week of the month. I can make the payments I owe, but there's nothing left for food. Everything costs a bloody fortune these days. Mum hasn't found a new job and she's too depressed to get out of bed to get signed off, so no benefit either. I bloody need Sam's cash, or I'll be living off the meeting room biscuits.

Sam and Wayne are confabbing in the conference room when I hear raised voices. Sam bursts out towards the fire escape. Desperation makes me reckless, and I follow, even though people could see us.

He's leaning over the railings, smoke puffing out of his nostrils.

'What happened to the cash?' I blow out a cloud of candy-floss vapour.

He waves his hand in front of his face like it stinks of shit, not burnt sugar. 'I'd love to oblige, Maz, but funds are low right now. I did say you were jeopardising your income, talking to my wife.'

'She approached me,' I say. 'I listened to Baz's jokes all night to get away from her. Not my fault.'

'I'm afraid it is. The texts you sent . . . She suspects we're having an affair.'

'Oh shit.' My stomach flips.

'Yeah. "Oh shit". Why should I pay you when my wife's suspicious of me anyway?' He gives me the evils.

I shrug. *About bloody time she cottons on to who her husband really is.*

'She's tracking my every move thanks to you,' he growls.

I shrug. 'Your own fault. Should've paid on time.'

He runs his hands through his hair. 'Why don't you get it? You're not thick. The agency's on its knees. Until we sign some new clients there *is* no extra cash.' He starts to push past me. I smell coffee on his breath, mixed with the sour reek of fear.

But it's nothing like the fear I have of losing my home. I block his way. 'Yeah, well, I'm sure HR would love to hear what I . . .'

'Really?' He grabs my wrist, pushes me against the railings so the metal digs into my back. 'Just try it.' Spittle lands on my cheek. 'I'll tell them the truth. You faked that video. You've been blackmailing me. Who d'you think they'll believe? The respectable partner and family man? Or a blackmailing slapper on the make?'

He shakes me so hard my teeth judder. He won't throw me over, will he, Ben? 'There's a flat roof one floor down, you won't die,' you reassure me.

Thanks. I'm just thinking I'm seriously in danger, when he lets go. I sink to the ground as the fire door slams. I'm shaking, I'm crying, and my wrist hurts.

The door swings open. I jump up. Is Sam coming to finish me off?

Anthony strolls out, holding a mug of tea.

I exhale with relief. 'Oh hi, Anthony. Didn't know you smoked.' I scrub away my tears.

'Just getting some air.' He cops a look at me. 'You OK? What's up?'

'Can't a woman have a cheeky vape, freelancer? Baz thinks you might be stalking me.' Baz told me Anthony was asking about me.

Anthony's cheeks turn red. 'Sorry. No, I . . . I was after Sam? Someone said he was here?'

'Haven't seen him. Could be downstairs.'

He peers at me closely. 'Sure you're all right, Maz?'

'Fine. Just . . . Personal issues.' I slide past him and head back in.

Chapter Thirty-One

Jade

It's been sweltering all day, and the tube is like an oven as I make my way to the bar Christina booked. I feel like I'm going through the motions. Nothing's been the same since I stopped trusting Sam.

Just outside Leytonstone the train grinds to a halt. The cotton of my blue polka dot dress clings to my damp skin and the seat covers scratch the backs of my legs. Trust there to be delays. I can't even text to let Sam know, as I've left my phone at home.

When the tube finally pulls into Tottenham Court Road, I race up the escalators and hurry down the narrow streets of Soho. I arrive at the Velvet Rooms panting and sticky under the arms. I slip past two dark-clad security guards at the door. The cool air-conditioning feels delicious. Mirrored panels on the wall reflect my harassed reflection and I take a minute to smooth my hair and swap my frown for a smile.

I scan the room, noting how perfectly Christina has gauged Sam's taste. Groups relax on slouchy leather sofas, and couples whisper in intimate booths. A roar of laughter from the far corner draws my attention to a gathering on a raised platform.

I glimpse a red swishing ponytail on a tattooed back. Mazza is perched on a barstool, chatting to Wayne and others I recognise from the awards ceremony. *What's she doing here?* She crosses her legs, and her denim skirt rides up over fishnet-clad thighs. Suddenly my navy polka dot dress seems more frumpy than elegant. As the group shifts, I spot Sam, looking relaxed and amused.

Anger spirals through me. It will be hard enough acting the couple in love when I want to scratch Sam's eyes out, but I didn't expect Mazza and the rest of his agency to turn up. Christina hadn't mention booking for a group. Sam must have invited them. My chest aches with the proof that he's given up trying; he doesn't want to celebrate his birthday alone with me.

I pin a smile on my face and thread through the crowd, my gaze fixed on Mazza who is throwing her arms up in the air in a performative way. Everybody laughs again. Sam's eyes are dancing, his cheeks flushed, a wayward lock of hair curling on his forehead. He looks happier than I've seen him for a while. I can't help feeling a spike of jealousy.

When I reach the reserved area, a black velvet rope bars my way. 'Sam.' I raise my voice over the babble.

He notices me and unhooks the rope. 'Darling, you're late.' He flashes me a grin, but his eyes are tinged with red. My heart sinks. *How many's he had?*

'Sorry.' My smile feels strained. 'Bloody tube was delayed, and I forgot my phone. Happy birthday.' I lean in for a kiss, but someone bumps me as they pass and my lips miss his mouth, brushing the rough texture of his hair. I inhale the woody tones of his aftershave before we're shoved apart.

'The guys wanted to join us.' Sam raises his voice over the

chatter. 'I asked Christina to book a larger sch— space.' *Great. Slurring already.* 'You don't mind, do you?'

'No. Of course not.' My cheeks ache from holding in my irritation. Christina and Sam are obviously calling each other without telling me. Neither have bothered to let me know the change in plan. I fold my jacket carefully, placing it on the back of a bar stool. At least the others being here means I can avoid being alone with Sam until dinner at Teatro. I don't want to argue at his birthday drinks.

Wayne moves towards us, and pecks me on the cheek. 'This is hi and bye, I'm afraid, Jade. Mark booked us theatre tickets.' He slaps Sam on the back. 'Enjoy the rest of your birthday, mate.'

'Yeah – laters.' Sam pats Wayne back then turns to Mazza, lowering his mouth to her ear. 'A round of caipirinhas. Put it on my tab.' He rests his palm on her back for a second, touching her bare skin. Her lips twist, embarrassed, as she catches me watching them. Her cheeks flush scarlet. She disappears towards the bar. But her reaction re-kindles my doubts. *Is there something going on?*

'Shot! Shot! Shot! Shot!' The agency staff pass round a tray of shot glasses that ends up with Sam.

He hands me one. I tip back the glass and liquid fire slips down my throat.

Sam winks and mouths, 'All right?'

I'm about to reply but a young Asian guy with a quiff asks, 'How old are you, boss?'

'Bloody ancient.' Sam's smile is brittle. It must be hard to be constantly surrounded by kids in their twenties.

Mazza's back. She hands me a cocktail but avoids my eye.

I attempt a smile. This is my chance to get to know her. 'Hi . . . Mazza, isn't it? We met at the summer party, I'm Jade, Sam's wife.'

'Hi,' she mumbles, edging away.

I sip at the frozen tumbler. The alcohol warms me up. I turn back to Mazza but she's already deep in conversation with her friends.

Sam hasn't noticed I'm feeling awkward. He keeps his arm around me, but he faces the Asian guy, and I catch the occasional word like 'pitch' and 'strategy'. It's hard to relax when I'm conscious Mazza could be the Unknown Number. She shares a joke with the two girls who I'd heard gossiping in the loos at the awards ceremony. Do they recognise me? They must remember I heard them talking about Mazza's crush. If I still worked at the agency instead of having kids, we might all be friends. But those days feel light years away.

'Jade?' I turn and sigh with relief to see Anthony's familiar face. He bends to kiss my cheek and Sam catches my eye, raising his eyebrows, surprised to see him. *Wasn't Anthony working at Sam's office? Why else would he be here?*

'Happy birthday.' Anthony slaps Sam on the back and they grin but the tension's thick between them. Anthony points to our glasses, already drained. 'Drink?'

'Well, if you're buying,' Sam jokes, but sounds a touch belligerent. 'I'll have a whiskey sour. Jade?'

'Thanks – caipirinha.' I'm so tense, I can't think of a different drink. He heads for the bar.

'I heard you're freelancing for Anthony.' Sam's voice is cold. 'You didn't mention you were working for him.'

I flush. 'I meant to say. But . . . I've hardly seen you lately.'

'No.' His tone softens. 'I know, I'm sorry.' He pulls me towards him. 'If we win the pitch, I'll have more time.'

Mazza's laugh breaks the tension and Sam moves towards her, listening intently to her story, leaving me watching the vibe between them.

Anthony's back with my drink. 'Having a good night, Jade?'

'So – were you in Sam's office today?' I feel awkward. Does he remember my questions about Sam and Mazza?

'Yes. I'm in a couple of days this week. Actually, I'm glad I caught you – great news ...' He pauses. 'Teatro's approved our campaign.'

'Yeah? Brilliant.' His face sways from left to right. I should've asked for water, not another cocktail.

'The CEO's away so feedback's delayed.' I strain to hear him. 'Are you OK, Jade?'

'Stronger than they look,' I mumble, clinking my glass on his.

'Cheers,' he grins. 'You know, I just swung by to say hi. I have dinner plans. Enjoy the rest of your evening. Sam, I'm off.'

Sam lifts a hand, jovial in front of the others. 'Already? Thanks for coming.' He turns back as the group laughs.

I wave goodbye to Anthony and go in search of water. There's a jug at the bar and I pour myself a glass and gulp it down, holding on to the counter to steady myself.

When I get back to our area, Sam's gone to the loo. My nose is running, and I'm out of tissues. Sam's leather satchel is looped around the back of his chair. I pick it up, looking for the pack of tissues he keeps inside.

My fingers feel a smooth flat box and I pull it out. The dark blue box is wrapped with a satin ribbon. I can tell it's from an expensive jewellers.

221

For an improbable second, my heart leaps, but it can't be for me. My birthday isn't for ages. The gift must be from someone else. Unless he'd bought someone a gift.

My head spins. Who could it be from? Mazza? I still don't know if she's the unknown number but her crush on him is pretty obvious. Every time I smile at her, her eyes slide away. Before I can check what's in the box, I hear Sam's back, saying goodbye to the others. I quickly push the gift to the bottom of his satchel.

There's a collective shout of 'Happy birthday, old man!' I zip up the bag and pass it to Sam with his jacket. It's nearly eight and time for our table booking.

We stumble down Wardour Street, turning into a side street towards Teatro. The cocktails have hit me hard. I'm barely aware of the throng of tourists and Friday night revellers. We push through the revolving door to the refined atmosphere of the restaurant.

'Good evening. If you'll come this way.' The maître d' recognises me and seats us near the podium again.

Once seated, I ask Sam, 'Did anyone at work give you a present?' I keep my voice casual.

He barks with laughter. 'I'm forty-two, not four.'

'My old man,' I try for a light tone but it's not working. 'No one had a whip-round for you?' I flick through the menu, wondering if he'll tell the truth about the box nestled in his bag. Or will it be something else he's forgotten to tell me about?

The white satin ribbon smacks of romance. I can't concentrate on the performance. Sam doesn't seem that interested in the trapeze artist or the clowns. He works his way quickly through the bottle of Malbec, slumped in his chair, his face puffy and tired.

He could be telling me the truth, and no one's bought him a gift. He could have bought it for someone – maybe the person sending him text messages? I still suspect it's Mazza. I think of him touching her back, her embarrassed reaction.

Teatro is wasted on us. The wine might as well be water. The sea bass with samphire and crushed garlic potatoes could be cardboard.

I don't bother with dessert. Instead I down a glass of dessert wine and the sickly-sweet liquid coats my teeth like syrup.

Knowing Sam is lying makes me coldly sober.

Chapter Thirty-Two

Jade

S am lies next to me in a stupor. A hangover pounds at my skull and images flicker through my mind on a loop. The gift with the satin ribbon. Sam's hand on Mazza's bare back. Her guilty blush. Anthony arriving. His look of pity as he sensed something was up.

As the sun peeks through the blinds, I turn towards Sam, only to get a blast of alcohol-stewed breath.

Leo pushes open our door and pads in. 'Mumma!'

'Sssh.' I throw on a dressing gown and lead him out. 'Let Daddy have a birthday lie-in.' The longer he stays in bed, the better. I don't have to face him.

The kitchen is spotless, except for the glass of water I knocked over last night in a vain attempt to ward off a hangover. I soak up the water with some kitchen towel, then sit Leo down in front of the TV with a bowl of cereal. I cuddle up to him on the sofa, sipping a glass of fizzy C. *I'm giving up drinking after this weekend.*

I must have dozed off. I wake to see Christina, peeking round the living-room door. 'Hi, would you like a coffee? I've made a fresh pot.' My chest tightens. I'm annoyed that she hadn't told me that Sam's work colleagues would be there.

'Sssh,' scolds Leo, frowning at the interruption.

I move him off my lap, and head for the kitchen. The smell of freshly brewed coffee fills the air. Amber's at the table, eating her cornflakes and reading *Mallory Towers*. 'Morning, darling,' I kiss her, but she barely acknowledges me, eyes glued to the page.

'So, how'd it go last night?' Christina presses the plunger. 'Did Sam have a good birthday?'

'It was ... fun, thanks.' My tone's short. I don't say more while Amber's there.

Christina pours milk into a pan, and starts whisking. 'What about the bar? Live up to the five-star reviews?'

I lean towards Amber. 'Darling ... take your cornflakes to the living room. The boys are watching *Finding Dory*.'

Once she's gone, I can be frank with Christina. 'So, a couple of things about last night ...'

She brings the coffee to the table. 'Any sign of Mazza? Still mooning after Sam? No men in the office more her age?'

I say nothing, but make a face and she smiles, as if amused, which irritates me.

'Are you OK?' She touches my arm.

My head is throbbing, and I flinch. 'Look, even if Mazza has a crush on Sam, there's nothing going on.' I don't feel comfortable discussing my suspicions about Mazza and Sam with her.

'I mean, Sam's a good-looking guy – he must get a lot of attention?' Christina smiles, indulgently.

I think of his fingers, pianoing on her shoulders, and how she gazes at Sam through her lashes. My pulse races. 'Christina,'

I snap, 'I wish you'd told me Sam invited his colleagues for drinks. I thought it was just the two of us.'

'What? Didn't he tell you?' She looks surprised for a second, then pours the coffee.

I shake my head, not trusting myself to speak.

'I'm sorry, I presumed he'd told you.' Her smile is apologetic. She adds frothy milk and a sprinkling of chocolate and places a mug in front of me.

Her pity makes me feel worse. *Of course* she'd assume Sam would have told me. It's what normal couples do. Talk to each other. Tell each other if they change arrangements.

'It's fine. I just wish I'd known it was going to be a party.' I don't add that she's caused more trouble between us. *Is she really as innocent as she pretends?*

She bites her lip. 'I must apologise. I should have mentioned it.'

'Look, I'm sorry. I'm hungover. I didn't mean to shout.'

'It's understandable. But you had a good time at Teatro? Your romantic dinner?'

I don't tell her Sam was too drunk to appreciate it. 'It was fine. But I don't think circus acts are really Sam's thing.'

I blow on the drink I hadn't asked for. The froth on the cappuccino has already flattened and the powdered chocolate resembles scum.

When I come down after my shower, Christina's disappeared into her room. I'm glad. I just want to forget about the previous night. Mazza. Anthony's pity. The hordes of women who apparently fancy Sam.

I help Amber prepare Sam's birthday breakfast of strawberries and croissants.

My heart swells with pride as I watch her carry the tray carefully up two flights of stairs, biting her lip. The boys fake-tiptoe behind her, trying not to giggle. Their arms are full of homemade cards and presents.

'Happy birthday, Daddeee!' chorus the kids, while Amber sets the tray carefully on the side. 'Happy birthday to you-hooo!'

Sam blinks his eyes open and yawns. Leo jumps on him and Eddie and Amber climb on the bed, their infectious laughter tugging at my heart, despite my worries.

'Wow! What's all this?' Sam smiles sleepily as the boys pile their carefully wrapped presents on top of the duvet – a box of fudge and the hip flask I'd ordered online.

He tousles Leo's curls and cuddles Eddie and Amber. 'Wow – did you guys make these cards?' He takes the time to comment on every scrawled message and photo.

'Kiss Dadda, Mumma,' says Leo and pushes me over to Sam.

I force myself to kiss him. It's not the children's fault Sam and I have hit a bad patch. But it's a huge effort to pretend everything's fine.

Chapter Thirty-Three

Jade

I'm underwater, in the deepest, darkest part of the ocean, where danger lurks. I'm frozen with terror. A sea creature reaches out a tentacle, but a dark energy swirls around it. *Can I trust it will pull me to safety?*

A familiar voice burbles from a distance, calling my name. 'Jade. Jade ah, wake up.'

Fingers grip my shoulder and gently shake me. I catch a whiff of wine mixed with an old-fashioned perfume. Opium. Mum's favourite. Has she come to rescue me? The weight of water presses down. Pins and needles prickle my arms and legs.

'Jade, come. Wake up.'

I peel open my eyelids, flinching at the light and attempting to move, but the weight of my duvet is pinning me to my bed, not the ocean. A dull ache pounds at my skull. My mouth is gritty, my tongue dry as paper. This isn't a normal hangover. I've had a headache on and off since we got back from hospital. I wonder if I picked up a bug.

'Jade!' my mum shouts. 'You are missing Sam's birthday dinner.'

I force my eyes open. After the late breakfast, we'd planned to ride our bikes to the park. But it was pouring with rain by the time Sam was ready, so we'd settled in front of a movie instead. I kept drifting off and eventually retired upstairs for a nap.

It's tempting to sink under the covers, but my mum looms over me, face red with drink, a frown creasing her forehead. Coral lipstick is smeared in the cracks of her lips. Her gold chain dangles towards me, but she straightens before my fingers can reach for the teardrop pendant I played with as a child. She helps me sit up. 'What's wrong with you? You sick?'

I blink and rub my eyes. 'What's the time?'

She pulls at the duvet, swaying slightly. 'Gone eight o'clock. Time for cake.'

'What?' I reach for my phone and my stomach roils with nausea. I squint at the screen: 20.08. 'Sam was meant to wake me. I have to cook the lasagne.'

'Good thing your friend Christina already cook. Sam said, you very tired, need to rest.' She holds out a glass of water, spilling a little on the sheets. 'Come, drink.'

I sip gratefully, swishing the cool liquid round my mouth to get rid of the stale taste.

'Come have cake. Better than nothing.' She whisks the duvet off briskly, like she used to when I was a teenager.

I swing my legs out, smoothing my crumpled dress. The blood rushes into my muscles with a painful tingle. I came up just after five. I've been asleep for three hours.

Mum crosses to my wardrobe. She flips through the hangers and pulls out a wrap dress in a shade of green I hate. 'Put this on. Quick, let's go.'

'All right. I'll be down in a minute.' I shoo her away, then shuffle to the bathroom. In the mirror, I see black eyeliner is smudged down my cheeks. My skin looks dry and wrinkled. I wash my face, refresh my make-up, then slip on a clean dress, a silver one, not the green, and make my way downstairs.

The kitchen is an assault on my senses. There are balloons and streamers hung around the room and a birthday banner is strung up behind Sam, at the head of the table. My mum's at the opposite end, Christina is sitting in my usual seat next to Sam, Leo by her side and Amber and Eddie opposite. For a moment I stand unnoticed, and survey the happy scene. On a glass cake stand, the chocolate fudge cake I'd bought is barely recognisable, covered in gold and silver dragées, sugar flowers, and studded with 'Happy Birthday' candles.

'Hi . . . Sorry, I overslept.' Their chatter pauses, and all heads turn towards me. I feel like I'm interrupting a stranger's dinner party.

'Jade.' Christina jumps up, as if her chair is too hot.

'Awake at last.' Sam's unsmiling eyes are bloodshot. He grabs the bottle, tops up his glass and fills another for me.

'Mumma!' Leo runs to me, burying his sticky face in my legs.

Christina crosses to the stove where there's a dish covered with foil. 'We saved you some lasagne. I can reheat it?'

'Thanks, I was going to come and finish cooking . . .' I've missed the main course. On the counter stands an empty champagne bottle and an empty red wine bottle. I know Sam will have drunk most of it.

Leo drags me to the table, and I sit down in my usual seat, still warm from Christina. 'Daddy should have woken me up.' I look at Sam, pointedly.

'I tried.' He shrugs, alcohol lacing his voice with belligerence. *Not very hard.*

'And I didn't stir?' Leo won't move from my lap.

Amber glances up, nervously. 'We tried to wake you, Mummy.'

'You were snoring,' says Eddie. Everyone laughs, breaking the tension. But my cheeks flame.

'Mummy was dead to the world, but luckily, Christina took over – she's been amazing, right, kids?' Sam grins appreciatively at her.

She's moving a stool to my mum's end of the table and sits down next to Amber. My mum pats her arm. 'Lucky Christina cooked dinner or we would be hungry. You know, when Mummy teenager, I call her Sleeping Beauty.' My mum talks to the children. 'She never can get up.'

The children snigger. I feel hot with shame and change the subject. 'Thank you, Christina – seems you saved the evening. Didn't expect all this.' I wave a hand at the decorations.

Christina's eyes sparkle. 'It's my pleasure, Jade. The children enjoyed it. Why, Amber's turned your supermarket cake into a work of art.' I feel the word 'supermarket' like a slight.

I smile stiffly. 'The cake does look wonderful, darling. Well done.' Amber gulps her juice, ignoring my praise.

Christina puts an arm round her. 'She's turning out to be a great cook.' Amber's cheeks turn pink as if Christina's approval means more than mine.

Eddie pipes up. 'I chose the balloons and sparkling candles, Mummy. I know you don't like the sparkling candles from Amazon, but Christina said the ones in the shop are fine.'

'I . . . just worry they're a fire hazard.' I sip my wine to hide my burning cheeks, instantly regretting it as my head swims.

Christina smiles at Eddie. 'These ones are safe enough, from Party Zone in the high street. Every yummy mummy in the area would complain if they set fire to their precious kitchens.'

I pretend to laugh. 'You shouldn't have gone to so much trouble.'

'No worries,' she beams. 'After all, not every day is their dad's birthday.' She glances over at Sam through her lashes, and he grins. *She's won over the whole family.*

'Don't you like the balloons, Mummy?' Eddie looks worried. I realise I'm frowning.

'Darling, I love them!' I inject enthusiasm into my voice. 'It all looks amazing – I just wish I'd been here.'

'Too much fun last night, eh?' Sam claps a hand on my shoulder. I shrug him off.

'You have hangover?' My mum giggles, tipsy. 'So that is why you turned into Sleeping Beauty. You should be grateful to your friend.'

Anger rushes through me. Can my mum make it any clearer that she thinks Christina's doing a better job than me? 'Of course I'm grateful.' I force my lips into a smile. 'Thanks, Christina. Sorry for leaving it all to you.'

She tilts her head at her plate. It's like a nod of approval.

I pick at my lasagne, desperate for something to do so Mum can't see that her thinly veiled criticism is getting to me. 'It's late, the children need to go to bed,' I say. 'Shall we have cake?'

Leo cries, 'Yay! Choc choc cake.'

Christina holds up a lighter. 'Eddie? You wanted to help?'

'Leo light candle.' Leo scrambles off my lap and he and Eddie jostle each other to reach the cake.

Christina glances at me for permission. 'I promised Eddie he could help. But it might be a bit dangerous for Leo?'

'Me! Leo light!' he whines.

'Mummy'll help so you can light some too.' I hold out my hand for the lighter. I feel petty, as if lighting the candles will give me a semblance of control.

'If you're sure.' Christina hands me the lighter, despite the doubt in her voice.

It's hair-raising trying to control the boisterous Leo without burning any fingers. I'm aware of Christina and Sam chatting softly, while I struggle with the candle-lighting, wax pooling on the icing.

'Amber, dim the lights,' I say. 'Happy birthday to you . . .' I start singing. Mum, Christina and the children join in. As Amber and Eddie carry the cake over to Sam, the sparkler candles start whizzing and popping. Brilliant white sparks flare out, releasing plumes of smoke into the air.

An ear-splitting beeping fills the kitchen as Eddie and Amber place the cake in front of Sam. They slap their hands over their ears.

'I don't like it – make it stop!' Leo screeches.

'It's just the fire alarm, baby, it's fine.' I put my hands over his ears. My head's in agony.

Sam opens the back door and lets out the smoke. I find the broom and press the reset button on the alarm. The beeping stops but the shock of it still rings.

Amber and Eddie are half screaming, half laughing. Leo's crying. My mum tries to soothe him, but he won't relax, so she ends up telling him off.

'I'm so sorry, Jade. You were right about the candles. I'll go into Party Zone and complain,' says Christina, frowning.

'Cake now!' shouts Leo, standing on his chair. He's over-tired, about to have a tantrum.

'OK, darling, one minute, let's get a knife,' I say, and slice it up into chunks.

'I make a move, let you get the children to bed,' says my mum. 'Good to see you again, Christina. You can visit my house anytime. Thank you for dinner. The lasagne was very good.'

'Bye, Mum. Thanks for coming,' I snap. 'I would have cooked if someone woke me up.' I move everyone into the hall.

'You are working too hard,' says Mum. She leans forward to kiss me on the cheek, but I pull back. 'How long is Christina here for?'

'Until Monday – the day after tomorrow – isn't that right, Christina?' I say.

She doesn't answer and my mum hugs her. 'My daughter is lucky you are here.'

I shut the front door with a sigh. Eddie chases Leo upstairs, roaring like a lion and Amber follows.

'Thank you, Christina.' Sam throws an arm round her shoulders. 'Great birthday!' She smiles awkwardly at me, ducking away from his arm. Sam turns to me, a cool tone entering his voice. 'Thank you, darling, you woke up in the end.' He doesn't bother to hug me, and I'm glad.

A moment later, Christina brushes at his sleeve. 'Hang on, I think you have some . . .' She scrapes her nail at his shirt. 'Just a piece of wax. All gone now.' She steps back, darting an apologetic smile at me.

Sam starts up the stairs. 'Thank God that's over for another year.'

I agree. It's been hard to keep up the pretence of happy families for his birthday. Whatever the next year brings, at least Christina won't be here.

Chapter Thirty-Four

Mazza

Anthony's working on a credit card brochure in the studio when I go look for him. Could I tell him about my money troubles? He's always been a good listener and I'm bursting to confide in someone. 'Look, sorry about earlier. I've a lot on my mind. Fancy a drink?'

He stretches and moves his neck from side to side. 'Sure – I'm not being paid to work overtime.'

'You're buying, then, freelancer?'

He laughs. 'Oh, all right. Four-pack of Special Brew in Soho Square?'

'Sure you can do better,' I banter.

'Coach and Horses?'

I grin and nod.

There's at least two Coach and Horses in Soho, but there's one that hasn't changed much in the last fifty years, with a varnished wooden bar and a tiled floor.

Anthony goes to the bar and comes back with a pint, and a bottle of pear cider. We chat a little. Who fancies who in the office. Who's going to shag who in the latest Netflix show. He tells me about the design studio in his living room. How he can be faster and more competitive than big corporate agencies with their massive salaried creative directors and account directors.

By the time I've downed my second bottle of cider, my tongue's loosened up. There's a pause in the conversation. 'So . . . I love that you're too polite to ask, by the way.'

'Ask what?' He pretends he doesn't know what I'm talking about.

'Earlier today. When you met me on the fire escape? Don't you want to know why I was upset?'

'Er . . . no. You said it was personal.' He looks uncomfortable. Which makes me want to tell him. I'm contrary like that, as you know, Ben.

'Truth is, I'm in a bit of trouble. Financially.'

I tell him about Mum losing her job and us nearly being evicted. I sink another bottle of cider and there's no stopping me. Anthony's like a priest or something. He makes all the right noises, and he looks like he cares. And since you've gone, Ben, I haven't anyone who listens to me. Really listens. Mum's hopeless. And Heidi and Lauren are great for a laugh, but I can't tell them what a mess my life is.

We're both silent. And then I ask, 'Why've you been asking Baz about me?' Baz told me last week that Anthony's been asking questions.

He turns red. 'I'm sorry. It's Jade, Sam's wife. She's a mate, and I – I care about her. She thinks you've been texting Sam. She's curious. Wants me to find out what it meant, should she be suspicious?'

'And what did you tell her?'

'Well, I'm hardly in the agency, so I asked Baz. I thought he'd know if there are any rumours floating around – about you and Sam. He said you guys were doing coke at the office party. He said he left to go and buy more, and when he came back, you'd both gone.'

'Well, good of Baz not to invent anything. There's nothing going on with me and Sam. Not like that. Jade needn't worry.'

Anthony looks concerned. 'Is it really a good idea to get into coke when you have debts? Not that it's any of my business . . .'

'No, you're right, ain't your business. But I'm not a coke fiend. It was a party.'

'So that's it?'

'So, you're wondering if I texted Sam? Sounds well dodgy, to be fair. But – well – he's been helping me with some cash payments every month. The text was just a friendly reminder.'

'And did he? Lend you some cash?'

'Well, he did last month. But he can't help anymore. That's why I was upset. I can't afford to eat this month.' I drain the rest of my drink.

'So, you need money?' Anthony looks concerned.

'Yeah, Sam's been sorting me out. Kind of like a private loan, but one I don't need to pay back.'

'Funny, I never saw Sam as an altruistic type, he must really value you. But why doesn't he tell Jade? I don't understand.'

Can I tell him? What do you think? I pick up my empty glass. 'S'your round.'

Another bottle of Kopparberg and a chaser of tequila later, Anthony says, 'There's just a point I'm not quite clear about.

237

I mean, you don't mind me checking again – there's definitely nothing going on between you and Sam, right?'

'Sexual, you mean? No, *definitely* not. I'm . . . well, I like girls,' I admit.

'I find it . . . slightly unusual that he'd help you, with his own money as you say, when . . . Well, he's got his own family to keep afloat?' Anthony's bright red.

'Yeah, you're right,' I say. 'He needed some persuading before he'd help me.'

'Persuading?'

'If you must know, I have a rather compromising video of Sam.'

'What?' He looks shocked.

'Yeah. I threatened to send it to HR and his wife, and he paid up. Until now.'

'So, spill.' He leans nearer. 'What's on the video?' I wonder what he thinks Sam is capable of? Has he guessed?

I feel a flash of guilt for not dobbing Sam into the police. But you'd said it. 'We have to carry out our own justice.'

'Let's just say I have some dirt I could reveal unless he helps me out with a loan. Oh, Anthony, when I met his wife I could hardly speak to her. The video's of something . . . Something he's done. Something bad.'

'I see.' Anthony's silent.

'His wife's lovely, isn't she? What does she see in Sam, eh? You knew 'em both in the old days, right?'

His face scrunches up like his drink's turned bad. 'Look, Mazza, let's keep to your problems. You've been blackmailing Sam. What are you going to do now he won't pay up?'

'I haven't quite decided. And, hey, blackmail's a harsh term. I'm a good worker. I save them money instead of pocketing the discount from the printers, like Kevin. And he wouldn't want me to be on the streets.'

'So, how much did you ask him for?'

I shrug, like it's no biggie. 'Just the extra payments to the council. £300 a month.'

'So that's what you were upset about on the fire escape, when he said there's no money this month?'

'Yep. Got it.'

'So now . . .' He frowns, and I see cogs turning. 'There's no reason for you to keep quiet, right?'

'I—I guess not.'

'So . . .' His eyes gleam with hope. 'You could tell Jade the truth. You could tell her what Sam did?'

I hate to kill his dreams, but I shake my head. 'Sorry. If I tell her, then there's no money. And I need the money more than Jade needs to know.'

Chapter Thirty-Five

Jade

The next morning, I'm woken up by a light tap on my door. 'Wake up, Mummy.' Leo and Eddie pile on top of me as I peel open my eyes. The sun's streaming through the blinds. A fresh breeze wafts through the window.

Sam's gone. My head's sunk deep into the pillow, my limbs heavy and numb. Glancing at the clock on the bedside table, I quickly calculate I've been asleep for twelve hours. *Why am I still so tired?*

'Tea and fizzy C?' Christina hovers in the doorway with a tray.

Eddie helps me sit up and hands me the glass of vitamin water. 'Here, Mummy. This will make you better.'

'Are you hungover? Could you be coming down with a cold?' says Christina. 'I thought the children might like to go to the park?'

'Want Mumma to come park.' Leo burrows into my side, his hands grabbing my belly.

'Amber's finishing her homework and then we can go,' she says.

Eddie says, 'I did my maths, Mummy. Christina helped me.'

'Where's Daddy?' He should be helping Eddie, not Christina.

'Sam's gone to meet Wayne,' Christina replies. 'He asked me to keep an eye on the children. After the park, we could finish those collages, boys? Jade, you can catch up on your sleep.'

'Don't you need time to pack?' I say, remembering she's leaving tomorrow.

She shakes her head. 'Oh, there's not much to do. I've time for one last trip to the park.'

'All right.' My head's fuzzy, like it's filled with cotton wool.

She takes the empty glass from me. 'You're still catching up from the sleepless nights.'

Eddie hands me the mug of tea. 'We added honey.'

'For energy,' adds Christina. 'You could do with a boost.'

'Thanks.' After the sharpness of the vitamin water, the tea tastes too sweet, but under Eddie's eagle eyes, I drain my mug.

Christina perches on the armchair. 'I'm going to miss you, Jade. I've felt so at home these last two weeks. Thanks for being so welcoming.'

'I should thank *you*,' I say gruffly. 'You've been such a help.' I'm glad she's going. I won't need to compete with her for my family's attention anymore.

'I can come back and babysit anytime.' She ruffles Eddie's hair. He flicks me a glance and pulls away. 'How about I cook dinner later? There's no need for you to do anything. Just rest.'

Her voice is soothing and my eyelids droop. When Christina's gone everything will be down to me again. 'Yes, thank you. Sounds great.'

It's a relief to slip back under the softness of my duvet.

THUD.

I wake with a start, the duvet's thrown off my body and

tangled at my feet. It's dark, so I fumble for the bedside lamp switch and glance at the clock. 10.05 p.m. I've been asleep for hours. *All day.*

Is it flu? I don't feel feverish, but my bones feel heavy, my eyelids feel like they've been glued shut. I'm tempted to go back to sleep but the window's wide open, a breeze rattling the blinds. I swing my legs off the bed and shuffle towards the window to close it.

A photo frame has fallen to the floor. Is that what woke me? I crouch down and pick it up. The glass is cracked. A shame, it's one of my favourites. Five of us, in Sardinia. I smile, thinking of that holiday. Happier times. We're sat on a stone wall, eating gelato, Leo in the sling. The sea behind us is fiery with the sunset. I place the frame safely on the dressing table.

A door slams downstairs. Sam must be back. Echoing up the stairwell are muffled sounds. I creep down to check on the children. Amber's fast asleep, her arm flung up against her headboard. Asleep, her face is relaxed instead of wearing her usual anxious expression. In the boys' room, Eddie has burrowed under the covers and his snores make me smile. Leo's limbs are spread like a star. I cover him with his puppy paw-print duvet, breathing in his delicious baby scent before I leave the room, shutting the door quietly.

Sounds echo up the stairs. It must be the TV. Sunday night, Sam likes to watch a film. But the volume's too loud. *He'll wake the children.*

Irritated, I pad downstairs.

The living-room door's wide open. A moan drifts out from an action scene or a love scene. As I reach the doorway, there's another loud moan.

'For God's sake, turn it down,' I say.

Then, I freeze.

The TV isn't on. Only a side lamp glows.

There's a couple on the armchair. Moaning, panting. A musky sweaty smell fills the air.

It's Sam. He faces me, eyes shut. His shirt is unbuttoned, his chest bare. Astride him gyrates a half-naked woman, her back to me. Sam's hand holds her waist, his gold wedding band glinting in the lamp light.

I'm numb. My mind can't believe what it's seeing.

Who the hell is fucking my husband?

Mazza? But no, this woman has black hair, not red. Her back is pale, no tattoos.

The room sways. I gasp. The woman whips round. Her black bob is tousled. Her eyes smudged with black.

It's Christina.

The shock knocks the air out of my lungs.

Chapter Thirty-Six

Jade

I gasp.

Sam peels his eyes open. 'What the hell?' he slurs, confused. 'What's going on?'

Like it's my fault I've caught them.

He stands up, unsteady, pushing Christina away. She pulls up her dress and I catch a glimpse of her small breasts and dark nipples. Her eyes gleam. With desire? Triumph?

And then her mouth twists. 'I'm so sorry.'

It feels like a shard of glass is stabbing my heart.

'Get out. How dare you.' My voice is a harsh whisper, as the pain wraps round my chest and clutches my throat.

'Jade? I fell asleep,' Sam mumbles, looking at his shirt like he didn't realise it was unbuttoned.

Christina sobs, and runs past me, out of the room.

'Bitch!' I shout. The study door slams shut. I turn to Sam. 'You disgust me.'

'I swear I didn't do this.' His voice trembles, his skin is grey.

'I just saw you!' I can't listen to excuses. I stomp to the study and rattle the handle, but she's locked it. I bang on the door. 'Get out! Christina! Get out of my house.'

I hear the creak of footsteps. A door opens upstairs. 'Mummy, what's going on?'

Oh God, Amber. She's peering down through the balustrade.

'It's nothing, go back to sleep.' I rush upstairs and lead her back to her room. 'Sorry, darling. Go to bed, or you won't wake up for school.'

When I've settled her, I go down to the living room to confront Sam. He's buttoned his shirt and sits in the armchair, holding a glass of whisky, eyes red and glaring.

'Get. Out.' My voice can't seem to go above a whisper. 'And take your ... your girlfriend with you.'

'No way.' His voice is cold. 'You're jumping to conclusions. Get rid of your crazy friend, but I'm staying in *my* house where *I* pay the mortgage.'

'Leave!' I clench my fists. 'I won't stay in the same house as you. I can't!'

'We need to sort this out.' He stands and tries to take my hands.

But I'm shaking with rage, I can't stand to be near him. I run to the door. 'If you won't leave, then I will!'

My legs march me upstairs. My hands grab my overnight case.

It's like I'm outside of my body, watching myself act as I pack. Pyjamas. Toothbrush. Underwear. A change of clothes.

Amber's back in bed, door shut. The boys are sleeping, blissfully ignorant of this seismic shift in our lives. I decide not to wake them. I can't deal with a grumpy Leo.

Sam hovers by the front door. 'Jade, please. I fell asleep. And when I woke up, there she was.'

Her lipstick's smudged round his mouth and he's still lying.

How could you? I want to howl.

I cannot stay in the same space as him and her. I slip on my shoes, grab my keys, my handbag.

'Jade. This is not what it looks like.'

What a shit.

'The kids are asleep,' I grate out. 'Drop them at school in the morning. I'll pick them up. And I want you gone by the time we get home.'

I'd mistaken the danger. I'd been worried about Mazza when the danger had been closer to home.

Christina. Who I invited into our home. *My friend.*

The betrayal is killing me.

'She did this. Not me.' The blood rushes in my ears. Sam sounds far away.

I walk out of the door to my car.

He doesn't follow.

Chapter Thirty-Seven

Mazza

As the date of the pitch draws nearer, the studio guys work later and later. All apart from Anthony. He refuses to work late unless we bump up his day rate, but we don't have the budget until we win some new business.

One evening, he hands me his boards and mimes drinking. 'Fancy one?' We've been going to the pub regularly, since I opened up to him about Sam, sometimes with Baz and the others, but they're too busy to join us tonight.

It's muggy outside. Flying ant season. They land on my clothes, buzz in my face, crawl out of cracks in the road. A couple of tourists with backpacks block the pavement and I step into the road to avoid them.

'Wanker!' A driver blares his horn and a gust of air whooshes past as a trishaw practically crashes into me.

'Fuck right off,' I scream to its flashing lights and fluffy boas shedding pink feathers.

Anthony raises his eyebrows. 'Stressed, are we?'

'Fucking need that drink.'

In the Coach and Horses, I slide into our favourite corner seat while he goes to the bar.

He hands me a bottle. 'Here, get that down you.' He gulps at his pint, wincing with satisfaction. 'Can I ask you a favour?'

'Depends.' I'm curious, noticing his forehead is gleaming with sweat.

'Mazza, you should come clean about Sam. Whatever you've got on him, is it fair his wife's in the dark?'

'Whoa, hang on there, mister. What's it to you? It's me he's not paying. I'm the one who's going to be on the street if I don't keep up my payment plan.'

His eyes crinkle with concern. 'Look, mate, I *am* worried about you. And Jade. It drives me insane to think of her playing happy families with that shit, right? Her marriage isn't worth saving. You said it. Sam's a sleaze – she deserves better.'

So, that's his game? Rescuing his damsel in distress? "Better" meaning you?'

Anthony laughs. 'If you like? I'd certainly treat her better than Sam does.'

'And the three kids? You'd take them on too?'

'Yeah, I like children. Jade means a lot to me. Sam's not who she thinks he is. He's a creep. I can't stand men like him. Full of it. They think their money buys them immunity. Normal rules don't apply. They can get away with grabbing someone's butt, or worse.'

I nod, considering his words. 'Sam's no Harvey Weinstein.'

'Not yet. But do you think Weinstein started off trying to stick his cock into young actresses? It starts with a grope, a slap on the bum. But he never got reprimanded. So he moved on to worse. The film industry enabled him.'

'I get you. But if I tell Sam's wife what he's like, and the truth comes out – the agency could run into trouble too. And there goes my job. How'm I going to pay my rent arrears? What's going to stop the council kicking me out to the street?'

'How much do you owe?'

'I've paid off nearly two grand, so I owe just over seven grand. How'm I going to get seven grand if I lose my job? I might just have to kidnap some rich kids and ask for a ransom at this rate. In fact, I could kidnap Sam's kids, so he pays up.'

I kill myself laughing, like it's all a joke. But Anthony's giving me a strange look. I realise I find it funnier than he does.

'I think you'll find kidnap slightly more difficult than blackmail.' Anthony looks at me sternly. 'And Jade says her children are a handful, especially her youngest. Kids know all about stranger danger. They'll scream the house down.'

I nod and laugh, like I'm joking around. But I turn it round in my mind as if it's a serious proposition. Kidnapping Sam's kids. What do you think, Ben? Could I do that?

'Another round?' I fish in my bag and show Anthony my empty purse. 'How about you go, since I'm just as brassic now as I was earlier?'

While Anthony's at the bar, I amuse myself wondering if I could do it for real. Kidnapping. I'm good with kids. You always said I'm a kid at heart.

I bet I could pick up Sam's kids from school. Teachers are so stressed these days, it's not that hard. I'd pretend to be a babysitter or an auntie. Remember how Mum was always sending different people to pick us up when we were little? It might not be quite as easy these days, but I bet I could call the school office in advance. Say I'm the parent giving permission for so and so to pick them up. Easy-peasy.

I'd get to know them a little, get them to trust me, before I throw a sack over their heads. I'm laughing out loud, amused with myself, when Anthony comes back with the drinks. He asks what I'm chuckling at, and I manage to persuade him I'm just joking about the kidnapping idea. I'm getting quite drunk, to be fair.

Before last orders, Anthony has a final pop. 'Seriously, yeah, won't you tell Jade what Sam's really like? No solidarity for the sisterhood?'

I shake my head. 'Sorry, Anthony. I'm not here to help you with your love life. Not while I'm expecting my big fat envelope.'

'But mate, what if he doesn't pay up?'

I pretend to think about it. 'Oh well, then all bets are off.'

Chapter Thirty-Eight

Jade

I pull up outside my mum's house in Ilford. But I can't bring myself to get out of the car. I sit for a while, staring at the dim light glowing through the frosted-glass panels of her front door.

My mum had warned me. My dad had had an affair, and she was permanently scared it would happen to me. I almost hate her for it, the way she kept telling me I wasn't making an effort.

I think of how she approved of Christina. Her medical degree. How she kept saying what a good daughter she was. How I was lucky to have a friend like her.

No. I can't go in there. Mum can't stop herself criticising me. She'd say it was my fault. She'd even blamed me for Dad leaving, because she'd been too stressed, working and looking after us.

And maybe it is my fault in a way. I chose Sam. I let Christina stay.

Tears of self-pity scald my cheeks. I slap my palms on the steering wheel, chest heaving with sobs.

I scream out my anguish.

At Sam. At Christina. At my mum and dad.

After some time, the sobs lessen. I wipe my eyes and blow my nose.

I start the car and drive, I don't know where, anywhere. I drive down dark streets, mindlessly. But I can't go anywhere near our house.

Eventually, I find myself on the North Circular. I stop at the nearest Premier Inn and book a room.

I'll go home tomorrow, when Sam's at work and Christina's gone.

Then I'll decide what to do.

I can't sleep. Images chase round my mind all night. The moment I caught Sam and Christina plays on a loop. I only doze off as it's getting light.

When I wake it's nearly eleven. In a daze, I check out and drive home. I park in our drive, staring up at the windows. There's no movement inside. No one's home.

I can't bear to go into the house yet. Not on my own. I'll go in once I've picked up the children. I need their noise, their chatter, to block out my thoughts.

Restless and jittery, I walk to the high street. It's warm but muggy. My armpits prickle with sweat. There's already people sitting at the whisky barrels outside the posh wine shop sipping tall glasses of frosé. The Green's full of sunbathers. To avoid bumping into anyone I know, I head away from the High Street, towards Hollow Ponds.

What am I going to do? Can I ignore what's happened for the sake of the children?

I want to kill her. I want to kill him too, but ever since

I found those text messages, it's like I've been waiting for this moment, to find out my fears are true. Except it's so much worse because I never thought he would cheat on me with Christina. Or that she'd betray our friendship like that.

Mazza. Christina. Maybe he's cheating with both of them. It's obvious he's a complete sleazebag. I can't trust him ever again.

But can I be a single mother like Fran? She makes it look easy, but I know it can't be. Working all hours. Hardly seeing her kid.

Should I turn a blind eye to it like Kate did with Daniel? Go to a marriage counsellor?

What should I do?

I'm starting my freelance career. If I divorce Sam, life will be harder. We'll have to sell the house. I might have to move away. The kids might have to leave their school and friends.

But how can I stay?

A storm's brewing and the air's humid and heavy. I walk round the lake. The murky water reflects grey, pregnant-bellied clouds. I used to come here when Amber was a baby. She barely napped in the day and would get more and more grouchy. I'd walk and walk, singing to her, desperate for her eyes to shut.

My phone beeps. I ignore it. I don't want to speak to anyone.

Why did I invite Christina to live with us?

Is it my fault for letting myself go, like my mum says? Or are some men like Sam hardwired to be unfaithful? Is the proximity to other attractive women too much temptation?

I clench my fists. No. This is not my fault.

I am *not* going to take the blame.

This is on him.

Even before Christina moved in, we'd drifted apart. Sam was hardly home. The zoo trip was the first time in months we'd spent time together as a family. I have to ask myself, do I actually want to fix this?

At the coffee morning, Kate had alerted me to Christina's flirting, I'd suspected she might be a threat. But the betrayal had still blindsided me. I can't believe it.

I walk round and round the ponds, barely noticing where I'm going. The clouds are getting darker, and spots of rain break the surface of the pond, forming concentric circles.

I glance at my phone. It's nearly three. I head towards the school.

I'm the first in the queue at the nursery and I peer through the gate, searching for the first sign of Leo. I look forward to him running towards me, his chubby face creased with dimples, throwing his arms around my legs.

At 3.15 p.m., the bell rings, and the assistant unlocks the gate. She throws me an uncertain smile. 'Hi, er . . . Leo's – already been picked up?'

A cold fist clenches round my heart. 'What? What do you mean? Did something happen to him? An accident?'

The assistant guides a child out to their mum. 'Oh, nothing like that. Your childminder came early.' The fist loosens a fraction. *He's not hurt.*

But I'm confused. 'I . . . I told my husband I'd get the children.' *I can't bear to think of them with Christina.*

Maybe Sam didn't think I'd come back. Did he ask Christina to pick them up to be safe? But why so early? The fear is back.

Something isn't right. I can feel it in my gut. 'I don't understand. Did something happen? The office didn't phone me.'

The teacher approaches the gate with more children. 'Is something wrong?'

The assistant explains, 'Leo's mum didn't know he was leaving school early.'

The teacher raises her eyebrows. 'We had a note? You wrote to say you were going away this afternoon, and your childminder would collect the children at lunchtime.'

'But we're not going away.' My throat tightens, my heart hammers against my ribs.

The teacher frowns. 'You'd better go to the office. Find out what's happened.'

I'm shaking. 'Eddie and Amber,' I say faintly. 'Did Christina pick them up too?'

The teacher shrugs. 'I don't know – talk to the office. They'll have signed them out.'

I push past the other mums and carers, heading for the school office. My hands fumble for my phone and I dial Sam's number. It goes straight to voicemail. I leave a frantic message. 'Please phone me immediately. I've come to get the children, but Christina's picked them up early. What's going on?'

Oh God. *Why did I leave them with Sam last night?*

I call Christina but again it goes to voicemail. Is it a coincidence? Or are they both somewhere with no phone signal?

At the reception desk, the woman smiles behind the glass, but there's a crease between her eyebrows. 'Mrs Callahan, is there a problem?'

'Eddie and Amber. Were they picked up early, with Leo?'

'Why yes. Your childminder came and got them at lunchtime.'

'No . . . please . . . no . . .' My voice is strangled by fear. 'I did not give my permission. I can't believe you let them out!'

She frowns. 'But it was your usual childminder – Christina, isn't it? It'll be in the book.'

I look at the registration list. There, printed in Christina's neat handwriting, are Eddie, Leo and Amber's names. Signed out at 12.25 p.m.

'But I didn't ask her to get them! She wasn't looking after them!' My voice is a hoarse whisper, my face pressing up against the glass.

The receptionist shrinks back. 'Now hang on a minute, Mrs Callahan. First you need to calm down. Then we can sort this out.'

'Did she say anything, when she took them out?' My knees sag.

'She gave us a note from you. She said she'd been asked to collect the children after lunch. She said that you knew it was against school policy but that you're going on holiday with the children's grandparents and needed to leave this afternoon.'

Oh God oh God oh God. Nausea rises in my throat. I grip the reception desk to steady myself. 'I *did not* make those plans. And I *did not* write a note.'

'Oh dear.' Her face falls. 'Let me find the note. Let's see exactly what it says.' She disappears into the back office and comes back with a piece of A4 paper. She holds it up to the glass so I can see. Black type, printed from the computer, saying exactly what she'd told me.

'I don't usually write on the computer. I handwrite my notes to the school,' I tell her, voice shaking.

Her face pales. She finally realises this is serious. 'Sorry, I've just noticed. It's signed from Mr Callahan, not Mrs. Your husband wrote in.'

The signature is Sam's. A large S and C and a squiggle for the rest. I stare at her, I can't speak.

'Did he forget to tell you? Look, I'm sure it's just a misunderstanding. They're probably at home.'

Did Sam really write this note, asking Christina to pick them up early? The typewritten letter spells it out in black and white. But they could still be at home waiting for me to get back.

I run out of the office, crossing the road without looking. I'm vaguely aware of a horn blaring and a Golf swerving to avoid me.

As soon as I cross the threshold, I shout the children's names, but the house is empty, the silence deafening. In the study, the bed's been folded back into a sofa, the duvet and pillows piled neatly on the seat. The clothes rail is empty, apart from a few wooden hangers.

Christina's gone.

On the desk I notice a paper bag from one of the posh boutiques in the high street. I look inside and find a receipt for a silver-plated hip flask plus engraving. *Was that the gift I saw in Sam's bag on Friday night?* Christina heard me say I was ordering one off Amazon. I guess she thought she'd go one better.

I call Sam's mobile again, then Christina's, but they're both switched off. I leave voicemails and follow up with a text, my fingers trembling so much it's hard to type. Maybe they've both turned their phones off.

Could the answer be in Sam's messages? I dial through to my voicemail, gritting my teeth at the sound of his voice. 'Jade. You

257

have to believe me, I had nothing to do with what happened. Please call me back. Let's talk.'

I listen to the next message. 'You really don't believe me? Jade. Please.' His voice breaks. He sounds genuinely heart-broken. What a good actor.

The next message is angry: 'How can you believe her and not me? I didn't even want her to live with us.' I can't listen anymore. There's nothing about the children and that's all I care about – not his excuses. Instead, I glance through his text messages.

Jade. I love you. Please. Let's work this out.
We can't let the kids suffer.
Why won't you listen?
Please give me a chance. Even in court a man is innocent until proven guilty.
Really? No chance to explain? All these years I've supported you?

I stop reading. Pain knifes me. Sam and I are over. I don't want to hear his excuses. How dare he act like he's been wronged? And 'innocent until proven guilty'? When I caught him in the act!

Breathe. Think.

The staff at the school said they were going on holiday with their grandparents. Sam has the Paris presentation later this week. Could it be, that when I didn't return his calls, he pan-icked and asked his dad for help? And then wrote the note for Christina to give to the school?

Back in the kitchen, I check the cupboard above the sink. Eddie's EpiPen is gone. There's no sign of the spare inhaler, or the bottle of Cetirizine.

258

Only last week we'd disagreed about his parents' holiday home. Sam knows I don't want them to miss school. I can't believe he's taken them anyway. It's so irresponsible.

I try his phone again. Straight to voicemail.

Where the hell is he?

Has he taken the children to Devon?

Chapter Thirty-Nine

Jade

I try calling Sam's dad, but the mobile goes straight through to voicemail, so I try their landline. The answerphone message plays. Sam's stepmum Victoria's cut-glass accent says they are away and will check their messages when they get back.

I'm wild with fury. Sam needs to work flat out on the pitch, yet he's taking a week off? Is he planning to work from Devon via Zoom?

Will he dare turn up at his parents' holiday home with Christina in tow? Or will she be staying in a hotel nearby?

I pace the hall. I have to do something.

I call 999.

An operator answers. 'Emergency services. Fire, police or ambulance?'

'Police,' I croak.

The operator is sympathetic when I tell her what happened. She says a police detective will contact me shortly. A few minutes later, my mobile rings and I answer immediately.

'Hello, am I speaking to Mrs Callahan?' It's a woman's voice.

'Yes, yes, I'm Mrs Callahan,' I say.

'This is DS Anna Collins, you called us regarding your allegedly missing children. Please could you walk me through what has happened, giving me as much detail as possible?' She's not as reassuring as the operator.

'Th—thank you. My children have been taken. I arrived to pick them up from nursery and school – to find that they had been collected already.' My voice shakes. I take a breath. 'My childminder, Christina Lee, picked up my children. She had a note from my husband, saying they were going to their grand-parents'. But I didn't give my permission.'

'Are you currently separated or divorced? Has a violation of custody occurred?' She's polite but detached.

'No. No, nothing like that. We're still married.' But maybe not for much longer.

'Oh.' She pauses. 'I see. Both parents have equal rights over their children if they are married. It sounds like your husband instructed the childminder to pick them up from school. What was his state of mind? Has he been suffering from depression? Do you believe the children are in danger?'

'No, not depression. But . . . we had an argument. I didn't want him to take them to my in-laws' holiday home.'

'Can't you call them and check if he's there?'

'I've tried. No one's answering but the signal is patchy in that part of Devon. My in-laws left a message on their landline in Kent to say they're on holiday.'

'If you don't think the children are in danger, and if it's a dis-agreement about a holiday in the UK then it's a domestic dispute. Not something for the police.' Her tone is weary, like she has to explain this all the time.

'What?' I sink onto the stairs. 'That can't be true.'

'Do you believe your children to be in danger?' she repeats, slowly.

'Possibly. Christina . . . she knew my son was allergic to fish, but she gave him food containing fish sauce. She said it was a mistake. But how do I know she was telling the truth? My husband, their father, wouldn't hurt them. But I never agreed to them going to Devon. He can't take them without telling me.' There's a hysterical note in my voice.

She speaks calmly. 'I'm sure this must be hard, but as their father, he's perfectly within his rights. Look, it could be a misunderstanding. Wait a while at home, they might turn up soon?' Her voice wasn't unkind, but she was dismissive. 'If you don't hear from your husband, or if the risk to your children changes, then call us back.'

I have to make her understand. 'This is not just a domestic dispute. My husband and I are currently separated. We had a bad argument Sunday night.' I take a breath. It's important the police know what happened. 'I caught him with Christina, my friend and childminder. They were together, half . . . half-naked. But she locked herself in the study and he wouldn't leave. So – stupidly, I realise now – I left. I asked my husband to drop the children at school in the morning. I said I would pick them up. But they weren't at school at home time. He wrote a note saying they were going on holiday with their grandparents and had Christina pick them up early. You have to help me get them back.' Sobs shake me and my last words are incoherent.

'I'm sorry, Mrs Callahan.' She doesn't sound the least bit sorry. 'As I said, we can't get involved in domestic disputes. I would advise you to employ a family lawyer who can advise you about your custody rights. If your children are not in danger, there's not much we can do to intervene. It could be a simple misunderstanding. It happens.' She rings off with a curt goodbye.

She's wrong. There's no way on earth that Sam misunderstood me. I specifically told him I didn't want the kids to miss the last week of term. I refused his parents' offer of a week in Devon. But it seems he's taken them anyway.

Sam must have been angry I didn't answer his messages or accept his lies. He's punishing me by taking the children on the holiday I didn't agree to – with Christina's help.

I look up an email Sam sent me a while back, when his dad and Victoria first invited us to the holiday home. I write down the postcode and address and get into my car.

If no one's answering their phone, then I'll drive to Devon myself. Sam won't want a showdown in front of his parents. But there's no way I'm letting him get away with this.

Chapter Forty

Jade

The traffic on the M25 is at a standstill because of an accident. Eventually it starts to crawl but by the time I get to Fleet services, it's past nine and my legs are shaky from working the clutch for hours.

A black Audi cuts in front of me to nab a parking space.

'Bastard!' I yell, revving. I pull up, kill the engine and rest my head on the steering wheel. I can't drive for much longer. Every time I step on the clutch my leg shakes. I decide to book a room at the Days Inn. I'm desperate to see the kids but it's past nine now and I've only just reached the M3. They'll be in bed by the time I got there. I'll leave first thing in the morning and be there for when they wake up.

The room is tiny and stinks of a chemical cleaning fluid. I force myself to eat a sandwich in the restaurant, almost gagging at the cardboard-like texture.

I try Sam's phone again. I try Christina's. I even try Anthony in case he's heard anything at Sam's office, but it goes through to voicemail. I leave Anthony a message, briefly summarising what's happened.

I lie on the bed fully dressed. With all the thoughts buzzing round my head it's hard to sleep. As soon as the light comes through the synthetic curtains, I have a quick shower and check out.

It's so early there's hardly anything on the road. Four hours later, the satnav tells me I've reached my destination, and I pull up outside a stone cottage, one of a few clustered along a quiet road. The Callahan's holiday home is a dream cottage, with stone walls and a thatched roof, a blush pink rose rambling over the porch. I open the gate and walk up the path. The morning dew's damp on the lawn and the sky is golden and fuzzy in the sunshine. The sweet scent of the roses fills my nostrils, making me nauseous.

The drive is empty. I can't see Sam's car anywhere, but he could be parked around the corner. Or did he leave the kids with his parents and drive back to London? But their car isn't there either.

My heart hammers. I'd pictured them all together, playing happy families in Devon. *Have I made a mistake?* I pick my way through a border filled with snapdragons and lupins and peer through a window. The blinds are closed but through the slats I detect the faint glow of a lamp. I can't detect any noise or movement.

I ring the doorbell and rap hard on the knocker. The sound echoes loudly in the hall. No one answers. This is definitely the right address. Rosebriar Farm is painted on a circular plaque, next to the door. I scroll through my phone and check Sam's email. Yes. It's the right house. I bang again, louder this time.

I stand back and look up. The windows are shuttered. A swoop of dread is building in my stomach. *Where are Sam and the children?*

I glance around, wondering what to do. A plume of smoke puffs out of the cottage next door's chimney. I stride round and ring the bell. A dog yaps, claws scamper. The door opens.

'Yes?' A silver-blonde woman in a dressing gown holds back a panting terrier. 'Down, Cosmo.'

'Hi, I'm sorry to disturb you.' I try to smile but my face is frozen with anxiety. 'I'm looking for the Callahans – next door? Rosebriar Farm? Victoria and Edward? Do you know where they are? I'm their daughter-in-law.'

She frowns. 'Aren't they renting it out this week? They're in Spain. It's an Airbnb until September.' She says 'Airbnb' like the word is toxic.

'What?' My knees sag. I can't compute what she's saying. 'They ... they haven't been here this week? What about their son, Sam – my husband? – he was bringing the children.'

She shook her head. 'No one's been here. The house has been shut up since, now let me see, they left last Wednesday.'

The ground tilts. I cling to the door jamb.

'Sorry,' I gasp. 'I thought my husband ... I thought he was here with my children.'

'Are you all right, my dear? Do you want to come in and sit down?'

Panic grips my chest. There's a rushing in my ears. Her voice comes from miles away. *Where are the children? Where's Sam taken them?*

Somehow, I make it back to the car. I fumble open the door and collapse in the driver's seat, shallow breathing. My heart's fluttering like a bird in a cage. *Where are they?*

After a while I realise there's a distant buzzing. It's my phone ringing. I empty my bag on my lap. It's Anthony.

I answer but for a moment I can't speak.

'Jade? Hello? Jade, are you there?' Anthony sounds worried. 'My phone died last night, and I only just got your message. Have you found the kids? What's happened?'

'No, no. I thought Sam would bring them here, to his parents'.'

'Where are you?' Anthony asks.

'In Devon. Sam's dad and stepmum have a holiday home here. We had a fight and I thought he brought them here to spite me. But there's no one here.' My voice cracks. Pain scythes my heart and I'm overwhelmed with sobs.

'What? Jade, oh my God.' He pauses. And then he speaks and his voice sounds . . . reluctant. 'Listen. I, er . . . it's a long shot, but I might have an idea about who could have your children.'

'W—what?' It feels like a brick is pressing on my chest. *What's he saying?* 'Who? Who's taken them?'

'Take a deep breath, Jade.' His voice is steady, calm. I blow my nose and wipe my face. I can't lose it. It won't help me find my babies. 'How long will it take you to get back to London?'

'I . . . I don't know, five hours or so? Depends on the traffic. Last night was terrible but if I leave now I should be back before rush hour. Please. Tell me who has them.'

'I'll tell you everything when I see you. Are you in a fit state to drive? If you're near a station you could catch a train back?' he suggests.

'Trains take ages. It's quicker for me to drive.' I *have* to keep it together.

'All right. You should be back around lunchtime. Come and meet me at Sam's agency. There's someone who might know something.'

'Sam's agency?' I'm confused. 'Who? I don't understand.'

'We need to talk to Mazza. I've a feeling she knows something.'

'Mazza?' I can't make sense of what he's saying. 'But why? Can't you tell me now?'

'It's best we talk to her when you get here.' His voice is irritatingly calm.

I want to know what he knows now. But the sooner I start driving, the sooner we can talk. 'All right. I'll text you when I get there.'

'And Jade. Please drive safely.'

Chapter Forty-One

Mazza

It's nearly half one and I'm emailing a file to the proofreader before I dig into my sarnie, when Anthony texts me to meet him in the Hush-hush Room. I can't remember booking him but someone could've called him without telling me. Bloody art directors. Think the rules don't apply to them. There's a system for a reason. Stick to the budget, so the client loves us, and I can prove how efficient I am.

I'm already in a mood when I get to the meeting room. And who's in there next to Anthony? Jade. *The Wifey*. My heart pounds, my guilty conscience working overtime. *Does she know her husband's a complete shit?*

'Hiya, Anthony. Didn't know you were in today?' I mock glare at him and mouth, 'What's she doing here?' Not very subtle, but I mask my rudeness with a smile. 'Hi, Jade, isn't it?' I know full well what her name is.

'I asked Jade to meet me here.' Anthony's eyes aren't twinkling for once.

I raise my eyebrows. 'O—kay . . . What's this about?' But

I think I know. He wants me to tell her what I have on Sam. *Maybe he's right and it's time.*

'Mate. You need to tell Jade everything that's been going on.' He's gone all headmaster-ish on me.

I sit down, opposite Jade. I notice how tired she looks. Her eyes are bloodshot, and her face has a greyish tinge. Her hair's a mess and there are deep lines on her face. Gone are her model good looks – she's every bit a worn-out, middle-aged mum.

'Where's Sam?' Her voice breaks. 'Where are my children?'

'Er . . . Sam's gone to Paris? To the pitch for the yogurt people.' Sounds like Sam's been a naughty boy. Why does that not surprise me?

'No. I didn't know. Your receptionist just told me. I thought the meeting was later this week.' A tear runs down her cheek.

She's in a right state. I feel sorry for her, married to that creep. I speak slowly. 'It was brought forward. One of the yogurt bosses is having a medical procedure or something. Didn't Sam tell you?'

She looks at her hands. 'We—We had a fight Sunday night. But I . . . left the children with him . . .' Tears stream down her cheeks. Her nose is red and running. 'Please, tell me if you know where they are?'

'Sorry. Haven't a clue.' I frown at Anthony. 'Why would I have anything to do with their kids?'

Anthony glares at me. 'Don't you remember what we talked about the other night? At the pub? Tell her, Mazza. Tell her what's been going on, yeah?' He rakes his hair. 'She should know what kind of a man her husband is.'

Oh. My. God. What? I remember my joke about kidnapping rich kids. Surely Anthony doesn't think I was serious? Sam might be a sleazebag, but it's not his kids' fault.

Jade glares at me. 'Do you think Sam could have taken our three kids to Paris?'

'Unlikely,' I say. 'I booked the Eurostar for Sam and Wayne – just the two of them. They have a double room each at the Hilton. Not really room for any kids.'

'No, of course not.' She stands, paces the room. 'They went to school Monday morning. Sam must have dropped them off like I asked him to.'

'I believe he did.' I remember now. 'Because he was running late. Wayne called me asking where he was. Sam only just checked in on time.'

Jade looks confused. 'Anthony, I don't understand why you asked Mazza here? She obviously has nothing to do with the children going missing. It's Christina, their babysitter, who has them. Christina picked them up. I thought she was with Sam. That he'd written a note to the school, that they were going on holiday with their grandparents. But why would he do that if he was going to Paris?'

Anthony grabs my arm. 'Mazza, are you sure you don't know where Jade's children are? You didn't – I don't know – conspire with the babysitter?'

'No. I don't.' I stand up, pushing my chair back. 'You're mad. What would I know about a bunch of kids I've never met?'

He shakes his head. 'No. Sorry, mate. I'm clutching at straws. I thought . . . maybe you knew where they'd gone. That joke you made the other night?'

'Yeah right.' I feel my face grow warm. 'I was gonna ask for a huge ransom. It was a joke?' I mutter.

'I'm sorry,' he flushes. 'Stupid theory.'

'Because of that drunken chat? You're mental. The only time I spoke to their babysitter was when she called the office about Sam's birthday drinks. I've had enough of this. I have work to do.' I head towards the door.

Anthony quickly bars my way. 'But you *have* been blackmailing Sam, haven't you? So not quite so innocent.'

'Blackmail?' Jade eyes me, curious. 'Why would you *blackmail* Sam? Were you— Are you having an affair with him? Is that why you thought she'd have the children, Anthony?'

I burst out. 'No! For fuck's sake. I don't have your children and I'm not having an affair with Sam. Yuk.'

'And the blackmail?' she repeats.

'I – am – not – blackmailing – him,' I say through gritted teeth.

Anthony won't shut up. 'But you hid something Sam did, didn't you? He paid you off, and promised you a promotion if you didn't tell.'

'Tell what?' asked Jade.

I'm shaking, Ben, what should I do? Should I tell her what he did that night?

I hear your voice in my head, as clearly as if you've spoken. 'If you tell Jade what happened, there goes your leverage. How will you get him to pay if he's in prison?'

There is something I can tell her though. Anthony thinks he knows. So why not tell her too?

'All right. If you must know, Sam, Mr Callahan, groped me when he was wasted at the Christmas party. He'd been drinking

272

all day. We all had. Then we came back here and moved on to coke. He put his hand up my skirt, groped my bum . . .'

'Did you . . . report it to HR?' Jade says faintly, leaning on the table.

Blood rushes to my face. Sam's done a lot worse than a bit of groping.

'So . . . I might have *hinted* I had a recording on my phone. And I might have used it to persuade Sam to give me a – a cash bonus, and maybe a promotion.'

Jade looks confused and I don't blame her. To be fair, all this must be too much when she's already worried about her kids. 'So, you say he *groped* you? He sexually harassed you – at work?' She rubs her knuckles into her eyes, then turns to Anthony. 'But what does this have to do with the children going missing?'

Anthony looks at me. 'You needed money, didn't you, Mazza? Didn't you ask Sam for more cash? And didn't he refuse to give it to you?'

A dry laugh escapes me. 'Oh my God.' I stand up. I put a hand on Jade's arm. 'I'm really sorry your kids have gone walkies, Jade, but it's nothing to do with me. My man here's been watching too much Netflix.'

Anthony glares at me.

'Er, yeah?'

He grabs my arm. 'You told me you were desperate. You needed money to pay your rent arrears. You'd do anything.'

'For fuck's sake, it was a joke, OK?' I turn to Jade. 'So I'm about to lose my flat because my mum hasn't paid the rent for months. I made a joke – about kidnapping Sam's kids to get money. But there's no way – NO WAY – I'd actually do something like that. For God's sake, it was just drunken banter.'

'Anthony,' Jade turns to him, eyes shooting out the evils. 'You *joked* with Mazza about kidnapping my children?'

Anthony goes bright red. 'Oh, God. I'm sorry, Jade. We were in the pub, half pissed. She made a sick joke and I shut her down immediately. But I've been worried . . . well, when I got your message – I . . . I thought maybe Mazza had done something, that she wasn't joking.'

Anthony reaches for Jade's arm, but she strides away to the door. She turns and stares at me. 'My babies. I can't believe you'd joke about kidnapping them!'

'No way would I put your kids in danger, OK?' I say. 'I suggest you call the pigs. The police. I've nothing to hide.'

'Not even a bit of *extortion*?' Anthony's voice is mean.

'It wasn't like that, all right? Call the police, Jade. Stop mucking about with Poirot over here and his made-up theories. I mean, if I wanted to, I could make up a little story about you, couldn't I, Anthony? I could tell lovely Jade how you feel about her? How you'd love her to leave Sam and run off into the sunset with you? Maybe *you* paid the babysitter to take the children so you can play the hero?'

His face turns purple.

'Anthony.' Jade fixes a hard stare at him. She's a real mamma tiger. 'Please tell me you don't have anything to do with Christina taking the children?'

'Of course not!' he protests, voice hoarse.

'And Mazza, you say Sam is definitely in Paris for a meeting, without the children?'

I nod. 'I have an email from Wayne when they arrived.' I check my inbox on my phone. 'Look. Sam's just emailed. *Meeting went well. On our way back.*'

Jade looks exhausted, but there's a steely glint in her eyes.

She picks up her phone and dials. 'Hi, is that DS Collins? My husband isn't with my children. The friend who was babysitting – she must have forged the note. She has my children. They're in danger.'

Chapter Forty-Two

Amber

I open my eyes. Too bright. I snap them shut.

My head. It hurts.

My throat's scratchy. There's a funny taste in my mouth.

What's happening? I try to remember.

We were outside school. There was a horrible smell.

A stinky cloth, on my nose and my mouth. Pressing hard so I couldn't breathe. Yuk.

What *was* that smell? Chemicals burning my throat. Drugs?

In Special Agent Scarlett Book Two, *Kidnapped!*, Russian secret agents drug Scarlett and she wakes in the boot of a car. She works out where the baddies are taking her by counting the bends in the road.

Can I work out where I'm going?

An engine hums. There's crackly piano music on the radio. I'm in a car but not the boot like Agent Scarlett. Am I in the silver car I saw parked on the yellow zigzag lines? Before they pounced on me and stuck something stinky over my mouth?

The road is smooth but sometimes there's a bumpy bit that

makes me jolt. A seat belt's buckled across my chest. I'm safe, but not safe.

Next to me, Eddie's slumped and asleep, breathing heavily. Alive. I can't see Leo, but there's another set of heavy breathing over the noise of cars and lorries whizzing past. He could be in his booster seat, next to Eddie.

Where're we going?

I peek through my eyelashes. Something tells me to hide that I'm awake. I can see the back of a head in the driver's seat. I shift like I'm sleeping, and turn my head towards the window.

Green and brown swishes past. It's a fast road. Could it be the motorway? Too green for London. I'll count the bends. But right now, we're going straight.

A big square blue sign rushes past. *Manchester 85*, I read.

Manchester. A city in the north. *Is that where we're going?*

The piano music makes me sleepy. My eyes want to shut. I dig my nails into my legs to stay awake.

We drive for ages and ages.

After a long time, I hear the ticking of the indicator. The car slows. We turn off, pull into a car park and stop. The handbrake creaks on. My heart beats quickly. *Could this be my chance to escape?*

A hand tugs at my arm. I shut my eyes, but not too tight. I breathe heavily through my nose.

I hear the door open. The driver gets out of the car, slamming the door shut. A key beeps, and the locks click down.

I open my eyes, lift my head, and look out of the window. Still daytime, but the sky's cloudy and grey. There's rows and rows of cars. I unbuckle my seat belt and shake Eddie's shoulder. 'Wake up, Eddie!' My voice is all croaky.

I lean over Eddie to reach for Leo. He's asleep, a trail of orange dribble crusted on his chin. 'Leo, wake up! We need to escape!'

But the boys won't wake up. They're drugged. Like me.

I have to get out. I don't have much time. I try to open the doors, but they're locked. I push the buttons to unwind the window, but it's locked too.

A woman walks to her car. I bang on the window. 'Help! Help me!' I shout and thump the glass as hard as I can. The car shakes, but the woman doesn't hear me.

I climb over to the driver's seat and press the horn. *Beep beeeeeep beeeeeeeep.*

The woman turns, looks at our car. Frowns.

'Help! Help us! We're being kidnapped!' I shout.

Leo wails and stretches. Eddie murmurs and turns his head from side to side. But they don't wake.

'Help! Please . . . help!' I yell.

The woman walks to our car, bends and peers in.

'Please! Rescue us!' I scream through the window and bang.

The woman tries the front door, but it doesn't open. She straightens and looks around. Footsteps run up.

Too late.

So sorry . . . just left them to pop to the loo . . . asleep . . . didn't want to wake . . . thank you so much . . . won't leave them again.

The door opens. I slide to the passenger seat and grab the door handle. A strong arm pulls me back. The doors lock.

'Get back in your seat, Amber.' The voice is cold, hard. 'You upset that woman. And you woke Leo and Eddie. Mum won't be happy.'

'I hate you, I hate you! Get away from us! I want my mum!' I scream.

The woman walks away, shaking her head.

'Don't make me angry. Sit down. Right now! Do you want to be left on your own in the middle of nowhere? Your mum'll never find you.'

I'm scared. I'm crying. I know Mum would want me to stay with Eddie and Leo. I climb back to the back seat.

'Do up your safety belt, Amber. We've a long way to go.'

I was too slow.

Next time, I'll have to be quicker.

Chapter Forty-Three

Jade

Blue lights flash outside our house as I hurry down our street. Curtains twitch. Two mums holding buggies openly stare at our house. There's a trouser-suited woman and two uniformed police officers waiting for me on the drive. Their expressions look too grave for good news.

'Mrs Jade Callahan?' The woman holds out her badge, her red lips curving in a polite smile. Dread winds round my gut. 'I'm Detective Sergeant Collins and this is Police Constable Miller and Police Constable Khan. May we come in?'

'Yes. Of course.' Fear grips me, I can only take short breaths. I've barely had time to process what Mazza told me about Sam, how he groped her. I can't think about that yet. The children's disappearance – no, *abduction* – is all too real now.

'Constable Miller and his team will conduct a search of your premises while I ask you a few questions, if that's all right.' Her tone is matter-of-fact.

The floor sways, and I reach a hand to the wall to steady myself. 'Of course, anything. But shouldn't your team be out looking for the children? They won't find them here.'

The detective glances at the photos in the hall. Amber on the day she started school, the sleeves of her red jumper long on her wrists. Baby Leo, showing his first tooth. Amber, Eddie and Leo on the swings, all three beaming with delight. *Amber will look after the boys.*

When the detective speaks, her tone is more sympathetic. 'It's standard procedure to search the home. I know this must be difficult, but we need to ascertain exactly what happened. We have spoken to your husband in Paris. He confirmed that he did not authorise Christina Lee to collect your children from school.'

I nod. There's a lump in my throat and I can't speak. Sam should be with me, answering their questions.

PC Miller interrupts. 'I understand Christina Lee was staying with you? Which was her room?'

'The study,' I point to the door. 'But she's taken all her things.'

'Your husband was about to board the Eurostar when we spoke. He told us he is due home around six – is that correct?' Detective Collins asks.

I nod, leading her into the kitchen and offering her a seat. Sam called me after the police rang him. He was on the train to Calais and he'd switched his phone back on. He'd been shocked. Angry. He denied asking Christina to pick up the children. I could barely bring myself to speak to him. I was in shock, disgusted with him after Mazza's revelations.

'Would you ... like some tea?' I look at the kettle, innate politeness kicking in.

She shakes her head. 'Maybe later. I'm sure you want to get started.' She opens a notebook and puts her phone on the table, setting it to record. 'I hope you don't mind.'

I shake my head.

She lists the date, time, address and our names into the phone. 'Mrs Callahan, I understand you're the main caregiver to your children? And your childminder, Christina Lee, is a friend who was staying with you?'

'You can call me Jade. Yes. I'm at home with the children.' I explain about Christina needing a room and how I needed childcare.

She asks the children's names and ages and a brief description of each. And then, 'Mrs Callahan, if you could tell me exactly what happened when you discovered your children to be missing?'

I go over what happened when I went to pick the kids up at home time. About what the office receptionist said. About the note.

She assures me that they would be speaking to the school, interviewing the staff and any parents who were around.

'And just to be clear, you hadn't planned any holiday with grandparents?' She pauses scribbling.

'No, of course not. I can't believe they let the children out early like that, without actually speaking to myself or Sam.' I'm furious. The school had been easily fooled.

She frowned. 'I guess they didn't question the note.'

'My husband's note. I was fooled too. Because I thought they were together.'

I explain again about Sunday night. Finding Sam and Christina together. How I left the house when I couldn't get them to leave. How I'd stayed in a Premier Inn.

'And what did you do when you left the school?' She's writing more notes. *Was she commenting on how stupid I'd been?*

282

'I came home in case they were here. They weren't. I searched the house and noticed some of the kids' clothes were missing. Their overnight cases. Sam's case was missing too. All Christina's stuff was gone. I assumed they'd gone to Devon together. I called 999, but you refused to help. You called it . . . a domestic dispute. My children could be home now!' I shouted.

She stops scribbling. 'I'm so sorry, Mrs Callahan.' There's a steely tone in her voice, not at all apologetic. 'We were working with the information you provided. You informed us that your husband had taken them on holiday. You believed Christina Lee was acting on your husband's instructions.'

Blood floods to my face. Her face stays neutral, but it's obvious what she's thinking. The mistake was mine. If only I'd realised the note was fake, they'd have treated it as an abduction straightaway. They'd have started the search immediately, perhaps even found them by now.

We've lost valuable hours. Christina and the kids could be anywhere.

Chapter Forty-Four

Christina

Then

Christina didn't recognise her own reflection in the tinted mirrors lining the dance floor. The striped stockings and the lacy minidress were tartier than she'd normally go for. So was the thick black eyeliner and dark purple lipstick Jade had plastered on their faces.

Jade had bought tickets to the annual Halloween Ball, and insisted Christina went with her, when she'd rather have stayed at home in their New Town flat, working on her essay or revising. Jade had made so much effort, even finding them matching outfits. She couldn't refuse to go.

Jade pulled her hand. 'Come on – let's dance.'

Christina had learned to let Jade drag her onto the dance floor and not worry about people staring. The first few minutes were the most excruciating, then Jade would find other friends to dance with and Christina could melt into the edges. While she watched the crowd, she ran through the principles of binary fission for next week's test, sipping slowly on her lemonade, making it last as long as possible so she wouldn't be forced to down shots.

'Boogie Wonderland' blared from the sound system. 'You have to dance to this.' Jade grabbed Christina's hand and bounced. Damp bodies pressed against her. She didn't want to think about the bacteria from their sweat that could land on her and start multiplying.

Jade spoke in her ear, but the music was too loud. 'What?' she yelled.

'Tom's!' Jade shouted. The music quietened as the next track started. Christina heard her this time. 'I'm going back to Tom's.'

'Oh. OK.' She smiled, relieved they were leaving.

But Jade pressed her back. 'You stay, it's early. There are tons of medics here. I'll get Izzie and Eleanor to keep an eye on you.'

Christina nodded. She rarely socialised with Izzie and Eleanor without Jade. As for the other medics, sharing lectures and seminars hadn't made them friends. The only friend she needed was Jade.

'Are you sure it's not too soon for you to be going to his place?' Christina asked.

Jade laughed. 'We're not getting married or anything. It's just a shag. At least I hope so.'

'Have you . . .?'

'Yes, don't worry – I bought condoms in the loos. You're OK, aren't you? Want me to book you a cab for later?'

'No. It's fine. I'll walk home.'

Abba's 'Dancing Queen' came on. They'd been dancing to it at the flat, getting ready.

'I love this!' Jade grabbed Christina and twirled. Tom appeared with Jade's coat, and they bopped up and down together. Christina's bones felt too stiff to bop.

Jade yelled. 'We're going. Wish me luck.' She winked. 'See you tomorrow. Late.' She moved towards Izzie and Eleanor, shouted something in their ears. Telling them to look after her, probably. Christina squirmed. It was so embarrassing, to be treated like a child.

Eleanor and Izzie waved Christina over, but she shook her head and threaded her way back to the dance floor. She'd prove she was having a good time. She didn't want anyone feeling sorry for her. It worked. Eleanor and Izzie only hovered round her for a while. Soon, Izzie disappeared to the bar for drinks, Eleanor to the loos and Christina saw her being waylaid by a friend.

Christina decided to leave. Eleanor and Izzie wouldn't miss her, and she didn't mind being in the flat on her own. She'd put on some classical music, have a bath.

Then she saw him. The guy from the library. The one she'd fancied for ages.

You couldn't miss him. He had that indefinable something, the charisma that drew people, like a magnet drew iron shavings. His hair grew to his collar, curling at the ends and sometimes he tied it back with a scrunchy. The trend for long hair was outdated now it was the noughties, but he didn't seem to care.

He was older – Christina would guess a couple of years above them – with the confidence that came with it. She'd noticed him from George Square library. He often had his arms round a pretty, dark-haired girl, who Christina presumed was his girlfriend, but she wasn't with him now.

As Christina watched him, the hairs on her arms raised. The public-school crowd surrounded him and Christina recognised Izzie's cousins, Digby and Mungo. She'd seen them once or twice since the holiday by the loch, but they were usually surrounded by the other ex-public-school kids and didn't acknowledge her. She shrank to the back, listening to the thump of the music and their braying shouts. An overconfident student bumped into her, slopping cold lager over her. 'Whoops!'

'Hey, Tristan, apologise to the lady.' It was him. Christina's heart started to thud.

'Sorry!' grinned Tristan and danced away.

'Excuse my friend,' he grinned. 'No manners. Can we help mop you up?'

'I'm fine,' Christina croaked. She couldn't believe he was speaking to her.

He picked up a paper serviette and she held her breath while he dabbed at her dress. 'Can I get you a drink? Make up for my mate's rudeness?'

She was about to shake her head, but out of the corner of her eye she could see Izzie looking concerned at her. Instead, she smiled at him and nodded. 'L-lemonade – thanks.'

'Vodka lemonade?'

She opened her mouth to say, 'Just lemonade,' but he'd already started making his way to the bar.

Guys like him never waited long to be served. A few minutes later, he was back, thrusting a plastic cup into Christina's hand, slurping from a fresh pint. The Rolling Stones came on and he hip-swivelled at Christina. She sipped her drink, and moved her hips too, the vodka relaxing her. Soon, she was bopping.

'Love the seventies!' he roared at her.

'Celebrate!' sang Kool & The Gang.

Christina took Jade's advice to go with the flow. His friends were buying rounds and Christina was always included. She drank another vodka lemonade. Shots of tequila. Somehow, she became part of the braying group of rugby players and rowers and blondes called Fi and Flo and Amelia, all pink-faced with posh accents.

For once, she allowed herself to relax, let her hair down. Party.

And he never left Christina's side. The rugby players and rowers drank all night. And the drunker they got, the drunker Christina got too. She was on a high. Excited to be noticed by him. Part of his crowd. Seen.

At 6 a.m. the music stopped and the lights came on, the bouncers decanting them into the darkness.

The night was over, but Christina didn't want it to end.

Tristan, Digby and Mungo had knocked back bottles of tequila and gallons of beer. They could hardly stand, and had to go off one by one to piss, urine splashing, steaming, onto the cobbles.

Maybe it was the fresh air, but the vodka seemed to hit Christina all at once. She stumbled towards the Playfair steps.

'Want to share a cab?' he asked, still by her side.

'I'm not far,' she replied. 'I can walk.'

He walked with her.

It was dark, although the birds were tweeting, and the cobbled streets were slippery with dew. Christina clung to his arm all the way home. And somewhere along Dundas Street, to her excitement, she found her hand in his. Her fingers were numb with cold but in the clasp of his hot hand, they were warming up. His thumb drew tiny circles on her palm. His heat transferred to her skin, travelling up her arm and through her whole body. Her nerve-endings tingled. It was like her very consciousness had moved into her hand. They shuffled up the steps to her flat. She only let go of his hand to fumble for her keys, zipped up as usual for extra safety, in an inner pocket of her handbag.

He pulled her towards him, and his lips touched hers in a clumsy kiss. His mouth tasted of whisky and cigarettes. But it was magic. Fireworks. All the enchantment she could wish for. Every inch of her skin fizzed with pleasure. She didn't feel the draught of cold as he pulled her coat towards him, she didn't feel the soft fingers of rain drenching her hair. They giggled as her keys slipped from her grasp and jingled onto the stone steps. She kneeled, picked them up and soon the front door was open.

His face was a silent question, and she grabbed his hand and pulled him into the hallway. His tongue thrust into her mouth, making her jump. She nearly bit down with shock as his palms cupped her face and drew her even closer. But after a while she got used to it. It felt weird but fine. She held her mouth open, trying to get used to the in and out of it.

They clattered along the hall, falling into the living room and onto the sofa, not pausing from the kiss.

The floor tilted as the alcohol kicked in. She couldn't quite believe it. The cute guy from the library was here, in her flat.

He was so drunk he could hardly stand but he was here.

This was the kind of thing Jade would do. What girls do after a night out with a guy. Jade and Tom would be snogging right now.

Just like Christina.

Chapter Forty-Five

Jade

'Why would Christina Lee want to take your children? Why do you think she forged that note? You say you found her with your husband. How long had this – affair been going on? Did you ask them?' The detective's gaze fixes on me, her pen ready to jot down my answers.

My neck prickles and my face burns. I can't bear to talk about it. 'I don't know.' My voice is a whisper. I think about how he assaulted Mazza. Disgust constricts my throat.

'Take a minute, Jade. Deep breath. This must be upsetting.' Her voice isn't unkind.

'I should have stayed with the children. But Sam refused to go. Christina locked herself in her room. I couldn't stay here with—with them as if nothing had happened. So I—I left.' Even as I say the words, I rail at myself. I must have gone temporarily insane to leave my children. Leave them with Sam and her – Christina – still in the house. I feel like a fool. 'It was a stupid thing to do. But – I was so angry.' My voice shakes. 'He should have been the one to leave. Sam, my husband, but do you know what the fucker said? He ... He said he paid the mortgage, it was his house. He refused to leave.' I clench and unclench my fingers. 'I just *couldn't* stay. I felt like . . . I was going to explode.'

I'd felt betrayed. Angry. Simple emotions. Now, after speaking to Mazza, everything felt far worse.

Detective Collins nods, face neutral. 'A difficult situation. But why didn't you take the children with you?'

'I've been asking myself the same question. If only I had. But they were asleep. I didn't want to wake them. I was in such a state, and I honestly never thought Sam would let any harm come to them. I told him to take them to school on Monday, and I'd pick them up at the end of the day. I just needed to get away.'

'Where did you go?' Her voice is gentle. Has she experienced that level of betrayal? How can she know what it's like?

'I drove to my mum's house. But – I couldn't get out of the car.'

She makes a note. 'Why not?'

'My mum is very . . . critical. I knew she'd blame me. So I booked into a Premier Inn. Oh God,' I howl. 'Bloody Christina. Fucking bitch. First my husband. Now my kids.'

'And you're certain your husband isn't involved?'

'Didn't you say you spoke to him?' I snap. 'You said he'd be back after six. Let's hear what he has to say.'

She pours me a glass of water. The kindness of the gesture makes my tears flow for real. I can't stop crying as fear for the children overwhelms me.

When the worst is over, the detective passes me tissues. 'I just have a few more questions, if you don't mind,' she says gently. 'Can you tell me about your friendship with Christina Lee before this happened? How long have you known each other?'

'We were flatmates at university in Edinburgh, nearly twenty years ago. We lived together in halls, and then we shared a flat.'

'And you've had a good relationship all these years?'

'Well, we lost touch for a while. She . . . she took a break from uni, and I had to find another flatmate.' We were best friends once. *How could she have done this to me?*

'Why did she take a break?'

I haven't told anyone Christina's secret. But it's time I did. 'In second year, we rented a flat together. In January she had a medical emergency – I think it was a miscarriage. The night it happened, I was out. An ambulance took her to hospital.'

I'd come back to find blood all over the bathroom floor. I shudder, thinking of it now. I knew she must have miscarried. What else could have happened? I hadn't been able to clean the blood out of the rug. I'd bought a new one and thrown the old one away.

'And once she moved out, did you stay in touch?'

'I tried to call her a couple of times, but no one answered.' The usual guilt grips me. I should have tried harder. 'How has this anything to do with my children?'

'We need to establish what Christina's motive might be for taking them. What she might be planning. You say she had a miscarriage? Does she have her own children now?'

'No. She doesn't have children. Do you think she's taken mine – because she can't have her own? Do people really do that?'

The detective shakes her head. 'I can't comment on that.'

'The miscarriage – it must have been an awful thing to go through on her own. Traumatic.' She says nothing but I feel her judgement. Why hadn't I been there to help that night? *What kind of friend am I?*

'So, how did you reconnect, after all these years?'

I explain about meeting up with Christina on Instagram.

292

How her mum had thrown her out and how it had made sense to give her a room in return for childcare.

'How was she with the children? Did she show any sign that she might . . .?'

'That she might want to steal them? Of course not. I would hardly have asked her to look after them.'

Had I been too trusting? I think back to the marble incentive scheme. *Did she think she was a better carer for the children than I was?*

The detective gazes at me. 'You had no doubts about her? No concerns that your children could be in danger?'

'Not at first. Not until Eddie had an allergic reaction – he suffers from anaphylaxis. Christina knew he was allergic to fish, but she put curry paste with fish sauce on the chicken, and Eddie . . . we had to call an ambulance. She said it was a genuine mistake but . . .' I put my head in my hands. The thought of Eddie's face going blue fills me with fear. Both his EpiPens and the bottle of Cetirizine are missing. *Surely that's a sign she doesn't want to hurt him?*

'After that happened – did you suspect she might want to hurt them?'

'I wanted her to go. I asked Sam to tell her to leave. But he wouldn't. Said she could stay and help me.' *And now I know why.*

'Do you have any idea where she could have gone?'

I shake my head. 'Back to Scotland? She said she'd separated from her husband.'

'Why was she separated?'

I shrug. 'She never wanted to talk about it. I didn't want to intrude.' The truth was, I hadn't bothered to find out what had happened. I never managed to find the time to ask her even though I knew I should. I didn't have the emotional energy to give her, despite all the ways she'd helped me.

Talking to the detective makes me feel like a terrible friend. Christina owes me no loyalty. I've done nothing for her.

But that's no excuse for what she's doing to my family.

I think back over the past couple of weeks. Christina planting seeds of doubt between Sam and me. She encouraged him to go to his parents' holiday home even though I didn't agree to it. What if she gave Eddie the curry paste on purpose? Did she intend to hurt him? Make me feel the loss of losing a child? Or was it just to get rid of me for a couple of nights, so she could move in on my husband? And then, on Monday, she'd forged the note, and I believed she'd taken the children for Sam.

Detective Collins scribbles on her pad.

I blow my nose and wipe away the tears that keep streaming. I need to stay strong if we're going to find the children.

'Can I just ask, up until the argument on Sunday night when you found your husband with Ms Lee, what was your relationship like with your husband?'

I flinch, thinking about what Mazza told me. *Do I know Sam at all?*

'I thought it was fine.' I decide I need to speak to Sam before I say anything about Mazza. 'He was . . . distracted by work. His agency was pitching for new business. They lost a lot of clients. With the recession, often the first thing to go is the advertising budget.' I parrot my headhunter's excuses. 'Things weren't brilliant. But I didn't suspect anything like – this . . . ' I spit out the words.

She stares at her notebook. 'I'm sorry but I have to ask this,

Jade. You ... you haven't ... formed any attachments, friend-ships with any other men?'

'What?' Disbelief makes me laugh. 'Of course not!'

She gazes at me sharply. 'You're sure?'

'Er ... I think I'd know.' Should I say something about Anthony? He used to have a crush, but – no. There's nothing between us.

She turns off the recording. 'Right, we'll go and talk to the school, and we'll knock on doors and ask neighbours if they've seen anything. We'll be checking local CCTV at the stations and main roads. We'll need photos of the children and Christina and if possible, details of what they were wearing. We are going to do everything we can to find your children, Jade. Don't worry. Oh, and we'll need items of their clothing. And some-thing with their DNA on it. A toothbrush is the easiest.'

DNA. Those letters fill me with horror.

'Three children can't have gone far without someone seeing them, right?' I say, more to reassure myself.

She nods. 'You're right. We'll do our best to find them. Do you have her husband's contact details?'

'I have her mum's address and number but not her husband's. I'm sorry – I don't know much about him.' I dig out my old address book and give her Christina's mum's address.

'We'll pay her mother a visit after the school. Are there any neighbours or parents from school that she's become friendly with since she's been living here? Anyone else we can contact to see if they've heard from her?'

I give the officer Kate's number. 'Is there anything else I can do? I'm going crazy here.'

295

'Constable Miller will type up your statement and a family liaison officer will be round soon. They will keep you up to date with our investigation. If you'd like to do a public appeal, we'll arrange it. Meanwhile, is there anyone you can call to support you until your husband returns? A family member maybe?'

'I'll be fine, I have some friends I could call.' I'll call Kate, not my mum.

One of the police team searching the house comes in and gives the detective a plastic bag with something in it.

'What is it?' I ask.

'This was found in the study, down the side of the sofa,' he says.

'What is it, detective?' I repeat. 'Please tell me.'

She holds the bag out to me. Inside is an empty blister packet. 'Temazepam. Prescribed for insomnia. They're sleeping tablets.'

Chapter Forty-Six

Amber

We're back on the motorway. We are past Manchester when the piano music goes all fuzzy and cuts out.

The boys wake, but they're given bottles of juice and they fall asleep again. I don't drink mine. I'm sure there's something in it. In the last Scarlett book, the baddie mashes up sleeping pills and drugs Scarlett's milk. Is that what's happening to the boys? Normally, Eddie'd be annoying me, chatting on and on, making me play I Spy.

Leo always sleeps in the car, but not this much.

I close my eyes, leaving a teeny tiny gap so I can see the blue signs. We'll have to stop to get petrol. How long does a tank of petrol last? How many miles? Eddie would know.

I have to be ready. To get help. Or to escape.

I'm drifting off to sleep, even though I didn't drink the juice. Outside, it's getting darker. We've been driving for hours.

Then I see a sign. *Welcome to Scotland.*

Scotland! That's another country. Miles and miles away from our house.

My eyes are full of tears and a dribble runs out of my nose.

The air in the car is stuffy and the clouds outside are grey. It's been raining.

The indicator ticks and we turn off the motorway. The car slows down. On the signs are strange town names like Kirkcaldy and other places I've never heard of. A sign says: *City Centre*. The last road sign said, *Edinburgh 4*. Is that where we are?

'Amber,' a voice says. 'I know you're not asleep. The holiday home is far away. So I've booked a hotel for tonight. I need you to help me with the boys. You're the oldest. Eddie and Leo look up to you. I hope you can help without making a fuss. If you do, I'll buy dinner. Pizza. Or burgers and chips. But if you make a fuss like you did in the service stop, I'm afraid you'll go without dinner. The boys will be hungry and cry all night. I'll have to take steps to make you quiet. I'll have to give you the sleepy hanky again. Amber, did you hear me? Answer me.'

I keep my eyes shut. I don't want to agree.

'I know you can hear me. Or do you want to sleep all night instead?' A pause. 'Will you help?'

'Yes,' I mutter.

'What did you say? Louder, please. I can't hear you.'

'Yes,' I say, loudly.

'You'll help?'

'Yes, I'll help.'

'Good. You can wake the boys when we stop.'

The car stops in an underground car park. I have to shout at Leo and Eddie and shake them for ages before they wake up.

Leo, eyes closed, wails, 'I'm hungry!'

'Where are we?' asks a sleepy Eddie.

'We're stopping for dinner. What does everyone want? Pizza or burgers?'

'Burger, but no cheese,' says Eddie.

'Want chips!' shouts Leo.

'All right. Burger and chips for children who walk nicely into the hotel.'

'Don't want to walk,' whines Leo. 'Want carry.'

My tummy rumbles. I'm hungry and weak. I want to cry. I will try and escape but not until after we've eaten. I'll save my energy.

I help push Leo in his buggy. We go up in a lift and get out at the second floor. We walk down a corridor to a door. There's no one in the lift or in the car park.

We reach a door. There's three stars on a sign that says 'Braeside Hotel. Bed and Breakfast'.

We ring the bell. A grey-haired man with a pink face answers the door. *Can I tell him we've been kidnapped?*

'Hello, are you Mr Laird? I rang earlier and booked a family room.'

Agent Scarlett is good at noticing details. There's Scottish tartan on the walls and there are carved wooden stags' heads and pictures of thistles in wooden frames.

'Hello there, your name is Callahan, isn't it? Come this way – do you need help? Oh, I see you have young helpers, how wonderful.' He smiles at me and Eddie but he's looking at Leo's sippy cup like it's disgusting. *He won't believe me.*

He leads us down the hall and up a flight of stairs. Eddie helps me carry Leo's buggy. 'Come this way – here's the key card. Little bit of technology at Braeside.' He speaks with a singsong voice. Scottish.

Once Eddie made Mum read *The Last Wolf* by Michael Morpurgo in a Scottish accent because Mum said she used to live in Scotland. And Eddie wouldn't believe her until she did the accent.

The story's about a boy who escapes to America on a ship, and the wolf who sneaks on the ship to protect him.

There are no wolves here with me, Eddie and Leo.

I will have to be the wolf.

Chapter Forty-Seven

Jade

Christina's been drugging me. No wonder I've been feeling so horrendous lately. I thought it was exhaustion, from those sleepless nights at the hospital. I suspected I'd picked up a bug that made my bones ache. But no. She's been drugging me with sleeping pills.

At 3 p.m., the detective phones with more news. Christina's mum, Mrs Lee, has given them the address of Michael Anderson. But it turns out he and Christina aren't married. He's not her ex-husband. Not her husband at all, the detective tells me.

'I guess you don't have to be married to be in a relationship,' I say. It doesn't surprise me Christina lied about her divorce. *What else has she lied about?*

'No, you don't understand.' Detective Collins' tone is clipped. 'Michael Anderson denies he was ever in a relationship with Christina Lee. He was her tutor at medical school. It seems she developed an unhealthy obsession with him. In fact, she was cautioned for stalking and harassment twelve years ago.'

Why did Christina invent her relationship? I remember how she'd talked about finding my family photos on Instagram. How warm and homey my house was. *She joked she sounded like a stalker.*

My throat closes with fear. Why did she target my family, take my children? *What is she planning to do to them?*

Detective Collins is still talking. 'Jade – are you there?'

'Yes,' I reply faintly. *I'm going to throw up.*

'I'm afraid there's more.' She sounds grave. 'Maybe you'd better sit down.'

I grasp for a chair and sit. 'What is it?'

'We contacted the General Medical Council to find out where she was last employed. Christina Lee was involved in a negligence case at the Patterson Memorial Hospital just outside of Fife. A baby died because she made the wrong diagnosis. I'm afraid she's been suspended, pending investigation.'

'What?' The blood rushes in my ears. The detective's voice seems to be coming from miles away. Then the floor rushes towards me and I'm retching.

The Family Liaison Officer, Rashmi Patel, arrives an hour later. She busies herself making tea for the forensic team who are still here. The smell of bleach in the kitchen triggered them to do a full Luminol inspection of the house. Rashmi explains that Luminol is used to detect blood. I tell them about Christina's paranoia about germs, but she's quick to say it's a precaution, to rule things out. So far, no significant amount of blood has been found but even the thought of it fills me with horror.

Rashmi's also here to help with an appeal. 'Jade, when we do the public appeal, it might be useful if you persuade Mrs Lee to join you. She could offer her love and support, and ask her daughter to turn herself in.'

She obviously doesn't know Mrs Lee. Love and support? She's more likely to scold Christina for shaming their family. But I agree. 'Yes, I'll contact her. I'll try and get her to help us.'

In my heart, I doubt it will make a difference. Christina doesn't get on with her mother. Even if she sees her appeal, why would she listen to her? But if the police think it might help, I have to try.

Sam calls me from the Eurostar.

'What's happening, Jade? Have they found them?'

'No.' I want to scream at him, but instead I ask, 'Why was your phone turned off? If we'd known Christina forged the note . . .'

'I'm sorry, I'm so sorry. But I told you all along I didn't do anything wrong. That evil bitch set me up. Why didn't you believe me?'

Why should I believe him now, after what Mazza told me? He might not have initiated the affair with Christina, but how can he claim he was innocent? *I saw them!*

I can barely stomach the sound of his voice. But right now, the children are all that matter. I need him to cooperate. 'We need to do an appeal when you get back. I'm going to speak to Mrs Lee, see if she'll do it with us.'

'Does she know where Christina could have taken them?'

'Just get home, Sam. We can talk then.'

I decide to appeal to Mrs Lee face to face. Surely she'll help if I speak to her in person, rather than on the phone? I tell Rashmi my plan and she offers to come with me. But I can't bear her to watch me, so I drive there on my own.

Mrs Lee lives in Bounds Green, a twenty-minute drive on the North Circular. The suburban 1960s block of flats looks more run-down than I remember. The lawn is overgrown and the outer door's been left ajar. I let myself in and climb to the first floor. I bang on the door, and it opens a crack, the chain still on. Mrs Lee peers out.

'Auntie Lee?' I say. 'It's Jade – Jade Chan. Christina's friend.'

'Yes?' she croaks. 'What do you want?'

'Can I come in?'

The door shuts but seconds later she opens it fully, shuffling aside to let me in. Mrs Lee has aged. Her hair is completely white, permed in tight curls, as was fashionable in Hong Kong years ago. Her plastic-framed glasses are too big for her thin, lined face.

'Jade Chan.' Her lips are pressed tightly. If she's surprised to see me, she doesn't show it. I could be a stranger, not her daughter's once-best friend. I take my shoes off and she leads me down the narrow hall. My feet slide on the varnished parquet. The living room hasn't changed in twenty years. The beige carpets are worn thin, and the cream leather sofas are covered in clear plastic and draped with crocheted doilies. She makes no attempt to make me feel welcome.

The remote controls are covered in clingfilm. To a western eye this might look like an extreme case of OCD, but I know from family trips to Malaysia that it's not unusual for people in Asia to take cleanliness too far. Even before the pandemic, people like Mrs Lee were afraid of germs.

'What do you want?' Mrs Lee blinks at me. Her eyes are dry. There are no tears for her daughter or for me or my children. Is she good at hiding her worries or does she not care?

'Christina – she is a sensible girl. Clever. A doctor. You – you say you're her friend – but you go to police? Why not call her? Find out what happened from her?'

'I have been calling. Her mobile's turned off. She picked up my children from school without my permission, and we don't know where she is. I *had* to call the police.'

'Christina – your good friend – she lives in your house. She is taking care of your children. Naturally she will pick your children up from school.' Her eyes narrow, accusing me, putting me in the wrong.

I shake my head. 'I'm sorry, Auntie Lee. She forged a note that said they were going on holiday. She was lying. Please tell me, have you seen Christina in the last forty-eight hours?'

She crosses her arms over her chest. 'No. I have not. Maybe she gone back to Michael. Gone back to Scotland.'

'I'm sorry,' I say, gently. 'The police told me Christina isn't married to Michael Anderson.'

'I know. They separate. Soon to divorce.'

I tell her what the police told me. That Christina and Michael were never together. That Christina's been suspended by the hospital. That she's under investigation for malpractice.

Her face turns grey and she starts shaking. 'What? I don't believe you.'

'I'm afraid it's true. You can ask the police yourself.'

She sits in shock. A tear slides down her cheek.

'Have you any idea where she could be?'

She goes to a drawer, takes out an address book and shows me. 'I have the address. I send her Christmas card. To Christina and Michael.'

'I believe that's Michael Anderson's address. Not Christina's.'

'What do you mean?' She looks confused and my heart breaks for her.

'Mrs Lee, I'm so sorry. We're going to make a public appeal, on the news. In case anyone has seen anything. In case Christina watches it. I wondered – the police asked – if you would join us?'

Now she glares at me. 'Appeal? So they can arrest my daughter? So they can tell everyone these . . . these lies! She was your good friend. You let her down. Why did you come here? Let the police do their job. Please. Get out of my house.'

She advances on me and even though she's barely five foot, I jump back at the force of her anger. 'OK, OK. I'm going.' I make my way to the hall.

While I slip on my shoes, she opens the door, spitting out her words. 'You are a selfish girl. Your parents spoil you. I wish my daughter never met you. I should have stayed in Hong Kong, not come to UK. You – you are no friend to my daughter. Where were you when Christina needed you? When she stressed out at medical school, did you call her? Say "Come come, let's watch movie or go shopping." No. Never. Christina stay at your house to help you. She look after your children. How you repay her? She want to take children on holiday. But you call police.' She continues the tirade in Cantonese. I can't understand the words, but I know she's cursing me.

Tears spill out of my eyes. 'I tried my best to be a friend to Christina. I *was* there for her when we were students. She found out she was pregnant, and she went through hell, terrified of letting you down. But she didn't want a – a termination. She thought you would force her to have one.'

'What do you know? She knew what was good for her, for her future. But you. You use her. When you need a friend to help, she was there. But you – you never there for her. As soon as you are happy with your boyfriend. Pah – gone! You should be ashamed. You give her wrong advice. My daughter is not like you – good for nothing. Unfilial. She regret every day that she listen to you. Good friend? You are no friend to her.' She shakes her fist at me.

I run into the hallway and down the stairs. I can't get out of there fast enough. Tears stream down my face.

Christina and I were friends once. But her mum is right. I haven't been a friend to Christina for a long time. The night of the Halloween Ball, I left her in a club on her own. I know something happened to her that night. Something that ended in her getting pregnant. I'd advised her as best I could. She hadn't wanted to go ahead with an abortion, despite her parents' pressure. I told her not to listen to them. To follow her heart.

How was I to know how it would end?

Chapter Forty-Eight

Christina

Then

It was New Year's Eve and Jade had dragged Christina to a party at Izzie's in Eyre Crescent. They planned to watch the Hogmanay fireworks from the roof. Jade was in full 1960s make-up, false eyelashes and all, and wore a sequinned mini dress. But Christina couldn't fit into any of her vintage dresses. Her belly had ballooned. She refused to think about why she'd put on so much weight lately. She would shut it away in her brain until after the party. She pulled on her old maroon cords, and the baggiest jumper she could find. Jade was in a rush to see Tom, and just raised her eyebrows at her trousers.

Christina had never celebrated New Year's Eve before. Her brother and her dad would stay up late in the living room, listening to the countdown on the radio, but Ma would always be in bed by midnight. Christmas, Ma took them to church, and they put up a fake tree. They even gave each other useful presents. But the only new year they celebrated was Chinese New Year.

When they arrived at Izzie's, Oasis had killed the dancing in the living room and the party was happening in the kitchen. Jade and Izzie were giggling, tipsy on white wine, but Christina sipped a glass of room temperature gin and tonic. No one had thought to buy ice. Izzie had dished up cheesy pasta to line their stomachs and the taste of garlic and cheese coated her mouth. Christina had only managed a couple of spoonfuls. The smell of cheesy garlic hung heavy in the air.

At five to midnight, they piled up a step ladder onto the roof. But it was freezing, and the fireworks display was tiny, so they trooped back in and turned on the television in time to catch the bagpipes playing 'Auld Lang Syne' from The Mound. Everyone held hands in that weird cross-armed position and sang along. Then everybody was kissing each other and shouting 'Happy New Year'.

Christina squeezed past Jade and Tom snogging, trying not to look at his slobbery lips. If one more person kissed her with their garlic breath, she might throw up.

She topped up her gin and retreated to the bathroom. Maybe she should run a hot bath.

She might be a scientist, a medic, but she was desperate enough to believe in old wives' tales. If only the dull ache in her back would magically turn into period pain. But her period stubbornly stayed two months late.

She peed and examined her underwear. Was that a spot of dried blood? Last month she'd found a smear of blood on her knickers that could have been a very light period. It could be stress stopping it. She closed her eyes and willed her period to start.

Her heart hammered so hard it filled her ears. No. That was someone banging on the bathroom door.

She flushed the toilet, washed her hands, opened the door.

Jade swept in. 'Christina! There you are! Are you OK?' She grabbed her hand, not letting her leave the bathroom. She locked the door, and sat and peed, intent on one of her confidences. 'What do you think of Tom? I think I'm in love.' She couldn't find the loo roll, so Christina passed it to her. 'Oh my God, are you OK?' She jumped up, pulling up her tights and flung an arm around her, bracelets jangling. 'Christina, what is it?'

Christina pulled away, her face wet with tears.

'Sorry – I'll wash my hands, don't worry.' Jade hurried to the sink and ran her hands under the tap. 'What's wrong?'

'Nothing,' Christina mumbled. 'Too much gin.' And then quickly, like an afterthought, 'I haven't had my period in two months.'

Jade washed her hands with soap. She checked her eyeliner and re-did her lipstick in the mirror.

Had she even heard her? Christina repeated, louder this time, 'I said, I haven't had a period in two months.'

Jade looked round, as if surprised she was still there. 'I heard you. But it must be stress, right? Have you been eating properly? I mean, it can't be because . . .' She paused, swaying. Then she focused on Christina's face. Finally, she registered what Christina meant. 'Oh my God, you've . . . really? Who? I didn't know . . .' She reached out a hand, steadied herself on the sink. 'OK. Look.' She snapped into efficient mode. 'You need to do a pregnancy test. I've got one at home – I had a scare last month and bought extra. Come on. Let's go back to ours.'

Christina felt seen for the first time that night. She attempted to protest. 'But. But . . . what about Tom?'

'Oh, he'll be too pissed to be any use.' Jade smiled and linked her arm with hers. 'Come on. Let's get out of here.'

Chapter Forty-Nine

Jade

It's nearly seven when the key turns in the front door, and I hear Sam's familiar tread. I hurry to the hall. He looks exhausted, his suit crumpled, forehead creased with worry.

'Still no sign of them?' His voice breaks, and he moves towards me. Disgust curls in my gut and I step back. I can't forget his lies. The vision of him half-naked with Christina. Mazza's story about him groping her.

He grabs my arm and pulls me towards him. 'Jade, please.'

I hammer my fists on his chest. 'This is your fault!' My voice is fierce but low. I'm aware of Rashmi, in the next room. 'If anything happens to my babies . . .' Sam takes the blows. His eyes are rimmed with red like he's been crying. I don't care.

Eventually, his hands circle my wrists, holding me away.

'Let go of me. Fuck off.' Stress makes me hysterical.

'No,' he says. 'I refuse to take all the blame. Nothing happened with Christina on Sunday. She faked the entire scene. She must have drugged my whisky. I fell asleep and when I woke up – well – you were there.'

She drugged him. Just as she'd drugged me.

'Are you really saying it's my fault because I didn't believe you?' I ground out.

He sighs. 'You can play the blame game if you want, Jade, but we need to focus on the children.' Before I can mention Mazza, he turns and strides into the kitchen. I follow.

Rashmi's there and she introduces herself to Sam, explaining how she's here to support us, and keep us updated with the investigation. Her manner is more sympathetic than Detective Collins' but I know we're being observed. How much of our exchange in the hall did she hear? I've watched enough TV police dramas to know she'll be listening, in case we do anything suspicious. *When children disappear, the first suspects are the parents.*

Sam listens to her explanation, his cobalt eyes crinkling at the corners. 'We appreciate how you're helping us to find our children.' He needs to charm any woman he talks to. It's like a reflex. *How did I not realise?* 'I guess you heard what happened? How the crazy babysitter took our kids?'

'I've read the report. I can assure you we're doing our best to find them.' Rashmi's eyes are warm with sympathy. She squeezes his arm gently. She might be a police officer, but she's not immune to Sam's 'little boy lost' act, even if his smile is currently a pale shadow of its usual self.

His behaviour turns my stomach, but I can't quite bring up what Mazza told me. Not in front of Rashmi. Not yet.

'Mr Callahan . . .'

'Sam, please.' A brief smile.

'Sam . . . Now you're back, can we talk about the appeal?' Rashmi asks.

'Of course, we'll do anything. Anything to help find them.'

The lines at the corner of his eyes make him look like he's smiling, despite the stress.

'We need to flood social media – all platforms,' she says. 'Plus, we'd like to film a public appeal for the local news. We need to get the word out there. A woman with three children might be a common sight, but we will find them.'

Sam nods, flexing his fingers. 'I can help with the appeal. My staff can handle social media – someone will have seen something. She could have travelled by tube, or bus—'

'Melinda's been helping to get the word out,' I add quickly. 'She's posted on Facebook and tweeted to all her followers.' As soon as I'd spoken to Kate, she'd suggested how Melinda could help. The mums had been a real support to me.

He frowns. 'Melinda? What makes her the social media expert?'

'You weren't here. She offered to help.' An accusatory tone creeps into my voice. 'Her blog and Instagram have a huge following.'

His brief smile is for Rashmi's benefit. 'Of course, I'm grateful to Melinda. But now I'm back, I can handle it.'

He wants to control the appeal. He likes to be in charge. 'Surely the more noise the better. You could both put the word out,' I say.

'That's great.' Rashmi squeezes my arm. 'I'll let DS Collins know. We can go over what to say before the camera crew get here.'

A light glares into my eyes while I sit on the sofa next to Sam. I'm clutching Leo's Blue Bear, a bead of sweat trickling down my neck. The curtains are drawn but we can hear the chatter and laughter of the journalists gathered outside. Lily Reeves, the local news presenter, has just arrived, and her heavy perfume makes me nauseous.

Sam shifts next to me, restless and on edge. DS Collins had interviewed him alone. Before I had a chance to ask him what she said, the camera crew had invaded our living room.

We should be holding hands. But I can't help shrinking from him. I knead my fingers into Blue Bear's soft fur instead.

The cameras start to roll, and I catch a few words from the presenter's introduction. 'Missing children', 'parents', 'Jade and Sam Callahan'. Lily Reeves holds the mic out to me. 'Mrs Callahan? Jade? What would you like to say to Christina Lee?'

I open my mouth, but my throat has seized up. Sam reaches over and squeezes my hand. I resist the urge to snatch it away. I force the words out, my voice strained and unfamiliar.

'Christina, if you're watching this. Please. I beg you. Bring our children back safely. We won't be angry. I know you—you care for them as much as we do. But they need us.' My voice breaks. I sob. '*We* need them.' I swipe at my eyes and whisper, 'Please, don't make them pay for our mistakes. I haven't always been the best friend. I don't blame you for—for wanting to hurt me. But I'm worried about you. You don't want to do this. Please.' Tears stream down my face. I sense Sam, bunching a fist in his palm. 'Amber, Eddie, Leo – be good for Auntie Christina. Mummy and Daddy love you very much. We'll see each other soon, my darlings. I love you.' I kiss my fingers and hold them to the camera, wishing I could kiss my babies for real. Sobs overwhelm me.

The microphone moves to Sam. He clears his throat. His voice is thick, and a pulse ticks at his temple. 'I'd like to thank

315

the police team who are helping to find our children. And please, if anyone, any member of the public, has seen our children with their babysitter, Christina Lee, please get in touch. Call the number. Email or text. Please. Amber, Eddie and Leo. We love you. Wherever you are – stay safe.'

Detective Collins relays some last words and the phone number to call, before the camera stops rolling. I let out my breath and turn to Sam but he's already standing up. He crosses over to the presenter. He turns on his broken smile and she puts a comforting hand on his arm.

I feel sick. Our children are missing and he's still trying to charm someone. Surely he should be too stressed to flirt? It's as natural to him as breathing. I've always excused it as a symptom of his motherless childhood. But now I see it for what it is.

I need air. I escape to the kitchen and let myself out into the garden.

How can Christina cope with all three kids? Amber will be knotted with anxiety. Eddie will try to be helpful, but Leo is bound to be tired and grizzly. Is she still bribing them with those bloody marbles? With sweets? *How else could she be controlling them?*

The door slides open. It's Sam. He sits next to me, glancing round to check we're alone. 'Are you crazy?' He drops his cultivated image of a father in distress. His voice has an ugly tone. 'This woman, your supposed friend, has taken our children. God knows what she's going to do to them, how she's going to hurt them. And you – you *apologise* to her?' His eyes glitter with rage.

I grind out, 'I'm desperate to see the children again. And I keep wondering: why's she doing this? She needs help.'

He scowls. 'She needs to be locked up. I still can't fathom that you believed her over me. If I find out that this is some kind of . . . set-up to . . . to take the children away from me . . .'

'A set-up? You're the one who encouraged her, flirted with her! Why would I be colluding with her? I'm terrified we'll never see our children again.' I clench my fists thinking of how he'd enjoyed her flattery, the meals she'd cooked.

He glares at me, but the sliding door opens and Rashmi joins us. We both bite down our anger.

'What happens now?' Sam is polite enough, but his easy smile is absent.

'Now we wait.' Her dark eyes are liquid with concern. 'It can take a while. But someone must have seen something. Meanwhile, would you like me to order some takeout? You need to eat. Keep your strength up.'

In the end she orders Indian food from a local takeaway. Sam shovels up the curry and rice, lips shiny with grease. But I can't do more than push the food around my plate.

I make coffee. The caffeine will keep me going, in case the police call with news. Every time Rashmi's phone beeps I jump. By half eleven there's still nothing, and Rashmi finally leaves for the night.

As soon as she's gone, Sam pours himself a whisky. He downs the glass of amber liquid without looking at me. 'I'm shattered. I'm going to bed.'

He strides upstairs and I hear the shower running. A few minutes later our bedroom door slams shut.

I pace the living room, checking the news sites, my email inboxes and social media. I know the police are monitoring them, but I need to do something. I stare at the landline, willing it to ring.

317

It's past midnight, but there's no way I can sleep. I can't lie down in the same bed as Sam. He might be telling the truth about what happened with Christina on Sunday night, but he's not totally innocent. He's been flirting with her for weeks. He says she set him up, intending that I find them naked together. But at the same time, he's been encouraging her. Mazza's revelation about Sam groping her has opened my eyes. I can't excuse him any longer. The creepy way he checks women out. The tactile way he touches their arms, brushes up against them. How he uses his charm to get what he wants.

These days we often hear about the latest sleazebag who's sexually harassed women. I've always wondered about the long-suffering girlfriends and wives. Did they really not know what a creep their man was? Did they make excuses for him?

But I'm not the clueless wife anymore. The thought of Sam making unwelcome advances to young women like Mazza makes the bile rise in my throat. I can't bear to lie in the same bed as him. But the police will be back in the morning. I need to rest.

I go to the study and pull out the sofa bed, making it up with the spare sheet. I lie for a while, trying to relax. The mattress isn't comfortable. There's something sticking into my back. After an hour of tossing and turning, I get up and look.

An object's wedged underneath. I swipe a hand under the mattress and pull out a small photo album, like the ones they used to give you when you got your film developed. I open it, my breath catching in my throat. The faded prints are from the early noughties, and I recognise them instantly. Christina and me in the canteen at Pollack Halls. The two of us dressed in our matching witch outfits in our flat before the Halloween Ball. We look so young.

I turn the page. There's Izzie's aunt's cottage, from our holiday by the loch, grey stone with a steeply pitched roof. There we are, dancing on the shingle beach, waving our arms in the air, I'm holding a bottle of whisky. We look happy. I think back to that summer years ago. After the first dull day, there'd been a mini heatwave. The sun shone, the sky was cerulean blue. The colours have faded on the print, the sky and water merging in a flat expanse of grey.

I put the album in my bag, ready to show the police in the morning. I lie down again, thoughts spinning. I keep seeing that cottage. We'd had such fun. We'd lived off wine and crisps, apples from the garden, and danced every night.

'Magical,' Christina had called that week. It really was. I think back to our lunch in Teatro. How she mentioned trying smoked salmon for the first time. *What had she said?* That holiday was the best time of her life. Her whole face had lit up when she spoke about it.

My heart thuds faster and the thought comes to me in a flash. *Could she have taken the children to the loch?*

My gut says yes.

She'd loved that holiday, where she felt happy and free. Where else would she go, to escape real life?

Plus, it's an isolated cottage. The nearest village is across the loch. Ideal if you don't want to be disturbed. Could it be a holiday cottage now?

I get up and grab my laptop. I remember where it is. A quick search on Airbnb and I find the listing. We'd travelled to Inverness by train, then another train to the local station. Then we'd caught a cab. If she's there, I'd find her and the children. We could sort this out.

I look up the time of the trains and plan my journey.

Should I tell Sam where I'm going? But, no, he'd insist we involve the police and that's the last thing I want to do.

I don't want to scare her. I need to find out what she's up to.

I lie down, head buzzing with plans. If I leave before Rashmi gets here, the police won't know where I've gone. I can call them later.

Soon birds are singing outside the window. At about five, I give up trying to sleep, and creep upstairs to our room. Sam snores, oblivious, rolled up in the duvet.

I pack a few things, careful not to wake him.

He doesn't deserve to know where I'm going.

Chapter Fifty

Amber

I chew on greasy chips and stodgy burger bun. I force them down. I only pretend to drink the hot chocolate. I saw her stir in liquid from a bottle when she thought we weren't looking. It must be the drug. Greedy Leo and Eddie drink theirs. But I tip mine away, behind the bed.

She makes us lie in the big bed, still wearing our normal clothes. Leo and Eddie fall asleep quickly, even though they slept all day in the car. I cross my arms over my chest, pinching the soft skin under my arms, forcing myself to stay awake.

I lie still, making my breathing deep and snorey, like I'm asleep. I listen to the sound of the TV. There's a whistling coming from Leo's nose when he breathes. After a while, footsteps pad around the room, making the floor creak. A door opens and the bathroom fan hums. The toilet flushes, the water runs, and the sound of an electric toothbrush buzzes. She spits, then the bathroom fan goes off, the lights too. The room is dark and shadowy. She pads back into the room and the bedsprings creak, as she settles into the bed next to ours.

I wait, digging my nails into my palms. When I hear another

set of deep, sleepy breathing, I slip out of bed and creep to the door. I grope around for my shoes, but I can't find them. *Never mind.*

I draw back the bolt. Slowly, bit by bit. Metal scrapes. It's loud in the silence. I stop. Wait. My heart's thumping hard, but I can still hear three sets of breathing.

I open the door a crack and squeeze through, closing it gently behind me.

The air is cool out in the corridor. I let go of my breath. It's dark and scary here. A blue nightlight glows on the wall. The tartan carpet is a shadowy grid. I'm not free yet.

I head for the staircase. As I move, a light pings on and makes me blink. I creep down the steps.

I go straight to the front door. I turn the handle but the door is bolted shut. I slide back a bolt in the middle and a bolt at the bottom but when I try the handle it still won't open. I look up. There's a top bolt. I reach up, jumping. But there's no way I can jump that high.

Beep beep beep beep beep.

Oh no. My jumping's triggered an alarm.

A door opens. It's the grey-haired Scottish man, wearing stripey pyjamas.

'Hallo there? What's the matter, lassie? Where're you going in the middle of the night?'

'That woman's not my mum. She's kidnapped us. She's taking us away somewhere we don't want to go. Please. You have to help.' I make my voice loud, but he just stands and blinks.

'What did you say, lass? I cannae hear ye. Need my hearing aid.'

He edges closer to me, but there's another set of footsteps.

She's here.

'Amber, darling. Oh dear. Not this again. I'm *so* sorry, Mr Laird, she's so . . . well, challenging.'

'Och, is this wee lassie your daughter? She said something about her mum?'

'I'm the children's nanny and I'm taking them to their parents' holiday home in the Highlands.' She speaks loudly and clearly.

'No. That's not true. My mum and dad are in London.' My voice won't go above a whisper.

'Come on, sweetie, what did I say about making a fuss?' She grabs my wrist with strong fingers. 'I'm so sorry to wake you, Mr Laird. Kids, eh?' He frowns but she's an adult. Adults believe each other.

'Och well, wee one, you better behave for your nanny over here.' He smiles and pats me on the head.

'She's lying. Please help me!' It's no use. He can't hear me. He's at the door, fastening the bolts.

'Amber!' Her voice goes all mean. 'Really now, that's enough. What will Mr Laird think of us? Mummy won't be pleased to hear about this, but she doesn't have to know if you come back to bed.'

Her hand clamps round my wrist until it hurts. I have no choice. I have to go with her.

'Go on with youse! Off to bed, wee one.' The man shoos us up the stairs. 'We'll say no more about it.'

'Thank you. And just to let you know, we're leaving very early, six a.m. We will not be requiring breakfast.'

I follow, kicking the carpet. The man didn't listen to me. I've lost my chance to escape.

Back in the room, she locks the door. She pours juice in a

glass and stirs in the yucky liquid. 'Drink, Amber dear. I can't trust you.'

I clamp my lips. I refuse to drink.

'What'll it be? Drink or the hanky?' Her pinchy fingers pull my chin forward, hold the glass to my lips.

I drink. Anything is better than the stinky hanky. The one she used outside the school. But I hold the juice in my mouth. I don't swallow it.

She grabs my chin and pinches my nose. 'Swallow – or it's the hanky for you.'

I can't breathe. I'm choking.

I swallow.

Chapter Fifty-One

Christina

Then

Two blue lines. Christina stared, willing it to be one line. Surely it was a mistake.

But in her heart, she knew. She was pregnant.

Jade asked who the father was, but Christina refused to tell her. It didn't matter. It was a problem she had to make go away, so she'd made an appointment to talk through her options with a doctor. Not that she needed to talk. She knew what she had to do.

If only she'd had the procedure the same day. But the appointment wasn't until the following week. Lectures hadn't started yet and Christina had too much time to think. She walked around the city. The more she thought about it, the more she wasn't sure if she could go through with it.

A termination. It sounded so final. She wasn't against abortion. Not at all. It was just a collection of cells in her body. Not a baby yet.

But she'd left it so late. She couldn't do it.

The morning of the appointment, she said to Jade, 'What if – I don't go through with it? The termination?'

'What? You can't possibly have a baby!' Jade was shocked. 'You want to be a doctor. How will you finish your training as a single mum? Who's the father? Will he support you? What will your parents say?'

Tears pricked behind Christina's eyes. It must be the hormones. Jade saw the truth in her face and hugged her tightly. 'But if you want to have it, I'll support you. I'll be here for you, whatever you decide. It's up to you.'

This was the most important decision of her life so far. *What should she do?*

The walls of the flat were closing in on her. A termination would be easier. The whole problem would just go away, and she could go back to her studies. *But what if she kept it?*

As soon as the thought entered her mind, she made a list of the steps she would have to take if she decided to keep this baby.

First, cancel the termination at the clinic. That was easy. Just a phone call. Check.

Next. Talk to her Director of Studies. Find out what the options would be for taking time out of her degree. She called and made an appointment to see him the following week. Check.

Next. Tell her parents.

She couldn't do that on the phone. She would have to go down to London. Tell them face to face. It would soon be Chinese New Year. A good excuse for a visit. She booked a train ticket and phoned home when she knew no one would be in. She left a message on the answerphone with her arrival time.

But her body had other plans.

That night, in the flat, Christina's stomach started to cramp. She wondered if it could be the curry she ate for dinner. She'd cooked it fresh with vegetables and a few chunks of lamb, defrosted from the freezer. Surely it wouldn't have given her food poisoning?

Jade was out with Tom. Christina was alone. The cramps grew stronger, gripping her belly, ten times worse than any period pain. It wasn't until she was doubled up on the bathroom floor, pain flooding her every cell, that she worried she could be in danger.

Sharp pains pierced her whole body, travelling all the way to her shoulder. She lay in a wet and sticky puddle. It was blood. She moaned when she saw it. It soaked through her skirt and pooled on the floor.

There was so much blood, she wondered if she was going to die.

She crawled out of the bathroom into the hall, and scrabbled for her bag and her phone. Somehow, she managed to call for an ambulance.

'I'm pregnant,' she gasped through the pain. 'I think I'm losing the baby.' Then she passed out.

Chapter Fifty-Two

Jade

I'm careful to turn off my phone before I get on the train at Euston. I don't want anyone to trace me. It's late in the evening before I arrive in Inverness, so I book into a cheap hotel near the station. I wake early, and take another train.

It's the same journey that Christina and I travelled, nearly twenty years ago. Once I get to the right village, it's a long cab ride to the cottage.

The spiky-haired taxi driver with piercings hums along to eighties rock on the radio while he drives at precisely the speed limit. We wind down country roads edged by clumps of heather, spiky gorse and ferns, past bare fields and purple scrubland. I sit forward in my seat, willing him to go faster, clutching my bag and swaying with the curve of the road. My throat's tight with fear, my chest aching with hope. If I'm right, Christina will be at the cottage by the loch. I could be seeing my darlings very soon.

The taxi pulls up in front of an idyllic-looking cottage and my heart beats faster. I recognise the steeply pitched, slate roof and homely looking chimney stacks. It takes me back to the summer we stayed here. I note the changes too – the grey rendering has been white-washed, and the shutters have been painted a dark blue gloss. 'Sunset Cottage' is carved on a wooden slab on a low gate set in the stone wall which encloses the property. A tall rowan tree, berries red as blood, grows by the wall. It's a mature tree now, but I vaguely remember it as a sapling.

I hand the driver a few notes. 'Can you wait for me? I shouldn't be too long.'

He tucks the notes into his jacket. 'I've another job first. Give us a call when you're ready to return, lass.' He passes me a business card.

'Thanks. In about an hour? I want to catch the last train back to Edinburgh – with my children.'

My babies will be with me. They have to be. My heart thuds and there's a fluttering in my throat.

Oh God. Please.

The driver executes a slow three-point turn and drives away. I shiver, pulling my cardigan around me. It might be July, but up here, it's a few degrees cooler than London. Grey clouds scud over my head and a sharp breeze tears at the leaves.

I hurry up the path. I hope I'm right this time. The children must be here. A tired rose bush straggles over the door frame. The roses have lost most of their petals and their perfume is tinged with rot. I press the doorbell and sharp electronic tones echo in the hall, fading to silence. I knock loudly on the glossy front door but there's no reply.

I peer through the shutters to the right and left of the door, but all I can see are beige curtains, pulled tight against the square windowpanes. I rap on the glass. 'Hello? Christina? Amber, Eddie, Leo?' My voice shakes. 'Are you there?'

I walk round to the back of the cottage and look through the kitchen window. I spy the old range cooker I remember from before. The sink's piled high with dirty plates and bowls. It's not like Christina to leave such a mess. Maybe I've made a mistake, leaping to the conclusion she's brought the kids here. Could I be wasting valuable time, like when I travelled to Devon?

I walk down the overgrown lawn, and turn to look up into the upstairs windows, but the square panes of glass reflect nothing but the pewter sky. I glance at the untidy borders, clumps of thistles and tall foxgloves in faded yellow and blousy pink. There are the same old apple trees, loaded with misshapen fruit, rotting windfalls nestled in the grass. Sour saliva fills my mouth as I remember the tartness of those apples. The stone wall runs round the garden and at the far end, a small gate opens onto the path that leads to the loch. I have a recollection of Izzie bringing rugs to the shore. We'd drunk whisky and wine, feasted on crisps and oatcakes, cheese and apples.

Could Christina have taken the children away from the house? Could she be hiding them in a bothy or barn nearby?

I stride through the overgrown grass and let myself out through the gate. My footsteps crunch over gravel. I've no proof she's brought the children here. Only the photo album and an ache in my gut that tells me I'm right.

The gravel turns to earth, threaded with roots. My leather sandals slip on loose stones, skid over weathered rocks and clumps of moss. Brambles edge the path, catching my sleeve, and tiny thorns tear at my skin. The jagged edge of a boulder grazes my arm. It's like the countryside wants to hold me back from finding them. But panic drives me forward. My heart is craving my babies, fearful for them.

The path twists to the right round a rock, then there's a sharp bend to the left and up a narrow incline before it opens out on a familiar view.

The loch hasn't changed for thousands of years. The last twenty are a mere breath in the scheme of things. The vast expanse of gently undulating water reflects the steel sky, hills rising up on either side, patchy with forest. Moisture prickles the air and tiny midges dance round my face. I shiver, recalling the shock of the icy water, slicing into me. I remember how Christina had refused to swim or paddle until I was dunked by one of the boys. She'd helped me out, and we'd warmed up on whisky, drunk straight from the bottle.

As I gaze out to where the water meets the sky, I notice a silhouette, against the horizon. A bulky figure wearing an anorak with a fur-lined hood is pushing something, a buggy. They're not doing well on this path, stopping, then starting. The figure bends to adjust a wheel. My heart races. I hurry closer, till I'm fifty metres away. I spy something flapping on the handle. *My rose print scarf.* The one I gave to Christina so Leo wouldn't miss me.

That's *my* buggy. It's Christina. It has to be.

My knees sag with relief and I stop for a second and grab the trunk of a small fir tree, dripping with slimy moss. I steady myself before adrenaline propels me forward again. I spy a head of tousled brown curls, slumped to the side of the buggy. *Leo. Please let it be Leo.*

It's strange to see him sitting in the buggy, like a baby. Leo hates the buggy. I have to wrestle him in usually. Has she drugged him, like she drugged me? Where are Amber and Eddie?

'Hey!' I yell, running, heart aching. 'Christina!'

She stops and turns, eyes glittering from the depths of her hood.

331

I'm ten metres away, a stitch cramping my side, eyes fixed on my baby. I slow down, panting, walking the last few steps to the buggy, stretching my hand out to my darling.

Leo's eyes are shut. The straps cut into his jacket. I crouch, kissing his warm cheek. His chest rises and falls with his breath, and I hug his solid body, inhaling his buttery smell.

But before my trembling fingers can unclasp the harness, the buggy jerks away, I fall forward onto my knees, tasting dirt. The breath's knocked from my lungs.

It feels like an age before I can catch my breath and lift my head. Christina's dragging the buggy away, the rose scarf fluttering madly, Leo's head bouncing with every bump on the path.

'Please. Christina,' I gasp. 'Stop! Come back, it's me you want to hurt, not Leo, not the children.'

She pauses, half turning, keeping hold of the handle. 'Stay where you are, Jade.' Her voice is low and hoarse. 'Leo needs his nap.'

If she's worried about his nap, surely she can't mean to hurt him?

I stand up, and a pain shoots through my right knee. I must have jarred it.

'Christina, I've been so worried.' I limp forwards. 'Thank God I found you. Where's Amber? Eddie?'

Shadows gather under her eyes like bruises. The stress must be getting to her. 'Don't come any closer.' Something glints in her hand.

And then I see what she's holding, and my heart almost stops with fear.

332

Chapter Fifty-Three

Jade

Christina points the knife at the open water. Around the loch, the land rises steeply. 'It's so isolated.' She turns towards me, a wild look in her eyes. 'I feel vulnerable – a woman on my own. Anyone could attack me.'

I stretch a hand towards her, every cell in my body fixed on the knife's proximity to Leo. She's not intending to hurt him, surely. But there could be an accident.

He shifts and his head lolls to the left. My muscles freeze. I have to get him away. 'Christina, please.' Terror wraps round my chest. I can barely rasp the words. 'I'm here now. Put the knife away. T-two of us – we can – scare off attackers.'

She cradles the knife, eyes darting from side to side. 'It's better I keep my weapon. It's busy with tourists near the village. But here – anyone could creep through the trees.' She looks fearfully at the pine forest encroaching on this side of the loch. Then she glares at me, as if I'm the one being unreasonable. 'I won't use it unless I have to.'

'Amber and Eddie?' I repeat. 'Where are they?'

She gestures in the direction of the cottage. 'Napping. The children haven't had much sleep this holiday, with all the travelling. It's been hectic.'

Is she serious? The kidnapping's a *holiday*?

Her eyes burn, feverish. Her mental state is fragile.

I force myself to take a breath, keep myself calm. Until Leo's safe in my arms, I can't risk upsetting her.

'Christina, I've been so worried about you. Why'd you – disappear without telling me?' I push my stiff lips into something resembling a smile.

She closes her eyes for a second, then opens them. 'I can tell this is going to take a little explaining.'

'Let's go back to the cottage. Chat there?' I plead.

She starts walking, pushing the buggy onwards. 'I was taking a stroll to the boulder rock. Leo needs to rest.'

I follow slowly at a distance. Careful not to alarm her. She picks her way down a gritty slope, the buggy jolting from side to side. My heart's in my mouth in case she slips.

Soon, the lichen-covered mass of granite looms. The same boulder that's been here since the Ice Age. The one I jumped off years ago. I shiver, feeling echoes of the past catching up with us. Waves lap at the strip of shingle that passes for a beach.

Christina stops the buggy and sits on a protruding ledge. Her hood falls back, revealing her flat, greasy hair, far from her usual shiny bob. My mind flashes back to her pale naked body, riding Sam in our armchair. Bile fills my mouth and I clench my fingers in a flash of rage.

She holds the buggy's handle, rocking it gently.

She has my son.

Anger twists back into fear. My heart's hammering. My mouth dry.

I have to get Leo away from her, find Amber and Eddie. They must be back at the cottage. We have to escape.

'So how did you find us?' Christina asks.

'I – I found your photo album. You left it – in the study. Lovely pictures of the old days. Weren't we just talking about our holiday with Izzie? I made an educated guess.'

Christina's eyes are shining as if she's thinking of the past. 'I couldn't believe it when I found the cottage on Airbnb. Izzie's cousin manages it now. I've stayed a few times. It's lovely here. Peaceful. It's never been as magical as the first summer we came. But it's close.'

'Yes. It was a good holiday.' I try not to grit my teeth.

'The best time of my life. Remember when you went in the water and came out nearly blue?'

'Yeah, wild swimming's not for me,' I admit. 'You know, you didn't have to bring the kids alone, Christina. We – could have come together.'

She smiles and shakes her head. 'Really, Jade? You'd have agreed to come with me? Without Sam?'

I take a breath, trying to sound casual. 'Sam's been busy. He hasn't had time for a holiday. We could've had a nice time together. We still can.'

She stands up and rolls her shoulders. 'We were having a "nice time" in London. You were happy for me to move in and help you – until you didn't need me anymore.'

'I'm sorry, Christina. You're right, you've done so much for me. And I've been a terrible friend.' I glance nervously at her hand, tight around the knife's handle. 'How long've you booked

335

the cottage for? I'm happy to stay. Let me take Leo, please. I can settle him. And let's go check on the others.' I shuffle towards her slowly, legs shaking. *No sudden moves.*

Christina shakes her head. She adjusts the brake of the buggy, making sure it's secure. 'I'm not sure that will work. You know, Amber and Eddie are well behaved. But Leo needs a firmer hand. The parenting blogs say not to give in. He'll be fine with more consistency around the rules. He can be good as gold when you're not around.'

I clench my fist. She's discussing childcare methods as if they were her children. Does she think I'm an unfit mother? Is that why she's taken them? *She's not right in the head.*

'I've missed them, Christina. Can I give Leo a hug? Please?'

She shakes her head. 'Not a good idea, Jade. He only fell asleep a few minutes ago. He's been so grouchy.'

'Leo can be a nightmare. Let me take him off your hands.' My voice is a whisper as I inch nearer.

'He's calm, now. Asleep.'

I'm two metres away. *Kick her, grab the buggy and run.*

But she points the knife at me. 'Don't come any nearer, Jade. You'll wake him. And we need to talk.'

The blade glints. The breeze breaks up the clouds and there are patches of blue sky and a glimpse of sun, but I'm cold to the bone. 'All right. Let's talk. Put the knife away.'

'I was hoping you'd come, Jade.' She folds the blade back towards her and sits down. With the sharp point away from Leo, I can breathe again. 'But I couldn't be sure. I must apologise about the last time we saw each other ... Desperate measures.' Her cheeks turn scarlet. Anger spirals through me. *Pouncing on my husband.*

'Did you want to drive Sam and me apart? You didn't need to. We're over. You know, I enjoyed seeing your photo album. Lovely memories. Us at the Halloween Ball.' *Remind her we were friends.*

She blinks hard. 'That's one of my favourites. Don't we look so young? Before everything went wrong.'

My chest tightens with guilt. She's referring to the time I left her alone in the club. *I knew it.* She blames me for what happened to her. *Try an apology.* 'Christina, please, listen to me. Will you ever forgive me? For what happened that night?'

She looks at me, surprised. 'It was a fun night – while you were there.'

'I'm sorry I left you alone that night. I wasn't a supportive friend to you.' My eyes brim with tears. 'Can you ever forgive me?'

She frowns, puzzled. 'Exactly why are *you* sorry?'

She acts like I don't know what happened. *Does she need me to spell it out?*

'The night, the Halloween Ball. I know that was the night you got pregnant. You never told me, but somehow, I knew. It was my fault. I shouldn't have abandoned you.'

Dressed as a sexy witch, she'd looked so young. Like a child in her older sister's clothes. *How could I have left her?* 'I shouldn't have left you alone in the club. I was young and stupid and selfish. I only thought about me, and how I wanted to go off with Tom. But it didn't even last more than a couple of months. I was a bad friend. We were like sisters. No sister does that.'

She smiles like she's trying to humour me. 'It's OK, Jade, I . . . wasn't on my own that night, Izzie and Eleanor were there.' She tests the point of the knife on the rock.

337

'But I should have been there too.' My voice wavers. *Can I get the knife away from her?* 'And then, the night you had the miscarriage, I was out. I left you alone in the flat. You—you could have bled to death.' I rub my face, wishing I could rub that night away.

She glances across the water. *Is she remembering the horror, the pain? Is she thinking about how she can't have children?*

I have to make her understand. 'Christina, I know we didn't speak again until you messaged me on Instagram. But I did call your parents. I tried to find out how you were. I called a few times, but no one ever picked up. I left a couple of messages. I should have made more effort, gone round to your parents' flat.'

She shakes her head. 'Oh no, Jade. I didn't want to see anyone. It would have been pointless coming round. I wouldn't have let you in.'

I open and close my fingers. How can I make her realise how sorry I am? 'Please forgive me. I don't blame you for – for hating me, for tracking me down – for taking away the people I love most in the world. But please, it's not their fault. It's mine. Leo, Amber and Eddie are innocent. Don't harm them. Please. Give me the knife.'

She claps a hand over her mouth and giggles. *Is this a joke to her?*

'No, no, no, no, no.' She laughs. 'Oh, Jade. You have it completely wrong. You don't understand. Not everything is about *you*.'

I frown. Has she completely lost it? 'So – why then? Why did you track me down? Try to break up my marriage? Take my kids?' There's an edge to my voice. 'Don't you want revenge because I wronged you? Isn't it because of that night, because of me, that you can't have children of your own?'

She stops laughing and her face looks bleak. 'Do you know, it wasn't a miscarriage. It was an ectopic pregnancy. They're quite common. One out of ninety pregnancies are ectopic. There was a medical error, and they removed both my fallopian tubes. I don't blame them. Doctors are so overworked. Why, I myself have made errors of judgement. The hours are inhumane. But I don't blame *you*. How could it be your fault? Anyway, I told you, you didn't leave me alone at the ball. I distinctly remember you asking Izzie and Eleanor to keep an eye on me.'

'Really?' I exhale and the vice round my chest loosens. *If she doesn't blame me, then why's she kidnapped my children?*

Christina grips the knife again. 'There *is* someone I blame for that night. For not being able to have children. It's the man who I met after you left the ball.' She gazes across the water, a cold expression in her eyes. Then she stabs the knife at the rock.

'Who was he?' I murmur. But, somehow, I guess the answer.

He was a couple of years above us in Edinburgh. I never met him there, but she could have.

Over the loch, grey clouds gather, blocking the sun. A breeze turns the ripples into waves. I shiver and wrap my arms around my chest while Christina looks straight at me. Her eyes glitter with anger and when she tells me, I'm not even surprised.

'It's not you I want revenge on. It's Sam.'

Chapter Fifty-Four

Christina

Then

O nce they were upstairs in the flat, Christina felt queasy. The meaty thrust of his tongue was making her gag. She pushed him away and stumbled to the kitchen. When did the floor get so uneven? She lurched from the counter to the sink, turned on the tap, filled a glass and drank.

In the living room, he was rifling through the sideboard and the dresser by the TV. He picked up Jade's bottle of holiday ouzo, unscrewed the cap and swigged. He poured the aniseed spirit into Christina's glass, even though she shook her head.

The water had bloated her belly, making her feel worse. Pain gripped her skull and a wave of nausea travelled from her stomach to her throat.

Was she going to vomit?

She sank onto the sofa. He collapsed next to her, leaned back and closed his eyes. He wasn't going anywhere. Christina had a feeling Jade wouldn't be back soon. She was alone in the flat with the guy from the library. He was incredibly drunk. He looked like he was falling asleep.

Was there any harm in letting him sleep here?

'I'm going to bed,' Christina murmured.

In her room she shrugged off her clothes and dragged on her night shirt. She stumbled to the bathroom to pee and brush her teeth before she sank into her bed, head pounding and dizzy, waiting for oblivion.

Christina woke to find a large, warm body in her bed. It was still dark, and she could smell musky body odour mixed with stale, yeasty alcohol. She was rammed against the wall, the man taking up most of the space. She pushed him, but the guy from the library wouldn't move. She lay as still as she could, her face pressed against the ridges of the wallpaper, foul breath blowing into her ear.

The room was spinning despite the darkness. She was still drunk. What should she do? She tried to sit up, get out of bed. But a heavy arm held her close, a muscled thigh trapped her. And then he grabbed her shoulder and prised her from the wall, like a mollusc from a rock.

She wanted to scream but only a whimper sounded. So she froze, squeezed her eyes shut, and pretended she wasn't there.

After a while, loud snores filled the night. She pushed his arm off her and wriggled to the bottom of the bed. She slipped out to the living room, and sat on the sofa, shaking.

Was this her fault?

I had a crush on him for months.

I danced with him.

I let him buy me drinks.

I let him walk me home.

I invited him in and let him stay.

She shouldn't have brought him upstairs.

He must have thought I wanted this.

And maybe this is what grown-up women do. Go to parties, get drunk. Sleep with people.

Christina went into Jade's room and shut the door. She curled up in Jade's bed. It smelt of Jade's lily perfume. There was a painful throbbing between her legs. She sobbed quietly.

After a couple of hours, she heard him moving in her room. The front door opened and clicked shut. She got up to check he'd gone. Her room reeked of something musky, animal-like.

She opened the window and let in the cold, damp air.

She pulled off the sheets and duvet cover and pillowcases. She bundled them into the washing machine, set the temperature to sixty degrees.

She ran a bath as hot as she could bear. She scrubbed and scrubbed her body with her flannel, washing him off her.

And eventually, her tears flowed into the water.

She scolded herself. She wasn't the first girl to have a bad experience. She shouldn't make a fuss.

She couldn't help weeping for the rose-petal-strewn bedroom she'd dreamed of. She'd been too weak to stop him taking what wasn't his to take.

But she buried her shame.

Chapter Fifty-Five

Jade

As Christina relives the trauma, her voice lowers to a croaky whisper and she starts to shake. The tears don't come until she stops speaking. And then she collapses, shuddering.

I'm reeling.

Ever since Mazza told me how Sam groped her, he's filled me with disgust. But this. This is a hundred times worse.

He raped my friend.

The man I thought I knew. My life's partner. *How could he treat someone like that?*

My heart aches for her. 'I'm so, so sorry, Christina.' I crouch down in front of her. 'I can't believe that you had to live through that. I'm sorry I wasn't there.'

I think back through the years, to the Halloween Ball. If only I'd stayed with her. If only I hadn't gone home with Tom. Afterwards, when I realised something was wrong and made Christina do a pregnancy test, I thought she must have had a one-night stand. I had no idea she'd been raped. Why didn't it cross my mind at the time? Why didn't I ask her?

'I wish you'd told me. I could have helped. We could have gone to the police. I would have supported you.' I reach out, wanting to hug her. But she holds out the knife and I keep my distance.

'The police,' she grinds out. 'Like they would have helped. I let him stay. I didn't say no.'

'But you didn't say yes either.'

I shuffle closer to her. In the buggy, Leo's face is flushed with sleep. I yearn to hold him safe in my arms. If only Christina would put the knife away, but she clutches it tightly, knuckles white. It's like she wants to drive it into Sam.

'Christina. Please. I'm so sorry for what you've been through. I can't begin to imagine. But, please ... It's not the children's fault. We will get you the help you need. Please. Put the knife down and let me take Leo. Let's go find Amber and Eddie.'

She looks up at me, turning the knife away but not dropping it. 'You know, I was so happy when I found you on Instagram. Hashtag Ilovemyfamily. You, Amber and the boys. Flour on your noses, baking cookies. I recognised you instantly.'

That photo. We did look like the perfect, happy family.

'I sped through your grid, admiring your three wonderful children. And then, I saw *him*. In the background, while Eddie blew out birthday candles. I froze and the hairs on the back of my neck stood up. It was definitely him. The student who assaulted me. And the horror of that night came flooding back.'

She swallows and pauses, her face even whiter. Reliving the trauma must be agony. I reach a hand out, as if to comfort her, but she blinks and carries on.

'And then, I realised ... my lovely friend was married to my abuser.' She glares at me, like it's my fault for not realising Sam

344

had raped her. 'How did you even know each other? Was it from Edinburgh? Through friends of friends? And how did you end up married to him? I couldn't ignore what chance had shown me. I had to know, to check how you were. Your family life looked perfect. But social media photos are carefully curated. I saw you lived in London. I was suspended from my job at the hospital, and I hadn't seen my mother for a while. So I moved down.'

'I was so thrilled when you got in touch,' I say. 'I guess I hoped . . . we could be friends again.' I'd hoped to find out exactly what had happened. I knew something had gone horribly wrong when she'd left, that her parents hadn't wanted her to come back because of her pregnancy.

She shakes her head. 'That first coffee in Wanstead, it was so good to see you. I was relieved to see you so happy. But then you told me about the text from the unknown number. Things weren't so perfect. It didn't surprise me he might be cheating on you. He doesn't think rules apply to him. He takes what he wants. So I stayed at your house, half fearful he would recognise me. I haven't changed that much. But that night in Edinburgh he was drunk, almost comatose. You have to ask, how many other women has he forgotten?'

I feel sick to think that Sam could have done this to countless other women. He said he'd been no saint. How many times had he passed out drunk and abused a woman's trust?

'I thought – if you found out something was going on with the sender of that text, you would break up with him. And I wouldn't have to worry. So I offered to babysit. I was sure there would be no smoke without fire. That you'd find out what a sleaze he is. But he managed to convince you nothing was going on. I couldn't believe he'd changed. I tested him. I flirted with him, and you didn't seem to mind. You didn't seem to notice. Did you accept his behaviour as normal?'

I shake my head vigorously. How could she think I'd condone his behaviour? 'No! Of course not ... I ...'

She ignored me. 'It makes me quite furious. How wives and girlfriends can be fooled. Whether you know it or not, you enable these predators. I offered to childmind so you could take on that freelance job. I hoped to prove to you what he was like, so you'd leave him. He didn't deserve your happy life together. But you became suspicious of me, instead of him. Especially after Eddie's allergic attack. That was a mistake. I shouldn't have cooked with the curry paste with fish sauce. I wanted to prove you needed me as a doctor. I didn't realise he suffered from anaphylaxis, that he would end up in hospital.'

'Eddie could have died!' I grind out. He was her innocent victim. I shake with fury at how she'd used Eddie's allergy to score brownie points for herself. It was so dangerous.

'While you were in hospital, I managed to get close to Sam. He still didn't remember me and I convinced him I was a help to you. But when you came back, I felt I'd outstayed my welcome. I could sense my time in your home was limited.'

'So – you drugged me? The police found Temazepam!' A wave of anger floods me. Has she been drugging us all?

'I didn't *want* to drug you, but I had to do something – don't you see? How could I show you what Sam was like before I left? And the children. Amber, Eddie and Leo needed me. I was growing fond of them. Drastic action was called for. I'm sorry about the sleeping pills. I didn't give you anywhere near a dangerous amount. But that last night, I was desperate. You wanted me to go by Monday. It was my last chance to split you up. But I couldn't be sure it would work long term. He has a way with words. Maybe you would believe him eventually. Cast me as the villain. Well, you're an adult. If you insisted on believing him that was up to you. But the children were suffering. Those poor children. They are my baby's half-brothers and sister. I can't help feeling responsible for them, so I made a decision. I would take the children away for a short break. They deserve a holiday. And what better place than by this loch, where we'd been so happy.

'You and Sam don't deserve such wonderful children. Your parenting skills are so inconsistent. Leo is in danger of becoming very spoiled. I had to take them. Don't you see?'

She pauses to wipe her face.

I'm in shock. *Say something. Anything.*

She's still playing with the knife.

'Christina. I understand. You did what you thought was best. But the knife, please throw it over to me.'

She smiles. 'I don't want to hurt the children – why would I? This knife is for our protection. You never know who's hiding, in the trees.' Her eyes dart around as if expecting someone to jump out.

'Then pass it over.' I creep closer. 'Please. Knives are dangerous and I don't want Leo to get hurt. I'll make sure Sam doesn't go near them. I'm their mother and I love them. You should have told me about Sam. What I said earlier still stands. We had a magical week here years ago. We can now. I'll make it up to you. Give me the knife. Let me take Leo. Let's find Eddie and Amber.'

She stands up. 'Yes. Let's go back to the cottage. It's getting chilly. Leo will have napped enough by the time we get back.'

'I do appreciate everything you've done for me, Christina, I really do. But we need to get you help. Help to recover from everything you've been through – the trauma.'

She doesn't speak but she pushes the buggy along the path towards the cottage. I follow behind. She holds the knife, loose in her hand, but I fear she could attack me if I attempt to take the buggy away.

A clump of brambles blocks our way and I hold the trailing creepers aside so she can push the buggy through.

Then we hear it.

The wail of police sirens.

Christina freezes. The stone wall around the cottage is just ahead of us. Blue lights are flashing up the road.

Christina glances at me, accusingly. 'You called the police?'

'No! I didn't, I swear!' My voice is hoarse with fear. Had they traced my phone? I'd had to turn it on to call the taxi.

She reaches into the buggy, unclasps the harness and scoops up Leo. She shoves the buggy hard, towards me. Before I can jump out of the way, it crashes into me, pushing me into brambles. I struggle up with difficulty, hearing cloth tearing, feeling thorns gouging my skin.

By the time I untangle myself, she's running back towards the loch.

'Christina!' I rush after her. 'Where are you going, Christina, please come back! It wasn't me who called the police, I promise. I wouldn't!'

Legs shaking, I run. My fall in the brambles wins her some time but she's hampered by Leo. Asleep, he's a dead weight, over twenty kilos.

'Christina, please. Leave Leo. He's heavy.' I'm gaining on her.

'No!' She turns, pointing the knife. Leo's head flops against her shoulder. 'Don't come any nearer.' Her eyes are wild, and I step back, fear gripping me.

'Christina, please,' I whisper, throat closed. *Leo, my baby.* I fix my eyes on the knife, feeling sick. *Will she use it on my sweet boy?*

Leo wriggles and turns his head, but he doesn't wake. She must have drugged him, just like she drugged me. Surely it won't be too much. She's a doctor, isn't she? She'd know the right amount to knock him out but not kill him.

She turns from the path, heading for the forest, seeking cover under the pine trees.

I follow close behind. My breath is wheezing in my lungs, my feet sinking into the cushiony undergrowth. 'Christina! Please! Wait!'

My ankles sink deep into hillocks of moss. Then I'm wading through ferns. My gaze fixes on Leo's curls, bumping on her shoulder. Above our heads, creaking firs are whipped backwards and forwards by the wind. Something brushes my face, a slimy spider's web or skein of moss.

If she trips, if she falls, the knife could slice him.

'Please, Christina, drop the knife. Throw it on the ground. You don't want to hurt Leo. There could be an accident. Please!' But my plea is lost in the roar of the wind.

The forest floor rises steeply. My legs shake as I hurry after her. Fallen tree trunks threaten to trip us up, their unearthed roots devoured by toxic fungi, crumbling bark suffocated with webs of moss.

Christina mutters, 'It's easy for you! Such a pampered princess.

You have a charmed life – everything you wanted. Supportive parents, marriage, and children. You've always been taken care of. Some of us have to fight for what we want.'

'Christina!' I beg. 'Please. Leo hasn't hurt anyone. I know you love the children as much as I do, but I'm his mum, he needs me.'

She's scuttling up a path leading out of the forest. We emerge onto bare moorland, weathered hills covered with grass and moss and heather. I can hear the chatter of a stream, cutting through the rock.

It's steep here, up the side of the hill. We clamber over carcass-like rocks smothered in lichen.

She's not a killer, she won't harm him, I tell myself. But Leo's heavy, a dead weight. It can't be easy to climb the hills carrying him. She disappears behind a boulder.

A tired whine echoes out. Leo's waking up.

I'm panting, unfit for this climb.

Below us, a siren wails.

Leo's screeching in protest. I imagine him struggling to be put down.

Please, Christina. Put down the knife.

I scramble past the next boulder. Small stones rain on my head from above.

A voice through a megaphone booms out, echoes distorting the words.

'Please, please stop!' I shout. 'Christina!'

Leo's screams grow louder. My hands grasp at springy clumps of heather as I heave myself towards his cries. My soles skid over bare rock. My ears focused on my baby.

I pull myself up to the next ledge.

And I see them.

350

Leo's flailing in her arms, thrashing his body back and forth. He's trying to escape her grip, his mouth stretched wide in a screech.

The knife glints in her hand.

I edge forwards. 'Christina, please!'

She pauses to set Leo down on a rock. He stops screaming.

She glances down, mouthing something indistinguishable at me. Her lips curve.

Then she turns towards the next Munro.

She carries on climbing. But without him.

Leo whimpers. He looks towards me. 'Mumma!'

My heart's banging in my chest. 'Darling Leo, stay sitting down, please. Mumma's coming to get you.' He sits on the rock, dazed, his mouth wide in silent fear. His face is covered in tears and snot.

I suddenly realise the danger. A stream has sliced a gorge in the bare rock and we're right at the top edge of it. I can hear the rush of a waterfall, and the chattering river that feeds directly into the loch. The water glints, dark and treacherous. One false step and we could slide all the way down, into its freezing depths.

'Leo darling. Stay there. Wait for Mumma.'

Leo looks at me and holds his arms out. His eyes are glazed, drugged.

'My darling.' I pull myself up towards him. I'm nearly there.

Leo stands, ready to run to me.

And then a thrush flutters past. He turns away, and watches the bird land on a nearby ledge. It warbles a tune. His eyes light up. He smiles and points. 'Birdy, Mumma.'

'Leo,' I croak. 'Stay still.'

351

He stands, tiptoes onto a ledge by the thrush, reaching out a hand to stroke it.

My heart's in my throat.

'Leo, NO!'

But it's too late. Even as I shout, I see his look of surprise as he loses his balance and tips backwards.

His arms windmill.

He tips slightly forward again.

But then his feet slide out from under him. He falls on his bum and slides backwards. His hands reach out to grasp a clump of heather but it's not enough to support his weight.

My heart stops beating as I watch him slide off the ledge and disappear from view.

There's a thud, a wail, and then silence.

Chapter Fifty-Six

Jade

A piercing shriek echoes in the hills.

I'm screaming.

'LEO!' I slither along the ledge, on my belly.

A gorse bush grows on the side of the rock, and I grab on to it. Thorns spike my hands, but I don't feel pain. All I can think of is my baby.

And then I see him. Leo's lying on a tiny shelf. It's nothing more than a rock sticking out, and a patch of heather. But it's broken his fall. Below him is a sheer drop to the river.

'Mumma,' he bleats. 'Mumma!' My heart thuds hard, fast and I feel like I'm going to be sick.

'Just stay there,' I croak at him. 'Good boy. Don't move, my darling. The police are coming to rescue you, my big brave boy.'

He holds out his arms for me and the movement disturbs a few pebbles. I hear the distant splash in the water.

'Want Mumma,' he whimpers. 'Mummm-ma!'

'My darling. Mumma's going to be with you very soon. But

you have to keep really still so you don't fall. Stay really still, like a—like a sleeping lion.'

'Lion, Mumma?' More loose stones fall.

'You're good at that game, my darling, aren't you? You know how to keep really, really still, don't you?'

'Yes . . .' he murmurs. 'Leo lion.'

'That's it, just like that, really still. Don't move a muscle. The police are coming to help us. They're going to rescue you.' I hear footsteps scrabbling towards us. The police are here.

Thank God.

Sirens wail in the distance.

The muffled roar of the megaphone booms out.

And I cling to the side of the hill, every muscle frozen, my teeth chattering hard.

The police bring ropes and harnesses, and Leo is carried to safety. Once I see he's safe, I start to sob.

Finally, an officer climbs up to help me. 'Mrs Callahan, is it? Your son is safe. Now we have to get you down.' My arms and legs are paralysed. But eventually the drive to see my babies helps me uncurl my muscles, and move down from the ledge. I trek back, all the way to the shores of the loch.

Leo lies on a stretcher by the beach. I rush to him. I stroke his cheek while the paramedics check him out. They think his leg is broken but otherwise he seems fine, they say. They stretcher him back along the path to the ambulance outside the cottage.

The police broke into the house and found Amber and Eddie, dazed and half asleep from the medication Christina had given them. Luckily it was nothing worse than sleeping pills and some chloroform. They were confused about what's happened. But they will be OK.

Christina disappeared into the hills.

The police thought she might have thrown herself into the loch. A few divers are sent down but there's no trace of her.

Chapter Fifty-Seven

Jade

Sam bursts into the hospital ward where Leo, Amber and Eddie lie in beds next to each other. I'm sitting in an armchair, in between Leo and Eddie, watching them sleep.

The children are woozy. We're all suffering from shock. The doctors want to keep us under observation for a few hours.

Sam's eyes are fierce. He kisses and hugs the children tightly. 'Daddy,' Amber murmurs, hugging him back. But Eddie is asleep, and Leo's leg is strapped up and he can't move.

Sam sits, smiling through his tears. I look at him – the man I fell in love with, the father of my children – and I feel nothing. I'm totally drained. Numb.

'Thank God, thank God they're safe.' His shoulders shake and he scrubs at his eyes. 'Jade. My darling.'

I stand up, pointing to the door. 'Amber, Mummy and Daddy are just going out for a second – we'll be right back.'

I lead him into an empty side room.

'I guess the police told you where to find me.' My voice is clipped. I can't pretend to be happy to see him.

'The police traced your phone. How could you go without

telling me or the police? Thank God nothing worse happened. They're searching for that evil bitch.'

I'm silent. He won't understand. How can I tell him I wanted to help Christina? Be a good friend to her for once? That even now, I would do it again.

He shakes his head. 'That woman is evil. She tried to break us up. She took our children. Who knows what she'd have done if we hadn't found her?'

'*I* found her,' I say in a low voice.

'Thank God. If you hadn't, the children could be . . .' His voice breaks. His face creases with anguish.

I can never forget what Christina told me. What she'd had to go through in Edinburgh. How she'd felt. Did he think what he did to Christina was acceptable? What would he think if the same happened to Amber?

'You don't even remember, do you?' I glare at him.

'What? What don't I remember?' He looks at me, visibly confused.

'Cast your mind back to one Halloween in Edinburgh. Some twenty years ago.'

He wipes his face. 'I didn't know you then. I always thought it was a shame we hadn't met in our student days. We'd have had longer together.'

His expression softens but I recoil. 'But you were living in Edinburgh then, weren't you? You were in your fourth year while we were in our second.'

'Yes, I guess so.' His eyebrows draw together, puzzled. 'Jade, what's this about?'

'Do you remember having a one-night stand that Halloween? She was dressed as a witch?'

Confusion is all over his face. 'What?'

'The witch was Christina. You – slept with Christina. You got her drunk and you . . . you followed her home, back to our flat. I wasn't there – I was with my ex, Tom – and you assaulted her. Later, she found out she was pregnant. She had an ectopic pregnancy that resulted in her becoming infertile. You don't remember?'

He rubs his face, then barks out a harsh laugh. 'Twenty years ago? No. To be honest, I don't. My fourth year in Edinburgh . . . I slept with women, yes, of course I did. But assault? That's a harsh word, Jade. I don't know what she told you, but I would never do that. Christina – she's crazy. She was responsible for the death of a baby where she worked. A baby! She drugged me, she drugged the kids. She drugged you. That's why you were so tired all the time. That woman took our children. Who knows what she was planning to do to them. The police said she had a knife.'

A cold anger's been building in me, ever since I heard Christina's story. Mazza's. 'She's crazy? Then we're all crazy, aren't we? Crazy women, that enable *your* bad behaviour. Yours and all the other creeps out there. And guess what?' I shake my head and give him a bitter smile. 'You don't even remember. You told me about your dark period, after your mother died. How you used to get wasted and sleep around. But your behaviour had consequences. You changed Christina's life that night, destroyed her chance to have children. But to you it meant so little that you *can't even remember doing it.*'

'Jade, please. Let's not fight. Not now.' He reaches out a hand, but I brush it away.

'Don't touch me!' I speak through gritted teeth. 'We're over.'

'What?' He falls back.

To him, that night was just one of many casual shags. 'How many other girls did you traumatise? Just a night of drunken sex. A laugh. Do you know for sure that all those girls – Christina included – really wanted to have sex with you? Would you have known if they'd said no?' I'm screaming inside, but my voice won't go above a whisper. 'If you did it to her and can't remember, how many other girls were there? How many others might be living with the trauma of rape?'

Sam shakes his head. 'What are you talking about? It wasn't rape.' He tries to put a hand on my arm but I back away.

'It makes me sick to think how many men are out there, just like you. They shag a girl whether she wants it or not. They just want to get their end away. They don't care they're too drunk and shouldn't be having sex with anyone. And later, they just laugh it off. People think they're a bit of a lad. Lads getting leathered and shagging around. Totally excused. Boys will be boys, eh?'

Sam rakes his hair as if trying to push away my words. He looks at me, tries to smile and fails. 'Look, I can't remember Christina. I can't remember sleeping with her. She could be lying for all I know. It was that time – I told you, when my mum died I – I went off the rails – I'd get really bladdered. Maybe I did sleep with her. I wasn't a saint. I've . . . been around the block. I admit I've slept with countless women. You knew that when you married me. But rape? There's no way I'd sleep with a woman if it wasn't consensual.' He opens his hands, baring his empty palms to me, protesting his innocence.

The gesture enrages me even more. He doesn't believe that he's guilty. 'And out of all those women, how'd you know they wanted to have sex with you? Were there any that were more reluctant? Who you had to "persuade"? If you were so drunk you can't remember, how do you know it was always consensual?'

I remember how Christina was when we lived in Edinburgh. So shy. So young for her age. How many other shy young women had a drunken Sam forced himself on? I was filled with fury.

'Jade. Please, this is ridiculous. As far as I can remember, I never had to force anyone. I never forced you to do anything, ever, did I? The girls — they were up for it.'

'Really?' My voice drips with rage. "Up for it" were they? Because you bought them a drink? Or they wore a tight dress?'

He runs his hand through his hair. 'Look. Times were different then.'

'Yes.' I nod. 'Too right they were different. And not in a good way. We put up with a lot more than girls do now. Because we felt we didn't have a choice.'

'I'm sorry, all right? If I really did sleep with her, I don't remember doing it. I can only apologise.'

'But it's not just Christina, is it?' I think about Mazza's story.

'What do you mean?'

'Mazza told me how you groped her after the office Christmas party.'

'What?' He half laughs in disbelief. 'That was nothing. She's chancing it.'

I widen my eyes. 'Chancing it? She should've reported you for harassment.'

'It was just a drunken feel. It didn't mean anything. I regretted it straightaway. I wasn't going to shag her. You have to believe me.' He runs a hand through his hair.

'So what was it? A hand up her skirt? Because she wore a

short skirt? Or just a skirt? Or because she's a woman and she was there when you were drunk and out of control? She just has to expect it? Take it? Because it's just a bit of fun?'

'I'd been drinking all day. She knew that. We were in the office doing coke. What did she expect?'

'Oh my God. I can't even look at you. When will men like you realise? Just because you're too drunk to remember or she's too drunk to remember, doesn't mean it's OK to do whatever you want. It does not make groping a woman OK.'

I'm incandescent. Furious for Mazza. For Christina. For all the shy girls out there who couldn't say *No*, or *Stop* . . . Who were too afraid to speak.

And I'm furious at myself. And women like me. The guilt is a brick in my chest. Are we part of the problem? The enablers of men like Sam. The wives who turn a blind eye and think their husbands are every woman's dream, and they'd never behave like a creep.

I spin round and march out, banging the door behind me.

I never want to see him again.

Chapter Fifty-Eight

Mazza

I hate to think of Sam walking around somewhere, happily going about his business. His wife might be divorcing him, but he's still out there. Free. Alive.

The plan was for him to pay. And pay he will, for what he did to you, Ben. For what he's done to me.

That night will remain forever etched on my brain. You crashed through the front door, the noise jolting me awake. It was well after three in the morning, and I'd not long gone to bed. I immediately knew something was wrong by the way you were stumbling down the hall.

'Hey, Maz, still up?' Your speech had been slurred, your face drained of colour.

'You all right?' I'd asked you.

'Never better, Maz, my mate. I've solved all our money problems.' You grinned, even though you flinched when I hugged you.

'Whatcha going on about? You been on the lash?'

And then you told me what happened.

Some people might say your luck ran out that night. But

362

how you saw it, your luck had only just begun. You never were one of life's moaners, always one for making lemonade out of lemons. Except when it came to guys sleazing after girls who weren't interested. But you were never afraid to call them out on it, a vigilante in the bar. If you witnessed it, that was it. They were banned.

But confronting a drunk guy who's behaved inappropriately with a woman isn't always pretty. They don't always crawl back under the rock they've come from without a fight. And that's what happened with Sam.

See, that video I had on my phone wasn't just a clip of Sam groping me, was it? No. It included the security footage from your bar. Sam was harassing someone. Not me this time. It was some blonde he liked the look of that night. And he'd put his hand on some bird's bum one too many times for you. So you called him out, threw him out of the bar.

But Sam wouldn't go nicely. He yelled that he'd given me my job as a favour to you. He could just as easily sack me. The threat to me made you see red. Punches started flying. Then, God knows how, coz you've always been pretty nifty on your feet, Sam must've caught you off balance.

You went down. You cracked your head on the pavement. Luckily, you'd caught it all on your phone. It made me wanna puke but I watched it all.

Afterwards, you went back into the bar, shoved an ice pack on your head, downloaded the security footage of Sam groping women in the bar to your phone, and finished your shift.

After you stumbled home, that last night, we sat and made a plan. Sam would have to promote me. I was going to be the new production manager. Or else.

The security footage from the bar, plus the phone footage of the fight, would be our leverage.

The next morning, I let you sleep in. By six, you weren't up, and Mum sent me into your room. I tried yelling and shaking you, but it was no use.

Mum was hysterical and I called an ambulance.

But it was too late. A bleed on the brain, they said. You hit your head hard on the kerb when you went down. You slipped into a coma and never woke up. I wish I'd phoned A and E that night. I should have forced you to go to hospital. I'll always feel guilty I didn't.

I thought about giving your phone to the police as evidence. Sam would be done for punching you. But then I thought about what you said. Would he get sent to prison? Or would he get off with a fine?

You wanted to take justice into your own hands, Ben. I could honour your memory by sticking to your plan.

It took me a while to gather up the courage to ask Sam for actual cash. It took me and Mum nearly getting evicted before I showed him what I had on him.

When Anthony asked me to tell Jade what I knew about Sam, I didn't tell her the whole truth. I told her about the groping. But I didn't tell her about the extra footage we had. Sam harassing women in the bar. Sam knocking you down with that fatal blow.

I want Sam to pay forever, for what he did. Now he's won the yogurt pitch, he has the money.

So I'm sticking to our plan to make him pay, Ben. You'd be proud of me.

It kills me that he's walking around, free to live his life after what he did to you. You're right. The system is broken.

But our way, he will pay. And pay and pay.

For the rest of his life.

Epilogue

Jade

One Month Later

The postcard arrives towards the end of August.

The tropical beach featured on the front is a far cry from Wanstead, where I've stayed with the kids all summer, recovering. All we've managed are trips to the park and cafés in the high street for ice cream and milkshakes.

Amber and her friend Saskia spend most days acting out their favourite Agent Scarlett game. The boys have enjoyed riding their bikes and I've been getting fit running after them, not willing to let them out of my sight even for a second.

Who could the postcard be from? Maybe Sam's parents? They were in Spain. Perhaps they didn't get the message that Sam's moved out, or they posted it before they knew.

I flip the postcard. That handwriting. The precise way the J of my name is printed. I'm suddenly cold.

I know who it's from.

The one-line message reads: *Wish you were here.*

The hairs stand up on the back of my neck.

Christina.

So she did get away.

In her own misguided way, she wanted to protect me. I can't help hoping she's getting the help she needs. Despite what she did, taking my children, I can't hate her.

But I never want to see her again.

Acknowledgements

I have so many people to thank for this novel's existence.

Firstly, a huge thank you to my editor Bea Grabowska for believing in me and my story. Apologies again for blasting your eardrums with screams of excitement when you phoned to tell me I'd won a publishing deal. Thank you for holding my hand, explaining the process, and for your insightful edits and suggestions. You've definitely improved the novel greatly. Thank you also to the rest of the Headline team, especially Ollie Martin, Ana Carter and Rhys Callaghan. I also wish to extend my gratitude to copy editor Russel McLean, proofreader Jill Cole, and designer Lisa Brewster, for the wonderful cover.

Thank you to my agent, Hannah Schofield of LBA. You're always so encouraging, I really feel like my career is in safe hands with you by my side. Thanks also to Amy Strong, Assistant Agent at LBA. Thank you both for always being on hand for advice and help with my work at every stage.

Thanks in advance to all the published authors who've been kind enough to give up their time to read an early copy of the novel and have provided a quote on the book.

Thank you to Jenny Rees, ex police forensics, for our chat over coffee on police forensic procedure.

This novel is being published as a result of entering The Future Bookshelf's Modern Stories Headline Open Submissions. I am hugely grateful to the Headline Judging Panel, and the bloggers who read and selected my novel as the winner, including The Candid Book Club (@thecandidbookclub), Shikha Chopra of Unfolding Pages (@unfoldingpages_), Amyn Bawa-Allah of Lip-GlossMaffia (@lipglossmaffia) and Nicola Soremekun of Booked Up and Busy (@bookedupandbusy). It was reassuring to know that readers, as well as editors, enjoyed reading the early draft.

I entered the beginning chapters of my novel (then called *The Truth Between Us*) into various schemes, designed to help writers of colour get published. I'm grateful to the following organisations and schemes for reading the early chapters and providing me with opportunities for discussion with publishing professionals: Spread The Word and One More Chapter, with special thanks to Bethan Morgan; David Higham Associates New Writers Scheme, special thanks to Maddalena Cavaciuti; The Asian Women Writers mentoring scheme, special thanks to editors Kathryn Cheshire and Angel Belsey; The Greene Door Project, special thanks to Judith Murray; The Harper Collins Writers Academy; The Creative Writing Bursary and Amazon Literary Partnership for the Creative Thursday session at the Theakston Old Peculier Crime Writing Festival in Harrogate; Jacqui Lofthouse at The Writing Coach.

I'm indebted to some brilliant creative writing teachers whose courses inspired this novel. Thank you to Caroline Green for her City University Crime Writing course; Erin Kelly and the Curtis Brown Writing a Psychological Thriller course; and Sophie Mackenzie for her brilliant Zoom feedback sessions on my manuscript.

A huge thank you to Chloe Timms for hosting her Thursday Night Zoom Writing sessions, and all the writers who came along and provided a great atmosphere to get some words down.

Much thanks to Emma Christie for her Diary of a Debut Novelist Facebook Group and the useful Zoom sessions about publishing; thanks also to all the participating authors who've shared their knowledge and experiences. I'm lucky to have a community of wonderful writer friends who've kept me going through the years, with encouragement, support, and sharing of both the good and bad. Plus, writing pals are the best to hang out with, at writing festivals and retreats, drinking wine and even dancing into the early hours.

My eternal thanks must go to my critique partner, Susan Sandercock, for her feedback and insightful comments on the messy first draft of this novel. You believed in this novel more than I did. Thanks also to Susan for being a founding member of our online cosy crime and psych thriller book club, together with Annette Caseley Chapman and Cara Lovelock (C. L. Miller). Now called The Furies, this group of mainly children's writers who've turned to writing crime, has been amazingly supportive, discussing our writing journeys as well as dissecting commercial crime books (that aren't too violent). Thanks to all The Furies.

My heartfelt thanks to Maisie Chan for setting up the Bubble Tea Writers Network, invaluable for making connections with other British–Chinese writers. Thank you to our core group of London Bubblies for all the dim sum meet-ups, advice, laughs and WhatsApp chat. It was wonderful to run the ESEA Lit Fest at SOAS together last year and I hope we can do it again.

Thanks also to the Harrie Writers (thanks, Hannah Brennan, for the name!), our WhatsApp group of writers and bloggers who met at Harrogate last year.

Thank you to all supporting my kidlit journey. My SCBWI friends and volunteers, the Critique Group With No Name, everyone at Jasmine Richard's Storymix. Thank you for your belief, guidance and support.

Lastly, a massive thank you to my dear and wonderful family. Love and thanks to my mum and dad, for all the years of support, especially when I was struggling as a single parent. All my love and gratitude to my darling husband, Matt, who supports me unquestioningly. Without you, I wouldn't have the time or head-space to write anything. And lastly, thanks to my three amazing, inspiring children, Anushka, Jasmine and Louis. My love for you is so immense, the fear of losing you gave birth to this novel.